DEATH AND GLORY

A Soldier with Richard the Lionheart, Part III

Richard Cœur de Lion.

ROBERT BROOMALL

A Bluestone Media Publication

ISBN 978-1-7326275-5-0

Cover by bespokebookcovers.com

Books by Robert Broomall

California Kingdoms

Texas Kingdoms

The Lawmen

The Bank Robber

Dead Man's Crossing (Jake Moran 1)

Dead Man's Town (Jake Moran 2)

Dead Man's Canyon (Jake Moran 3)

Death's Head, A Soldier with Richard the Lionheart

The Red King, A Soldier with Richard the Lionheart, II

K Company (K Company 1)

Conroy's First Command (K Company 2)

The Dispatch Rider (K Company 3)

Murder in the Seventh Cavalry

Scalp Hunters (Cole Taggart 1)

Paradise Mountain (Cole Taggart 2)

Wild Bill and the Dinosaur Hunters

For James, Heather, Diane,

Claire and David

PART I

Chapter 1

AILITH POINTED. "LOOK."

Roger had already seen them, but he hadn't told Ailith about it because he didn't want to worry her.

Riders.

Silhouetted against the blue sky and high clouds. Coming fast. From the east—the direction from which Saracens would come.

Roger and Ailith were exhausted, thirsty, hungry. It had been three days since they'd escaped the Blue Fort, one day since they'd lost their horses. The sun burned down on them, leaching out what little energy they had left. There was nowhere for them to hide on the open plain. To the west, heartbreakingly close, the towers of Acre shone golden in the sun's rays.

Roger drew his knife. He had promised to kill Ailith with that knife rather than let her be captured. He hadn't been able to keep that promise yesterday when it looked like they were about to be taken, and he wouldn't be able to keep it today. Ailith would live out her life in Qaymaz's *harim*, but at least she would live. Roger, on the other hand, had no intention of letting himself be taken alive and tortured by Qaymaz.

The oncoming dust resolved itself into a group of about twenty men, and as the men drew nearer, Roger and Ailith saw not the

3

conical helmets and light chain mail of Saracens, but sky blue robes, flowing white cloaks, and white turbans.

"Turcos," Roger breathed.

Ailith sank to the ground, legs crossed, eyes closed in thanks.

Turcopoles were native-born Christian light cavalry. They were not heavily armed and were used mainly for scouting. Because of their exotic dress, they were the most glamorous unit in the Christian army, and the majority of them were only too aware of that fact.

The Turcos slowed and formed a semicircle around Roger and Ailith. At a gesture from the unit's leader, three scouts fanned out to make sure they weren't taken unawares by Saracens.

Ailith climbed to her feet as the Turco leader and his second-in-command walked their horses forward. The commander seemed hard bitten, while the young second-in-command appeared to revel in the glamor of his unit's reputation. Like all Turcos, both men wore closely trimmed moustaches and short beards.

The two men studied Roger and Ailith. Roger's fair hair and beard were long and matted with filth. His hose contained more holes than material, and his shirt was in the same condition. His skin was nut brown from endless hours of labor in the sun. Ailith's face was stained from dust and sweat, her nose and cheeks burned red by three days of sun after months of living indoors. Her embroidered silk robe was torn and her slippers were in tatters. Her braided blonde hair had come askew.

Roger sheathed the knife and raised his hand. "Greetings. We mistook you for Saracens, coming from the east like that."

The commander did not return Roger's friendly demeanor. "We patrol to keep Saracens away from the city. We've been out a week, and we're on our way back. Another patrol will take our place." He added, "We're also on the lookout for spies. The Saracens like to use Circassians as spies because they have blond hair. Like yours."

The commander paused and went on. "Your exposure to weather and your ragged appearance would make excellent cover for someone trying to infiltrate the city."

"We aren't Circassians," Roger said wearily. "We're Christian slaves, escaped from the infidel. Do you have any water?"

After a moment, the young second-in-command passed Roger a water skin. Roger nodded thanks and gave the skin to Ailith, who drank greedily. When she had her fill, Roger took some. The water was warm, but it was fresh, and it tasted wonderful. He felt his sun-baked body coming back to life, like a wilted plant after the rain. "My name is Roger of Huntley. I am an English knight in the service of the earl of Trent. I command a company of footmen known as the Death's Heads."

At those words, the two Turcos relaxed. The second-in-command raised an amused eyebrow. "We know of the Death's Heads. We lost a barrel of good wine to them not long ago. We couldn't prove anything, but I know it was them."

"It does *sound* like them," Roger admitted. He indicated Ailith. "The lady's name is Ailith. She is English, as well. She was taken by the Saracens during the siege of Acre. I was captured at the fight near Arsuf."

The commander rubbed his jaw, as though searching his memory. "Whose prisoner were you?"

"The emir Qaymaz."

"He's a bad one, they say."

"You'll get no argument from me on that," Roger told him.

The second-in-command eyed Ailith. "And you, madame? You were a prisoner of Qaymaz, as well?"

Ailith took another drink from the water skin. "Yes."

The young man took in her expensive clothes, lingering on the places where rents in the fabric showed her creamy skin. "In what . . .?"

"I was in his *harim*, if you must know."

"Oh. I—I'm sorry."

"Not as sorry as I was," she said. She handed the water back to Roger, who took another drink and returned it to the young Turco.

The commander still looked like he was trying to remember something. Suddenly it came to him, and he snapped his gloved fingers. "Wait! Roger of Huntley—Death's Heads! I knew I'd heard that name. Weren't you with the rear guard at Arsuf? Part of the charge that won the battle?"

Roger had led the charge, though it had been an accident. "I was."

"Why didn't you say so? Everyone knows who you are. You're a hero—except maybe to King Richard. They say he wanted to execute you for disobeying orders."

Roger's face fell, and the commander added hopefully, "No telling how he feels now, of course." His once suspicious face beamed in smile. "It's a pleasure to meet you. My name is Espiart. And this raffish young villain is Gaston."

Roger shook hands with the two men. The breeze caught the long white sash of Gaston's turban and blew it across his face. He flicked it back with a practiced gesture that probably impressed the ladies.

Roger went on. "Tell me, does the crusade yet continue?"

"Not for much longer," Espiart said. "You men from the west are preparing to leave."

"So we've taken Jerusalem?"

Gaston snorted, and Espiart said, "Alas, no."

Roger didn't understand. "Then why are we . . .?

"Your earl of Trent can explain it to you," Espiart said. "He is governor of the city, and we must take you to him."

Ailith spoke up. "Must I see the earl, as well?" Ailith had been Trent's mistress for half a year. There was no telling how he would react when he saw her.

The Turcos didn't know this, of course. They probably thought that—typical woman—she didn't want to appear before a great noble like the earl in such a disheveled fashion. Espiart said, "I'm afraid I must insist, madame. You may have valuable intelligence. The earl's wife may wish to question you, as well."

"Lady Bonjute?" Roger said. "I thought she went home to England."

"She was shipwrecked and returned to Acre."

"To the delight of one and all," Gaston cracked.

Espiart cast Gaston a sharp look while Roger and Ailith exchanged glances. What if Bonjute found out that Ailith had been

7

her husband's lover? What if she already knew? Even if she didn't, it would be easy for one of the nobles who had survived the siege to identify her, and Bonjute was famous for extracting revenge.

"It will be all right," Roger promised Ailith, though he had no idea whether that was true—for her or for him.

"Let's be off," Espiart said. He beckoned two of his men forward. To Roger and Ailith, he said, "Ride double with these fellows. We'll have you at the governor's palace by vespers."

Chapter 2

"ROGER!"

Beaming, Geoffrey of Trent lifted himself from his inlaid ebony chair and embraced Roger. "By all that's holy, it's good to see you, boy. We thought you dead."

"I thought the same myself, my lord," Roger grinned. "More than once."

"Your father will be overjoyed at your return."

Roger's eyes widened.

"Oh, yes—Henry told us all about it. We were quite moved—it's a wonderful story. I'd take you to him except he went to Tyre with the count of Champagne. They're escorting Lord Conrad here for his coronation. They'll be back sometime today."

The earl turned to Ailith, who curtsied as demurely as she could in her state of near exhaustion. "My lord." Her voice sounded puffy because of her cracked, sun-blackened lips.

The earl's tone became more formal. "Ailith, it is good to see you again."

"Thank you, my lord. It's good to be back."

The earl's eyes were conflicted with emotion, and Roger suddenly realized that the earl loved Ailith. She had been much more than a mistress to him.

They were in the earl's private chamber at the palace. The sea breeze wafted through the window, bringing with it the late-afternoon sounds of the city, along with the smells of salt and spices and animals. When Roger had first met Geoffrey of Trent, he had been red bearded and hearty, in the prime of life. Now, a year later, he looked grey and frail. He looked defeated. He clutched a narrow wooden box with a glass viewing pane as though his life depended on it. He was dressed for a formal occasion, in an ankle-length tunic of dark blue silk, embroidered around the neck and sleeves with silver thread, and a white surcoat with his red dragon emblem on it.

The earl turned to his elderly steward. "Pero, bring my guests food and wine. And give a purse to the Turcos who brought them in. Tell them, good work."

Pero bowed and left the room.

The earl offered Ailith the chair. It was the only chair in the room. She sat gratefully, relieved to be off her feet.

To Roger, the earl said, "You never cease to amaze me, Roger. First you become famous for the Arsuf battle. And now, it seems, you've risen from the dead."

Roger wasn't sure how to take that. "I never meant to lead a general attack at Arsuf, my lord. I was just trying to kill the traitor who sold Ailith into slavery." He hesitated. "Does—does King Richard still want me executed for disobeying his orders?"

The earl smiled. "The king is a man of mercurial temperament. What he says one day, he recants the next, and forgets the day after that. I believe I can talk him into leniency for you. Serving time as a slave is punishment enough. Besides, there are those who swear we'd have lost that battle if not for what you did."

Roger breathed a sigh of relief. Ailith reached up from the chair and squeezed Roger's hand—a gesture that did not go unnoticed by the earl. Then the food came—black bread and flatbread, butter, goat's cheese, grapes of several varieties, pomegranates, and lemon water.

"Don't stand on ceremony," the earl told Roger and Ailith. "Help yourselves."

They went at the food like half-starved wolves at a flock of sheep, and as they ate, the earl said, "I would ask you to tell me of your adventures, but I fear it would take too long."

Roger spoke through a mouthful of bread and cheese. "'Adventures' might be too mild a word, my lord."

"'Ordeal' is more like it," Ailith added. She spoke to the earl with a familiar ease, and again Roger saw conflict on the older man's face.

The earl cleared his throat. "Yes, I take your point."

Roger changed the subject. "You're looking well, my lord."

"I feel much better," the earl said. "I was close to death, you know, then my wife bought me this relic." He showed them the box. "It's a piece of the lance of Longinus. Bonjute found it at a shop on the Street of Bad Cookery. I swear the thing saved my life."

Roger and Ailith examined the relic, a large wooden splinter, grey with age, on a velvet cushion, with what appeared to be faded drops of dried blood on it.

Roger handed it back. "I'm happy for you, my lord." He changed the subject again. "The Turcos who picked us up said that the crusade is nearly over."

Trent nodded. "It is. King Richard must return to England. Prince John is usurping power there, and Richard must put an end to it."

"And Conrad of Montferrat is being crowned king of Jerusalem?"

"Tomorrow," Trent said. "You no doubt saw the flags and bunting in the streets. He arrives in the city today. That's why I'm wearing my best robe. We expect him at any time, so don't be surprised if I have to rush off suddenly."

"I won't, my lord. What will happen with the Holy City now?"

"Conrad will take it, of that I have no doubt. Burgundy and some of the others are talking about staying on to help."

"What about you?"

The earl looked out the window, toward the harbor, and he sighed. "I'm going home with the king. Perhaps I can regain my health there. This place has been a graveyard for too many good men—it was damned near a graveyard for me. I'm ready to leave."

A tall, commanding blonde woman with sharp-planed cheekbones strode into the room. "I heard you had—" she took in the ragged figures opposite her "—guests."

Roger had seen the woman during the siege. Ailith hadn't seen her before, but rose from the chair instinctively.

The earl introduced them. "Roger, Ailith—this is my wife, Lady Bonjute."

Roger bowed and Ailith curtsied. To Bonjute, the earl said, "Roger is one of my knights. He and Ailith have just escaped infidel captivity."

12

Bonjute cast appraising blue eyes on Roger and—especially, it seemed—on Ailith.

Does she suspect? Ailith wondered. *Does she know? But how could she?*

The earl went on. "Roger was a hero at Arsuf. And Ailith was a . . ." He appeared to forget where Ailith had gone after she left him.

Ailith finished for him. "I was a washerwoman, my lady."

"Indeed?" Bonjute drawled in her aristocratic voice. "And now you're back in the fold? Not many escape from slavery, I'm told."

Ailith said, "We were blessed by God, my lady."

Bonjute regarded what was left of Ailith's rich garments. "Aside from your sunburn, the Saracens seem to have taken better care of you than they did of the hero, here."

Ailith's burned cheeks turned even redder, and she lowered her eyes. "I was in . . . I was in the emir Qaymaz's *harim*."

"Good Lord. How awful."

"It was, my lady."

Unbidden, the old steward Pero brought two purses. The earl gave the larger purse to Roger. "Buy yourself some clothes, Roger—a horse, armor, weapons—you know the drill. Will you be staying in the city or at the camp with your men?"

"With my men, my lord. I'm anxious to see them again."

The earl gave the other purse to Ailith, his hand shaking slightly as it touched hers. "And what about you, Ailith? Where will you go? I'm sure we could find a position at the palace for you, should you wish it." He couldn't keep a hopeful note out of his voice.

Ailith was aware of Bonjute's keen gaze boring into her. She was aware of Geoffrey's pleading eyes, as well. He wanted her back so much, and she felt badly for him.

"I will be staying with Roger," she said.

"Oh," said the earl. Shock and disappointment registered in his voice, and Bonjute missed neither of them.

"How delightfully scandalous," Bonjute said.

The earl went on. "I didn't realize you two were . . . Well, it's too late to go out to the camp tonight. You'll both stay here. Get yourselves cleaned up and have a good night's sleep."

"Thank you, my lord," said Roger. "That's very kind of you."

"Believe me, it's my privilege. Pero will find you quarters."

Bonjute said, "I'll have my servant Jehan prepare a bath for you— Ailith, isn't it?"

She knows.

"That's very—very kind, my lady."

"Not at all. It will keep Jehan away from the stable boys, or kitchen boys, or whoever it is she fancies these days."

When Roger and Ailith were gone, Geoffrey regarded Bonjute thoughtfully. He knew his wife, knew she must have guessed that he'd had relations with Ailith. "You've changed."

"Changed?" Bonjute said.

"There's something different about you. You seem, I don't know, happier. Less your old self."

14

"I don't mean to seem happy. Perhaps I should have someone whipped. Just to keep my hand in."

"You know what I mean. You treated Roger and Ailith quite well, not the way you usually deal with social inferiors—especially the girl. Normally you would have had anyone who looked like they do thrown out of the house."

Bonjute shrugged. "They've suffered enough, I expect."

Geoffrey cocked his head. "Is there a man?"

She stared at him, taken off guard.

"I mean, I wouldn't blame you if there was. I know I haven't been—"

"There's no man," Bonjute told him.

"You're sure?"

Bonjute rolled her eyes and let out her breath dramatically. "All right Geoffrey, I'll confess. I'm having affairs with the bishop of Verona, the bishop of Ravenna, and the bishop of Beauvais. Sometimes with all three of them at the same time. Oh, don't look so shocked. If you can swyve a prioress, the least I can do is service the odd bishop or two. After all, I'm as holy as you."

Geoffrey reddened. "If you bring up that prioress one more—"

Without warning, the chamber door opened and Geoffrey's latest marshal, Blaise, burst in.

Geoffey erupted at this breach of protocol. "What the—"

"Sorry, my lord, but there's news from Tyre. The marquis of Montferrat has been murdered."

Chapter 3

CHE WOMEN'S BATH was a small, circular pool with steam rising from it, bordered with marble, with marble Roman columns all around. Fresh sponges were arranged on the side. It was nothing compared to the elaborate *harim* bath at the Blue Fort, but better than anything in England—as far as Ailith knew, anyway. The ancient pipes that once brought in water no longer functioned, so hot water was hauled in tubs from the kitchen by Jehan, whose put-out expression told Ailith she considered herself far too good for such work.

When Jehan finally left, Ailith unbraided her dirty hair and pulled her fingers through it. God, it would be good to be clean again. She stepped out of her torn slippers and was about to remove her robe when she became aware of a new presence in the room.

She turned.

It was Geoffrey's wife, Bonjute, carrying what looked like a bundle of folded clothes.

"I brought these for you," Bonjute said, handing Ailith the bundle. Ailith could tell by the feel that the material was expensive. "Some old clothes I don't wear anymore." She looked Ailith up and down. "They should fit you fairly well."

Ailith said, "Thank you, my lady, but you needn't—"

Bonjute waved her off. "You have nothing but those Saracen rags, and the cost of women's clothing in Acre is exorbitant. Believe me, I know."

Why is she doing this?

"Thank you again, my lady."

Bonjute lingered. "You said you were a prisoner of the emir Qaymaz?"

"I was, my lady."

"King Richard likes Qaymaz, you know."

"King Richard doesn't know him then," Ailith said. "He is an evil man."

Bonjute took that in. She moved as she talked, circling Ailith. Stalking. Like a cat waiting to pounce.

"You were captured during the siege?"

"Yes, my lady. In Saladin's last attack on our camp."

"And you're from England?"

Now we're getting to it. "Yes, my lady. Trentshire, actually. The manor of Lower Wynchecombe."

Bonjute shook her head. "I don't know it."

Ailith wondered if that was true; Bonjute seemed like the kind of woman who knew a lot more than she let on.

"And you left the manor and came to the Holy Land as a washerwoman?" Bonjute made a face as though that was an odd choice.

Ailith was tempted to tell Bonjute that she'd been the wife of a soldier who had since died, but she didn't want Bonjute to catch her up in lies. She needed to be careful here. Bonjute could easily have her killed, with or without Geoffrey's knowledge. Better to be as truthful as possible. "To be honest, my lady, I was accused of witchcraft by a monk whose advances I spurned—"

"Bah! Witchcraft." Bonjute made a deprecating gesture. "Men always use that excuse when you turn them down."

"—and I ran away to avoid being tortured. Roger helped me escape."

Bonjute's delicate brows went up. "Did he? Roger was a monk?"

"No, my lady. He was employed by the abbey as a woodcutter."

"How fortunate for you. So the two of you came to the Holy Land together?"

"No, my lady. We became separated in the forest during our flight. After that, I fell in with a company of your husband's soldiers heading to the Holy Land, and they took me in as a washerwoman."

As a whore, she knew Bonjute was thinking.

Ailith continued. "I met Roger again during the siege, and as fate would have it, we were both prisoners of Qaymaz, though Roger had it far worse than I did."

"An interesting story," Bonjute said. She paused and cocked her head. "You know what I find curious? You're a peasant girl, a washerwoman, and yet you have the speech and bearing of a noblewoman. How is such a thing possible?"

Careful, careful. "I fell in with a lord," Ailith said. "It happens out here."

"Will you go back to this lord?"

She didn't ask which one. Why? Because she already knows?

"No, my lady. I'm with Roger now. I would have stayed with him in England had we not been separated." That much was true, anyway.

Innocently, Bonjute asked, "Did you know that my husband attempted to have you put on King Richard's list of prisoners to be freed by Saladin?"

Ailith's eyes widened. "No. No, I was not aware of that."

"Why would he do that, do you think? You, a washerwoman?" The cat had trapped the mouse.

"I—I've no idea, my lady."

To Ailith's surprise, Bonjute smiled, and the smile actually seemed friendly. It was as though she had found out what she needed to know, and there was no need to pursue the matter. The cat was letting the mouse go free. This was not the Bonjute of repute. She even offered Ailith a way out. "Perhaps it was because you're a friend of Roger's? Or perhaps Roger asked him to do it?"

Ailith tried to keep the relief from her voice. "Yes, I suppose that's possible. Your husband is very fond of Roger. Roger saved his life during the siege."

"Is there anyone whose life that fellow hasn't saved? Aside from me, of course."

Ailith ventured a smile. "There's still time for that, my lady."

Bonjute's sharp look seemed to say, *Don't push it.* "I rather doubt it. Geoffrey and I will be leaving for England soon—I'd say leaving for home, but it's hard to think of a place like England as home."

Ailith made no answer, and Bonjute said, "Enjoy your bath. You'd better get in while the water is still warm." She turned away, then looked back over her shoulder. "Don't worry. I'm not going to have

19

someone come in and slit your throat. The idiots around here would probably bungle the job anyway."

And with that, she left.

Chapter 4

ℜOGER AND AILITH were given quarters at the earl's palace. Roger slept on a straw-filled mat in a chamber with the earl's marshal, Blaise, and several of his higher-ranking knights, while Ailith shared a room with Bonjute's maid, Jehan, who complained and acted put out until Ailith threatened to break her arm.

The next morning, the earl's ancient steward, Pero, brought Roger a new shirt, hose, and braies. After dressing, Roger went to the palace hall for breakfast. There were few people in the hall. The earl and most of his staff were attending to business occasioned by Conrad of Montferrat's murder. No one knew where Lady Bonjute was.

Ailith entered the hall. The blue kirtle that Bonjute had given her was a bit tight in the shoulders, but otherwise it fit well. A white leather belt showed off her narrow waist. She had arranged a linen wimple over her hair and neck, hiding her long blonde braids.

She kissed Roger brightly on the lips—outraging the clerical staff who were present—then stood back, arms spread. "How do I look?"

Roger grinned. "In truth, my lady, it would take one of King Richard's *trouveres* to do you justice."

She made a face and kissed him again, outraging the clerics even further.

After breakfast, one of the earl's squires, a pimply, muscular lad called Regimbaud, brought horses around and led Roger and Ailith to the English camp. Courtly fashion compelled Ailith to ride sidesaddle, which she didn't like. As they departed the city, people in the street stared at them, pointing and whispering.

"What's going on?" Roger asked Regimbaud.

"Everyone thought you were dead," the squire told him over his shoulder, "and now you're back. Some are already calling it a miracle. If you don't watch yourself, they'll make you a saint."

Ailith laughed at that.

Roger had been shaven after his bath, and the raised scar stood plain on his cheek. He ran a finger along it self consciously. "Is there any more news about Marquis Conrad's death?"

Regimbaud replied, "It is said that the killer was a member of a sect called the Assassins. Before he died, he 'confessed' that it was King Richard who paid to have the marquis killed."

"No one seriously believes that, do they?" Roger asked.

"Unfortunately, they do. There's plenty who heard Richard swear that Conrad would never be king of Jerusalem, and they reckon he's made good on his promise. Word's been sent to King Philip that four more of these Assassins are on their way to France to kill him."

"Is that true?" said Ailith. "About King Philip?

Regimbaud shrugged.

"Sounds more like someone trying to sow discord in our camp," Roger said.

"So what will happen now?" Ailith asked Roger.

"I don't know, but I can't imagine it will be good."

The English camp was in a different location than it had been before last September's march on Jerusalem. It was still south of the city, but more westerly, on a stretch of level ground. There were row after row of conical tents, those of the knights painted with the emblems of their owners. The streets were once again laid out with whitewashed rocks, but the camp's atmosphere was more relaxed than of old. There were no footmen drilling—no cries of vintenars and centenars. Knights and men-at-arms lazed in the shade.

Ahead was the Death's Heads' section of the camp, with the red skull banner flying over the captain's tent. The banner was ragged from wear, and in places it had been torn by arrows, giving it an even more forbidding appearance than it had possessed before.

As they approached, there were excited shouts and men ran out to greet them. Roger saw Tatwine, then Short Peter, Slowfoot, and the chaplain, Father Ambrose—thank God they were all still alive. He saw someone else, as well, and he jumped from his horse and embraced the big man in wonderment.

"Ralph—you're supposed to be dead!"

"So are you!" laughed Ralph the Red.

Roger held Ralph by the shoulders and looked him up and down. "The last time I saw you, you were in the sick tent, gutted like a new-caught fish. They even gave you Last Rites."

Ralph made a deprecating gesture. He was emaciated and worn, but his red beard was braided again, tied with brightly colored ribbons. "Takes more'n a few Goat Fuckers to kill me." Then he thought of something, and he turned to Father Ambrose. "You can only get Last Rites once—right, Father?"

"That's right," the ebullient priest replied.

"So every sin I commit from here on out is already forgiven?"

"I never thought about it before, but I believe you're correct."

Ralph rubbed his big hands together and raised his voice. "So who's going into town with me, then?"

There was a roar of laughter. Behind them, Tatwine handed Ailith from her horse, surprise on his face. "Lady Ailith. We didn't know you were back."

"'Twas Ailith who organized our escape from the infidels," Roger told him. "If not for her, I wouldn't be here."

Tatwine made an awkward bow. "It's a pleasure seeing you again, my lady." There was loud agreement from the old timers. Ailith had nursed many of them through famine and disease during the siege, and a number of them would not be alive were it not for her.

Ailith beamed at all the familiar faces, laughing with the sheer pleasure of it. "Stop calling me 'lady.' My name is Ailith."

"You'll always be 'lady' to us," Tatwine said. He added, "Where's Miss Margaret?"

"She was killed during our escape."

Tatwine hung his head and shook it sadly. "Always liked Margaret, I did." Other men murmured assent.

To Roger, Tatwine said, "We been waiting on you, Roger. We heard you was alive, thought you'd be here last night."

"We were guests last night at the governor's palace," Roger explained.

Amid the requisite "Ooh's" and "La-di-da's," the squire Regimbaud bade Roger and Ailith good day and started back to Acre with the horses. The men crowded round, the old timers shaking Roger's hand. They took Ailith's hand as well, some of them kissing it, while the newcomers stood in the background, taking it all in. In the heat, most of the men wore only their knee-length shirts. They had untied their hose from their braies and the hose hung loose around their ankles.

Tatwine turned to the men behind him. "Bring them new lads here." To Roger he said, "They come in two days ago, looking to join up. Said they knew you from when you was a slave."

Two ragged figures were ushered forward. Ailith clapped her hands with joy, and Roger laughed heartily. "Pentecost! Yves!" He and Ailith hugged each man in turn.

"So you do know them?" Tatwine said.

"We were at Qaymaz's pleasure palace together." To the two men he said, "What happened to you? Ailith and I looked all over for you the next day. We thought you'd been taken by Saracens."

"What happened to *you?*" the crossbowman Pentecost shot back. "We come out of them woods next morning and you was nowhere in sight. Figured you'd got ahead of us somehow, so we made our way here."

"I'll tell you about it later," Roger said. To Tatwine he said, "Get these reprobates cleaned up, and for God's sake get them a good meal."

"Maybe two meals?" Yves offered hopefully. His wild black hair and bushy, matted beard gave him the look of an untamed forest creature.

"Aye," said Pentecost. "Starvation does wonders for a man's appetite." He turned. "Lady Ailith, if I may make so bold, you look even more beautiful now you got proper clothes."

Ailith blushed. "Why, thank you, Pentecost."

Roger said, "It will be good having the two of you with us."

"Don't know how long we'll be staying," Pentecost said. "'Pears you lot are headed home soon."

Roger said, "The kingdom will need good men after we're gone. You can join up with my father—I'll put in a word for you."

"Your father?" Pentecost said.

"Henry of Deraa. He's a—"

Yves cut him off. "Henry the Falcon is your father?"

"You know of him?"

"Everybody in the kingdom knows him," said Yves. "'Scourge of the Saracens,' they call him."

"Aye," Pentecost added, "Saladin's got—what?—ten thousand dinars on his head?"

"Something like that," Yves replied.

Tatwine produced two jugs of arrack, which were passed around, Roger and Ailith being afforded the first drinks. A camp chair was brought for Ailith, and the men crowded around her and Roger, reminiscing and laughing.

While that was going on, Tatwine and the new cook, Barnabas, brought out trenchers of cold chicken. "Real chicken," Barnabas said proudly, "not camel meat."

Roger marveled. "How the Devil did you come by chicken out here?"

Tatwine shrugged and replied with a straight face. "Found 'em runnin' loose. Free as ever you please. Gift from God, I reckon it was."

Roger and Ailith had dined last night at the earl's palace, but this meal of chicken and soldier's bread—the kind of bread with sawdust in it—washed down with cheap arrack, seemed infinitely better. As they ate, Tatwine said, "Will Conrad's death affect our situation, d'ye think?"

Through a mouthful of chicken, Roger replied. "I've no idea."

Ralph the Red weighed in. "I'm for going home as much as the next man, but I'm damned if I like leaving the Holy City in the hands of them Goat Fuckers. Fancy another go at them, I would."

There was a rumble of approval, and Slowfoot growled. "I agree with Reds. This crusade's been a shambles so far. What have we accomplished 'cept to get most of our friends killed?"

The centenar Oswy spit. "Could 'ave stayed at home for all the good we done."

"King Richard should've marched on Jerusalem last winter, when he had the chance," Short Peter said.

"Last winter?" Oswy scoffed. "He should have marched right after we beat them bastards at Arsuf."

Slowfoot nodded. The branded "B" for *bracierre*—"poacher"— stood pale on his deeply tanned cheek. "I love the king as much as any man, but I blame him for all that's gone wrong."

Ailith was puzzled by this talk. "I seem to have missed a lot since I was captured," she murmured to Roger.

"I, as well," Roger said. It made him uncomfortable hearing King Richard spoken about this way. Richard had been his hero. He owed his knighthood to Richard.

More arrack was produced, and criticism of the king turned to yarning and the usual soldierly grumbling. This continued till early evening, when the group gradually broke up. Tatwine said, "It's getting late for Lady Ailith to return to the city. We'll find a tent for her."

Roger looked to Ailith, then back to Tatwine. "Ailith will be staying with me."

"Oh," said Tatwine. Evidently he had not expected this. "Oh. I see. Right." He hesitated. "I left something in your tent, Roger. Kept it in case you . . . case you ever came back."

Roger and Ailith repaired to the captain's tent. Tatwine had already removed his belongings and moved in with Slowfoot. Roger held the tent flap for Ailith and entered behind her.

Leaning against the tent pole was Helvise's crossbow.

Roger picked up the crossbow and ran his hand over the carved tiller with its dragon's head, over the nicks and scars in the varnished wood, and he fought back a tear.

"Was that hers?" Ailith asked him, taking his arm.

Roger nodded. "Yes."

"It's beautiful."

Roger said nothing.

"You're going to keep it?"

"Yes." He turned. "You don't mind?"

"Of course not." There was a pause, then Ailith said, "Did you love her?"

Roger remembered Helvise, her wavy black hair and fierce dark eyes, and he let out a long breath. "I did, but not the way I love you. With you, it's more . . . it's like you're part of me, burned into me somehow. Does that make any sense?"

She nodded. "It does, because I feel the same."

"It's been that way since the first time I saw you."

"It's been that way for me, too."

He was about to kiss her when a familiar voice called from outside, "Hello?" and the tent flap opened.

"Fauston!" Roger cried.

Ailith removed her hands from Roger's arms and hugged Fauston. "Fauston! It's good to see you."

Fauston's grin seemed to stretch from ear to ear. "I came as soon as I learned you were in Acre. Didn't know Ailith was with you, though. Makes it all the better."

Now it was Roger's turn to hug his friend. Fauston went on. "It's like old times, isn't it—us all together? You back from the dead, and Ailith—we had no idea what had happened to you. We thought you had vanished into the depths of Araby."

Fauston still wore the wide-brimmed pilgrim's hat. Roger took in his well-cut clothes. "You're looking prosperous."

"Business has been good," Fauston admitted.

"Business?" Roger said. Then he drew back. "Wait—don't tell me you're still selling relics?"

Ailith didn't understand. "Selling relics?"

Fauston gave them a sheepish look. "I have a shop in town. You must come see it."

"Selling relics?" Ailith repeated, mystified.

Fauston went on. "I even have one of your old men working for me—Francisco."

"The *morisco*? I wondered why I hadn't seen him in camp. I assumed he must have been killed."

29

"Got his knee caved in at Arsuf and had to leave the army. Makes our reliquaries now. Fantastic work."

"Selling relics?" Ailith demanded.

"Good for him," Roger went on. "I never knew he had that kind of talent." He paused. "I thought you'd have departed the Holy Land by now. It's all you ever talked about."

"Things have changed," Fauston said. He added, "There is a woman."

"Ah. Will we meet her?"

"She's—she's married."

"Oh."

Fauston shrugged, as if there was nothing he could do, as if he were bound by a force greater than himself. "Let's talk about something else, shall we?"

"Yes," Ailith said. She grabbed Fauston's arm and shook it vigorously. "And you can start by telling me how you come to be selling relics!"

It was well after dark when Fauston left, promising to meet them again on the morrow.

Ailith let out her breath. "Finally, we're alone."

"Yes," Roger said.

"I thought it would never happen."

Outside the tent were sounds of the camp—laughing, singing, the braying of mules, neighing of horses. Inside, there was an awkward silence.

At last Roger said, "Well . . ."

"Yes?" Ailith said.

"I guess we should . . ."

"Go to bed?"

"I suppose. I mean, it's about that time."

She gave him an arch look. "Well past time, I'd say."

There was another pause, then Roger moved closer to her. There was a hitch in his voice as he said, "I've wanted this forever."

She raised an eyebrow. "Then maybe you should stop talking and do something about it."

So he did.

Chapter 5

ONE-EYED HENRY of Deraa and the young count of Champagne reached Tyre not long past dawn. Travelers on the road had told them about Conrad of Montferrat's assassination, and the two lords and their escort had ridden hard through the night.

They arrived to a scene of chaos. The city gates were closed. A mob of travelers and merchants was camped outside the city, clamoring to get in. The French forces under the duke of Burgundy, some ten thousand men, were camped there, as well, so that it seemed as though the city were under siege. When Burgundy saw the blue-and-white banner of Champagne and the red falcon of Deraa approaching, he mounted and rode out to meet them.

"Thank Christ you're here, my lords," the grizzled duke said. Like Henry of Deraa, the duke was indifferently dressed, while the count of Champagne was, as always, meticulous about his appearance.

"We heard about Marquis Conrad's murder," the count said.

"Aye," said Burgundy. "Looks like Richard was as good as his word."

"You really think it was Richard?" the count asked.

"Who else?" said the duke.

"Saladin's my guess," the tall, rangy lord of Deraa said. "He had the most to gain from Conrad's death. Damned clever of him to try and pin the blame on Richard. I don't like Richard, but murder's not his style."

"Don't be so quick to blame Saladin," the count of Champagne said. "What about Guy of Luisgnan?" Guy of Lusignan was an adventurer who had once been king of Jerusalem by virtue of his marriage to Isabelle's sister, Sybelle. He had lost the crown when Sybelle died, but he still claimed a right to it from his exile in Cyprus. He had also been Conrad's bitter enemy. "Could have been Humphrey of Toron, as well," the count went on. "He's never forgiven Conrad for stealing Isabelle from him."

"It could have been a lot of people," Henry said. "My money's still on Saladin."

Burgundy looked unconvinced, and the count of Champagne changed the subject. He indicated the throng outside the city. "What's this about?"

"Queen Isabelle has closed the city," Burgundy said. "Says she won't open it to anyone but King Richard or Philip of France. I am King Philip's representative, but she says that's not good enough."

Pointedly, the count said, "Isabelle wouldn't be offering to surrender the city to Richard if she thought he ordered her husband's death."

Burgundy made a growling noise. "Where *is* Richard, anyway?" he asked.

"In the south," said Henry the Falcon, "laying siege to Daron."

Burgundy swore. "What the . . .?"

The count of Champagne explained. "Saladin has been slow to sign the peace terms, so Richard thought he'd give him a prod."

Burgundy shook his head. "This is a pretty mess. Just when everything was going well at last. What are we to do now?"

33

The count tapped a gloved hand on the high pommel of his saddle. "I'll go to the city. Queen Isabelle and I are friends. She'll speak to me."

"I'll go with you," said Henry of Derra. "I've known Isabelle since she was a babe. We'll take no escort. It will be less threatening that way."

"Why should she feel threatened?" Burgundy said. "We're on her side."

"Put yourself in her place. She doesn't know what's going on. Conrad's murder could be part of a plot to seize the kingdom. Someone could be planning to eliminate her next and take the throne for himself."

Henry and the count left Burgundy and started toward the city. "Does Isabelle like you?" the count asked Henry.

"Very few people like me," Henry said. "She respects my opinion, though."

They approached the outer city. A considerable suburb had grown up around Tyre in recent years, fueled by the city's prosperity. This suburb had been destroyed by Saladin during his siege of Tyre but had risen from the ashes like the proverbial phoenix. The streets were nearly empty as Henry and the count rode through. The tension in the air was palpable. No one knew what would happen next, and they wanted to avoid danger. A number of Muslims had been killed since Conrad's murder, suspected of being Saladin's agents; and their bloated, fly-covered bodies littered the streets. The count's horse—a new horse, untrained for war—shied at the smell, and the count had to curb him.

Henry and the count crossed the mole toward the walled Old City. Tyre had originally been built on an island. Long ago, it had been besieged by Alexander the Great, who had constructed a causeway to the city in order to attack it. During the ensuing centuries, the area around the causeway had been silted in. Conrad had held the city for two months against Saladin, who had attacked from land and sea, but had finally admitted defeat and retreated. If not for Conrad's defense of Tyre there might have been no crusade, because the Christians would have possessed no safe harbor for men to land, and the German emperor Barbarossa's fate demonstrated the folly of an overland expedition.

They reached the city gate. From above, the guard commander cried, "Halt, my lords! What is it you wish?"

"I am Henry, count of Champagne, and this is the baron of Deraa, whom you know well. We wish to speak with Queen Isabelle."

The guard commander, a knight wearing the red-and-white livery of Montferrat, said, "I'm sorry, my lord, but the queen will treat with no one but the kings of England or—"

"She'll speak with us," said the count, impatient with this underling. "I am nephew to both those men, and Lord Henry here was her husband's close ally."

"My orders are to—"

"Just tell her we're here, would you? There's a good fellow."

The knight hesitated, then disappeared. Henry and the count had a long wait in the sun. Sweat trickled out of Henry's greying hair and down his back. "What's your plan?" he asked the count.

"In truth, I do not know. But Isabelle must open the city or there will be panic—perhaps even civil war. The fate of the kingdom is at stake."

The sun rose higher, and the count said, "Tell me, what are you going to do when this is over? Assuming that it's ever over."

"Go back to Deraa and have a long bath," Henry said.

"Then what?"

Henry shrugged as though the answer was obvious. "Wage war on the infidel."

"What if we sign a peace treaty?"

"There will never be peace between me and them, my lord. Not while Saladin reigns and that bastard Qaymaz still draws breath."

At last came the sound of the heavy iron bar being raised. There was a metallic squealing of hinges, and the gates slowly opened.

Henry of Deraa and the count of Champagne rode across the dry moat into the Old City. Behind them, the gates ground shut.

Chapter 6

𝕴NSIDE THE CITY, a crowd grew around them—men, women, children. There were shouts of approbation for the handsome young count of Champagne, while salty veterans greeted Henry of Deraa, who acknowledged them with a curt nod of the head.

Queen Isabelle had shut herself in the citadel, where she would presumably be safe from whoever had ordered the murder of her husband. The citadel gate was opened. Servants took Henry's and the count's horses; and Conrad's grim steward, Kurt, escorted the two men into the citadel's hall, which was small and sparsely furnished.

The queen awaited them there. At twenty-one years of age, Isabelle was strikingly beautiful. She was also worn and haggard beyond her years. She had already been married twice. Her first marriage, to the scholarly Humphrey of Toron, had been brutally dissolved on grounds of expediency by Conrad of Montferrat and his allies. Now her second husband, Conrad, was dead at a murderer's hand. Isabelle wore a patterned Byzantine robe, swept up and gathered with a brooch at the shoulder. A Byzantine wimple covered her hair, and a necklace of ebony and precious stones was at her neck. With her in the hall were Josicus, archbishop of Tyre, and Balian of Ibelin.

The count of Champagne bowed low to Isabelle. He knew her well from the siege. They had often been thrown together at parties and banquets, and they had spent many hours in pleasant, and sometimes flirtatious, conversation. "Your highness. May I express my deep regret at your loss."

"And I," added one-eyed Henry of Deraa, bowing as well.

"Thank you, my lords," Isabelle said formally. "It is good to see the both of you again. We have missed the pleasure of your company."

"Hullo, Balian," Henry said, straightening. "Thought we'd find you here."

"I arrived last night," said the normally dapper Balian, who looked almost as haggard as Isabelle. Balian was Isabelle's stepfather. He had married Isabelle's mother, King Amalric's second wife, Maria Comnena, after Amalric's death. The kingdom's inheritance had passed to Isabelle's sister, Sybelle, and then to Isabelle after the death of her half-brother by Amalric's first marriage—Baldwin, the Leper King. Balian, the Leper King's closest advisor, had been one of the chief movers at making Conrad king of Jerusalem, but now his plans to restore the kingdom's glory lay in ruins. Beside him, the purple-clad Josicus looked gloomy.

"Now," said Isabelle to her guests, "why have you come to see me?"

"To make sure you are well," the count said, "and also to say that it is imperative for you to open the city."

"Why? So that whoever killed my husband can come in and kill me, too? We don't know who designed my husband's death, or for what purpose."

"As to the first, my lady, if the gates are not opened and normal life resumed, we may soon see discord and fighting in the streets. As to the second, the purpose is obvious—to keep your late husband,

Conrad, from becoming king, to keep him from taking Jerusalem from the Saracens."

Balian said, "Thank you, lord count. That's what I've been telling her." Balian, Champagne, and Henry of Deraa had become good friends over the course of the crusade, but circumstances—and the queen's presence—forced them to assume a more formal attitude today.

Beneath her outwardly cool demeanor, Isabelle seemed scared, like a trapped animal. Josicus tried to ease her fears, his voice, like his appearance, smooth from years of practice. "I think we're agreed that our first order of business must be to keep the queen safe."

"Yes," said the count of Champagne.

"We'll keep her safe," Henry of Deraa growled. "You have our oaths on that."

Isabelle fell back on her previous terms, reciting them as if by rote. "I will open the city to no one but the kings of England or France."

The count of Champagne spoke in a soft voice. "That is physically impossible, madame. The king of France is long gone from this land, and the king of England is busy in the south. I am related to both men, as you know, and on their behalves—and, more importantly, as your friend—I will assume responsibility for keeping order in the city and for the safety of your person."

Balian said, "Thank you, Count Henry. Your words are appreciated." He took a deep breath. "It grieves me to say this, but there is a more important matter before us. To avoid civil war, the kingdom needs a ruler, as soon as possible. The queen may not like it—*we* may not like it—but she must be married again, and quickly."

The blood drained from Isabelle's face. "Married? I've only been a widow for two days."

"I know, Isabelle, and I don't like it any more than you do, but we live in perilous times. When the crusaders from the west go home—and they will go home very soon—we will be on our own against the Saracens."

"I am queen," Isabelle protested. "I can lead—"

"With respect, you cannot. The barons would never accept a woman as their leader, even with me to back you. There would be civil war—Guy of Lusignan might well return—and the kingdom would cease to exist within a few years. We need a strong ruler, one whom everyone can respect. We can't afford to have Lusignan and his friends back in power."

The color returned to Isabelle's cheeks. "And who is this strong ruler to be?" she demanded.

"I have no answer for that, unfortunately," Balian said. He turned. "Archbishop?"

Josicus shook his head. "Nor do I. Lord Henry?"

Henry of Deraa scratched his beard and cast a sidelong glance with his remaining eye. "My lord of Champagne, you're unmarried, I believe?"

The count nodded, not comprehending at first. "That's right, I—wait. You want *me* to marry the queen?"

Josicus picked up on Deraa's idea. "You'd be an ideal candidate, my lord. You're related to the kings of France and England. You're young, good looking, and popular with both the nobility and the people."

"But . . . I'm going home when the crusade is finished. I miss my lands in Champagne. I have a duty to my vassals there."

Henry placed a hand on the count's shoulder. "You have another duty, my friend. A duty to God and His kingdom. You came here to save the kingdom, this is your chance to do it."

"But—"

"I agree with the lord of Deraa," Balian said. He saw the count's surprise and added, "My lord, we wouldn't ask this of you were it not of paramount importance. Were our old comrade James of Avesnes still with us, he'd urge it of you, as well. You know he would. He wouldn't have wanted to come all this way and die for naught. To die so that pimp Lusignan could come back and destroy the kingdom."

The count felt like he had fallen into a trap. This was the last thing he had envisioned. He turned to the lord of Deraa. "You're unmarried, why don't you do it? God knows, you'd make a good king."

Henry laughed. "I am not of high enough rank, and I am too old and too ugly for such a beautiful lady." He grew serious, "Besides, I swore an oath never to—"

Isabelle stepped forward, irritated. "Perhaps you'd be so kind as to consult me about this?"

Josicus said, "My lady, such matters are best left to—"

"To men? Leaving matters to men is what's gotten us into this mess. It's the rest of my life you're talking about. The first part hasn't been all that wonderful, in case you hadn't noticed, so I'd like some say in the next."

Henry of Deraa inclined his head gallantly. "A reasonable request, my lady."

Balian of Ibelin said, "I agree, Daughter, and you'll excuse me us if this has been hasty. It's just that—"

"It's just that time is of the essence. Yes, yes, I'm not stupid, Father. I understand your concerns, and believe it or nòt, I share them. I have no wish to be queen of a kingdom that doesn't exist. And I'll kill myself before I let Guy of Lusignan destroy my life as he did my sister's."

Archbishop Josicus spread his arms. "So . . .?"

Isabelle let out a long breath. Suddenly she was no longer a hardened queen, but a vulnerable young woman. "This is all so . . . sudden. I haven't even had time to absorb the fact that Conrad is dead."

Josicus said, "We realize that, my lady. Nevertheless—"

She silenced him with a wave of the hand, a queen once again, and practical. "By Church law, wedding banns must last a year," she reminded them.

"We can work around that," Josicus said. "Once the Pope learns of the wedding, it will be too late for him to do anything about it. He would not dare annul it."

Balian put an arm around the queen's shoulder. "Your happiness is my concern, Isabelle, you know that; and if we were at peace, I would say take your time and marry the person of your choosing. But we are at war. We have just lost our greatest leader, and we will quite soon be without our most powerful military force. We must present a united front to the enemy, or we are lost."

Isabelle closed her eyes for a moment, then opened them and turned to the count of Champagne. "If I must be married so quickly, it should at least be to someone I like. I would as soon that someone be you, my lord count, your reservations notwithstanding."

The count hesitated. He and Isabelle were friends. More than friends. They might have become lovers had a jealous Conrad not spirited her back to Tyre. Still, the count longed for the green fields and rolling hills of Champagne. If only he could take Isabelle there, he would agree to the union happily.

"There is one thing you must know," Isabelle went on, holding the count's gaze. "I am pregnant."

The room fell silent.

"This changes everything," Josicus said at last.

Balian nodded. "If the child is a boy, it means that Count Henry's children would not rule. It means their futures would not be secure." To the count he said, "It is a lot to ask of you, my friend."

Count Henry looked at Isabelle. He did like her. Had she stayed on the Toron during the siege, he might well have fallen in love with her. And he knew how rare it was to marry someone you loved. He would be placing a great burden upon himself for the sake of another man's son, though—assuming that Isabelle's unborn child was a boy. He would also be placing another burden on himself—he would have to assume command of the kingdom's army. He was a good soldier, and he had experience commanding the army during the siege of Acre. He had done well, all things considered, but command was not something he relished—not this command, anyway, and the expectations that went with it. He knew the army would demand to

43

march on Jerusalem before the duke of Burgundy's men went home, and he felt inadequate to lead such an undertaking.

The lord of Deraa was right, though. Count Henry had a duty, and he believed in duty.

He looked at Isabelle again. She was so beautiful, and her expression seemed to be pleading with him. "I'll do it," he said.

As Isabelle's face brightened, he held up a hand. "On two conditions."

Balian said, "Which are?"

"One, that my uncle, King Richard, approves the arrangement."

"We should have no trouble persuading him to do that," Balian said.

"Two, that we ask Richard to lead one more attack on Jerusalem before he leaves the Holy Land. We have his army here; we should use it while we yet may."

Balian and Henry of Deraa shared uneasy glances. They did not want to get Richard involved in military matters again. As far as they were concerned, the sooner Richard was gone, the better.

For all his smoothness, Josicus did not pick up on their misgivings. Before Balian or Henry could try to talk the count out of letting Richard back into the picture, Josicus said to the count, "Those conditions are immutable?"

The count wavered. He was already starting to picture himself as Isabelle's husband, to picture her in his arms, and that picture was not an unpleasant one. He was looking forward to it, in fact. He knew that, if they pressed him, he would give in, but he pretended to stiffen. "They are."

Balian turned to Isabelle to dissuade her from accepting these terms, but she had her own mind. She advanced and put her arm through Henry's. "I accept the terms. I will surrender the keys of the city to Count Henry."

"Very well," said Archbishop Josicus, looking relieved. Before Balian or Henry of Deraa were able to object, he said, "Send a messenger to King Richard. Let the marriage be held in two days' time, in the city of Acre."

Chapter 7

ᛕING RICHARD AND his retinue of knights and men-at-arms rode back to Daron. It had been a successful hunt. The heads of six Saracens were tied to Richard's saddle—three on each side, for symmetry. Blood still leaked from the heads; it splotched the horse's shoulders along with the front of Richard's saddle and his legs. Alart of Vouzin and Andrew of Chauvigny, who rode with Richard, disapproved of this new habit of taking heads. They said nothing about it, but Richard could tell. Richard didn't care. The crusade was over, at least his part in it was. He was going to do what he wanted until he left this Purgatory and went home. He was going to have fun. And lately his idea of fun was hanging a daily harvest of pagan heads from his saddle. Tomorrow it might be something else. Just like taking Daron. Oh, it was true that he wanted Saladin to stop dawdling over the peace terms, but he had really laid siege to the city for the fun of it. The siege of Acre had been no fun. Those fools had made a botch of it. Had he been there from the beginning, it would have fallen in a month, probably less.

Richard had taken Daron in five days, showing that he hadn't lost his touch, then put the garrison to the sword. Taking castles was what he was good at. Maybe that old goat herder Saladin would sign a peace agreement now. Despite endless negotiations, the framework of a peace had changed little in the past six months—the Christians would hold the land they currently possessed and would have access to

Jerusalem. The sticking point was still Ascalon. Saladin wanted the new fortifications there torn down, but Richard refused. The city was the crusaders' most commanding position on the coast. It had also cost Richard a fortune to rebuild, and he was loath to see all that money go to waste.

"Sire," Alart warned.

Riders were coming—from the north, where Ascalon lay. Richard dropped a hand to the axe at his belt, then relaxed. The riders were Christian.

There were about fifty men in all—safety required a large number in this country. At their front were the banners of the bishop of Beauvais and the count of Soissons.

"They're coming on fast," Alart said.

"Wonder what they want?" said Andrew of Chauvigny. "I'm surprised they have the nerve to show themselves around you, sire."

Richard and his retinue halted to wait for the men, who adjusted their course to intercept the royal party. "You know, I've never liked Soissons' banner," Richard remarked to his companions while they waited for the riders to get close. "Yellow perch on a red background? It makes the house of Nesle look weak. Real men have lions, or hawks, or boars for their emblems—not fish."

Alart and Andrew laughed. Richard had not forgiven either of these newcomers—especially his one-time ally Beauvais—for turning on him and supporting Conrad of Montferrat for king of Jerusalem.

The newcomers reined in, dusty and travel stained. Beauvais and Soissons were both in their early forties. Of the party, they alone were not wearing armor. The stolid, unprepossessing Soissons looked worn, and Richard knew that he longed for home and family, while the warlike Beauvais planned to stay in the Holy Land a while with the duke of Burgundy.

"Greetings, sire," said the bishop of Beauvais.

"My lord bishop," Richard intoned. "You are not under arms"— *and without a whore*, Richard sneered inwardly—"so this must be a social call."

Before things could turn ugly, Soissons said, "The marquis of Montferrat is dead, sire."

Richard paused, not quite believing what he had just heard.

Soissons plodded on. "He was killed by a member of the sect called Assassins, for what reason we do not know."

Richard was stunned. He was not sorry to hear of Conrad's death. He had never liked the fellow. Conrad was a nobody trying to put himself on an equal footing with his betters. Still, this was momentous news.

Beauvais continued. "I'd best warn you, sire, some are blaming you for Conrad's death. Saying that you paid the Assassins to kill him."

"Who says this?" Richard demanded. "Burgundy, no doubt."

"And others," added Beauvais.

"And what think you, my lord bishop?"

There was a threat in Richard's voice, but Beauvais gave it no heed. "We have had our differences, sire, but I do not believe you would stoop to having Conrad murdered."

"Nor do I," said the count of Soissons. "My guess is that Saladin was behind it."

The bishop nodded agreement.

"Saladin is behind it, yet I get the blame," Richard said. *"Plus ça change, plus c'est la même chose.* So what is to become of the kingdom?"

"That is why we have come to see you," Beauvais said. "Your nephew, the count of Champagne, wishes to marry Conrad's widow, Queen Isabelle, and he asks for your approval."

"That was quick," Alart remarked.

"The kingdom needs a leader," the bishop snapped.

The poor girl is lucky to be rid of Conrad, Richard thought. He had known that Henry and Isabelle had feelings for each other; a man would have to have been blind not to have seen it. "He has my approval, and most heartily given." Richard almost added, "I wish he had taken Berengaria instead," but he realized that a joke would be in poor taste under the circumstances. "He will make a good husband to the queen and a good ruler for the kingdom."

Soissons cleared his throat. "There is more, sire. Count Henry also requests that you put off going home and lead one more advance on Jerusalem."

Richard felt like he had been struck by lightning. He sat straighter in the saddle and made a show of gathering his reins while he thought.

Conrad's death, the call to lead the army again—it was a sign from God. It had to be.

This was redemption. It was fated, decreed in the ancient halls of time. He was to get a second chance at immortality, and this time he would not fail. He felt the hand of God upon him, and he was both humbled and raised up by it.

He crossed himself and addressed the two messengers as if there had never been bad blood between them. "Brothers, tell the count that I will lead an advance on the Holy City. Tell him further that in assurance of this, I promise to remain in the Holy Land until Easter next."

There were mixed emotions on the faces of Beauvais and Soissons; Richard couldn't tell whether they were happy with his decision or not. Alart showed no reaction to the news; he would do whatever Richard wanted. Young Andrew of Chauvigny was downcast, though he did his best not to show it. He had been hoping to go home and see his father before the old man died.

Richard went on, expansive now, almost jovial. "Let us take up our weapons and repair to God's Holy City, that we may punish the heathens who have made themselves its masters. Have our men begin assembling at Ascalon and Jaffa. We will rendezvous at Bet Nable in the first week of June, and then march on Jerusalem. Come, gentlemen, there is work to be done."

He untied the Saracen heads from his saddle and threw them on the ground. He wouldn't be needing them anymore.

Chapter 8

"**JT'S A PITY** Fauston's been so busy," Ailith said.

"Yes," said Roger. "I wish we could see more of him."

"Is it his work, do you think, or is it this mysterious woman of his?"

"Both, is my guess."

Arm in arm, the two of them strolled along the road from the city, where they had dined with Fauston at the Golden Keys. Roger had never been as happy as he was right now. Paradoxically, he felt guilty about that, because he'd thought he'd been happy with Helvise. He wondered if he was in some way betraying Helvise now, betraying her memory, her commitment to him. He couldn't help it, though. He had always loved Ailith and he always would. Everything seemed perfect—even the weather, which was unusually mild for this time of year. The sun glared off the sea; gulls cried. A man could stare at that blue sky and dream his life away. Roger had dreamed about Ailith like that, and now here she was beside him.

Ahead lay the English camp, sleeping under the late afternoon sun. Ailith was used to camp life, having lived on the Toron during the long siege. She knew a lot of the Death's Heads from those days. She had renewed her acquaintance with Celia and Mary and the other washerwomen who had survived the siege, and she spent time with them when Roger was on duty. She even helped with the washing, to keep her hand in.

"When do you think King Richard will be leaving?" Ailith asked. Her eyes were partially closed, as though she, too, didn't want this moment to end.

"Probably soon," Roger said. "They say he's vexed with Prince John and eager to get back to England. The earl will no doubt be going with him."

Ailith stopped. "And what will you and I do then?"

The perfect moment had ended. It was a question that had obviously been on Ailith's mind, a question Roger hadn't wanted to think about.

Ailith went on. "I want to go back to England, but what would we do there?"

Roger was almost afraid to answer. "I—I cannot return to England."

Ailith's brow clouded. "You were ready enough to leave the Holy Land with Helvise."

"Helvise had a home to go back to, in Germany. She had money and an estate where we could live. I'm wanted for murder in England. And even if I could get pardoned by King Richard, what are my options? I could be a knight for hire, but that's not the life I want. I'm not as fond of warfare as I thought I would be."

"Because you keep getting scars?"

"Because I want to be with you, not off killing people."

That seemed to mollify her. They began walking again and entered the Death's Heads' camp. Men lazed about, or tended to the transport animals, mended clothes, or collected dried animal dung for the fires. Drill was largely forgotten these days, but Roger insisted that tents and equipment be kept clean and that the men stay out of serious trouble, and for the most part they did.

Ailith said, "So what is your plan if you remain here?"

"Join my father, I suppose."

"Isn't that the same as being a knight for hire? The war out here is never like to end."

"He's the only family I have, Ailith. The only family I've ever had. Anyway, he's a chief baron of the kingdom. His estates will one day be mine—ours."

They had reached his tent, and Roger held the flap open as she entered. "You say 'ours,'" she said when they were inside. "What am I to be to you?"

Roger spread his hands. "My wife. I thought you knew that."

She let out her breath. "You wish to marry me?"

"It's all I've ever wished."

"And have a family?"

"That's usually part of marriage."

"But how can we be married? In the eyes of God, you're still under the vows of a monk."

"I'll take my chances if you will."

Her brows arched playfully. "And when does this marriage take place?"

"As soon as possible, if you say yes. I can get Father Ambrose to marry us."

She pirouetted. "You say you wish to marry me, sir knight, yet you have never asked for my hand."

Roger stammered. "Well, I . . . I mean, I thought that you—"

"On your knees," she commanded.

Roger obeyed and clasped his hands together, as though in prayer. "Ailith of Wynchecombe—"

"Lower Wynchecombe," she corrected imperiously.

Roger rolled his eyes. "Ailith of Lower Wynchecombe, I formally request that you do me the honor of becoming my wife."

She pretended to mull over his request. "No ring?" she said.

"I'll get a ring. Fauston will find us one."

"Arise, sir knight."

Roger got to his feet. Ailith put her arms around him, kissed him and held him close, her voice soft. "I know you want to stay here with your father. Of course you do. I'll be happy to stay here with you. I'll stay with you anywhere, you know that."

"What about going back to England?"

She shrugged. "All it ever does there is rain."

Roger stepped back. "Does this mean you accept my proposal?"

For an answer, she pulled her dress over her head. She wore nothing beneath it. "I don't know. Show me some of your knightly prowess that I may judge whether your words are true."

Roger moved toward her.

Outside, a horn sounded—three long blasts, three short.

Roger stopped, swearing. "Commander's Call. Wonder what that's about?"

Reluctantly, Ailith picked up her dress. As captain of the earl's footmen, Roger would have to answer the call. "Most likely they're telling us when the army will return to England," he said.

Roger kissed her, fondling her breast as he did, massaging her nipple between his thumb and middle finger until it got hard, making her gasp and drop the dress. He let go of her and winked. "Don't go anywhere."

He left the tent. On the patch of open ground that was used for drill and inspection, Geoffrey of Trent sat his horse. His marshal, Blaise, was beside him, along with the usual crowd of squires and heralds—Roger recognized Regimbaud, who had escorted him and Ailith from the governor's palace. Before them the high-ranking lords and unit commanders of the earl's division were assembling. All around the Christian camp, horns and trumpets sounded, so the news must be important. Roger took a place in the rear, as befitted a captain of foot. Behind him, a number of curious knights and common soldiers had turned out as well.

The earl was still weak from his long illness, but he gutted his way through his announcement. "Gentlemen, I bring news."

There was a stirring among the lords in front of Roger, and the earl went on. "As you know, the marquis of Montferrat is dead, and the count of Champagne is to marry his widow and become ruler of the kingdom of Jerusalem."

More stirring, but not much; the men knew this already. "As his first official act, Count Henry has requested that King Richard lead another march on the Holy City."

That caused a buzz, and the earl paused to let the news sink in.

Then he said, "King Richard has agreed."

The buzz became a low roar, and the earl raised his voice. "We're not going home just yet, men. We have unfinished business. We are to make all haste to Jaffa, and from there repair to Bet Nable, on the Holy City's outskirts."

The roar grew louder. "Are you going with us?" one of the barons called to the earl.

The earl rose in his stirrups. "Nothing could keep me away!"

The roar turned into cheering. It started among the watching footmen in the rear, then spread to the knights and men-at-arms, then to the commanders.

"There is much to be done," the earl said, barely able to make himself heard above the noise. "I wish to be in Jaffa within the week."

The cheering grew louder and louder. There was similar cheering all round the vast camp. Something made Roger look behind him.

Ailith stood in the tent entrance, dressed now. She was watching him, and she looked worried.

Chapter 9

WHEN THE ASSEMBLY was dismissed, Roger walked slowly back to his tent. Around him, cheers and shouts resounded through the English camp, from the highest lords to the lowliest servants. Similar cheers sounded from the other camps scattered around the city. These men longed for home, but they longed for Jerusalem more.

Ailith waited for Roger at the tent entrance. She was composed, but that composure seemed fragile. "Must you go?" she asked him.

"It's my duty," Roger said.

Ailith said nothing, and Roger went on. "This is why we've come here, Ailith. To take Jerusalem."

Ailith sighed. "I know, but I'm worried."

Roger tried to make light of her foreboding. "I'll be all right. The worst that can happen is that I'll get another scar. I'll try to get one on the right side of my face this time, for balance."

"That's not funny," she snapped, and her eyes gleamed wetly. "I know I'm being selfish, but I've waited all this time for you, and I don't want to lose you now."

He took her shoulders. "There are more important things in this world than us."

She lowered her eyes.

"Besides," he said, "you won't lose me."

"Your saying it doesn't make it so."

Roger didn't reply to that.

She punched his chest lightly. "Just promise you won't try to be too much of a hero."

"I won't. I'm hoping for a short campaign. King Richard had bad luck last time. This time he'll take the city, you'll see."

She put her arms around him. "Can I go with you as a washerwoman?"

"There'll be no washerwomen on this campaign."

"I could cut my hair, then, and pretend to be one of your squires."

Roger wasn't sure if she was serious, but he said, "No. I don't want you anywhere near the fighting. I don't want to lose *you* now, either."

She looked up at him. "Then I suppose I'll ask Fauston to find me a room in the city. I'll be safe there till you get back."

Fauston was only too happy to find Ailith a room. In fact, he procured her a suite of them, near the Church of St. Andrew, with a balcony and a view of sea.

"This is lovely," Roger said as the three of them stood on the balcony. The sea air made everything, even the city, smell fresh. "I can't afford it, though. The only money I have is—"

"I'll pay for it," Fauston said.

Roger looked to Ailith, then back to Fauston. "I appreciate that, Fauston. I'll repay you after we—"

Fauston waved him off. "Consider it a gift. You two are my oldest and best friends. I have money for once in my life, the least I can do is see it put to good use."

❧

There was much to do be done before the army set out, especially since no one had anticipated this turn of events. Armor had to be repaired; weapons needed to be honed. The men had to be drilled. They had gotten out of shape and complacent. Some of them had forgotten the evolutions they'd learned, while the newcomers had never learned them at all. Men from other units whose terms of service were over were transferring to the Death's Heads. The Death's Heads were considered a prime company by these men because they always seemed to be in the thick of the fighting, where the glory—and the loot—was. The thick of the fighting was also where death lay, but these men—young men, who thought themselves invincible—were willing to take that chance. Roger had no idea where the earl was finding the money to pay them—borrowing it, probably. All the nobles were. Roger had heard that King Richard had been forced to sell his jeweled sword Excalibur—named after King Arthur's weapon—to help defray his mounting debts.

Besides drill, there were a thousand and one things for Roger to worry about—supplies, equipment, animals. He also had to obtain new equipment for himself. Trained war horses were prohibitively expensive. The earl had not given him enough money for that—and as a captain of foot, he did not need one—so he purchased two palfreys—a deep-chested bay with a black mane and a chestnut with a white blaze. Arms and weapons were plentiful—from dead men and from men who had sold them before returning to Europe. Roger bought a long-sleeved hauberk, with mail more tightly woven than that of his last one. Mail mittens at the end of the hauberk's sleeves could be tied back to the wrist when the user wasn't in combat. He bought mail leggings with foot coverings, which would come in handy if he was on horseback and fighting men on the ground—he'd seen more than one knight with feet or toes chopped off by Saracen footmen.

He found a conical helmet with a nose guard, similar to the one he'd worn before. Tatwine painted both the helmet and its cloth cover with the red death's head. Roger's new shield was more triangular than the kite-shaped shield he'd used before, and Tatwine painted that with the death's head, as well. Tatwine also sewed a death's head on Roger's white surcoat. There was a time when wearing the death's head had bothered Roger, but now he was proud of it. Saladin himself had recognized the symbol—and spared Roger's life because of it. More than that, he was proud of it because his men liked it. It gave them identity.

For arms, Roger purchased a dagger with a foot-and-a-half-long blade and a sword. The sword was of good construction and had a longer hand guard than his last one. He preferred an axe in battle, though, and he found a good one in the city market. It was nicely balanced with a spike on the cap for thrusting. The letter "A" had been burned into the oak handle by some previous owner, but Roger had no idea what the "A" stood for or what the owner's fate had been.

~

Before dawn on the seventh of June, the feast of St. Willibald, the earl of Trent's men began assembling for the march south. Trent's rival, the earl of Leicester, had chartered ships for his division, but Trent didn't have that kind of money. Besides, it was a short march to Jaffa.

In the space of time between matins and prime, the English camp virtually disappeared, as most of the tents were taken down and stowed in wagons to be used in the upcoming siege of Jerusalem. What had yesterday been a bustling tent city was largely open plain again.

Tatwine packed Roger's new armor and equipment into a wagon as well. Knights weren't wearing armor for the march to Jaffa; the route was deemed safe. A screen of Turcos would give ample warning in case of a Saracen attack.

As the sun rose, those who were staying behind—the sick, the wounded, washerwomen, clerics—gathered on one side of the plain to see the earl's division off. They were joined by curious onlookers from the city. Roger stood with Ailith and Fauston, watching the spectacle—horses being saddled for the knights, spears and hauberks bundled onto wagons, foot soldiers packing sacks, servants and squires running about on last-minute errands, transport animals hitched to wagons. Gradually the bustle slowed, and in small groups the men began forming.

It was almost time.

Roger took Ailith's hand in his. "I'll miss you," she told him.

Roger's heart felt so heavy, he thought it might burst. "And I, you."

Fauston held out his hand. "Goodbye, my friend."

Roger clasped Fauston's hand. "Goodbye. Take care of Ailith."

"I will."

"Don't worry about me," Ailith told Roger, "you take care of yourself."

"I will," Roger said.

A horn blew the two long notes of Assembly.

Roger kissed Ailith goodbye. She clung to him hungrily, the way she had clung to him last night, digging her nails deep into his back and trying not to cry, neither of them wanting it to end. Roger started away, holding onto her hand as long as he could, then reluctantly letting it go. He gave her a last look and joined his men.

The Death's Heads were formed in marching order—spearmen, axe men, archers. Their armored jacks were rolled up and tied behind their backs, with their helmets attached to them. On their heads most wore keffiyehs, which had largely replaced the conical straw hats that used to be the headgear of choice.

"Morning, Roger," said Short Peter as Roger approached. "Good day for it."

"Morning, Roger," said Oswy.

"Morning Roger," said Pentecost and Yves and just about every man he passed. Hardly any of them called him by his title, "Captain," and though that was a breach of discipline, Roger didn't mind. He had once been one of them, and in his mind he still was.

Roger took his reins from Tatwine and mounted the bay. Beside him Tatwine carried the worn Death's Heads banner with its leering red skull.

The earl's men were drawn up in three ranks—knights in front, followed by men-at-arms and squires, then the footmen. Behind them were the supernumeraries, spare horses and wagons, along with a herd of camels that would be eaten on the march to Bet Nable. As the division moved south, they would be joined by the count of Hungary, the Latvians, some Poles, and a contingent from Naples. Other units had already left Acre; more would follow.

Banners and pennons snapped in the sea breeze as the earl and his marshal, Blaise, rode down the lines of men, inspecting them. The earl was pale and thin after months of confinement, but he seemed eager. He came to the Death's Heads and smiled. "Your men look good, Roger."

Roger said, "They'll do, my lord."

"They always have."

Their inspection complete, the earl and Blaise retired to the front of the formation to join the rest of his retinue. A horn sounded, and the Turcopole scouts cantered out. The earl's chaplain recited a longish prayer and blessed the men. When that was done, Blaise cried, "By the right! Column of fours!"

The knights wheeled and formed column, and Blaise cried, "Forward!"

The knights set off, followed by the others. They passed the earl and his retinue, dipping their banners in salute. When it was the Death's Heads turn to go, Roger cried, "By the right—march!"

By fours, the men turned and set off—axe men with weapons in their belts, spearmen with heavy spears resting on shoulder pads, archers with cased weapons slung over their shoulders. They were followed by the spare animals and transport and the soon-to-be-eaten camels. As they passed the earl, Tatwine dipped the Death's Heads banner, and Roger held his chin high in salute.

The division took a turn around what used to be the parade area for the benefit of the onlookers and those who were staying behind. Roger raised a hand to Ailith and saw her wipe an eye, Fauston with her, wearing his wide-brimmed hat. Then the division turned south, where they would meet the Hungarians and the others. The new band—the original band members were all dead—started playing "Girls of Falaise," and the men sang lustily, reveling in the tune's bawdy lyrics.

The earl and his staff waited until the entire division had passed, then they galloped to the head of the column and set off on the road to Jerusalem.

PART II

Chapter 10

June 1192

ℭRUNCH OF HOOFS, tramp of feet, jingle of armor and accoutrements. A cloud of dust in the still air.

The earl of Trent's division was approaching Bet Nable.

"Don't look much different than it did last time we was here," Tatwine observed as they entered the town.

"Probably don't look much different than it did last time Jesus was here," the centenar Oswy said.

"Or Moses," said Slowfoot.

"What makes you think Moses was here?" Tatwine asked.

"Stands to reason," Slowfoot said. "He were a Jew, weren't he? Every Jew ends up in Jerusalem, and you have to go through here to get to Jerusalem."

Tatwine looked to Oswy for assistance, but Oswy shrugged. "All I remember about Moses is them commandments, and that he turned the sea red."

Tatwine turned to Roger, who rode alongside them. "'Ere, Roger, you know about these things, working at an abbey and all. Was Moses ever in Jerusalem?"

Roger smiled. "Moses was born in Egypt and died in the desert. He never set foot in Israel, much less Jerusalem."

"Ha!" Tatwine said to Slowfoot. "Told you."

"Christ save us," Slowfoot muttered. "Tatwine, the religious scholar."

Bet Nable was a straggling village of shabby, flat-topped clay houses. Around them, troops drilled and scouting parties rode out. A long pack train was being readied to go back to Jaffa for supplies. There were cries of vintenars and braying of mules; there was music and shouting. There were the familiar army smells of animals and shit and thousands upon thousands of unwashed men, mixed with the aromas of dung fires and baking bread and whatever meat the men could find. Vari-colored tents clustered the hills, along with three great parks of siege engines, packed and ready to be assembled before the walls of Jerusalem.

The men of Trent's division were hot and weary, the infantry footsore. The march from Jaffa had taken four days on the flinty, winding trails, with the armored horsemen walking as often as they rode, sometimes ploughing through thick scrub as high as a man. The men had eaten meals off their shields, contesting the food with furry spiders and swarms of small, biting flies that left their skins covered with red bites. All of them—even the highest nobles—were covered with a layer of dust so thick that at first glance they seemed like inhabitants of some distant world. The singing had ceased long ago, they were too tired for that. They wanted water; the last time they'd had any was at Latrun. They were hungry, too; the camel herd was a distant memory.

"Lousy country for foraging," Oswy said, looking around.

"Lousy country for much of anything," Tatwine said. "Thought this was supposed to be the land of milk and honey?"

Some of the men who were already there came out to watch them march in. "Smarten up, lads," Short Peter ordered. "Don't let the Frenchies—" he called any Christians who weren't English "Frenchies" "—see you slacking." The Death's Heads straightened and tried to put some liveliness into their step.

Roger looked around. Two years had wrought many changes in the Christian army, so many that Roger felt he was hardly a part of it anymore. Most of the men encamped at Bet Nable had arrived since the fall of Acre or late in the siege. There wasn't much left of the old crowd. Those bright, eager faces from the early days of the siege had become toothless veterans, pocked and scarred from disease and battle and malnutrition. The hymns they had sung then had been replaced by satirical songs about their leaders. The once-vast host of Scandinavians was down to little over a hundred men. They, with the Frisians, Scots, Irish, Spanish, Germans and some of the Italians were finished as individual units and had taken service in a kind of international division under King Richard. When the crusade ended, these men were not certain of getting home. They could not afford passage, and their liege lords were dead or far away. But they would worry about that when the time came.

King Richard's heralds showed Trent's men where to camp, where to draw water, where to dig their latrines. Trent's division was situated next to the earl of Leicester's men, who had arrived two days before, and, as latecomers, they were at some distance from the springs.

The men fell out, and Roger dismounted. To Short Peter, he said, "All right, Shorty, detail water parties and find something to start fires with. When the men and animals have drunk their fill, get the tents up."

"Right, Roger."

As Short Peter turned away, Roger noticed Tatwine slouching off. "Where are you going, Tatty?"

"See if there's any meat to be had," Tatwine said.

"Be careful, I don't want you hanged for a—"

"Roger!"

Roger turned to see Henry of Deraa riding up.

The one-eyed baron swung himself from the saddle and approached. Roger wanted to embrace him, but Henry was not that kind of man. He stopped in front of Roger, looking him over, then he nodded and clapped Roger's shoulder, raising a small cloud of dust. "Good to see you, boy," he said.

"And you," said Roger.

Henry wore an out-of-fashion straw hat against the sun. "I heard you were alive, but I wasn't able to get to Acre to join you."

"I understand, Father."

Henry shook his head. "'Father.' That still takes some getting used to." He grew serious. "They say you were Qaymaz's prisoner."

"Yes. Saladin wanted me—"

"Saladin? You met Saladin?"

"Yes."

"What's he like?"

"Hard to say, I only saw him the one time. Qaymaz wanted to kill me, but Saladin had me kept alive because we wouldn't kill those prisoners at Acre."

Henry grunted, and Roger went on. "Qaymaz wasn't happy when Saladin ordered him to let me live. Later, when I was his slave, Qaymaz arranged for me to have a fatal 'accident.'"

"Sounds like him," Henry said. "How did you get away?"

"Ailith—you remember her—"

"Geoffrey of Trent's woman?"

"Not anymore, but that's a long story. Anyway, she found out I was at the Blue Fort, and—"

"Wait—Ailith was Qaymaz's prisoner too?"

"She was. He'd made her part of his *harim*. Anyway, she found out I was there, and she arranged for us and some others to escape."

Henry took off his straw hat and scratched the back of his head. "That's a hell of a story, son. You've become quite the hero, you know—both for what you did at Arsuf and for escaping. Hard to tell which you're most famous for. Half the lords in the army are jealous of you."

"I'd gladly have traded places with them," Roger said. He looked round the great camp. "When do we march on the Holy City?"

"We're waiting for the count of Champagne to bring up the last men from Acre."

"We shouldn't have to wait long then. The count was supposed to leave the city a day or two after us."

❦

71

Nearby, a huge man in a red surcoat rode up to the earl of Trent and his staff. The Holy Land had changed King Richard. The boyish handsomeness had been replaced by the lined face of a veteran. His once luxuriant hair and beard were cut short, the reddish gold flecked with grey.

"Lord Geoffrey," he said in his booming voice, "I prayed you would be able to join us. The last I saw you, you appeared sick unto death."

Geoffrey drew himself up. The ravages that the crusade had wreaked upon him made Richard look like a babe. Even his voice sounded older. "Sire, I have lost my brother to this enterprise. I have lost most of the men I brought with me. I have lost my health. Our goal is finally within reach, however, and I will give whatever I have left to assure its success."

Richard put a hand on the earl's shoulder. "Well said, Geoffrey, well said."

From the corner of his eye, Richard spied the red skull flag of the Death's Heads. "Excuse me, if you will," he said, bowing to Geoffrey. He and his retinue trotted their horses over to where Roger stood with Henry of Deraa.

"Well, well," Richard cried, "if it isn't the hero of Arsuf."

Roger turned and blanched. He couldn't tell from the tone of Richard's voice whether he was angry or not.

Richard reined in and glared down at Roger. "You disobeyed my order, Huntley. I could have your head for that. He waved an arm at

Henry. "You take after your father here. He pays no attention to what I say, either."

Roger stammered. "Sire, I was just trying to—"

Richard's grim mien suddenly lightened, and he beamed a smile. "Yes, yes, I had the story from your father. You're in no trouble. Damn me, but I might have done the same thing were I you."

Roger was relieved. "Thank you, sire."

Richard went on. "It's good to have you and your band of pirates with us." He raised his brows. "Though I must tell my stewards to place a guard on the wine."

Alart of Vouzin laughed at that. Roger thought of Tatwine scrounging the camp, and he stared blankly, as though he had no idea what Richard was talking about.

As if on a whim, Richard said, "Tell me, Huntley, are you up for a bit of action?"

Roger was dead tired. He wanted nothing more than to remove his hauberk and helmet and lie down, but there was only one answer he could give. "Yes, sire. Of course."

"My scouts tell me Saladin's put an outpost on that hill—" he indicated a distant rise "—so that his men may spy on our movements."

Roger stared at the hill but could see nothing. Richard went on. "I'm going to take some fellows and winkle them out. Care to join us?"

"I'd be honored, sire."

"Give me time to arm myself. Then get a fresh horse and meet me at my tent. Deraa, you come as well. We'll see if we can't give these pagans something to think about."

Chapter 11

KING RICHARD'S PARTY made its way through rocks and brush and stunted olive trees. They were guided by the Turcos who had discovered the Saracen outpost. At Richard's direction, the Turcos had taken a roundabout route out of Bet Nable, hoping to surprise the outpost from behind. Along with Roger and his father, Henry, the king's companions Alart of Vouzin and Andrew of Chauvigny were in the company, as well as swarthy William of Mello, Ralph of Mauleon, Robert of Saci, and a score of other knights. There were also a number of mounted footmen, or sergeants.

The knights were more lightly armored than usual. Spears had been left behind; they would be of little use in these hills. The knights had eschewed cumbersome mail leggings, and some wore mail coifs or flat-cap helmets instead of their regular helms. Some had abandoned their hauberks altogether in favor of lightly armored jacks. Bells and been removed from bridles, and anything else that could make noise had either been discarded or tied down.

The country was so broken that Richard's men could see little in any direction. Thus far they had encountered no one, though tracks and droppings showed that men and horses had passed this way not long before.

From the front, the dashing Turco captain, Guibert—it seemed a requirement that Turco captains be dashing—motioned the small column to halt. He dropped back and conferred with King Richard.

Then Richard turned to his men in a low voice. "Not far now. We'll advance the rest of the way on foot. The sergeants will remain here with the horses."

On foot, the knights picked their way up the slope, trying to make as little noise as possible. It was a hot day and, with no one else about, they might have been on a leisurely, if somewhat grueling, stroll. The outpost was at the top of a hill, and, according to Guibert, it was guarded only on the Bet Nable side.

They neared the top of the hill.

Ahead were voices.

The men tensed, kept going.

From somewhere a horse whinnied nervously. Others joined in.

From the hilltop, a cry of alarm.

"Come on!" Richard shouted, and he and his men ran for the top of the hill.

They emerged onto the top to find the Saracens taken by surprise. Some frantically tried to arm themselves. Others ran. Still others scrambled for their horses. The hilltop dissolved into a melee. An arrow bounced off Roger's helmet just above the nose guard, stunning him and causing him to miss a step.

He recovered and spied a Saracen to his right. The man wore no armor and was aiming a bow at King Richard. Roger ran at the man and crashed into him with his heavy shield, knocking him to the ground. Roger recovered his footing, and before the man could get up, Roger hit him with his axe, the blade taking off the side of the man's head, splashing Roger with blood and gore.

That quickly, it was over. The Saracens broke, some running down the far side of the hill, a few riding away bareback.

"Horses!" Richard cried.

The horses were hurried forward by the sergeants, and the knights set off in pursuit of the fleeing Saracens. Most of the Saracens on foot were quickly caught and killed—there was no quarter in this kind of fighting. Those on horseback—the ones who were not ridden down immediately—seemed to vanish in the broken hills. It was a slow chase as the Christian horses picked their way down slopes, along ridges, up more slopes, looking for tracks and wondering where the Saracens had gotten to. Distant screams told when some of the Saracens were overtaken.

Roger found himself alone in the rocks and scrub. He might have been alone in the world for all he knew. The only sounds were the buzzing of flies and the clopping of his horse's hooves.

Below and to his right, he sensed movement. He watched intently.

There—a Saracen in a green-painted helmet.

Trailing the Saracen in a ragged line, half hidden by boulders and brush, were three other men, all riding bareback. They were half a mile off, maybe a bit more. Roger turned after them.

Hooves sounded to Roger's left. Close.

Roger cursed himself for being caught off guard and wheeled his horse with his knee, at the same time raising his shield and axe, all the while knowing it was too late and he was going to die.

It was King Richard.

Roger lowered the axe and Richard flashed his boyish grin. "Lucky for you, I'm not a pagan—eh, Huntley?"

Roger let out his breath in relief. "It is indeed, sire."

"Never let your guard down, my boy. Never let your guard down." Richard pointed to the distant man in the green helmet. "You're after those fellows?"

"I am, sire."

The Saracens had become aware of Roger and Richard, and they had picked up their pace. It was going to be difficult to catch them.

Richard looked around, studying the ground, glancing at the sun. "If I'm right, we're between them and their camp." He pointed left with his shield. "If we go that way, I believe we can drop down the hill and cut them off. Does that sound good to you?"

Roger was amazed; the king of England was speaking to him as an equal. "It does, sire."

"Come on, then."

They set off round the other side of the hill, letting the horses pick their way over the difficult terrain.

Suddenly the rocks parted and a stunning vista opened before them. They could see for leagues in the bright sunlight. In the distance was a city. Roger saw long walls with square towers. He saw two large domed structures, and what could only be the famed Jaffa Gate.

"Jerusalem." The words spilled from his mouth. He halted his horse and crossed himself. Excitedly he turned. "Sire!"

But Richard had covered the left side of his face with his shield, blocking the view.

"Sire, it's—"

"I don't want to see it. I'm not worthy to see it. I have failed to return it to God's keeping."

"But we'll be there in a few days," Roger said, puzzled. "We'll deliver it then."

Richard made no answer, and Roger added, "Won't we?"

Still shielding his eyes from the city, Richard turned his horse on the rocky ground. "Let's go back."

"But the Saracens, sire. We can still—"

"It's not worth the effort," Richard said, and of a sudden he looked and sounded very tired.

Roger cast a last glance at the Holy City, burning its beauty into his memory, filled with joy and longing for the time when he would see it again, when he would enter its holy places and worship. Then he turned and followed Richard back to the outpost.

Chapter 12

SULTAN YUSEF, ALONG with his brother, al-Adil, the sultan's oldest son, al-Afdal, the emir Qaymaz, and a company of the sultan's guards were making their way to the new outpost in the hills.

Saladin and Qaymaz rode in front of the others. "We should have been there by now," the sultan grumbled. "We *woul* have been there, if you hadn't let me sleep. I gave instructions to be awakened before dawn."

Qaymaz replied, "You seemed unwell last night, lord. I thought it best to let you rest."

Only Qaymaz could violate the sultan's instructions in such a manner and go unpunished for it.

Saladin knew that he sounded petulant, but he was too old and too tired to care. "I need to observe Rik's dispositions. I need to know the moment he advances. It has to be any time now."

"A few hours won't make that much difference, lord," Qaymaz said patiently. "Besides, Rik does not seem eager to advance. Were I him, I would have attacked long since."

"As would I," Saladin said. "For the life of me, I cannot understand why he delays."

"Perhaps he does not realize how dire our situation is."

"Perhaps," Saladin mused.

Qaymaz went on. "If that supply caravan does not reach us soon, we may not be able to hold the city."

"We may not be able to hold the city in any case."

Qaymaz gave the sultan a look.

"Don't act surprised," Saladin said. "You're far too able a general for that." Saladin turned his head to see if the others had heard what he said, but they were at a distance behind him and Qaymaz.

Qaymaz nodded, acknowledging the gravity of the situation. "There must be something we can do. Poison the wells between here and Rik's camp?"

"I don't like to do that," Saladin said, "it hurts the villagers." He sighed. "We can try, I suppose, but I doubt it will make a difference. We are too few, with too few resources. One determined assault will carry our walls."

Saladin pinched the bridge of his long nose between his thumb and middle finger. He felt tired all the time; there was a dull ache in his stomach that never went away. "I thought we had solved our problems when al-Markis was killed. But now it is worse than ever. The blood and treasure we expended on taking al-Quds are about to go for naught. If we lose al-Quds now, we may not regain it for a hundred years, and I will be remembered as a failure." He let out his breath. "I do not have long to live."

Qaymaz protested. "Sire—"

Saladin cut him off with a wave of the hand. "We both know it's true. After I die, my sons will fight over my throne, even though they have pledged not to. Plus, war with Damascus looms." He sighed again. "Ah, well, Allah wills it."

He reached over and put his hand on Qaymaz's shoulder. "Do your best to keep what I have built intact, old friend."

Qaymaz's eyes glistened. "I shall, lord."

"That reminds me—that prisoner of yours, the feringhee who commanded the Red Skulls. Is he—?"

"Listen," Qaymaz said suddenly, holding up his hand.

From far ahead came shouts and the sounds of fighting.

Saladin and Qaymaz halted. Qaymaz turned and waved the men behind them forward. Al-Adil and al-Afdal rode up ahead of the company of guards.

From ahead, more yelling, the distant clash of steel.

"The feringhees have discovered our outpost," al-Adil swore.

As if in answer to this statement, four horsemen appeared ahead of them. The four men were disheveled. They lacked any kind of order, and their horses were without saddles. Their apparent leader wore a green-painted helmet, marking him as one of al-Adil's Egyptians.

The men saw Saladin's party and rode toward it as though pursued by djinns. They reined in. With shock on his sweaty face, the breathless leader recognized Saladin and bowed deeply. "Lord Sultan."

"What is going on?" Saladin demanded.

"We were attacked by feringhees, lord. The outpost is overrun. There are two infidels right behind us."

"The four of you are running from *two men*?" Qaymaz snapped. "Where is your pride?"

Al-Adil motioned Saladin's company of guards to form a double line. They unsheathed their weapons, while a scout rode ahead.

"Do you see two men?" Qaymaz shouted at the scout.

"No, lord. They must have turned back."

"If they ever existed," Qaymaz said with a sharp look at the man in the green helmet.

"They did exist," the man in the green helmet swore, "we saw them. But there is more, lord. The feringhees were led by Malik Rik himself."

Saladin's dark eyes flashed. "You're certain of this?"

"I am, lord. I recognized his shield."

"How many men does Rik have altogether?" Qaymaz said.

The man shook his head. "I am not certain. Half a hundred, perhaps. It all happened so fast. One moment it was quiet, and the next, they were upon us."

"Perhaps if you had kept proper watch, you would not have been surprised," Saladin's pugnacious son al-Afdal told the man.

The man in the green helmet lowered his head, chastised.

Meanwhile, Saladin and Qaymaz exchanged glances. If Qaymaz had not let Saladin sleep, he and Saladin would have been at the outpost when the Christians attacked.

"It seems you were right, and I needed the extra rest after all," Saladin remarked dryly.

Qaymaz smiled, and Saladin continued in seemingly good spirits. "All is not lost, my friend. If what this fellow says is true, we have twice as many men here as Rik does. Take our men and cut Rik off from his base. He has tricked us well; let us return the favor."

Chapter 13

KING RICHARD AND Roger started back to what had been the Saracen outpost. "This cursed country all looks the same," Richard said. "If I get lost out here, I'll never hear the end of it from Alart."

Roger laughed.

From ahead came the sounds of fighting.

The two men spurred their horses over a rise. Below them a trio of knights was being attacked by about five times that many Saracen horsemen. One knight fell from his horse even as Roger and Richard rode to their aid.

The Saracens turned at the sound of horses. Then Roger and Richard were among them. Roger struck at a Saracen on his right, hitting him in the collarbone, shattering the bone and slicing into the man's chest. Roger jerked his axe free. He raised his shield, warded off a mace strike from his other side, reached across his body and struck back, then rode on.

The air was thick with dust. Roger clashed shields with a long-bearded Saracen, trying to knock him off his horse, but he didn't have time to see if he had been successful because another Saracen aimed a blow at him with a curved sword. Roger leaned away and the blow glanced off his hauberk. He righted himself and swung wildly at the man, backhanded, missing his target and gashing the hindquarters of the man's horse.

King Richard's voice boomed through the dust and the noise of fighting. "Fall back to the outpost!"

It was difficult to fall back to anywhere in the swirling melee. Singly and in small groups, more knights joined the fray, men who had been hunting the refugees from the hilltop. The fighting spread over a large area, with more Saracens seeming to arrive by the minute. The Christians tried to keep some kind of order. Men who were separated from the group were surrounded and killed. For their part, the Saracens tried to cull the Christians, to herd them away from the group and overwhelm them by force of numbers. There was no level ground over which to charge. Men barged into one another and swung away, and as the momentum of their horses took them past one opponent, they looked for another.

Roger made his way forward, guiding his bay horse with his knees, blocking blows and giving them, though it was hard to see what effect they had because of all the dust. He emerged into an open area and stopped to catch his breath. He saw a Saracen watching the battle from a far rise, waving more men into the fray. The Saracen rode a black horse, and there was a blue sash around his helmet.

Qaymaz.

Roger had no more time to observe because from out of the dust a Saracen rode at him, sword raised. Before the Saracen could strike, his horse stepped in a hole. There was a loud crack as the animal's leg snapped. The horse screamed and the rider was catapulted to the ground. Ralph of Mauleon's horse trampled the man with its hooves.

The Christians were surrounded. Their perimeter, if it could be called that, was shrinking. King Richard seemed to be everywhere, rallying his men, urging them to keep together, to get back to the relative safety of the hilltop.

There was a cry and a clash of steel, and the Saracens were assaulted from behind by the mounted sergeants who had been left at the outpost. The sergeants opened a hole in the ring that surrounded Richard and his men.

"Come on!" Richard cried.

Emboldened by this new attack, the Christians battered their way through the opening, while the sergeants covered them. Near Roger, a Christian horse was struck in the head by a Saracen war hammer. The point of the hammer penetrated the horse's brain, and it went down, throwing its rider, William of Mello. Roger wheeled his horse to go back for Mello, as did Alart of Vouzin, but one of the sergeants got there first. The sergeant slipped his foot from the left stirrup and held out his arm. "Get on."

Roger reined in as Mello straightened his flat-cap helmet, which had been knocked askew. "Give me your horse," he told the sergeant.

"My lord—"

"The horse, damn you. Give it to me."

"But—"

"Do it now, or I'll have the skin from your back."

The sergeant dismounted. Mello got on the horse and rode back into the fighting.

Roger made for the sergeant, a young fellow with a sun-blistered nose. Before he got there, he was intercepted by two Saracens, one to either side of him. He blocked an axe blow with his shield, swung his own axe at the man on his right, missing the man and almost falling from his horse. Then he was past them. As he regained his seat in the saddle, they came at him again, but one was knocked from his horse by a sword blow from Henry of Deraa, and the other disappeared in the confusion. Roger looked for the young sergeant, but he was gone.

Roger and Henry joined the rush for the hilltop. Roger tried to stay close to his father, but it was impossible in the dust and confusion, and they became separated. The Christians fought their way forward. The men in the rear—the sergeants—were hardest pressed, and seemed to be taking the most casualties. King Richard, along with Alart and Andrew of Chauvigny, dropped back to give them assistance.

Then the Christians were through, spilling over the hilltop, one of the wounded falling from his saddle, with Richard bringing up the rear. Richard wheeled and waved his Danish axe defiantly at the Saracens. Then he cried, "Dismount! Form a line!"

Knights and sergeants hurriedly made a line along the hilltop. The Saracens were too few to press an attack uphill, where they would be at a disadvantage, so they drew back a short distance. Then a horn sounded, and the Saracens turned and rode out of sight. They had suffered more killed and wounded than had the Christians, and it appeared they were done fighting for the moment.

The Christians regrouped. Men and animals were splashed with blood that, when combined with sweat, was turned into a kind of mud by the omnipresent dust. Some of the horses were wounded so badly that they had to be killed. Roger saw a knight weeping as he slit his animal's throat.

Henry walked over to Roger. "Are you hurt?"

"No," Roger said.

"That was close."

"It was. Where did those Saracens come from?"

Henry shrugged. "We probably ran into some reinforcements they were sending up here."

King Richard stood nearby, looking down the hill and brooding. "We were lucky to get out with our lives," he told Henry and Roger. "Had they brought footmen and archers I doubt we'd have survived."

Henry said, "We definitely wouldn't have survived it if not for those sergeants. Whoever ordered their attack saved us."

That attack had been led by a senior centenar from Dijon named Priyo. He had disobeyed orders to remain on the hilltop and ridden to the knights' rescue, and King Richard knighted him on the spot for it. "See to the wounded," Richard ordered Alart. "Those who can ride will go back with us, the others will stay here. We'll leave the sergeants and some of the knights here, then send up a proper garrison as soon as we get back to Bet Nable."

The men refreshed themselves as best they could, saving most of their water for the horses. A few of the men tried to quench their thirst by sucking blood from wounds on their arms. The walking wounded were treated, then they mounted or were tied to their horses. The more seriously hurt would be brought down on mules later.

Richard and his men departed the hilltop and started back to Bet Nable. As they made their way along the winding trail, they came to a level spot. A crude pole had been erected there, and atop the pole was a human head.

The head belonged to the sergeant who had given William of Mello his horse.

Mello rode by the head with scarcely a glance, though Roger was certain he recognized the man. It was all Roger could do not to go after Mello. Instead, he pulled his horse out of line.

Beside him, Henry of Deraa said, "What are—?"

Roger halted his horse next to the pole and dismounted. "I'm going to bury him," Roger said. "He's a Christian, he deserves that much." This wasn't like Joseph and his friends during the march to Arsuf. Those men were fools and deserved what they got. This young sergeant died through no fault of his own; he died because he was trying to help a fellow Christian.

Henry dismounted as well. Roger didn't want to dig with his dagger or hack at the rocky soil with his axe; both would damage the blades. "Help me get my helmet off," he told his father.

Henry unlaced Roger's helmet, and Roger used the edge of the helmet to scoop a shallow depression in the soil. Henry joined him, digging with his hands. They couldn't dig very deep because the ground was so hard.

Clatter of hoofbeats. "What's going on here?"

It was Alart of Vouzin, come to check on them.

"We're burying this poor fellow," Henry told him.

Alart said, "The king's orders are that no one is to—"

"Damn the king's orders," Roger shot back. He didn't care that he was speaking to one of the king's senior advisors. "This man was a Christian. You were there, my lord, you saw how he died. William of Mello should be punished for what he did."

"William is a trusted companion of King Richard," Alart said stiffly.

Henry placed a warning hand on Roger's arm, but Roger went on. "That doesn't excuse what he did. He as good as killed this man himself."

Alart drew himself up. "As you—and your father—well know, William was perfectly within his rights to take this man's horse. Knights are trained for war almost from the day of their birth. That represents an investment of great time and expense. A knight's loss is far more serious than that of a common foot soldier. I'm sorry, I know that's not the answer you wanted to hear, but it's reality. I wouldn't have done what William did, but I won't fault him for doing it. He is a noble and this man was a commoner."

"But—"

"I understand, but there's nothing to be done. Go on, finish burying him."

Roger was speechless with anger. Henry nudged his shoulder. "Come on."

From the head of the column, King Richard cried, "What's going on?"

"It's all right, sire," Alart cried back, waving a hand. "Keep going. We'll catch up."

Alart drew his sword and stood guard while Roger and Henry finished the hole. Roger removed the head from the pole. The head was still warm, the neck sticky with blood. Roger tried not to look at it, tried not to see the youthful expression, the sun-blistered nose, tried not to stare into those empty, accusing eyes.

Roger placed the head in the depression. He and Henry covered it with rocks to keep it from animals. They formed the rocks in the shape of a cross. Alart dismounted and led the three men in a *Pater Noster*, after which they crossed themselves.

Roger hung his helmet from his saddle, and the men remounted. Alart said, "You may have once been a woodcutter, Huntley, but you're a good Christian and a worthy knight. I wish we had more like you."

Roger said, "Thank you, my lord," but his words rang hollow. Would Alart say that if knew that Roger had killed his son?

Chapter 14

𝕱AUSTON AND BONJUTE were riding, as they did whenever Bonjute could get away. When the earl of Trent had set off for Bet Nable, he had appointed Bonjute governor of the city, for lack of a suitable male candidate, and the job kept her busy.

Bonjute rode a milk-white palfrey; Fauston, a borrowed sorrel mare. They were headed to a long-abandoned eremite's hut that they had discovered and made their own. They slowed as they made their way up a winding valley, riding side by side, a small stream to their left. It was quiet, peaceful. Birds chirped.

Bonjute said, "Can I ask you a question?"

"Of course," Fauston said.

"You'll give me an honest answer?"

"I would never lie to you."

"About anything?"

"About anything."

"Are the relics that you sell real?"

Fauston took a deep breath. "No." He let that sink in. "Gregory, Francisco, and I make them."

She nodded as though she'd expected that answer. "So that piece of Longinus's lance you sold me is . . ."

"Just an old bit of wood." He paused. "I hope this doesn't . . ."

She shook her head. "I think I suspected all along. It's just that I *wante*, to believe. Geoffrey wanted to believe, as well. And he did believe, and it's helped him. So perhaps the 'relic' has powers after all."

They rode a bit further and Fauston said, "Maybe I should become an honest man. Sell real relics, if there are any. Or go into trade."

Bonjute chimed her bell-like laugh. "Brock the Badger—a merchant? How would mothers scare their children with stories about you then?"

Fauston looked embarrassed, and she went on. "Tell me, would you ever go back to highway robbery? I mean, if things got bad for you?"

Fauston thought about it. "If I did, would you stay with me?"

"To be honest, I don't think so. I couldn't bear to see you on the gallows, which is where you would end up. Why, would my opinion make a difference?"

"You know it would. I'd never do anything if it meant losing you." He laughed at himself and shook his head, "Listen to me. I sound like Lancelot."

"And I am your Guinevere?" Bonjute raised her eyebrows. "You know the stories of Chretien of Troyes, then?" Chretien had popularized the adulterous love of Lancelot and Guinevere.

"Some of them," Fauston said. *Trouveres* had recited them during the long days of the siege, when he'd been chronicler to her husband, but he didn't want her to know about that part of his life, not yet. "Well-born clerics tell them at the Golden Keys. They think it makes them fashionable."

"Historians claim to have discovered the tomb of Arthur and Guinevere last year," she said. "At Glastonbury."

"Yes. It's all the talk at the Golden Keys these days."

"Do you think it's real?"

Fauston shrugged. "Hard to tell. My guess is no, but as you say, people want to believe."

The eremite's hut was visible ahead of them. It was a low structure, built of stone. Fauston did not know how old the hut was—though he suspected it was very old—or who had built it. Someone had destroyed the makeshift altar inside, but otherwise the hut had been left alone. Fauston and Bonjute had cleaned the place up. Fauston had constructed a bed frame from olive wood and fashioned a straw mattress for it. He'd made a table and built a roof over the side porch where they could eat. It was cool and surprisingly comfortable inside the hut, and he and Bonjute had begun to consider it their "home."

They bathed the trail dust from their bodies in the stream, then they made love, starting in the water and ending in bed. Afterwards, Bonjute lay naked in Fauston's arms, eyes half closed on this dozy afternoon. Fauston stroked her blonde hair, kissed the top of her head. "You know how I feel about you, don't you?"

Bonjute looked up and ran her fingers along his cheek. "Yes. And I feel the same about you."

He kissed her again. "I wish this day would never end."

"So do I. When I'm with you, I feel different than I ever have before. For the first time in my life, I feel like I can be myself." She sat up suddenly. "But who *am* I? Really? I have no idea. I've never been allowed to find out. All my life I've had to play a role, to be what other people expected me to be." A distraught look crossed her face. "What if I really am the ogre people make me out to be?"

"You're not," Fauston assured her.

"How can you be sure?"

"I just know. I wouldn't love you if you were that person. I *couldn't* love you."

She squeezed his hand in both her own. "I wish I could be with you always."

"You can," Fauston said.

She let go of his hand and looked away. "No. The crusade will end soon, and I will have to return to England."

"Why?" Fauston said. "You can hide in the city—or even here—until the ships leave, and then—"

She turned, peering into his eyes. "I'm married, Fauston. I took a vow and I must honor it. No matter what it costs me." She paused. "If something happened to Geoffrey, of course I would stay here with you. Our son is old enough to manage the estates; he doesn't need his mother helping him. But Geoffrey seems to be getting better. As a Christian, I want him to get better. He attributes his improved heath to that relic I bought from you. Ironic, isn't it?"

Fauston knew he should wish for Geoffrey to die, either from sickness or in battle, but he could not. The earl was a good man, and Fauston liked him. "Then the day you sail will be the last day we see each other?"

Her eyes were moist. "Yes." She took his hand again. "Oh, Fauston, I'll miss you. I'll miss what might have been. Being with you is the best thing that's ever happened to me."

"And to me." Fauston let out his breath. "You're not even on the ship yet, and already my heart is breaking."

Through her tears she laughed at his weak joke. Then she got to her knees and straddled him. "Well, then, my gallant Knight of the Cart, we had best enjoy the time we have left."

Chapter 15

AILITH PLUCKED THE lute, tinkering with the notes to her new song.

She sang: *"Hath any loved you well in the ground, all the seasons through?"*

The song fit her mood, but it didn't sound quite right. She tried again.

"Hath any loved you well down there, all the seasons through?"

Better, but still not right. She sighed. She missed Roger. She had finally found him, and now he was gone again. There was no news from the army. If Jerusalem had fallen, gallopers would have been sent with the word. Something must have held them up.

Or gone wrong.

She wondered if it would always be like this and realized that it probably would. The kingdom of Jerusalem was perpetually at war for its survival, and if Roger remained here with his father, he would likely be absent for long periods of time. Even if Roger were somehow pardoned for killing Auberie, and they went back to England, things wouldn't be much better. King Richard or Earl Geoffrey would always need him for something, or, because he had no land, he would have to hire himself out to a lord in need of knights. She would never be certain of his safety.

She sat in the window seat that overlooked the sea. It was morning, and the sun already cast its harsh glare off the water's surface. The gentle breeze brought smells of salt and brine and fish and a thousand and one other things. The view didn't fit her mood; it should be cold and raining.

"Hath any loved you well down there, summer or winter through?"

There—she liked that. Please God, she hoped Roger was all right and that she wasn't writing this about him.

Her accommodations were paid for and she had money to spend—Fauston saw to that. But she lacked companionship. She helped at Fauston's shop from time to time, particularly when Fauston was off with his mysterious woman that he couldn't talk about. Sometimes Ailith wondered if the woman even existed. So she had taken up the lute to fill her time. It was similar to the *ou*, which she had learned at Qaymaz's command, so that she might entertain him. The lute was larger and heavier than the *oud*, but the fingering was similar. She was far from an expert, but good enough to accompany her singing.

She plucked the instrument again. *"Down there, have you found any fair laid in the grave with you?"*

She had always liked music. She'd been the best dancer in Lower Wynchecombe, not that that meant much. With so much free time, she'd taken to writing songs, like the troubadors. Like Pere Vidal and Eble of Ussel, whom she'd heard during the siege. Or Ambroise, Richard's minstrel, who was with the king, keeping a record of the crusade.

A knock on the door.

Ailith hesitated. She had no idea who it might be.

Another knock. Light. Polite, but insistent.

She couldn't pretend she wasn't there; whoever was out there would have heard her singing. She put down the instrument, crossed to the door and opened it.

She faced a tall woman in a lime-green dress, with a gauzy veil across her face. Behind her were two native Christian bodyguards.

The woman looked familiar, and when she let the veil fall, Ailith saw that it was Hugoline of Montjoie, one of the wealthiest women in the city. Ailith knew her from Fauston's shop, where she was a frequent customer. Ailith suspected she had designs on Fauston. She was handsome, in her mid-forties, deeply tanned in the manner of the natives of Outremer.

"Lady Hugoline, this is a surprise."

"Good day, Ailith," Hugoline said. "I trust I'm not intruding?"

"Of course not. It is good to see you." Ailith motioned Hugoline and her guards through the door. "To what do I owe the pleasure of your visit?"

Hugoline wasted no time on formalities. "You were referred to me by the Countess of Trent."

How did Bonjute know I live here? Ailith thought.

Hugoline went on. "Lady Bonjute says that you sing."

"Well, I . . ."

"She claims you're better than most of the fools who follow King Richard around, or who lay about the taverns, trying to find employment with nobles of the city."

When could Bonjute have heard her sing? She had been in Fauston's shop one day; it must have been then, when Ailith had been practicing in the back room. "Lady Bonjute does me too great an honor," Ailith demurred.

"I am giving a banquet next week for the bishop. The troubador who was to entertain has fallen ill, and his life is despaired of. I need someone to replace him."

Ailith waited for her to say more, then understood. "You want *me* to do it?"

"I have nowhere else to turn. The rest of the singers I know are spoken for or with the court at Bet Nable."

"But . . . I've never sung in public. My songs aren't . . . I don't know if I—"

"I'll make it more than worth your while," Hugoline told her.

Ailith and Roger would need money after the crusaders went home. Right now they had none. "Well . . ."

"You'd have to disguise yourself as a man, of course."

Ailith stared.

Hugoline said, "Women are banned from performing in public by both Church and civil law. The bishop would be scandalized, and you and I would face arrest or heavy fines. You might even be tried for heresy."

"You make the job sound most attractive," Ailith joked.

"It will be all right if we're careful. You'll have to cut your hair of course."

"No," Ailith said. "I can't do that. I won't."

Hugoline made a gesture with her hand. "Nonsense. It will grow back. You'll have to wrap your bosom, as well, and I can get you a man's clothes."

Ailith knew that women could not perform in public. That was the reason women's parts in mystery plays were taken by boys whose voices had yet to change. It could be dangerous for her to do this. Still . . .

"How much money were you thinking of?" she asked.

Hugoline shrugged. "Say, ten gold bezants?"

Ailith's eyes widened. She and Roger could live a good while on ten gold bezants. *It might work*, she thought. "I know someone who could fashion a false moustache and chin beard for me."

"Excellent!" Hugoline exclaimed. "You'll do it, then?"

"Well, I . . . all right."

Hugoline clapped her hands. "Wonderful. Don't worry, my dear. It will be fun, you'll see."

After a bit of polite conversation, Hugoline and her bodyguards left, and Ailith wondered what she had gotten herself into.

Chapter 16

"WATCH OUT, PRETTY boy," Hugoline's steward sneered at Ailith. "You're in the way." The steward's face resembled a lump of dough that had been punched repeatedly by a heavy fist, and he ran Hugoline's household in a no-nonsense fashion.

Ailith stepped back behind the wooden screen that separated the door to the outside kitchen from the hall. Harried servants—most of them hired for the occasion—pushed past her, carrying trenchers groaning with pork, lamb and mutton, with roasted quail and doves, with oryx and Persian deer. There were kebabs of spiced meat and fruit, as well, and, of course, jugs and jugs of wine.

Ailith squeezed even closer to the wall to avoid two heavily muscled Nubians carrying a roast ostrich, its plumes plucked and spread in a fan behind it. There were gasps of amazement as the bird was brought into the hall.

Fauston's reliquary maker, Francisco, had cut Ailith's hair short, letting it come just below the ears, as was the fashion for young men. Her bosom was tightly wrapped, and she wore a loose scarlet tunic with short sleeves that showed off a green shirt beneath. The tunic had a square neck embroidered with gold thread. Her hose were dark blue. At her belt hung a wicked-looking dagger—troubadors and *trouveres* got into *lots* of tavern brawls. Francisco had also fashioned a thin moustache and chin beard for her and glued them to her face as through she were an actor in a mystery play—which, in a way, she was. She propped her lute against the wall to prevent its being trampled by the passing servers.

The noise in the hall swelled to a roar—talking, shouting, laughter. Hugoline's house had been built by her husband, Rotrou, a wealthy trader in silks and spices, who had been knighted for his financial contributions to the kingdom. He was from Troyes originally and wanted his house to resemble those at home. As a result, there were long benches and trestle tables, and rushes on the floor. There was a gallery around the hall, and the ceiling was vaulted, with thick stone columns. The capitals atop the columns had been decorated with figures—saints and martyrs, knights and ladies, bishops, burghers, and peasants—painted in gay colors. The kind of figures one might see on the portico of Troyes Cathedral. At one time, the faces of these figures must have been a mixture of heroic and tragic and comic. Now it was impossible to tell what the faces were, because the Saracens had smashed them off during their occupation of the city. They'd made fair progress on destroying the rest of the bodies, as well. Hugoline was attempting to restore them, but it was slow—and costly—work.

The banquet was in honor of Bishop Jean's feast day. The guests were a mixture of merchants and high-ranking clerics, both local and visiting, along with nobles who were either too old to be with the army or who were recovering from illness or wounds. The men, including some of the clerics, were accompanied by their wives or by high-priced whores pretending to be noblewomen. *I used to be like them,* Ailith thought bitterly. As acting governor of the city, Bonjute of Trent sat at the guest of honor's left hand, while Rotrou and Hugoline occupied the chairs to the bishop's right.

The noise subsided, and Ailith peeked around the screen to see what was happening. The steward scowled but didn't move her back.

Bishop Jean had risen to his feet and was motioning for silence. The bishop was handsome in a fleshy sort of way—almost too handsome, Ailith thought. His purple robes were of the finest silk, and his jeweled ring of office seemed far too big for his hand. He blessed the crowd, then folded his hands as if in prayer and spoke in a silky voice. "I wish to thank my dear friend, Lady Hugoline, for having me here tonight. I also wish to thank Lord Rotrou and Lady Hugoline for their sizeable contribution to the cathedral's building fund."

Applause.

The bishop went on. "As you know, occupation by the infidels and the long siege have left our cathedral in dire need of repair, and I pray that I may persuade others of you to pledge a contribution, as well."

More applause, not as loud.

The bishop then preached a brief sermon, the gist of which was that anyone who gave a sum of money to the church fund would receive an indulgence for their previous sins.

The applause this time was louder and more sustained. Everybody liked indulgences.

As Bishop Jean returned to his seat, Hugoline stood. "That was most inspiring, your grace. We will certainly miss you when you are archbishop of Tyre."

The bishop spread his hands, smiling in an overly humble way. "I pray that is not for many years to come, my lady. Archbishop Josicus does an admirable job, considering what he must work with."

More applause. Then sherbet, honey cakes, and sugared nuts were served, while jugglers performed with balls and clubs.

"Get ready, pretty boy," the steward told Ailith. "You're next."

"Stop calling me pretty boy," she told him.

"Why? Bless my balls, but you look like a girl." He grinned menacingly. "We knew how to deal with your type in the army."

She fingered the handle of her dagger. "I know how to deal with your type, as well."

He looked like he was going to hit her, but he probably realized that would cost him his job. Instead he growled, "Just get ready."

Ailith took a deep breath, picked up the lute and adjusted its strap around her neck and shoulder. In the hall, the jugglers finished and ran off.

"Now," the steward told Ailith, giving her a none-too-gentle shove.

Ailith rounded the screen and entered the hall. The hall was hot because so many people were packed into it. It smelled of food and sweat and perfume, with an overlay of the cinnamon and lemon that the guests used to sweeten their breath.

Ailith didn't know what kind of reception she had been expecting, but she'd been expecting *something.*

The guests ignored her.

They continued eating and drinking and wandering between tables. Ailith saw Bonjute watching her from the corner of one eye.

Bonjute had recommended Ailith, and if this proved to be a disaster, it would be Bonjute's fault—hers and Hugoline's. Ailith still wondered how Bonjute had known where she lived. Hugoline was watching, as well. She gave Ailith a subtle uplift of the hand, urging her to begin.

A stool had been placed before the high table, and Ailith perched on it. She tuned the lute, cleared her throat and sang her introductory song. She cursed inwardly as she sang, because her voice sounded weak, when she had wanted it to come off as strong and confident:

> *Ah, what a lovely thing*
> *To sing your praises, Lady,*
> *And what an honor to*
> *Sing with heart devoted,*
> *Sing with . . .*

Her voice tailed off. No one, absolutely no one, was paying attention to her. No one had heard her. No one cared whether she was there. No one cared whether she was alive or dead. Bonjute and Hugoline looked worried.

At first Ailith wanted to slink out of the hall in shame, but her reception from the crowd angered her. She'd rather they booed her, rather they threw food at her, than pretend she didn't exist. She pictured the dough-faced steward laughing at her, and that really made her angry. She'd been looked down on by these people all her life, and she was tired of it. She didn't care if they discovered her true identity, but they were going to *notice* her. They were going to know she was there.

She got off the stool and kicked it over, sending it flying and getting everyone's attention. She strolled down the hall, close to the long trestle tables, so close that the guests couldn't ignore her, so close that they had to turn and listen to her. She sang loudly, swaggering like a young man. She curled her lip, made eye contact with the better-looking women, singing to them and daring their men to do something about it, as a cocky young troubadour would. She snatched a meat pie from the fist of an elderly nobleman, took a bite, then washed it down with a leisurely drink of his mistress's wine. The mistress—or maybe she was the noble's wife—smiled at Ailith.

Ailith sang of love, love unrequited, the love of a man for a woman he could not have, the sorrow of a man as he left his love for the war. She sang of love in the spring and love in the summer, with the birds were chirping and the meadows green. She sang of love in winter, when all that was left were memories.

And as she sang, the sounds of eating and talking gradually died away. Heads turned until the eyes of the entire chamber were on her, and she seemed to hold a kind of power over the audience.

This is fun, she realized.

She returned to the head table. She started to sing to Bonjute, then thought better of it. Even *she* wasn't that bold. Instead, she hopped onto the table and sat so that she had a view both of the head table and the rest of the audience. She took the bishop's cup and drank deeply from it, drawing gasps from the guests. Then she sang the new song she'd been working on:

> *Hath any loved you well down there,*
> *Summer or winter through?*
> *Down there, have you found any fair*
> *Laid in the grave with you?*

Is death's long kiss a richer kiss
Than mine was wont to be—
Or have you gone to some far bliss
And quite forgotten me?
What soft enamoring of sleep
Hath you in some soft way?
What charmed death holdeth with deep
Strange lure by night and day?
A little space below the grass,
Out of the sun and shade;
But worlds away from me, alas,
Down there where you are laid.

When she finished, there was silence. Several of the women in the audience were misty eyed. A few of the men were, too, though they tried not to show it. Hugoline looked both pleased and relieved; Bonjute looked surprised.

Then came a loud handclap—from Bishop Jean. This was the signal for others to join in. Some people clapped, others banged tables with fists or cups, there were even a few cheers.

"Magnificent, young man," gushed Bishop Jean. He held out his hand. Ailith swung off the table, bent and kissed the bishop's oversized ring. "How is it I have not heard of you until now?" he asked.

Remember, you're a man. Lower your voice. Talk slowly. "I've not been in the Holy Land long, your grace. I recently arrived here from Famagusta."

"You're a bold fellow, drinking my wine like that."

She cocked her head. "I was thirsty, your grace."

There was nervous laughter around them. The guests didn't know whether this would be received as brashness or insolence.

"Were you now?" said the bishop. "And what do they call you, my thirsty friend?"

She almost said, "Ailith," but caught herself. "Alan, your grace." She thought furiously. "Alan of the Dale. I'm from England originally, though it's been many years since I set foot in that land."

The bishop produced a purse. "Well, Alan of the Dale, here's for your efforts. Perhaps you can purchase your own wine now."

Relieved laughter from the audience.

Ailith took the purse, felt its weight. heard the clink of coins. She hadn't expected this. "Many thanks, your grace."

The bishop turned to Hugoline. "You are to be congratulated, Lady Hugoline, for finding such a talent."

Hugoline beamed. "Thank you, your grace."

Bonjute met Ailith's eyes and smiled.

The bishop turned back to Ailith. Around them, the sound rose in the hall as people went back to eating and talking amongst themselves. "Are those your own songs?" the bishop asked Ailith.

"Some are, your grace. The rest are songs I've learned on my travels." She'd heard them during the siege, but that answer was close enough.

"Travels?" exclaimed the bishop. "Why, you're scarce more than a boy." He looked her up and down, appraisingly. "A very attractive boy, too—I'm sure the ladies like that." He winked and lowered his voice. "Some of the men, as well, I'll wager."

Ailith felt her face redden. "I wouldn't know about that, your grace."

The bishop smiled knowingly, then said, "How come you by your trade?"

"I was an orphan. I was raised by the Church—that's where I developed a love for music. One day, a troupe of musicians came along. I didn't want to stay with the Church any longer, so I ran away with the musicians."

"Fascinating." And, just like that, Bishop Jean waved a dismissive hand at Ailith and began talking to Hugoline's husband, Rotrou, about the cathedral building fund.

Even though the bishop was no longer paying attention to her, Ailith bowed to him before turning away.

Remember—you're a man. Placing the lute behind her back on its strap, she squared her shoulders and swaggered from the packed hall, curling her lip arrogantly and making eye contact with any woman who chanced to look her way, "accidentally" brushing the shoulders of the more attractive ones with his hips.

As she neared the screen, she encountered an attractive young woman on her way to the steps leading to the *garderobes* in the gallery. It was the mistress, or wife, of the elderly noble from whom she'd taken the meat pie. The woman was dark haired and almond eyed, and Ailith wondered if she had Arabic blood in her. The two of them were shoulder to shoulder in the press of people, and it occurred to Ailith that their meeting was not coincidental.

The woman touched Ailith's arm. "I enjoyed your singing," she said, her voice covered by the commotion around them.

Be bold, dashing, Ailith thought. "I'm glad, my lady."

"I am Odelina of Bellaire." She hesitated. "I would like to hear you again."

"It would be my great pleasure to sing for you again," Ailith replied. She held Odelina's gaze and bowed her head slightly.

"Somewhere more private, perhaps?" Odelina looked around to see if anyone was listening. "It could be arranged."

Ailith was having fun, playing the rogue, seeing how far it would go. "I would like that, Lady Odelina. I will compose a song in your honor for the occasion."

"A love song?" Odelina asked.

Ailith lowered her voice. "Is there any other kind?"

Odelina stood closer to Ailith than the crowd dictated, her leg brushing Ailith's. "I sing as well, you know."

"Then perhaps we could sing together."

"In harmony?"

Ailith lowered her voice still further. "In very close harmony. Joined together."

"Entwined?"

"Entwined as one."

"How may I contact you?" Odelina's voice was insistent—urgent, almost.

"What about your husband?" Ailith asked her.

She waved off the thought. "I don't want to talk about him. He is old and can no longer function as a husband. He hires prostitutes and watches them perform, and he pleasures himself while he watches. He wants me to join in, but I never do, and sometimes he beats me for it, and he pleasures himself after that, as well. Now, how do I—"

"Ah, there you are." It was the bishop of Acre.

Ailith and Odelina stepped apart. "Your grace," Odelina said, bowing.

"Your grace," said Ailith, bowing as well.

"Might I have a moment with young Alan here?" the bishop asked Odelina.

"Of course, your grace." Odelina withdrew, flashing Ailith a look that pulsed with desire.

Bishop Jean watched her go. He grunted noncommittally and turned back to Ailith. "I wanted to ask you, have you met the king?"

Ailith's eyebrows went up. "King Richard?"

"Mm."

"No, I haven't."

"Would you like to?"

Remember, you're a man. "Of course, your grace. It would be a great honor."

"He writes and sings, as well."

"I've heard that."

"As it happens, he's a friend of mine. I can arrange a meeting, if you like, should he return to Acre before leaving for England."

"That's—that's most generous of you, your grace."

"Not at all. I expect Lady Hugoline knows how to contact you?"

"She does, your grace."

"Good."

The bishop strolled away. *What was that about?* Ailith thought. She'd carried the game with Odelina farther than she should have, and before Odelina could approach her again, Ailith rounded the screen.

The dough-faced steward was watching her. She smiled politely to him. "Carry on," she said.

The steward stiffened with anger, but didn't say anything.

Ailith left the house, crossing the courtyard and out the gate. It had gone well—better than she had expected, especially with that extra money she'd gotten from the bishop. And she had not been revealed as a woman. Far from it, she'd made a conquest. She wondered about the bishop's invitation for her to meet King Richard, presumably to sing for him. The bishop was looking for something from the king before he left the Holy Land—money, most likely. If Richard liked the way Ailith sang, he might be amenable to the bishop's desires.

Or was the bishop looking for something from Ailith—from Alan? Something of the flesh.

She shuddered, then shrugged.

Nothing would ever come of it.

Chapter 17

Bet Nable – St. John's Day, 1192

ℜICHARD STEADIED HIMSELF against a table, hoping no one in the audience would notice, and sipped from a cup of lemon water. He was light headed and weak, and he wished he could sit. Sweat beaded his forehead.

Richard was ill again. It had come out of nowhere, not long after he'd returned from capturing Saladin's outpost. One minute, he'd been full of energy and drive; the next, he could barely function. He was alternately burning hot or wracked with chills. He threw off his clothes or bundled himself in blankets. He had no appetite for food. All he wanted to do was sleep. Unfortunately, that was not to be.

"My lords, I have received bad news," he informed the council. Next to him was a rough-looking Templar, presumably the bearer of this news, his face seamed by scars and his mail much mended. "Saladin is poisoning the wells between here and Jerusalem. There is no water for a siege."

There was a pained reaction from the assembled barons. They were in the large outer area of Richard's red pavilion, the pavilion's sides rolled up against the June heat. The men were sweating in their emblazoned wool surcoats, their matted hair and beards caked with dust. Even after all this time in the East, some of them still had sunburned cheeks and noses.

"The Devil there's no water," Hugh of Burgundy cried. To the Templar, he said, "Where is the closest unpoisoned well?"

The Templar thought. "Tekwa, my lord."

"How far from the city is that?"

"Two leagues," said the Templar.

"Then we'll get our water from Tekwa," Burgundy said.

"How will we transport it?" Richard's ally the earl of Leicester asked him acidly.

One-eyed Henry of Deraa had the answer to that. "We'll divide the army in half. One half will be at the well while the other half presses the siege. Each man visits the well every second day."

"That's how Godfrey of Bouillon got his water on the first crusade," Balian of Ibelin added. "And from the same well, if I'm not mistaken."

"That would never work," Richard told them. "As soon as one half of the army has left for the spring, Saladin will fall on the other half and destroy it."

"How do you know that, sire?" Balian said.

"Let him try," Henry of Deraa snarled.

Richard was exasperated; he wished he could lie down. "For the love of God, Deraa, you saw how much trouble we had in that fight for the observation post. Our horses are useless in this country. If Saladin brings footmen and archers against us in the numbers I believe he has, we will face a disaster as great as the one at Hattin."

"What if Saladin doesn't have those numbers?" Henry said.

"Of course he has them. His people breed like rabbits. Life is nothing to them." Richard paused to catch his breath. "I won't fight the Saracens in these hills. They have every advantage here. We would be destroyed ere we got to Jerusalem to begin a siege."

The Templar was dismissed, and Richard gulped more lemon water. He didn't want to argue anymore. He was too weak. He just wanted to drop the sides of the tent, lie down in the darkness and sleep.

He had thought it would be different this time. He'd been full of optimism when they'd left Ascalon. Then he'd gotten sick again, and things had fallen apart. And with the illness, he was once again confronted with the same old doubts—about himself, about Saladin, about the efficacy of besieging the Holy City.

He could follow the advice of the council and wager all on a throw of the dice, but what if the throw went wrong, as Richard believed it would. Richard was beginning to think those lofty goals the world had set for him might never be achieved. And that scared him.

The bishop of Beauvais spoke. The bishop had once been Richard's most ardent supporter, but had turned against him after Richard had declined to besiege Jerusalem last winter. "What are you telling us, sire?"

"It's obvious, my lord bishop. In light of this latest news, it's best that we withdraw—"

He was drowned out by angry shouting.

With an effort, Richard spoke above the noise. "—that we withdraw and try to lure Saladin into a—"

"No!" cried Hugh of Burgundy. "We went through this six months ago. Why did you come with us if you were going to let us down again?" He rounded on the new ruler of Jerusalem, the count of Champagne. "Why in the seventeen names of Christ did you insist that this incompetent lead us?"

Both Richard and the count flared with anger at these words, but the count replied first. "I insisted because King Richard is the greatest warrior in Christendom. If he cannot take the Holy City, who can?"

"Bah!" Burgundy shook his head in disgust.

Haggard Geoffrey of Trent tried to make peace. "Let's not lose our tempers, gentlemen. There's too much at stake. If we just—"

"If we just what?" said Henry of Deraa. "'The greatest warrior in Christendom' is afraid to fight. There's no other way to put it."

The tent grew quiet.

"Be careful or I'll fight you," Richard told Henry.

The quiet became tense. Men edged away.

Richard and Henry faced each other, neither man backing down.

Henry stared at Richard with his good eye. "It's funny. You seem more interested in fighting your fellow Christians than you do in fighting Saladin."

"What's that supposed to mean?" Richard said.

"You figure it out," Henry said. Insolently, he added, "Sire."

Richard swelled with rage and his hand went to his sword. Balian, the earl of Leicester, Alart of Vouzin, and others jumped between the king and Henry.

Just then, there was a commotion at the tent's entrance. Harsh words were spoken by the guards, harsh words uttered in return.

A Turcopole officer and a Bedouin forced themselves inside. There were met by drawn swords and oaths from the assembled nobles, who, mindful of Conrad's murder, feared villainy of some sort. The guards tried to pull the two men back.

Richard pushed away from Alart and the others who had been keeping him from Henry. "What the Devil is this?" he demanded of the guards.

The lead guard said, "These men claim to have news of the utmost importance, sire. We tried to tell them that they had to—"

Richard made an impatient gesture. "Let them in."

The two men came forward, with a baleful look back at the guards. The Turco was compact and swarthy. Above his trim beard, his face was brown and leathery from a lifetime in the sun. The Bedouin's face was partly hidden by his flowing robes. There was a curved sword at his hip, and bracelets on his wrists jangled when he moved.

The Turco put a foot forward and bowed low. "Si—"

Richard cut him off. "What is it that's so damned important?"

The Turco looked tough, but nervous—like as not, he'd never spoken to a king before. "We are part of a long-range scout, sire, and we have sighted a large caravan. It appears to be headed for Jerusalem. It looks like they've come up from Egypt then swung round in the desert behind Bethlehem, hoping we wouldn't spot them. The rest of our patrol stayed behind to shadow them."

There were murmurs from the audience.

"How large is this caravan?" Richard asked.

"Near a mile long, sire. Horses and camels. Looks like they're bringing reinforcements and supplies to the Saracens in the Holy City. There's a lot of foot soldiers."

"How many?"

"Four thousand, perhaps."

The murmurs rose, joined by low whistles.

"How long until this caravan reaches Jerusalem?" Richard said.

"Five days would be my guess, sire. Maybe four."

Richard nodded. "You were right to interrupt us. Get yourselves some refreshment, then have my steward give you a purse for your efforts."

"We thank you, sire." The two men bowed and left the tent.

Richard turned to the council, which was abuzz with talk. Richard brushed a fly out of his ear and motioned for silence. Gradually the tent fell quiet.

"We shall take this caravan," Richard announced. He had difficulty breathing in the stifling heat of the pavilion. "I would lead the raid myself, unfortunately, I am too ill."

A buzz ran through the tent. There was a shifting of feet.

Henry of Deraa said, "I'm sorry, sire. I had no idea it was that bad. I never would have said those—"

Richard waved him off. He hated admitting that he was sick. It made him appear weak. He would have given anything to lead this raid. It was the kind of bold gesture he loved, but he doubted he could sit a horse for more than a league or two in his condition. In truth, he doubted that he could even stand for much longer.

With difficulty, Richard held himself straight. "So, who is to command?"

He looked at all the eager faces hoping to be chosen as leader—Andrew of Chauvigny, William of Mello, the count of Dreux, the bishop of Beauvais, young Hacon of Denmark, a dozen others.

He turned. "My lord of Deraa, I believe you have experience in this sort of thing?"

There were gasps of surprise. A moment ago, these two men were near to blows. All eyes turned to the tall, rangy Henry. "I do, sire," Henry said.

"Would you be willing to command the expedition?"

"I would deem it a great honor, sire."

There was an outburst from the Western nobles. Leicester said, "See here, sire. There are men far more deserving than Deraa, men who are loyal to you. Why let this—"

Balian of Ibelin spoke over the noise. "No man is more qualified to lead this raid than the lord of Deraa. Before the current war, he raided Saracen caravans for a living. He was so good at it, Saladin placed a bounty on his head."

There were more outbursts, but Richard silenced them. "I have made my decision." To Henry he said, "How many men will you require?"

Henry thought. "My own men, of course, and my son, Roger. I'll take some of Lord Garnier's Hospitallers, a company of Turcos, and a hundred horsemen from my lord of Ibelin."

"Against four thousand?" the bishop of Verona asked skeptically.

"Speed is of the essence if we are to catch this caravan before it reaches Jerusalem. More men would slow us down. We can handle four thousand."

"No Templars?" Richard asked.

Henry shook his head. "They're too hot headed. I can't trust them."

As if to prove Henry's point, Robert de Sable, the Templar Grand Master, stepped forward, red faced, but Richard motioned him to stop. To Henry he said, "How soon can you be ready to leave?"

"By vespers."

"Get to it, then."

Henry bowed and exited the tent, followed by Balian, the Hospitallers' Grand Master, Garnier of Naplouse, and his marshal, William Borrel.

When the council was ended and the other nobles had departed, Alart approached Richard. "Why did you let Deraa command the expedition, sire? It doesn't seem like you."

Richard sank gratefully into a camp chair and allowed himself a small smile. "It's simple, my friend. If Deraa is successful, I will get the glory plus a nice share of the booty. If, on the other hand, he fails . . . well, then, he will be out of our hair forever."

Alart nodded, and Richard added, "A good day's work, either way. Now, if you don't mind, I need some sleep."

Chapter 18

THEY SET OFF at sunset, the western sky red and gold behind them, the eastern sky already darkening.

The men were nervous but tried not to show it, paying exaggerated attention to animals and equipment as they got ready, joking among themselves. The call came to form up, and the men led their horses to their assembly points.

Roger and Tatwine made their way through the crowd to Henry's red falcon banner at the front of the line. Roger was in full mail, his helmet laced, his Death's Head shield slung on his saddle. Tatwine wore his brimmed helmet with the Death's Head painted on it and his mail-ringed jack. His axe was stuffed in his belt, his round shield slung over his shoulder. He eyed his horse, a bay gelding, warily.

"Sorry, Tatty," Roger said. "I know you don't ride, but you said you had to come."

"Bloody right, I'm coming," Tatwine said. "I'm your squire, ain't I? I let you go off on your own, you might get into trouble." He cast another suspicious glance at his mount. "Besides, if this caravan's rich as what they say it is, we'll get us enough loot to last a lifetime—provided this horse don't murder me first. I'm going to use my share to build me a tavern at the edge of the forest. I'll hire a man to run it, stock it with whores, and you'll never see Uncle Tatty do a day's work again."

121

Roger raised his brow. "Whores? I thought you were done with sin."

"Depends on your notion of sin, don't it? Nothin' wrong with whores, far as I can see. Necessity of life, really."

"But the Church says—"

"Church ain't always right. Remember what I told you about Heaven."

Tatwine's pet theory was that Heaven consisted of fun things like drinking and gambling and consorting with women, while Hell was an eternity of sitting on a cloud, singing hymns. Roger couldn't argue with his logic.

They passed Rob and his band of poachers, who would be coming with them, attached to Henry's men. Few of the bowmen could ride, so they were mounted on the tamest horses Henry's seneschal, Guiles, could find for them.

Rob was tall and ruggedly handsome. Like everyone else, he seemed to have aged beyond his years while in the Holy Land. "Ah, it's the knight of Huntley," he said. "I hear it was you who talked the lord of Deraa into inviting us on this little excursion."

"I did," Roger admitted. "I've seen your fellows in action, and I thought you might come in handy if we find ourselves in a tight spot."

"I don't know whether to thank you or kill you," Rob said, only half joking.

Rob's large friend John, called "Tiny," was more sanguine. "Least it gets us out o' camp. Bloody boring, sitting 'round the tent all day, doing nothing."

"Better than having our heads removed by infidels," Rob told him.

Roger and Tatwine left the archers and joined Henry and his squire, Thierry—or Teary, as they called him—at the head of the line. "All set?" Henry asked Roger.

Roger nodded. Then he said, "I've been wondering. Why did King Richard put you in charge of this expedition? You and he aren't exactly best friends."

Henry was realistic. "He knows I can do the job, and he's probably hoping I'll get killed in the process." He rubbed his bearded chin. "Look, Roger, perhaps I made a mistake bringing you along. This could be a risky affair. Maybe you should stay here. You've already cheated death enough for one lifetime."

Tatwine looked hopeful at those words, but Roger said, "Of course I'm going. Aren't fathers and sons supposed to do things together?" He tried to sound brave, cocky even, but inside he was nervous. He wondered if he would ever see Ailith again. He wondered what she was doing right now, if she was thinking of him.

"You're sure?" Henry went on. "There's no dishonor in staying behind. You're not technically one of my men."

"I'm sure," Roger told him. It was too late to back out now, even if he wanted to. A knight's honor demanded that.

Henry sighed, as though he'd been hoping for a different answer but got the one he expected. "Pass the word to mount," he ordered Teary.

The command went down the line, and the men mounted. Tatwine climbed into his saddle awkwardly. "Nice horsie," he said, patting the animal's neck.

Henry nodded to Teary, who rose in his stirrups and waved Henry's falcon banner back and forth. The men wheeled right and started off by twos. There was the clop of hooves, the creak of leather, the clink of mail and accoutrements—bells had been removed from reins and bridles, along with anything else that could make noise. The knights had their spears slung behind their shoulders on cords.

Roger stayed with Henry as the column filed past. The two scouts—the short, swarthy Turco officer, whose name was Reynard, and the Bedouin—went first. They were followed by half the company of blue-robed Turcos. After them came Henry's men, then the knights and men-at-arms furnished by Balian and the kingdom of Jerusalem, and finally a company of Hospitallers, led by a veteran knight named Peter of Blessons. Each unit brought pack horses carrying grain and extra water, led by squires. The other half of the Turcos brought up the rear.

Altogether there were close to five hundred men in the raiding party. It sounded like a lot, but they would have to take on four thousand Saracen footmen, and if they encountered Saracen cavalry in force, they could find themselves in serious trouble.

When the column had ridden past, Henry and Roger, along with their squires, cantered to the head of the line. A number of men had gathered to watch the raiders ride out of camp, among them King Richard, his huge form silhouetted against the red sunset. Richard looked wan and unsteady on his feet. Alart of Vouzin and Andrew of Chauvigny stood to either side of him, to offer support should he fall.

Richard reached up and shook Henry's hand. "God be with you, Deraa."

"Thank you, sire," Henry said.

Richard acknowledged Roger. "Huntley, good luck." He grinned. "Try not to get taken prisoner this time, will you?"

Roger grinned back. "I'll do my best, sire."

Just past Richard was the bishop of Beauvais, resplendent in purple chasuble and gold stole, his head adorned with a low, two-horned mitre. He blessed the departing raiders, sprinkling them with Holy Water as they rode past.

"Good luck, Lord Henry," the bishop called. "I wish I was going with you."

Henry crossed himself and smiled. "I wish you were, too, your grace. We could use you."

Roger felt the sprinkle of Holy Water and blessed himself, as well. Then they were out of camp and riding into the darkness.

Chapter 19

ℌENRY RODE DOWN the column. "Close it up. Keep moving, men. No talking."

They had been on the march for hours, judging by the passage of the moon, but there was no sense of time, no sense that they had gotten anywhere. The rhythmic clump of hooves and jingle of equipment sounded unnaturally loud in the quiet of the desert. The men were alert, mindful that Saracens could come hurtling out of the darkness at any moment. The men had been ordered to tie themselves to their saddles, so they wouldn't fall off if they fell asleep.

The Turco Reynard and the Bedouin were about a half-mile ahead of the main column. The Turcos in the rear kept guard to watch for Saracens approaching from behind. The raiders planned to intercept the Saracen caravan somewhere between Hebron and Bethlehem. They hoped to link up with the Turco patrol that was shadowing the caravan, but if they didn't, they'd have to find the caravan themselves.

The vast sky was crystalled with stars, which, along with the quarter-moon, helped to light their way. The arid ground was broken, rising gradually, the hills around them blocking much of the view. Roger and Tatwine rode behind Henry and his squire, Teary. Behind them was Henry's second in command, Guiles. Tatwine shifted uneasily in his saddle. "My arse hurts," he whispered to Roger.

"You'll get used to it," Roger lied. By the time they got back to Bet Nable—*if* they got back—Tatwine's backside and inner thighs would be rubbed raw and soaked with blood. He'd told Tatwine to grease them and put some kind of padding on them before starting off, but even that wouldn't be much help for someone who had never been on a horse before.

Despite the night chill, Roger was sweating under the weight of his armor and padded leather gambeson. Flea bites on his scalp itched, but he couldn't scratch them because of his helmet. His nerves prickled with both excitement and fear, as each step took them further into the unknown.

The Turco Reynard cantered back and fell in alongside Henry. "No sign of the enemy," he told Henry in a low voice. "Ibrahim has gone ahead to a spring we know. I will guide you there."

"Very well."

Henry dropped out of line as the men rode past. "Keep going. Close it up. No talking."

On and on they rode. Roger's head jerked up with a start, and he realized that he had nodded off. He shook his head to get the blood flowing again.

From behind him came a metallic clatter that seemed to reverberate through the hills and across the countryside. This was followed by startled oaths and muttered curses. One of the knights furnished by the kingdom had fallen asleep and toppled from his horse.

"Get up, damn you," swore Daurel of Vitry, the native knights' commander.

Henry rode up. "Why weren't you tied on?" he demanded of the man who had fallen.

"Rope broke," the embarrassed knight replied, picking himself off the ground. The haft of his spear had cracked in the fall, and he discarded the now useless weapon.

"Halt the column," Henry said.

The word was passed down the line. Men licked their lips, waiting to see if the noise had been heard. Listening for cries, horns, the sound of hooves.

There was a scream in the distance, and hands dropped to sword and axe hilts.

After a tense moment they realized the noise had come not from a man, but from an animal that had fallen prey to another.

All appeared to be quiet.

Henry motioned the column forward again.

Around nocturns, as near as Roger could tell by the stars, Ibrahim the Bedouin ghosted out of the darkness and guided the raiders to a brackish spring, where they watered their horses, then drank in turn. The water tasted like it had been strained through unwashed braies, but at least it was water. Roger stretched his cramped legs as best he could, then they were back in the saddle—Tatwine groaning as his sore thighs made contact with the leather—and amidst whispered calls for more speed, they started off again.

❧

It was cool on the walls on Jerusalem, the night breeze dissipating the day's heat. Saladin wrapped his cloak around him. Worry and the pain in his stomach prevented him from sleeping, so he had gone for a walk on the walls, accompanied by al-Adil and the emir Qaymaz. Now the three men stood on the parapet, gazing to the west, where a distant glow marked the infidels' huge camp at Bet Nable.

"Why don't they attack?" al-Adil muttered to no one in particular. "What are they waiting for?"

Qaymaz paid no attention to the infidel camp. He was thinking about Ailith, as he did far more than was good for him. He thought of her with a mixture of longing and rage. He realized she didn't love him the way he loved her, but he'd believed she at least liked him, believed she would be glad to accept the wealth and privilege he could bestow on her, believed she would be appreciative. But she had tricked him, made a fool of him, and escaped. To his everlasting regret, he also knew he would take her back should the opportunity arise. By rights he should kill her, subject her to torture, but he wouldn't. He cursed himself for a fool, but he couldn't help it.

A man cannot pick whom he falls in love with.

Saladin turned to Qaymaz. "Is there news of the supply caravan?"

Qaymaz shook his head, clearing thoughts of Ailith from it. "None, lord."

"They should have been here by now," said al-Adil.

"There could be any number of reasons for their delay," Qaymaz pointed out.

"There could," Saladin agreed, "but I am worried. I fear that Rik has learned about the caravan and sent a force to attack it."

"That would be a disaster for us," al-Adil said. "We need the supplies and reinforcements, or we cannot withstand a siege."

"Precisely. Which is why I want you, Lord Qaymaz, to take a party of your men, find the caravan, and escort it here."

"Yes, lord. Shall I leave immediately?"

"That would be best."

Qaymaz bowed and left the group.

"Please Allah he is not too late," Saladin told his brother.

Chapter 20

𝔍N THE MURK and chill of the predawn, they entered a deep, winding *wadi*, and word was passed down the line to halt.

"We'll camp here for the day," Henry told his commanders. "There's a spring nearby. You'll be told off in sections to go for water. Aside from that, the men are to remain in place. No loud noise, no unnecessary movement. There are Saracens all over these hills, and it's our lives if we're discovered."

As the fresh scent of dawn filled the air, the men unsaddled, fed, and picketed their horses. Tatwine hobbled in agony as he took the saddle off his horse. "Rather eat this bloody beast than ride him," he muttered.

When the horses were seen to, the men removed their armor. With Tatwine's help, Roger unlaced his helmet and shrugged out of his mail hauberk and gambeson. He felt like he might float into the air without their weight holding him down. At this point, most of the men scurried to secluded parts of the *wadi* to relieve themselves. There had been a few quick breaks for this on the march, but it wasn't easy to urinate while wearing mail, even harder to defecate. For the men suffering from dysentery it was yet more difficult, and a number of those had voided themselves in their clothes and had to clean themselves up as best they could.

Guards were set and Turco scouts sent in all directions. The men led their horses to the spring in groups. When that was done, they jammed themselves into pools of shade on one side of the *wadi*. As the sun moved across the sky, they would cross to the *wadi*'s other side for shade, taking their armor with them so it wouldn't heat up in the rays of the sun. Some of the men ate or cleaned weapons, but most fell right asleep. Soon the *wadi* grew quiet as the sun beat at the dust around them. The only sound was snoring. Even the flies seemed to sleep.

Wearing only his long shirt and hose, Henry walked down the *wadi*, looking over the men. He snatched an earthenware pot of arrack from one of the kingdom's knights who was still awake. "I said, no liquor."

He threw the pot against the rocks, shattering it and startling the sleeping men nearby.

The knight started to protest. "Be quiet," Henry told him.

When he was finished inspecting the men, Henry stretched out beside Roger, propping his head on his saddle. His hauberk was neatly folded behind the saddle, his helmet placed on top of it. His sweat-soaked gambeson was laid out to dry nearby. "Damned fools," he said, "no matter how many times you tell them, they still try to bring liquor."

From the corner of his eye, Roger saw Tatwine hurriedly stuff something under his saddle blanket.

Henry closed his good eye. Roger hesitated, then said, "You've never told me how you became such a powerful baron. In fact, you've never told me anything about your life in the Holy Land."

Henry sighed and opened his eye. "Deraa was given to me by the Leper King, Baldwin, as a reward for my services at Montgisard. We beat the Saracens that day, and I almost caught Old Sidesaddle as he was running way on his camel. Would have—would've killed him, too, bugger the ransom—but my horse broke a leg and threw me. I'll always wonder how history would have been different if that hadn't happened. Anyway, the barony was open and Baldwin thought I'd make a good lord for it."

Henry was quiet for a moment, then he squinted at Roger. "I was a lot like you when I got here—about the same age, no money. I took service first with Reginald of Kerak, then with Reynard of Chatillon."

"Reginald of Kerak," Roger said, "I've heard of him."

"A great warrior, but no man of honor, and I couldn't abide that. That's why I left his service. Saladin struck his head off after Hattin. He'd do the same to me if he got the chance."

"Why does Saladin dislike you so?"

"I've been a thorn in his side for years. I've taken more gold from him than most of the other barons combined—certainly more than Reginald of Kerak ever did. But the real reason he hates me is . . ." his voice tailed off.

"Is what?" Roger said.

Henry took a deep breath. "Some years ago, my steward, Udo, and I hit upon the idea of building a fleet of ships and sailing them down the Red Sea to attack Mecca."

Roger's eyes widened.

Henry nodded, as though he knew the story sounded fantastic. "We felled timber and dragged it across the desert on rollers to Aqaba, where we constructed three warships."

Roger leaned on one elbow. "Then what?"

"We should have headed straight for Mecca, but the prospect of loot was too tempting. We destroyed tons of Saracen shipping in the Red Sea. They never expected to encounter feringhees there, and their ships were defenseless. We raided Saracen slave ports in Africa, as well—that's where I lost my eye."

"In battle?"

Henry shook his head ruefully. "I burned a mosque. As I looked up to watch the flames, a drop of melted lead from the roof fell into my eye. Ironic, eh? Maybe their god has some clout, after all. At any rate, we took so much gold and ivory and jewels in Africa that it slowed our ships down, which proved to be our undoing. The men were content with the loot and wanted to return to Deraa. But not me. No, I was determined to carry out the original plan. I wanted to raze Mecca to the ground. Well, the Saracens aren't stupid. Saladin guessed where we were heading and was apparently outraged beyond belief—one of his titles is 'Defender of the Holy Places,' or some such blather. He gathered fast sailing ships, filled them with troops, and sent them after us. A lot of them. They caught us, and, well . . ."

Henry paused for a long moment. "After many adventures, Udo, Guiles, and I and a few others made it back. The rest were killed." Henry's jaw tightened. "Udo was killed a year after, skinned alive by Qaymaz. He was under flag of truce at the time, conducting negotiations for King Baldwin."

Henry went on. "A lot of good men died because of my pride and stupidity. It was the same reason I lost your mother."

Roger waited, letting his father go at his own pace. "My days with Aethelflaed were the happiest of my life—maybe the only happy ones. Strange how your life can be influenced so much by a woman. I miss Aethelflaed every day, miss her even more as time goes by. There's an ache—a knot—in my heart that never goes away. Oh, I manage to put her from my mind for a while, but she always comes back, stronger than ever. They say the Lord works in mysterious ways, but I wish He'd worked a little harder for your mother. She didn't deserve to die. Not that way, not so young. If God had taken anyone, He should have taken me—I'm the sinner. And yet here I am, still alive, still sinning. I pray I'll get to see Aethelflaed again in Heaven, but I fear Heaven will be denied to me."

He turned to Roger. "If you get out of this in one piece, you go back to that girl Ailith—yes, I know about you and her, everybody does—and you never let her go. Do you understand me?"

"Yes," Roger said.

There was another pause, then Roger said, "Tell me about my mother. She was a villager?"

"Yes, but a free one, not a villein."

"How is that possible?" Roger said.

"Her free status was hereditary—I guess because her family had been nobles back in the English days. Her father was the largest landowner on the manor—aside from the lord, of course. Aethelflaed had received a calling; she wanted to join a convent and serve God. Then she met me. Her parents didn't like me—I was a Frenchman, and

135

a poor one at that. Her father wouldn't approve our marriage, so we ran off. Her father died not long after—of a broken heart, they say. Her mother sent that ring of yours to her—he'd willed it to her, not to one of his sons."

"How did you two meet?"

Henry smiled fondly. "I was resting beside the River Eal, one day, by a ford. There's a huge willow that overhangs the river at that point. Pretty spot. Anyway, here comes this girl—striking creature—leading a cow, trying to get it to cross the river. The cow didn't want to go. The girl whacked its rump with a switch, but the animal wouldn't budge. So I gallantly rose and offered to be of assistance. I tried to push the beast and ended up slipping and falling full length in the water."

Henry smiled again—hard to picture the ferocious lord of Deraa smiling at himself. "The girl couldn't stop laughing at that. At first I was angry, then I started laughing, as well. We got to talking, spent half the day there. She was bright and witty and beautiful, and I was entranced by her. After that, we began running into one another 'accidentally.' Before we knew it, we were in love."

Roger found himself smiling, as well. "What about the cow? Did you ever get it across the stream?"

"Damned animal crossed by itself while we were talking," Henry said. Then he became gruff Henry again. "Now, stop asking all these questions and get some sleep. We pass the Saracen outpost at al-Burj tonight, and with luck we'll catch that caravan on the morrow. We'll need to run like hell after that, so everybody better be rested."

He closed his good eye and fell fast asleep, but Roger lay awake for a long while, thinking.

Chapter 21

WHEN THE SUN was low, they fed and watered their horses, the men using their helmets as water buckets. There was a quick meal of salt pork and hard bread, washed down with water warm from the desert heat. They only took a swig or two of the water because they didn't know when they would find more.

They saddled the horses, armed themselves, and started off. It was sunset as they left the shelter of the *wadi*. "Keep the men moving," Henry told his commanders. "I want to catch that caravan tomorrow just before dawn, when they're most vulnerable."

The country was rugged, the going slow. Roger glanced over at Tatwine. "You seem more comfortable with the horse today."

Tatwine nodded; he was no longer holding the reins in terror. "Still going to eat the bugger," he added.

Roger grinned. "Remember, I warned you not to come."

Tatwine harrumphed, as though not coming had never been an option.

After some time, stark cliffs blotted out the sky before them. "Al-Burj," the guide said.

Henry motioned the column to halt. "Pass the word. Dismount."

The men climbed from their saddles. They tied leather pads that they had brought with them to their horses' hoofs. They made sure all their equipment was tied down. Henry and Guiles checked the pack animals, directing squires to right any imperfections.

"Single file," Henry whispered. "Keep a space between yourself and the next man. Anybody talks, I'll have the hide off him, I don't care if his father's a duke."

They started into the pass, hands across the muzzles of their horses to keep them from whinnying. Men stared into the shadows, half expecting Saracens—or maybe devils—to leap out at them. Roger followed Henry's squire, Teary, placing each foot with care. Tatwine hobbled painfully behind Roger.

Above them to the left, a faint light revealed the fortified watchtower of al-Burj. The garrison at al-Burj was too small to threaten the raiders, but if they spotted Henry's men, they would send gallopers and bring troops from Saladin's divisions quartered around Bethlehem and Jerusalem.

From above came a cry of alarm.

Every man stopped without being told.

They waited, eyes straining up into the darkness. Sweat ran down foreheads and cheeks.

Another cry—this one, it seemed, of derision. Sounds of an argument.

There was a pause, then something hit the floor of the pass with a loud *clack* and bounced three times, narrowly missing a pack horse. A rock. The squire holding the pack horse did a good job of keeping the animal calm.

A laugh from above, then silence.

The men waited a long time, until Henry deemed it safe, then they moved on, walking cautiously.

Ahead, the pass opened and the blanket of stars unfolded before them again. Henry dropped behind to see the column through. They stayed on foot a while longer, and when they were far enough away from al-Burj, they removed the coverings from the horse's hoofs, mounted, and started off again.

"That took more time than I had hoped," Henry told Guiles. "The Saracens will know we were here at some point tomorrow. The passage of so many horses can't be kept secret."

"Which means?" Guiles asked him.

"Which means we'd best not dawdle."

Beyond al-Burj, the ground started to fall away, the sere grass and brush becoming more scarce. They took a break, and Henry ordered the men to remove their armor and tie it to their saddles. With Tatwine's assistance, Roger took off his helmet, hauberk, and sweat-drenched gambeson. He stood in his long shirt and hose, fluffing sweat from his hair, letting the cool night air flow around him. Tatwine removed his mail-ringed jack and brimmed helmet.

Then they were back on the march. Monotonous clopping of hooves, swaying of horses. Some of the men slumped with chins on their chests, half asleep, but Henry was as alert as he'd been when they started—maybe more so. He rode down the column, urging the weary men to keep up the pace. Roger marveled at his ferocious drive and energy.

They stopped every so often to walk the horses and rest them, then it was back in the saddle. During one of these periods of walking, the swarthy guide Reynard came back to report. Henry and his commanders gathered around him. "Where is that Turco patrol of yours?" Henry demanded.

"Don't know, my lord," Reynard said. "No sign of them."

"I'm not going to blunder around the desert all night looking for them. We've lost too much time as it is. Find me that damned caravan."

"My lord, I think it would be better to link up—"

"I don't care what you think. Find the caravan, or I'll find it myself."

Reynard rode off.

"Let's go," Henry told his commanders.

"Perhaps we should rest a while," the scarred Hospitaller Peter Blessons suggested. "The men and animals are tired."

"They can rest all they want when they get back to Bet Nable. Get 'em moving."

The column trudged on.

Henry had hoped to attack the caravan at dawn, but it was already close to dawn when Reynard and the Bedouin Ibrahim clattered out of the darkness with the missing Turco patrol. The Turcos were led by Roger's old acquaintance Espiart and his second-in-command, the raffish young Gaston.

The column halted and the commanders rode up. Espiart spotted Roger. "By God, it's—" he tried to remember the name— "Roger, isn't it? What are you doing here?"

"Talk about old times later," Henry told Espiart. "Where's the caravan?"

Espiart gave Roger an apologetic smile and waved an arm. "About six miles to the northeast," he told Henry. He glanced at the lightening sky. "They'll be breaking camp about now."

Henry swore. "We're too late to attack them. Well, there's nothing for it." To Espiart he said, "Set us a course to intercept them. We'll need to swing wide so they won't see our dust."

"Very well," Espiart said.

As grey dawn spread across the eastern sky, Espiart and his Turcos set off, Henry and the raiders following.

The horizon turned red, then abruptly the sun rose, throwing its harsh glare across a landscape that had been in shadow moments before. It was hot already; the night time coolness dissipated as though it had never existed. Like most of the men, Roger and Tatwine wrapped checkered keffiyehs around their heads and faces to protect them from the sun. Far to the right rose a plume of dust—the caravan, separated from them by a range of low hills. They heard a faint wailing of horns, a beating of drums.

Roger frowned in disbelief. "Music?"

"Don't believe in the Rule of Silence, do they?" Tatwine said.

They rode for miles through the rising heat, turning west till the dust of the caravan fell behind them. When it had been gone for some time, they turned east again.

Henry halted the column. He and Espiart rode to the top of a low rise, watched for a moment, and came back. "This will do," Henry announced. "Tell the men to water the horses and arm themselves. And be quick about it."

The knights and men-at-arms assisted each other in putting on their armor. Roger's gambeson was still soaked with sweat, which seemed to add pounds to its weight. Tatwine helped him pull on his hauberk and lace his helmet until he was once again in his iron cocoon. He was glad for the loose cloth cover on his helmet, whose metal would otherwise have turned red hot in the sun.

When the men were armed, Henry summoned his commanders. "Roger, you come, too."

Henry and Roger, along with Guiles, red-haired Daurel of Vitry, Peter Blessons, and Vauquelin, the Turco commander, left the main column. They dismounted behind the low rise and crept to the top, where they lay down.

To the south, the dust cloud was again visible. They heard distant, high-pitched music.

The head of the caravan gradually appeared out of the dust, cavalry in the lead. "About a hundred," Henry mused. "Probably the same number in the rear."

The caravan came on. There were strings of camels and horses laden with packs, flocks of sheep and goats, musicians, gay flags and banners.

"It's like a traveling fair," Peter Blessons said.

Long lines of infantry marched to either side of the caravan. "Egyptians," said Daurel of Vitry. "See the helmets?"

Henry agreed. "That figure of four thousand seems about right, though it's hard to tell with all the dust. We'll wait till they get abreast of us, then we'll go."

The Turco Vauquelin said, "You don't want to follow and attack tonight after they camp?"

"There's no time. We have to assume we're being followed. I don't like it, but that's how it is. We'll spread out. Five companies. Guiles, you'll take my men and attack the van. Daurel, you take the center. Peter, you and your Hospitallers, the rear. Vauquelin, your Turcos will surround the bastards and cut off flight."

There were nods all round. Henry continued. "Take out the cavalry and infantry first, especially the cavalry. Don't let any of them get away to spread the news. Roger, you're with me. Keep those archer friends of yours with us, as well. They don't ride well enough to be in a charge."

He looked around. "Everyone understand what they're to do?"

More nods.

"No horns, no trumpets, no yelling. Just pitch into 'em. All right, form your men, then wait for my signal, and may God be with you."

The music from the caravan was louder as the commanders returned to their units, while Henry remained on the hill. The widely separated companies formed a line about a mile long. Men loosened weapons in scabbards and belts. They readied their spears, took last sips of water. Leaders assumed positions in front. Horses stamped and pawed the ground; they seemed to know what was coming and were eager to get on with it.

Roger waited with Teary and Tatwine behind Daurel's men at the center of the line, Rob and his archers behind them. Roger's throat was dry, his heart pumping. He adjusted the Death's Head shield on his shoulder for what seemed the dozenth time.

Henry waited until the center of the caravan was nearly opposite him, then he half scrambled, half slid back down the hill. Teary held the reins of Henry's horse and he mounted.

He nodded to Teary. "Now."

Teary raised the falcon banner and waved it so that the men up and down the line could see.

Commanders motioned their men forward, and the armored companies started over the rise.

Chapter 22

𝕿HE TWO LINES of armored men thundered over the ridge and started down the other side, picking up speed as they hit level ground. They started cheering now, yelling their war cries

The members of the caravan stared in shock. The screaming feringhee devils seemed to have been conjured out of the very air. Too late, the Saracens were jolted into action. Most turned and fled, both horsemen and infantry—the infantry throwing down their weapons. The crusaders piled into them, cutting them down from behind, first with spears, then with swords and axes. It was more like butchery than a battle, with the defenseless Saracens offering their backs and necks as targets. Small groups of footmen banded together and put up a fight. Their long spears did damage, gutting feringhee horses, while other Saracens rushed to kill the Christians who were thrown to the ground, but these men were soon chopped down by new horsemen or trampled by crusader mounts, the flailing hoofs crushing skulls and chests and backs.

Vauquelin's Turcopoles swept wide and cut off fleeing Saracen cavalry, who were in turn attacked from the rear by Guiles' men and black-surcoated Hospitallers. Camel drivers, horse tenders, musicians, and cooks fled into the desert or cowered under their beasts for protection. The caravan's commander, a bejeweled emir with a silver-inlaid helmet, fought bravely and tried to rally his men, until his head was split open by an axe. The air was filled with yells and screams, with dust, with the cries of wounded horses, the bleating of frightened sheep and goats.

It was over so quickly that Henry and Roger, following the main body of men, never joined the fight. The Saracens were dead, surrendered, or fleeing into the desert. Thirsty knights unlaced aventails and drank from water skins. Other knights dismounted and rounded up the Saracen prisoners. Still others hauled terrified Saracens from beneath animals or wagons and banded them with the prisoners or killed them.

Henry took off his helmet and replaced it with a keffiyeh while Teary blew Commanders' Call on his horn. The blood-splashed commanders rode up, dust from the battle still swirling about them.

"How many did we lose?" Henry demanded.

A rough tally came up with fourteen dead and thirty-one wounded.

"We were lucky," said the Hospitaller Peter Blessons.

"It's not over yet," Henry told him. "Detail one man in four to watch the horses. Water and feed them. See if you can find grain in some of these packs before you use what we brought with us. Same with the water. Take everything else and destroy it."

Henry's seneschal, Guiles, was wide eyed. "All of it?"

"Yes."

"King Richard won't like that," Guiles said. "He's expecting us to bring it back."

"I don't care. These supplies will slow us down, and I intend to make it back alive."

147

"What about the animals?" said red-haired Daurel of Vitry, slinging his shield behind his back.

"Kill them. Save some of the horses for our men who lost theirs."

"Kill the sheep and goats, too?"

"Especially the sheep and goats. They're food for the garrison at Jerusalem."

"And the men?" Guiles said.

"Kill the footmen and cavalry. The rest are harmless. Strip them naked and set them loose."

"Wait," Roger protested. "We can't kill them. Before, at Acre, you—"

"We'd given our word not to kill those men at Acre," Henry said. "We've given no such word to these."

"But it's not—"

"When you make war, make war. This isn't some game. Either kill these men now, or face them on the walls of Jerusalem in a few days. Which do you prefer?"

Roger said nothing. He couldn't argue with Henry's reasoning. Still . . .

Henry dismounted and gave his horse to Teary. He started down the long line of pack animals. "All this material. Get it down and destroy it. Hurry, we need to get away from here as quickly as possible."

"You think there's Saracens nearby?" Guiles asked him.

"I think I don't want to stick around and find out."

"What about loot?" said the Turcopole Vauquelin, wiping blood and someone's brains from his face with the tail of his white scarf.

"The men can take whatever will fit in their saddle bags. Leave everything else behind."

The Hospitallers began killing the prisoners and animals, whose screams filled the background. Other men walked through blood, stepping over bodies of men and animals. They pulled sacks of grain and flour off the animals, slitting some of them open, letting the breeze carry their contents across the sand. But that took too long, so the rest, along with the dried fruit and spices, the tents, the silks and armor and weapons, they piled and burned, using the wooden pack frames and the few wagons as tinder. Rob and his archers joined in, glad to be of use.

Attended by Roger and Teary, Henry continued down the line, amidst dead men and animals already beginning to stink in the heat. Amidst smells of shit and urine and blood and burning spices.

"Hurry," Henry told the men. "We need to get moving."

The Hospitaller Peter Blessons came up. "What about our wounded?"

"Patch up the ones who can travel and get them on their horses."

"And those who can't travel?"

Henry looked him in the eye, and Blessons' silent nod made Roger go cold inside.

"What about our dead?" Blessons added.

"Have one of your Hospitallers say a prayer over them, then burn them. I don't want the Saracens desecrating their bodies."

Henry looked for the Turco guide Reynard and found him going through the saddlebags of a dead Saracen noble. "We're taking a different route back to Bet Nable," Henry told him. "We can't chance using the one we took getting here. The pass at al-Burj will likely be blocked."

"I know a way," said the Bedouin Ibrahim, who stood nearby, admiring a jeweled sword he'd acquired.

"Good. You two scout it out. Espiart, go with them. Have Gaston and the rest of your patrol scout toward Jerusalem. They'll cover our back trail as we leave."

"Yes, my lord," said the world-weary Espiart.

Ibrahim stuck the jeweled sword in his belt, and he and Reynard started off, along with Espiart. Young Gaston waved casually to Roger as he went to gather his men.

Besides destroying supplies, the raiders—save for the Hospitallers, who were forbidden by their monastic vows to loot— plundered bodies and horses of anything valuable. There was a yell from the center of the caravan. Some of Daurel's men had discovered chests full of money, pay for the Jerusalem garrison. "There's enough here to make us all rich!" one cried.

There was ragged cheering, and men ran to see.

Henry shouldered through the crowd and kicked over one of the chests, scattering the coins it held. "We've no time for this, and these chests are too heavy to carry. Every man take a handful of coins, and let's get moving."

"Already?" said Daurel of Vitry. "The men and horses could use a rest."

"I told you before, rest when you get back to Bet Nable." Henry turned. "Teary, sound Assembly."

Teary blew two blasts on his horn. "Form up!" Henry cried. "Get mounted."

The order was repeated up and down the line. Men finished what they were doing and hurried to their horses. The wounded were tied to their saddles.

"Quickly!"

Some of Daurel's men, and a few Turcos, ignored the horn and were still rifling the treasure chests. "What about them?" Guiles asked Henry, jerking a thumb toward the looters.

"Leave them," Henry said. "They can catch up, if they're still alive to do it."

Henry mounted, followed by Roger and Teary. Rob and his archers were already on their horses. Henry looked around. "Ready? Move out."

"Move out!" The cry was repeated down the line.

The column set off, passing the remains of the caravan. Plumes of dark smoke rose into the sky. Bodies of men and animals littered the ground. Wounded animals and treasure hunters drifted through the mess. Already, vultures picked through the leavings.

"Thought we was going to get rich," Tatwine complained to Roger as they rode. Roger hadn't seen Tatwine since the fighting ended. "Maybe them fellows what stayed behind had the right idea."

Roger lifted an eyebrow. "I'm sure you picked up a few things."

"The odd bauble or two," Tatwine admitted. "One of 'em's still got a finger attached."

"Enough for your tavern?"

"The tavern, maybe. Don't know about the whores, though, and that's the part I was lookin' forward to the most."

They rode along, following the trail left by Espiart, Reynard, and Ibrahim. Most of the men still had their helmets off. They had gone about six miles and were settling into the rhythm of the march when cries came from the rear of the column.

Everyone turned.

A rider was approaching. Fast.

As the rider grew closer, they saw he wore the light blue and white of a Turco. He was slumped in his saddle, arrows protruding from his shoulder and back.

The column slowed. Commanders left their companies and galloped toward the rear.

The rider was young Gaston, Espiart's second in command, and he was covered with blood.

Henry reached him first and grabbed his reins, stopping his horse. "What happened?" Henry said.

Gaston looked up. "Saracens," he said weakly, and he dropped from his saddle to the ground.

Chapter 23

ᏀASTON LAY ON the ground, blood running from his wounds, staining his sky blue robe and white cloak. Henry snapped off the arrows, eliciting screams from Gaston, then he turned the boy over and propped his head against Henry's thigh. He fanned his face, gave him water from his skin. "Where's the rest of your patrol?" Henry asked.

"Dead," Gaston said. "I was lucky to get away." He took more water. "There's thousands of them. They're under . . . they're under a blue flag."

Henry looked at Roger and Guiles.

"Qaymaz," Guiles said.

"And our men who stayed behind at the caravan site?" Daurel of Vitry asked Gaston.

Gaston shook his head. "Gone."

Henry said. "How far behind us are they?"

"Seven miles. Maybe less."

Daurel said, "Which means that if we'd stayed behind to loot the caravan and bring the supplies back to Bet Nable . . ."

"Qaymaz would already have overtaken us," Henry said.

Daurel straightened. "My apologies, Lord Henry, for not seeing your point earlier."

"Forget it," Henry said. "Buy me a flagon of wine when we're in Heaven. Right now, we need to get moving."

Somebody fashioned a pillow from a blanket. Henry gently laid Gaston against it and stood, heedless of Gaston's blood soaking his leg.

"What about him?" Peter Blessons said, indicating Gaston. "He's in no condition to ride."

Henry looked at Gaston. They both knew the answer.

"I'll do it," Roger said.

Henry hesitated, then said, "Very well," and moved off to rejoin the column.

Roger bent over Gaston. "Come on, Tatty, help me get him into the shade."

Roger and Tatwine half-lifted, half-dragged Gaston into the welcome shade of a boulder. Roger drew his long dagger from its sheath and offered it to Gaston, but Gaston waved him off. "You may have need of that dagger soon. Get mine from my belt."

Roger pulled Gaston's blood-stained white cloak aside and drew his dagger—a curved Arab blade with an ivory handle. He placed it in Gaston's hand. He felt an affinity with the raffish young Turco. The young Turco who would never grow old, who would never become hard bitten and cynical like so many others out here. Roger remembered opening Egwulf's veins at Acre, when his big friend had been burned beyond hope by Greek fire. He remembered how he'd felt then.

"We'll leave you some water," he told Gaston.

Gaston flashed a cocky smile. "I'd rather have arrack."

Tatwine slipped a small jug of the forbidden liquor from his saddlebag and handed it to the boy.

"Thanks," Gaston said. He took a drink of the arrack, coughed heavily, then traced his fingers over the dagger.

Roger and Tatwine crossed themselves.

Roger said, "We've got to be going, Gaston. God be with you."

"Be seeing Him in a bit," Gaston joked. "I'll give Him your regards."

"Enjoy the arrack," Tatwine said.

Roger added, "Don't wait too long."

Gaston swallowed and his voice broke. "I won't."

Roger and Tatwine left Gaston and rode back to the column, where Henry was addressing the men. "For those of you who didn't hear, we are being pursued by the emir Qaymaz. There will be torture for those who survive, so if we get in a fight, make sure you don't survive."

There was silence, some of the men exchanging glances.

Henry went on. "Take off your armor. Make it easier on yourselves. There will be time to put it on if we have to fight."

While the men removed their armor, Henry turned to the Turco officer Vauquelin. "Ride for Bet Nable. Tell King Richard to send help. Go as fast as you can. Kill your horse if you have to."

Vauquelin nodded. He vaulted into the saddle and galloped away.

Henry said, "All right, men, move out."

The men hurriedly finished fastening armor to their saddles, mounted, and rode off, most of them wearing keffiyehs and their long shirts—save for the Hospitallers, who refused to remove their black surcoats, even in the stifling heat. Henry set as fast a pace as he dared, but it was tricky going. They needed to stay ahead of the pursuing Saracens, but they didn't want to wear out their horses and be overtaken because of that.

It seemed an eternity since they had first spotted the caravan, but by the sun, it was only about nones. They rode for a long time, then dismounted and walked their horses, to give the animals a rest.

Behind them, a dust cloud towered into the blue sky.

Tatwine and Roger looked at it. "A lot of men," Tatwine said.

"More than we can hope to fight," said Roger.

They remounted and kept going. The sun beat down. Men began discarding equipment. Knights who still had spears tossed them away. Not a few got rid of helmets and hauberks, as well. The heavy mail wouldn't be much use to them if Qaymaz caught up. They'd be dead either way. Other men got rid of loot they had taken from the caravan, anything to lighten their load. Coins and jewels were flung away as though they were worthless bits of metal and glass. The Saracen emir's silver inlaid helmet lay beside the trail.

At one point the pack horses were let go. "Kill them?" Guiles asked Henry.

"Let 'em run loose," Henry said. "Maybe the Saracens will stop to catch them. Anything to give us more time. If we can stay ahead of the bastards until dark, we have a chance."

The march continued. Behind them the dust cloud grew inexorably closer. The sun was getting lower in the west, but not quickly enough.

"We're not going to be saved by darkness," Henry said.

"So what should we do?" Roger asked him.

"Keep going. It's all we can do. Keep going, and pray for a miracle."

The column plodded on, the men resigned to their fate, glancing behind them anxiously as they rode. "Be on us soon," Tatwine muttered to Roger.

The Turco guide Reynard rejoined them and led them to a pass through the hills. Peter Blessons rode to the head of the column. "Perhaps we should make a stand here," he suggested to Henry. "Their numbers won't be as much of an advantage for them in this pass."

Reynard was quick to discredit that idea. "They can outflank us on two sides if we stay here, come in behind us and cut us off. If I know the routes, they'll have someone who knows them, too."

"How long would it take them to outflank us?" Henry asked him.

Reynard looked at the sky. "They'd be on us before vespers."

"Maybe we could leave a small party to hold them up," Daurel of Vitry said. "Buy us some time till it gets dark, and we'd be safe. At least till tomorrow."

Almost without thinking, Roger said, "I'll do it."

Heads turned toward him.

"I'll take Rob and his archers," Roger said. "We can hold the pass for a while."

Henry looked down the line at the ragged group of English archers. "With so few men?"

"They can do it," Roger said. "Trust me."

Henry rubbed his chin. "It's worth a try. I'll stay here with the archers. My lord of Vitry, you'll take over command of—"

"No," Roger said.

Henry stared at him.

"You command the column," Roger told his father. "You need to remain with them. See that they get through. I'll stay. It was my idea that the archers come with us, it's my duty to share the danger with them."

Roger saw the worry on Henry's face. Henry did not want to leave his son in this position. Then he squared himself. "Very well. I—"

"Get going," Roger told him. "Time is precious. Don't waste it talking to me."

Henry nodded. He clapped Roger's shoulder. "Good luck, son, I'm proud of you. Your mother'd be proud of you, too." He started away, then curbed his horse and looked back. "I still wish you'd stayed at that damned monastery." He turned and cried, "All right, men. Keep moving."

Roger pulled out of the line. "Rob!" he cried. "Bring your men."

As the column moved on, Rob and his men fell out of the formation. "We're going to stay here and hold this pass," Roger told them. "Buy time for the rest of the column."

The rest of the knights passed by, casting curious glances at these peasant archers who were supposed to save them.

Roger went on, speaking to the archers. "Sorry to do this to you, lads, but—"

"That's all right," Rob said. "I was tired of riding. Be nice to stretch my legs for a bit."

"Aye," said Tiny John. "We've yet to have a proper go at the buggers."

The other men growled assent, even if most of them didn't mean it.

Roger realized that Tatwine was still at his side.

"Go with the column," Roger told him.

"I'm your squire," Tatwine said, "I'm staying here."

"That's an order."

"And I'm disobeying it."

"Look, I know you don't really want to stay—"

"Course I don't want to stay, I didn't say I was stupid. Now stop yappin', and let's get on with it."

Rob and his men were already dismounted, leading the horses to safety, Rob and John shouting orders.

The dust cloud was closer, the drumming of hooves filled the air. The ground trembled.

Roger dismounted and gave his horse to Tatwine. There was no time to put on armor.

"You got a plan?" Tatwine asked.

"I'm working on one."

"You might want to work a bit faster. Bastards are almost here."

Chapter 24

IN THE END, Rob came up with the plan. "We're used to being chased," he explained to Roger. "We've done this sort of thing before."

The archers took a stand in a narrow part of the defile. There was a slight rise in the floor of the pass here, giving the men a good view; and the sides of the pass were high enough that the Saracens could not get around them on horseback, only on foot.

Rob stationed his eighteen men in two lines. One or two of the men had put on helmets, the rest still wore keffiyehs. About a third had donned their armored jacks. Roger stood to one side, Death's Head shield slung over his shoulder. Tatwine was beside him, axe in hand. The archers placed their three-foot arrows by their right legs in two rows of five, tips twisted into the dirt so they could be picked up easily.

The hoofbeats were louder now, the ground shook. They could smell oncoming dust.

"String your bows," Rob said calmly. He acted like he did this every day of his life.

The men bent the long bows and strung them, their huge forearms bulging.

Fierce cries and yells. The sound of approaching hoofbeats reverberated off the walls of the pass and through their heads, like hammering.

Dust filled the pass, obscuring vision.

"Five arrows," Rob cried over the noise. "Nock your arrows."

The bowmen put arrows to their bows.

Out of the dust the Saracens came charging down on them. Roger saw screaming faces, distorted eyes.

What is he waiting for?

"Draw! Shoot!"

Each man shot five arrows, plucking them from the ground one at a time and loosing them in a fluid motion. In less time than it took to load a crossbow, a hundred arrows were sent into the front of the Saracen formation, and at this range every one struck home. Men and horses went down in a welter of screams and dust. The men coming after them were unable to stop and piled into the ones already down in a mass of somersaulting horses and men flying from saddles.

The Saracen column was completely blocked by the smash-up of men and horses. Still more men ran into them from behind, coming at such speeds they could not stop and with no room to swerve out of the way. There were shouts from the Saracen leaders. Roger could have sworn he heard Qaymaz's voice among them.

"Five arrows. Draw! Shoot!"

A hundred more arrows went into the confusion, a rain of pointed shafts. More men and horses went down, making the jam at the front of the column even worse. Roger noted some alert Saracens dismounting and making their way along the sides of the pass on foot.

"Fall back!" Roger cried.

The archers ran back to the next position Rob had selected. It was just after the pass took a slight bend. The Saracens wouldn't be able to see them here until the last minute. With luck, they'd think the archers had ridden off after the first attack and be surprised to come upon them again. Qaymaz was a good commander and Roger assumed that he would normally send out scouts, but he also knew that Qaymaz wanted to overtake Henry's column before dark, and to do that he needed to abandon caution and come ahead at speed.

Rob lifted his bow to get his men's attention. "We'll shoot two flights of five again."

The men spread out. They stuck arrows in the ground in two rows.

It was taking a while for the Saracens to clear the pass. Roger heard them yelling. Each minute that passed was an extra minute for Henry and the column to reach safety.

"Where did you learn the use of this long bow?" Roger asked Rob.

Rob jerked a thumb. "Tiny brought one back from Wales. He was on campaign there."

"Awful place, Wales," Tiny said. "You wouldn't believe the gibberish they speak."

Roger said, "Are you fellows really poachers like they say?"

"Depends on what you consider poaching," Rob said.

"We consider it taking what's rightfully ours," added a barrel-chested fellow named Will, who wore a red hood. "No reason our forests and the game in them should belong to a bunch of people who aren't even English."

"Ever hear of Brock the Badger?" Tatwine asked them.

"'Course," Rob said. "Everybody's heard of Brock the Badger."

"He's a friend of ours."

"Go on," said Will.

"It's true," Tatwine said. "Ain't that right, Roger?"

Roger didn't want to drag Fauston into this, but he said, "It's true."

"He fought with the Death's Heads at the siege," Tatwine added.

"Well, strike me down," said Tiny. "Where's Brock now?"

Before Tatwine could answer, Rob said, "Here they come."

Hoofbeats rumbled. The rumble grew steadily louder.

"Nock your bows."

The Saracens rounded the bend in a compact mass.

"Draw! Shoot!"

A hundred more arrows plunged into the front of the column, wrecking it.

"Draw! Shoot!"

A hundred more. Once more the pass was blocked with downed men and horses, filled with cries and screams.

Roger cried, "Let's go!"

The archers fell back again, running about two furlongs to a rise on their left that overlooked the spot where the pass opened onto the plain. Their horses had been tethered there earlier.

"Get your other bows," Rob told his men.

Men fetched regular-sized bows from their saddles along with quivers of arrows for them. "Figured we might need these," Rob told Roger. "We've only got twenty arrows left for the long bows."

The men were breathing heavily. They took quick gulps of water, wiped sweat from their grimy faces with the tails of their keffiyehs.

One man had hurt his thumb and kept shaking it. They unstrung their bows so the strings wouldn't go slack.

"Think we've bought the column enough time?" Tatwine asked Roger.

"Till dark, maybe. After that . . ." Roger let his voice tail off. "The bad thing is, the Saracens will catch us before they catch the main body."

"Couldn't we just hide or something?" said Will, the man with the red hood. "Let 'em go by us?"

"If it was a small party, I'd say yes," Roger told him, "but there's thousands of them. They'll be between us and Bet Nable, and we don't know the country. They'll have trackers, as well, and I've seen what Qaymaz's trackers can do. Our best hope is to catch up with Lord Henry."

They waited in the heat. They watered and fed the horses, arranged their last arrows in the dirt. Took arrows from the new quivers and stuck them in the dirt, as well, for when the longer arrows ran out. They made sure the new bows were at hand for when they were needed.

"We'll do as much damage as we can, then go," Roger said. He added, "Save enough arrows for a last stand."

The men took this quietly. They had expected it. "Beats bein' hanged at the assizes," Tiny said with a shrug.

They heard horses coming again. More slowly this time, cautious. Roger said, "Lie down."

The men lay on their stomachs just behind the top of the ridge. Roger looked down the line. "Don't let them out of the pass. Kill as many as you can. If you see one with a blue sash on his helmet, aim for him. That'll be Qaymaz."

The horses grew louder. The men took deep breaths.

"String your bows."

Five scouts emerged from the pass and fanned out, following the archers' tracks. One of them cried to the others, and they joined him, headed for the ridge.

The archers stayed hidden behind the ridge, only Roger and Rob peeking over. "Wait for the main body," Rob told his men. "Tiny, you and Will take out those scouts when this gets started."

The main body of Saracens rumbled to the head of the pass. The blue flag was at its head this time, along with a rider with a blue sash around his helmet. Qaymaz was in a hurry.

"You time it," Roger told Rob.

Rob waited, then, "On your feet, lads! Draw! Shoot!"

The archers rose and unleashed a hail of arrows. Men and horses fell. Tiny and Red Will shot down the five scouts.

"Fire at will!" Rob cried.

The archers shot off their last volley of the longer arrows. They switched to the regular bows and began shooting them, taking their time, picking targets. The blue flag went down. The Saracens bunched up at the pass entrance, trying to break through the tangle of men and horses on the ground, and making excellent targets in the process. The helmet with the blue scarf pushed its way to the front, then it went down as well.

There was a wail, and the Saracens halted in disarray.

"Got him!" Roger cried. "It'll take them a while to reorganize. Let's get out of here."

The archers fired a last volley, then ran for their horses, mounted, and rode off. Those who still had helmets and jacks threw them away.

The pace was slow because most of the archers were not good horsemen. They followed the broad trail left by Henry and his men. They were still charged up by the fight and the damage they had inflicted upon the Saracens at no cost to themselves.

They rode for a mile in the still-blistering heat of late afternoon. Then Tiny looked over his shoulder. "Shit!"

Behind them the dust cloud had risen again, and not far behind. The Saracens were through the pass and after them. "They replaced Qaymaz already?" Roger said. "I thought it would take longer."

Rob scanned the horizon ahead of them. "No sign of the main column. They must have gotten away."

"Wish you could say that about us," Tatwine grimaced. He was in agony riding the horse again after being on his feet for so long.

Tatwine was right. They weren't going to make it. There was dust to either side of them now. Flankers, galloping ahead to surround them.

The sun was low, but they would be cut off before full dark.

To their left was a low line of cliffs. A small outcrop of rock had eroded away from it like a miniature castle. "No sense letting them ride us down," Roger said, pointing. "That looks like as good a place to die as any."

The company made for the rocky eminence, rode up it and dismounted, letting their horses go free. The animals would be of no use to them anymore.

Tatwine hobbled alongside Roger among the rocks, wincing at each step and drawing his axe from his belt for what was likely to be the last time.

The Saracens soon had the rise surrounded. There were, indeed, thousands of them. There could be no escape from such overwhelming numbers. The English archers formed a loose circle in the rocks, men crossing themselves, saying last prayers, taking last gulps of water, arranging what was left of their arrows.

The Saracen ranks parted, and the blue flag came to the front, accompanied by a rider with a blue sash streaming from his helmet.

"Damn!" Roger swore. "What does it take to kill that man?"

Qaymaz surveyed the rocky outcrop, then rejoined his men. The Saracen horns blew a command.

"Remember, don't let yourselves be taken prisoner," Roger reminded his men.

A group of about fifty horsemen detached itself from the Saracen lines, rode toward the hill, fired their bows, and rode away. One of Rob's archers fell. The other men sought deeper cover among the rocks.

"Don't shoot back," Rob told them. "They want you to waste your arrows. Save them for the final attack."

More Saracens rode at the hill. Another flight of arrows. Two more archers went down, one screaming with an arrow in his eye, the other with a shaft in his thigh.

The Saracens launched another attack. Arrows clattered off the rocks, but nobody was hurt this time.

"How long will they wait?" Rob asked Roger above the screaming of the man with the arrow in his eye.

"Not much longer. They want us dead by nightfall. They don't want any of us slipping away in the dark."

As if in answer to Rob's question, the Saracens began advancing from all side. Cymbals crashed.

"Get ready!" Rob cried.

Suddenly a horn blared from the west. Another. More.

"Look!" someone yelled.

Banners appeared against the western sunset, among them a white cinquefoil on a red field.

"That's the earl of Leicester!"

Men began cheering.

Gravedigger Leicester had brought a large force, as large as Qaymaz's. Roger saw Henry's falcon banner near the earl's.

The cymbals stopped clashing. The Saracens began falling back without being ordered to do so.

Leicester's force advanced in a line, coming at a canter, picking up speed, lances couched against their shoulders.

The Saracens went into full flight. They did not want to caught on the open plain by a Christian charge.

Qaymaz was last, staring up the hill.

Roger moved to the edge of the hill and raised his Death's Head shield high, so that Qaymaz would know who he was.

Qaymaz glared at him. Then he wheeled his horse and galloped off into the growing darkness.

Chapter 25

SALADIN PACED BACK and forth, as was his habit, listening impassively while Qaymaz told the assembly about the disaster that had overtaken the caravan.

"It was destroyed," Qaymaz said. He was still covered with dust and sweat from his ride back to al-Quds. "Everything. Supplies, gone. Sheep and goats slaughtered and left for the vultures."

"What about the reinforcements?" asked Saladin's brother, al-Adil.

"Dead," Qaymaz said. "Save for a few who were able to run away."

There was a collective sigh of resignation. They were in the ornate reception chamber of the governor's palace, which Saladin had taken as his headquarters.

Qaymaz straightened. "The worst part is . . ."

"It gets worse?" Saladin asked, feigning amusement.

"It does, lord. The feringhees were led by the one-eyed brigand who calls himself the lord of Deraa."

Saladin stopped pacing and clenched his fists.

Qaymaz went on. "We almost reached the caravan before the infidels struck. Just a few hours more, and we could have . . ."

His voice tailed off, then he continued. "We pursued Deraa and his men, but we were held up by an ambush from their rear guard. Before we could catch the main body, we were confronted by a large force which had been sent to rescue them, and we were obliged to withdraw."

Saladin stood still, reflective. "Henry the Falcon, lord of Deraa. I had rather taken his head than that of the Wolf of Kerak. The Falcon is more intelligent than the Wolf was. More dangerous."

Qaymaz hung his head. "It is my fault, lord. Had I pushed my men harder to reach the caravan . . ."

Saladin raised a hand. "You bear no blame, Lord Qaymaz. The fault is mine. I should have realized the threat to the caravan sooner. I should have realized that Rik would attempt to capture it."

There was quiet in the chamber. Emirs, officers—everyone— waited for the sultan's command. Even the Nubian slaves had ceased to wave their ostrich-feather fans.

Saladin paused for a moment, then he turned and addressed the assembly. "We have no choice. We must evacuate the city."

A low moan of dismay filled the room. Saladin continued, "Prepare the army to march. We will retire to Damascus and await developments there. We must hurry—Rik may be upon us at any moment. He must know how weak we are by now. We need to be far away when he arrives. Al-Afdal, your Syrians will lead. Qaymaz, bring up the rear. I will be in the center with my brother. I want the first units on the road by mid-day."

He waved a hand in dismissal, and the chamber quickly emptied. Already Saladin could hear orders being shouted outside.

Saladin retired to his private quarters. The room was small and spare, bereft of decoration. A bed, a rolled-up prayer rug, a table and candles. A jug of water and fruits in an earthenware bowl of the type one might find in any *suk*.

Saldin plucked a grape from its branch. He rolled it between his fingers absently.

He was beaten. Rik had won. He had not thought such a result possible, but such was the will of Allah.

He had done his best, but it had not been good enough. His life's goal had been to retake al-Quds from the infidel. He had done that, and he had come close to holding it—so close—but now it was slipping away. He knew he would never see the city again. Allah willing, his sons would—or their sons. But for now the dream was ended.

He placed the grape back in the bowl, careful not to bruise it. Tomorrow a feringhee would eat it—perhaps even Rik himself—and Saladin did not want to be thought inhospitable.

What had he done? What sin had he committed to make Allah look with disfavor upon him? He had tried to lead an exemplary life, but he ended by being punished. His people were being punished, as well. But they would not give up. They would be back. If not today, then tomorrow. If not tomorrow, the next day. They would never stop—

The curtain was yanked aside and the emir Qaymaz barged into his quarters, still covered with dust. "Lord, forgive me—"

"What do you mean by this?" Saladin demanded. "My privacy is never to be intruded upon, you know that."

Qaynaz went on, undeterred. "You must come see! Hurry, lord!"

"See what?" Saladin snapped.

"The Christians, lord. They are retreating. They have broken camp and are marching back to the sea."

Chapter 26

$\mathfrak{K}$ING RICHARD HAD feared that Saladin would learn about the raid on the caravan, or at least divine Richard's intent. So he had dispatched the earl of Leicester with a large relief force to escort the raiders back to safety. He couldn't fault Deraa's reasoning for destroying the supplies—it had kept him and his men from being killed—but it meant that there was no plunder. Richard had been counting on getting money from that caravan. He seemed to be paying for the entire crusade now, and his once-unlimited funds were running low. He had even sold his jeweled sword Excalibur—named after King Arthur's weapon—to help defray his mounting expenses.

He had expected plunder or Deraa's death from the raid, and he had gotten neither. It seemed an apt summary of his time in the Holy Land.

With the raiders returned, Richard had once again addressed the council of barons and made the case for not advancing on Jerusalem. "There's no room to maneuver in those hills. Our horsemen would be cut up by the Saracen infantry, and with the horsemen gone, our footmen would be helpless. It would be like the forest of Arsuf all over again, except that this time we wouldn't get away."

Richard's former ally the bishop of Beauvais said, "God's breath, Richard, what's come over you? You act like you don't want to take Jerusalem."

"Of course I want to take it, but this isn't the way to go about it."

"So what do you propose?" asked the bishop of Verona.

"I propose that we invade Egypt."

There were groans, along with shouts of outrage and frustration.

Old Hugh of Burgundy waved a paw at Richard. "This is no different than your ridiculous idea of drawing out Saladin by fortifying Ascalon."

Richard bristled. "That idea wasn't ridiculous, and neither is this one. Saladin needs Egypt, it's the source of his wealth. If we invade, he'll have no choice but to come fight us."

Burgundy spoke to Richard as though he were addressing a child. "Do you not understand, sire? We came here to recapture Jerusalem. Not Egypt. Not Ascalon. Not the kingdom of Prester John. Jerusalem."

A loud chorus of agreement filled the pavilion; it could be heard all over the camp. Richard knew that further argument was useless. These men would not be persuaded. He had Leicester, Vouzin, Chauvigny, and a few others on his side, but that was all.

He drew himself up. "Very well. If you do not approve my plan, choose another commander, and I will go with the army as a common soldier."

"Bah!" Burgundy rolled his eyes and turned away, shaking his shaggy head.

The count of Soissons said, "I don't understand, sire. Why did you agree to lead us if you never intended to attack the Holy City?"

"I came because you begged me to do it. At the time, I was over confident. I convinced myself that we could take the city. But I was wrong, and I refuse to lead this army to its destruction. Besieging

Jerusalem is impossible. If we attempt it, we'll be fighting Saladin on *his* chosen ground, not ours, and that's not what we should do. If we invade Egypt, *we* pick the ground on which to fight." The truth was, he was too ill to undertake a siege, and he didn't trust any of the others to take the lead. Only a few—Alart, Andrew of Chauvigny—knew how sick he really was. He hoped that the more salubrious air of the coast might revive him.

The meeting had ended, as these meetings always did, with nothing resolved. That evening a messenger brought Richard news, and the crusade was forgotten.

❧

The next morning, Richard announced that he was leaving for home.

There was the expected outcry. "You promised you would remain here until Easter," the count of Champagne reminded him.

"I apologize, nephew, but I cannot honor that promise," Richard said. "I have received information that *your* lord—" he indicated the duke of Burgundy— "King Philp, is conspiring with my brother John to rob me of my lands at home. In return for Philip supporting John to be king of England, my brother will recognize Philip's claim to some of my French possessions." He turned to Burgundy again. "I suppose you know nothing of this?"

"First I've heard of it," Burgundy said with a shrug. "I don't even know if it's true. We have only your word for it."

Richard slammed his fist on a table. "You have the word of a *king!*"

Richard looked like he might physically attack the French duke, so red was his face. He felt like he was going to pass out from his fever.

The earl of Leicester broke the ensuing silence. "So much for Philip's vow to leave your possessions alone for three years."

"That puking weasel," Richard said. "That . . ." His voice trailed off in inchoate rage. He pointed at the duke again, jabbing his finger. "I'll make him pay, I swear it. But to do that, I must start for home now." His temper eased, and he looked at the council. "I trust you gentlemen will appreciate my position."

"Let him go," Burgundy cried. "We don't need him. There's still enough of us here to take the city. We can break camp today. What say you?"

"I'm with you," said Henry of Deraa. "What about you, Count Henry?"

The count of Champagne, putative ruler of Jerusalem, and in whose name this march had been undertaken, let out a long breath. "No. I will follow the lead of my uncle, Richard. If he says the thing can't be done, I believe him."

Deraa rounded on his old friend. "My God, sir, what would James of Avesnes say if he heard you? Did he die for nothing? Is this how you honor his sacrifice?"

The count of Champagne could not meet Henry's eyes.

Balian of Ibelin stepped forward and put an arm round Henry's shoulder. "I speak with a heavy heart. No man loved James of Avesnes more than I, you know that. But I'm afraid I must agree with my liege lord of Champagne. Look around you—Deraa, Duke Hugh—there is no enthusiasm left for a march on Jerusalem."

It was true. Richard's announcement had taken the fight out of them. The pavilion was filled with gloom. Balian went on. "It is pointless to continue. It's done. We had our chance, and we threw it away."

And that was that. After all these years.

The reality of what had just happened sank in. The bishop of Beauvais summed up what everyone was thinking. "I feel naught but disgust at this moment. In the end, this enterprise was a giant waste of time and treasure."

"And of lives," added the earl of Trent, who looked unwell. "Let us depart this unhappy land and return to our homes as quickly as we may."

With a heavy heart, the count of Champagne addressed the kingdom's chief negotiator, Humphrey of Toron. "Go to Saladin. Tell him we'll sign the peace terms."

"Aye, my lord," said the slightly built Humphrey. "What about Ascalon? Saladin insists we tear down the fortifications there."

The count looked at Richard. "Sire?"

"Hold out for Ascalon," Richard told him. "It's the key to your position here."

The council broke up, not in rancor, but in despondency. The council members filed from the pavilion until only Richard and Henry of Deraa were left.

Henry faced Richard squarely. He spoke not with rancor, but honestly. "'Twere better you had never come to this land, sire. We had taken Jerusalem long since were it not for you."

There was challenge in those words, as well as judgment; and Richard did not take up the challenge because he knew the judgment to be true.

Chapter 27

"**H**E'D BE EASY pickings for the Goat Fuckers had they the wits to see it," Tatwine said.

"Let's hope they don't see it, then," Roger told him.

The retreating army was strung out, dispirited, men marching and riding with their heads down. Some of the footmen had started throwing away helmets and other bits of gear. A few of the companies discarded their banners. Tatwine was right—if the Saracens attacked right now, the Christians would be massacred. The Death's Heads were with the earl of Trent's footmen. The earl himself had fallen ill again. He was on a litter in one of the supply wagons, his squire Richambaud sitting beside him, shielding his face from the sun with a straw hat.

Roger adjusted the keffiyeh over his nose and mouth to keep out the gritty dust raised by hooves and tramping feet, but it still filtered through. He and Tatwine rode alongside the company, the tattered Death's Head banner planted in a holder on Tatwine's saddle.

"I thought you were going to eat that horse," Roger reminded his squire.

Tatwine looked aghast. "Lionheart?" That's what he had named the animal. "I'd never eat him. Why, he's me best friend. I wouldn't harm a hair on his head." He patted the horse's neck. "Would I, boy?" He shot Roger an accusatory look. "How could you even say that?"

Instead of bringing doom upon the horse as he had threatened, Tatwine now brought it treats of fruit and sugar scrounged from God only knew where. Tatwine was still in pain from days in the saddle, but a heavy coating of axle grease and fresh padding sewn to his hose seemed to have alleviated that somewhat.

Slowfoot, in charge of the axe men, blinked his eyes rapidly. "Don't seem right, us goin' back this way, without a fight." He blinked again, averting his eyes from the harsh sun.

"Eyes still bothering you?" Roger asked him.

"Can't get the grit out of 'em," Slowfoot acknowledged. "Gives me headaches somethin' fierce. Makes me vision blurry, too. Expect they'll come round when we get home."

"You'd better hope so," said Ralph the Red, marching behind him. "Ain't much call for blind poachers these days." The once bright ribbons in the big man's beard had faded to the color of the dust that covered them all.

Tatwine waxed philosophical. "Nothin's gone right with this crusade from the start. It's funny, us fightin' for the Lord and all. I mean, He ain't been much help, has He?"

Short Peter, who had been a cottar, a hired day laborer, at home, and who now commanded the spearmen, said, "What I want to know is why King Richard wouldn't march on Jerusalem."

"Said it can't be taken, is what I heard," said Ralph the Red.

"He should've at least tried," said Shorty. "Don't you think so, Roger?"

Roger hesitated. "Yes." He let out his breath, disappointed. "I never thought it possible that Richard would lose. Right until the end, I was sure he would find a way to win through. And now . . ."

"And now he's fucked us," Tatwine said.

There were nods and mutters from the marching men. Pentecost, Roger's friend from slavery, called out, "Where we headed, Roger? Acre or Jaffa?"

"Jaffa," Roger said. "Then Acre. Then home."

Ralph the Red brightened. "I like Jaffa. Nice whores there."

To Roger, Tatwine said, "Guess you'd rather we was goin' right to Acre, so you could see Lady Ailith."

Roger nodded. Getting back to Ailith was all he could think about. He longed to kiss her again, to taste her sweet lips, to take her in his arms and press her hard body against his. He wondered what she was doing right now, if he was all right . . .

"Christ's sandals!" blurted Tatwine. "You know what today is?"

"Tuesday?" guessed Short Peter.

"Thursday?" said Pentecost.

"It's the feast of St. Martin of Tours," Tatwine told them, "the fourth day of July. A year to the day since Acre fell. Five years to the day since that battle at Hattin that started this mess. Strange, ain't it?"

Slowfoot grunted. "Five years, and what did we accomplish?"

"Nothing," said Ralph the Red. "Not a damn thing."

"'Cept to get a lot of people killed," the centenar Oswy said.

Short Peter sighed. "What was it all for?"

There was only one answer to that, but Roger didn't tell the men because he knew it would upset them, just as it upset him.

God's plan.

~

The crusade was over.

This was not like the retreat from Bet Nable in January. This time there was no lingering for a last look, no wondering what might have been. This time Richard rode alone at the head of the column. This time he couldn't wait to get away.

Deraa's words still rang in his ears, the truth of them still stung. How could they have failed to liberate Jerusalem? The most powerful force ever assembled by Christendom had gathered here, yet after two and a half years of fighting they had barely left the coastline, when once Damascus and even Baghdad had seemed within their grasp.

No matter what his accomplishments in the years ahead, Richard knew he would always be judged by his deeds in the Holy Land. The glittering future—the immortality—that people had predicted for him was not to be. He was not the man everyone had thought he was. He was not the man *he* had thought he was.

He was not the next Caesar, the next Alexander or Charlemagne. He would be forgotten, a paragraph in some dusty chronicle. The crusade had been a failure, and it had been a failure because of him.

PART III

Chapter 28

𝕿HE ARMY STARTED breaking up even before it got back to Jaffa. Some units left and traveled to Acre overland, despite the danger from Saracens that way. Others split into pieces, the footmen separating from the knights and men-at-arms, though it was unclear how the footmen would get home without their lords to pay their way. Equipment and clothing littered the road, and by the time they reached Jaffa they were little more than an armed mob.

King Richard immediately commandeered a ship and left for Acre. The great lords occupied buildings inside the city, while everyone else camped outside, awaiting transportation north.

The Death's Heads camped with the earl of Trent's men and those of the English contingent that still remained with the army. The earl, now gravely ill, had been taken back to Acre by King Richard. Roger considered that a noble gesture from the king to a man who had rarely taken his side politically.

When they weren't brawling with Normans or other French soldiers, the Death's Heads lazed about, drinking, sunning themselves, or—for those like Slowfoot, with sun-damaged eyes—keeping to the shade as much as possible.

Almost every day the men bathed in the warm water of the sea, splashing each other, diving into the gentle waves. "What you going to do when you get home?" Tatwine asked Short Peter one afternoon.

"Bugger if I know," said Shorty. "I'd hoped to come out of this with money to buy some land, but that didn't work out. Reckon I'll go back to my village and hire out as a cottar again, till something better comes along." Roger thought it sad that a man who had risen to centenar, like Shorty, should be reduced to being hired labor in the fields, the lowest rung of village society.

Pentecost, who was bobbing about nearby, said, "I'm going with Roger and follow Lord Henry."

"You can be my squire," Roger told him. "I'll need one when Tatwine leaves."

"Me, a squire?" Pentecost said. "Who'd of thought that? You comin' with us, Yves?"

The dark-visaged Yves shook his head. "Think I'll take service with the kingdom. Should be plenty of room for advancement, with so many leaving. Should be able to start as a vintenar. Maybe even centenar."

Tatwine said, "What about you, Reds?"

Ralph the Red seemed unconcerned. He was trying to float on his back, the massive scar on his chest an angry shade of red in the sun. "Sign up for the next war, I guess. What I always do."

The lanky spearman Bern dunked his head into a wave and came up blinking. "I expect I'll take up the family trade again."

"What trade's that?" Pentecost asked him.

"I was a cutpurse, back in Badford."

"Don't I remember," scoffed Tatwine. "Getting caught was what got you sent here."

"It was that or the hangman," Bern said philosophically. "We all get caught eventually. Just a matter of when."

Oswy the centenar said, "Me, I just want to get back with the family. Three young 'uns I got, can't wait to see how they've growed. I'll help Dad in the fields till he's too old, then I'll take over, and I'll never leave the village again."

"Sounds boring," Bern said.

"Not a bad life, really," Oswy said. "Beats getting hung."

Bern was about to reply when there was a cry from the beach. Everyone turned. A squire in the green and gold livery of Vouzin danced away from wavelets lapping at his feet. He advanced again and called out, "Roger of Huntley?"

Roger raised his hand and waded to the shore.

The squire, who couldn't have been more than twelve, tried not to stare at Roger's nakedness. "The count of Vouzin's compliments, sir, and would you attend upon him at your earliest convenience?"

What's this? "I'd be happy to," Roger said. "Wait here."

Roger dried off, dressed, and accompanied the squire to the city.

"What's this about?" Roger said as they walked the narrow, teeming streets. His hair was still wet, and there was sand in his hose and shoes.

"No idea, my lord," the boy replied.

They found the count in the governor's palace. Apparently he had just returned from his devotions, because he was accompanied by a brown-robed monk. The count spied them approaching. "Ah, Roger! There you are. I have someone I want you to meet. Thought you two might know each other, you having worked at Huntley Abbey."

He stood aside. The monk moved forward and pushed back his deep, brown cowl.

Roger stared in shock.

It was Auberie. The count's son. The man Roger was supposed to have killed.

Chapter 29

ℜOGER STARED. AUBERIE had survived—but how? Roger had shoved a knife into his chest. Why hadn't he died?

Auberie didn't recognize Roger at first. The bearded, scarred knight before him bore little resemblance to the clean-shaven, tonsured youth he'd known back at Huntley.

Recognition slowly washed over Auberie's handsome face, and his mouth fell open. Count Alart noticed none of this as he introduced them. "Auberie, this is Roger, knight of Huntley. His is a remarkable story. He was once a woodcutter at your—"

Auberie swung his fist at Roger.

Roger casually sidestepped the blow. Auberie was four years older than Roger. Roger had fought him a number of times before, and, except for the last time, Auberie had always been victorious. Roger was so much more experienced now that a fight between the two of them would not be an equal contest. It would not be a contest at all.

Auberie recovered and rushed Roger, head down. Roger stepped aside once more, grabbing Auberie's arm as he passed so that he wouldn't fall.

Angry, the count grabbed Auberie's other arm. "What is the—"

"He's no woodcutter," Auberie said. "He was a monk, and not a good one. He tried to kill me. Stabbed me in the chest and left me for dead, then ran away."

Auberie was breathing hard. Alart stared at his son in disbelief.

"I can show you the scar if you'd like," Auberie told his father. "I lay on the verge of death for a month. My life was despaired of. 'Twas only by a miracle that I lived."

Roger tried to remain calm. He knew the danger he was in. As governor of the city, Alart could have him killed with a word.

Alart regarded Roger coldly. "Is what my son says true?"

Roger straightened. "It is, my lord."

"Ha!" said Auberie. "See, he admits it."

Alart frowned at Roger. "You stabbed him?"

"I did, my lord."

"Why?"

"He was trying to rape a girl, and I—"

"That's a lie!" Auberie said.

"—and I prevented him from doing it. To cover his crime, he claimed the girl was a witch."

"She was," Auberie cried. "A witch and a whore. She put me under a spell and led me into sin so that she might damn my soul to hell. I had no control over my actions."

With difficulty, Roger restrained himself from beating Auberie senseless. "The lady in question was neither a witch, nor a whore, my lord. You know her—Ailith."

Alart's brows went up.

Roger went on. "Auberie and the abbey circuitor, Gregorius, had the girl detained for 'questioning,' which meant they were going to torture her to death. I helped her escape—"

"Again!" Auberie crowed. "The fool admits it!"

"Auberie and Gregorius caught up with us in the forest. Your son attacked me with a knife and I stabbed him in self-defense. That's why I ran away from the abbey—no one would have believed my story."

"Because you were in concert with a witch!" Auberie said. To his father he said, "Arrest him."

Alart considered for a long moment. To Auberie he said, "I know of your proclivity for women, Auberie. I hoped you had been cured of that in service to God."

"I didn't do anything. He's—"

Alart held up a hand. "I have met the woman in question. She does not impress me as being a witch, though personally I don't believe in nonsense like witchcraft. I also know Roger, and he has shown himself to be a model knight. The main thing is, you're alive, and that's what matters to me. My advice to you is to let the matter drop."

"Let it drop? This peasant tried to kill me."

"Roger is far from a peasant. His father is one of the chief barons of this kingdom."

"I don't care. Roger must pay for what he's done."

"You'd have to see the king about that."

"I will," Auberie said.

Alart spoke calmly. "The problem is, the king likes Roger, and if you hope to be abbot of Huntley one day, I doubt you want to get on the king's bad side."

Auberie glared.

Alart went on. "Whatever is between you two, let it go. It ends here. Do you understand me?"

"Yes, my lord," Roger said.

"Yes, Father," said Auberie, seemingly chastened.

"Roger, you may go."

Roger bowed to Alart, nodded to Auberie, and started from the hall.

As Roger crossed the floor, he realized something. He had come to the Holy Land to atone for killing Auberie. But Auberie wasn't dead, so Roger's vow to remain here no longer counted.

There had been no Mortal Sin.

Footsteps behind him, sandals slapping marble.

Roger turned as Auberie came up, smiling. Auberie proffered his hand and spoke loud enough for his father to hear. "I'm sorry for any misunderstanding that's passed between us, Roger. I trust we can put it behind us."

Roger took his hand. "Very well."

Auberie's smile faded. Under his breath, he added, "I'm not finished with you, Foundling."

Chapter 30

𝔉AUSTON WAS SHOWING the countess of Perche a piece of Jacob's Ladder—authenticated by St. Sadoth, bishop of Seleucia—in a worn ebony reliquary. There was a time when he might have shown the countess—who, though older, was not unattractive—more than that, but those days were behind him.

"Look at the scrollwork on this reliquary," he said. "Unmatched. They don't do that kind of work anymore. They *can't* do it—they've lost the skills. This particular piece was discovered many years ago in Smyrna and came to us through the estate of a merchant in Beirut."

There was a commotion from the front room. Raised voices. Fauston started to speak to the countess again, but the commotion continued.

"Excuse me, my lady," he told her, bowing.

He parted the curtain and went into the front room. "What's going on?"

He found Francisco, who had been watching the front room, faced off with a tall, hook-nosed monk whose sallow complexion made him look like some night-dwelling creature that hid from the sun. The monk was accompanied by a pair of burly armed men, ex-soldiers by the look of them.

The monk regarded Fauston as he might regard a spot of dirt on his robe. "What's going on is that this shop is now closed and its

193

contents confiscated by the Church." His accent marked him as English, and he spoke with an arrogant drawl.

Francisco started to speak, but Fauston waved him off. "Closed?" he said. "By whose orders?"

The monk held up an ornate sheet of vellum. "By order of the Holy Father. This is a brief from Pope Celestine authorizing me to investigate the sale of fraudulent relics in the Holy Land, and I have found items in this establishment that are, to be charitable, of dubious authenticity."

Fauston gave the monk his most disarming smile. "I assure you—"

"Do you own this shop?"

There was something familiar about this monk. "I do."

"Are you Tolomei or Rico?"

"Neither. This is a venerable firm, and those gentlemen are long dead. I—"

"I'm not interested in your lineage, you buffoon." The monk stopped and peered at him. "Don't I know you?"

Fauston shook his head. "We've never met." *Where have I seen this fellow?*

The monk's eyes narrowed. "You're certain?"

"As certain as I can be." And even as he said it, he realized who the monk was.

The monk realized Fauston's identity at the same time. "Wait," he said, peering closer. "I *do* know you. As God is my witness, you're that so-called *scholar* who was with *Domnus* Roger when he fled Huntley Abbey."

"Roger?" Fauston crinkled his brows, as though he had no idea who the monk was talking about.

"Don't play the fool with me, boy. If you don't remember me now, you soon will. My name is Gregorius, and the joy of my life is rooting out heretics. Selling fake relics is heresy enough, and employing a vile Muslim to do it is even worse."

"I'm not a Muslim," Francisco cried.

"But consorting with a someone like Roger . . ." Gregorius drew himself up. "I intend to question you, young man, question you thoroughly, to learn what other sins you have on your soul."

At that moment, the bells over the door jingled and Ailith walked in. "Hello, Fauston. I wondered if you needed any help . . ."

Her voice tailed off as she saw the monk.

Gregorius stared at her, recognized her even with her hair cut short. "You!"

She turned to leave and Gregorius yelled to his guards. "Stop her!"

The guards grabbed Ailith's arms. She struggled but couldn't get away from them. Gregorius rubbed his hands together. "Truly the Lord has been kind to me this day. First I find a heretic with a shop full of false relics, and now a witch."

He moved close to Ailith. "You'll be pleased to know that your good friend *Domnus* Auberie is in the Holy Land, as well. I brought him with me. He's in Jaffa, right now, visiting his father, but he'll be back here soon. I'm sure he'll look forward to 'examining' you—" he could barely keep the excitement from his voice "—as shall I. And we'll both look forward to seeing you burn, for burn you most assuredly shall."

He turned back to Fauston with a smug smile. "As shall you, if you survive your interrogation, which I doubt." To his guards he said, "Take them away."

One of the guards advanced on Fauston.

"What's this all about?" said a voice.

The curtain to the back room parted and Bonjute entered, followed by the countess of Perche.

"What business is it of yours?" Gregorius sneered.

Bonjute straightened, her lips set tight. "I am Bonjute, wife to the earl of Trent and acting governor of this city. That's what business it is."

"Acting governor?" Gregorius scoffed. "A woman?"

"Your powers of observation are remarkable, sir. Now what are you playing at?"

"I'm not playing. I hold an appointment from the Pope to investigate the sale of false relics in this kingdom, and the relics in this shop are fakes."

The countess of Perche let out a little cry of surprise. Bonjute spoke coldly. "Nonsense, I've bought relics here. One of them cured my sick husband."

"I don't know what cured your husband, madame, but it wasn't one of these relics."

Bonjute looked to the two guards and Ailith. "Why are you holding this woman?"

"I'm holding her because she is a known witch."

Bonjute calmly turned to her servant. "Jehan, fetch the city guard."

Jehan pushed past Gregorius's two henchmen. One of them made to stop her, but she glared at him and he let her pass.

Gregorious went on. "I'm closing this shop. So if you don't mind, I'm rather busy—"

"Have you a warrant from the archbishop of Tyre?"

Gregorius showed her the vellum. "I have a document signed by the Pope."

"I don't care if it's signed by Michael the Archangel. There is a thing called protocol. If you wish to take any actions in Acre, you will need a warrant signed by the archbishop of Tyre and endorsed by Bishop Jean of this city. Until then you have no legal authority here." She turned to the guards. "Let that woman go."

"No!" Gregorius told them. "Might I remind your *ladyship* that Ecclesiastical law takes precedence over civil law? You have no authority over me. This woman is a witch, and I have the right to—"

"You wouldn't know a witch if one bit you on the bottom," Ailith told him. "This woman is no more a witch than I am."

"Is that so?" Gregorius smiled. "Perhaps I should investigate you then, as well."

Bonjute seemed to swell in size. "How dare you address me in such a manner?" She advanced on Gregorius, driving him back. "You talking turd, you bilious beanpole, you mosquito-buggering pile of pus. I'll have you flayed alive and hung from the city walls as food for the crows."

"You wouldn't dare," Gregorius said. "The Pope—"

Bonjute advanced further, pinning Gregorius against the wall. "By the time the Pope finds out, I'll be gone from this land, and you'll be long forgotten."

The two guards edged closer to Bonjute.

A look from her stopped them in their tracks. "One more step, and I'll have you two eating your balls for supper."

The guards hesitated.

From the street came the sound of marching men. Jehan entered. "The guard is here, my lady."

Gregorius's pale face blossomed red with outrage.

"Now take your tiny prick away from here," Bonjute told him. "And don't come back without that warrant. And if I learn that you're trying to act on your own before that, I'll have your precious brief set on fire and shoved up your rectum. Is that clear?"

Gegorius's eyes bulged. He looked like he might have apoplexy.

"*Is it?*" she demanded.

"Very clear." He almost choked on the words.

Bonjute stepped back. Gregorius hurried past her and left the shop along with his guards.

Just like that, Bonjute's rage disappeared. She turned and addressed the countess of Perche sweetly, as though nothing had happened. "This is all a misunderstanding, my dear. The man's obviously a lunatic. Please continue as you were. I'm sorry to put you through this."

The countess of Perche was shaken but tried to act like she wasn't. "Beastly fellow. It's a sin who they let into the Church these days."

As the countess returned to the middle room, Bonjute turned to Fauston. In a low voice, Fauston said, "Do you think he'll be back?"

"I know he will," Bonjute said, "and if he has a warrant from the archbishop, there'll be nothing I can do to stop him. This will blow over, but you and your friends need to leave the city until it does."

Fauston turned to Francisco and Gregory. "I'll finish with the countess, then we'll get the expensive things and hide them away. Let Gregorius have the rest. Let him think he's accomplished something."

"What if he destroys the shop?" Gregory said.

"We'll rebuild it," said Fauston. "When we're done here, I'll sail down to Jaffa and wait out the storm."

"I'm for Jaffa, as well," Francisco said. He sighed. "And I just met a girl I really like, too. Oh, well, we won't be gone long. What about you, Gregory?"

Gregory pulled his fingers through his long black beard. Now that he was affluent, the beard no longer contained bits of food and other detritus. "I believe I'll go to Tyre. I haven't seen my second wife in a while. Perhaps she'll be amenable to some company. While I'm there, I'll look for some product against the time we reopen."

The three of them left the room. When they were gone, Bonjute turned to Ailith. "That monk means to have you burned. If he charges you as a witch, Church law gives him possession of you. There's nothing I—or my husband—can do. You need to get out of the city."

Ailith nodded. "I'd leave right away, but Bishop Jean wishes me to sing for King Richard at Hugoline's two nights hence. I've never met the king, and I don't wish to let the bishop and Hugoline down. Lady Hugoline's been very good to me, and I gave my word."

Bonjute said, "I don't think that's wise, Ailith. You should—"

"Gregorius can't get to Tyre and back in two days," Ailith assured her. "I should be all right. After that, I'll go straight to Jaffa."

"Very well." Bonjute took her arm. "But be careful."

The countess of Perche emerged from the middle room, with the piece of Jacob's Ladder under her arm. Bonjute exchanged formalities with the countess, promising to visit her later, then returned to Ailith, her blue eyes cool as ever. "Now if you'll excuse me, I'll say my goodbyes to Fauston."

Chapter 31

ℜOGER ENTERED HIS tent and gulped water from a clay jug. It was early morning, but it was already hot. He had just made his daily inspection of the men. In the main this consisted of making sure none of them was dead or ill, and seeing that they hadn't let their arms and equipment rust. Roger didn't try to enforce discipline. Why should he? As long as they didn't get into serious trouble, he let them do what they wanted, which consisted mainly of drinking and brawling and chasing whores.

Heaven, Tatwine called it.

There were footsteps outside, and Roger's father, Henry, ducked into the tent. "I'm leaving for Acre," the one-eyed baron announced.

"When?" Roger said.

"Now. I need to be there to sign the peace terms when they're finalized."

Roger said, "I'll walk you to the harbor."

Roger left the tent, wearing a knee-length white shirt and scarlet hose. He adjusted the keffiyeh around his head to protect him from the sun. Henry's squire, Teary, had gone ahead with the baggage. "I thought you weren't leaving for a couple days yet," Roger said.

Henry inclined his chin toward the sea. "Favoring wind. Best go while I can."

"When is the treaty to be signed?"

"Soon, they say. They're still arguing about Ascalon, but Richard may give in on that. He just wants to leave."

"Will you be visiting Jerusalem afterwards?" Under terms of the proposed treaty, Christians would be allowed access to the Holy City if they came unarmed, and many of the nobles and common soldiers planned to visit before going home.

Henry's eyes hardened. "Me? No. It would just remind me that we lost, and I'm not a good loser. I can wait. We'll get Jerusalem back someday—Saladin won't live forever." He turned back to Roger and smiled. "I'm looking forward to having you at Deraa, you and Ailith." The smile broadened. "Your children, as well."

Roger blushed at that thought, then said, "What's it like, Deraa?"

"You'll like it, I think. It's in the middle of the desert, but we've irrigated, and we grow crops and fruit. There's excellent hunting and hawking. The castle itself is amazing—nothing like those little stone boxes at home. We can hold off Saladin's whole army there—and we've done it, more than once."

"Sounds like there's not a lot of peace and quiet."

Henry shrugged. "We're the most exposed fief in the kingdom. For us, the war never really ends, even when there's a truce."

They had reached the port, the smell of salt and fish strong, the sun glinting off the sea. Bright-colored sails and cries of fishermen and sailors. Cogs and galleys crowded the quay, lines of men boarding them. Horses in slings were being hoisted into the ships' waists by winches—the horses didn't like going up the narrow ramps.

Henry stared at Roger. "When I dropped you at Huntley Abbey that day, I never thought I'd see you again. Yet now we'll be living together. Funny how life turns out. I still wish you'd stayed at the abbey where it's safe, but it's the joy of my life having you here."

"Thank you, Father. I . . . I don't know what to say. It was only in my dreams that I thought I'd find you out here, and yet . . . here we are."

They made way for a column of Burgundian footmen, slouching along in loose formation. Behind them, sweating squires and grooms led strings of horses. Everywhere were wagons packed with arms, tents, equipment.

They reached Henry's ship, a dumpy Venetian transport, painted an even dumpier shade of green. Other vessels were already putting out to sea, some driven by sails, some by oars. "Before long, everyone will be gone," Roger said. "I wonder when it's our turn?"

Henry gave him a look of surprise. "You don't know? The Death's Heads are to remain here as part of the garrison until the treaty is signed."

"What?" Roger said. "No one's said anything about it to me."

"They should have. My men will be here, too, along with a company of Turcopoles and some fellows from the kingdom. And those archer friends of yours, I think. Richard wants men who are reliable."

Roger's heart sank. Would he ever get to see Ailith again?

"Who's in command?" Roger asked.

"William of Mello."

Roger remembered Mello commandeering the horse from the young sergeant who was later beheaded by the Saracens.

Henry apparently didn't think much of Mello, either. He shrugged by way of explanation. "Richard likes him. Word is, the count of Champagne may make him permanent governor." Henry put a hand on Roger's shoulder. "Don't worry. You won't be here too much longer. I'll see you in Acre soon."

Father and son stared at one another. Then Roger embraced Henry. Henry was caught off guard; he had probably never embraced a man before. But he recovered and returned the gesture, if awkwardly, and finished by slapping Roger on the Back. "Goodbye, son."

"Goodbye, Father."

Henry boarded the ship, whose grey-bearded captain was clearly impatient to cast off. Roger waved to Henry, waited for the ship to pole off, and started back. He entered the city gate and climbed the narrow, twisting path to the governor's palace, passing stalls and merchants' houses, the air perfumed with cinnamon and cloves, with oranges and lemons and smells of refuse, animal and human. He would present himself to his new commander, and maybe learn why no one had told him the Death's Heads were staying in Jaffa.

Even at this early hour, the city taverns rocked with laughter and music. Roger looked around as he walked, half expecting to see Auberie, but there had been no sign of Auberie since their initial encounter. He must have gone back to Acre with his father, who had left a few days earlier.

The governor's palace was far different than it had been when

Alart of Vouzin occupied it. William of Mello had taken over like he expected to be there for the next thirty years—and maybe he did. It would be a nice reward for him.

Roger found William in the governor's private quarters, sharing grapes with a good-looking native woman, who was sitting on his lap, wearing a diaphanous gown.

"Huntley," William said. "I've been meaning to contact you." He popped a grape in the woman's mouth, and she sucked it in and out of her lips, while William laughed. "Keep getting distracted, though."

Roger tried not to stare at the woman's firm breasts, which were visible through the material of her gown. "I was told my men and I would be here until the treaty was signed. I wanted to see if you had any orders for us."

Now the woman fed William a grape, setting it in her teeth and transferring it to William's mouth without breaking the skin. "Keep your fellows from burning down the town and we should be fine," William mumbled as he took the grape.

"What about standing guard on the walls?"

"My men will handle that." William placed a grape in his own teeth and gave it to the woman, his hand kneading her breast. When the woman had the grape, William broke it with his teeth and sucked the juice from her mouth, a bit of it dribbling down her chin.

"Shouldn't we send out patrols or something?" Roger said.

"Why?" William licked the juice from the woman's chin. "The war's over. Nothing's going to happen here."

"But what if—"

"When I want advice, I'll ask for it. Now if you don't mind, I have important matters to attend to."

The woman giggled, and Roger left.

Chapter 32

When the last leaf falls
From the highest limb,
And the cold wind rises,
Withering the hazelnut and willow,
I see the wood grow numb.
But I am warm,
For I have love . . .

Ailith strolled the packed hall of Hugoline's house with an ease born of practice, because she had been much in demand these last weeks. She was dressed as she had been for her earlier triumph here, save that she had cut her hair even shorter and she wore a jaunty cap with a feather in it.

By her joy, a sick man can recover,
By her wrath, a healthy man can die,
A wise man turn childish,
A fair man see his beauty change,
The most courtly man become a churl,
And the greatest churl become courtly . . .

Henry of Champagne and Queen Isabelle were here, along with the duke of Burgundy, the bishops of Verona and Beauvais, the earl of Trent and his wife, Bonjute—who smiled at Ailith—the counts of Vouzin and Soissons, the earl of Leicester, Andrew of Chauvigny, Hacon of Norway, Bogdan of Hungary, and others. Many of the great houses of Europe and Outremer were represented at this gathering, and those representatives were listening to Ailith. The feeling was indescribable. It was the proudest moment of Ailith's life. Her only regret was that she could not tell people who she really was.

> *Beneath your brows five beautiful things repose—*
> *Love and fire and a flame, the lily and the rose . . .*

Lady Hugoline and her merchant husband, Rotrou, presided over the banquet. Near them was Bishop Jean, whose idea it had been for Ailith to sing for King Richard. The bishop looked from Ailith to Richard and back again. The bishop seemed worried. So did Hugoline and Rotrou. They had probably never had a king in their hall, and they wanted him to enjoy the entertainment, which it appeared that he was not doing.

King Richard sat with his elbow on the high table, seemingly bored, with his chin in his hand and his eyes closed. Once, his ice-blue eyes opened, and they bored into Ailith's eyes with an intensity that almost caused her to lose the thread of her song. Then they closed again.

Richard's pretty wife, Berengaria, sat next to him. Ailith felt sorry for Berengaria, who managed to look both queenly and bewildered at the same time. She was so obviously in love with Richard, and he so obviously cared nothing for her. Berengaria still wasn't pregnant, and Ailith couldn't understand why. Either Richard hadn't tried, or Berengaria was infertile. If she was infertile, Richard should have had the marriage annulled and found someone who could provide him an heir. If he hadn't tried, why not? She was certainly attractive enough.

Ailith started her final song, her favorite and most popular:

> *Hath any loved you well down there,*
> *Summer or winter through?*
> *Down there, have you found any fair*
> *Laid in the grave with you?*
> *Is death's long kiss a richer kiss*
> *Than mine was —*

With a loud scraping, King Richard pushed his chair from the table. He rose and strode from the hall, men and women scrambling to give him room.

Ailith stopped singing. A gasp rose from the assemblage, followed by a loud buzz. Andrew of Chauvigny started after Richard, but the count of Vouzin held him back. Bishop Jean looked to Ailith, his hands spread as though he didn't know what had happened. Bonjute seemed at a loss, as well. Hugoline's face was ashen; her husband stared after the departing king with a stunned expression on his face.

The buzz swelled, then died to nervous silence. Ailith felt weak in the knees; she had been humiliated. But she refused to quit. She finished her song. As the last plaintive note of the lute died away, the silence in the hall lingered.

Then someone started clapping.

It was Berengaria.

Berengaria stood, smiling a brave smile and applauding. The rest of the hall joined in, slowly, then with more gusto, for they had enjoyed her singing, but because of Richard's actions the enthusiasm fell far short of what Ailith had experienced here previously.

Berengaria beckoned Ailith forward. Ailith approached the high table, doffed her feathered cap, and bowed low. "Your highness."

Berengaria still wore that same brave smile. It seemed to have been painted on her face. She held out a hand; in it was a purse. In her Navarrese accent, she said, "My husband is indisposed, but he instructed me to give you this reward. Your singing was most enjoyable." She was making this up, Ailith was certain of it. She was giving Ailith her own purse to cover for her husband's actions.

Ailith took the purse, bowed low again. "Thank you, your highness. Tell the king I am most grateful."

Berengaria nodded her head in return.

Still bowing, Ailith backed halfway down the aisle, then turned and started from the hall, trying to act as though nothing had happened, as though King Richard hadn't insulted her by walking out on her performance. As always, she caught the eye of attractive females—the few who still dared to meet her gaze. She winked at one or two, but it was a show of bravado, nothing more, to hide her shame. Across the room, Odelina of Bellaire sat beside her ancient husband with a pleading look at Ailith. Even at this distance, Ailith could see that Odelina's cheek was bruised.

With the lute slung across her back, Ailith headed for the exit. She wanted to get out of the house quickly, before she started crying.

As she quickened her pace, Gregorius rounded the screens and entered the hall directly in front of her.

Ailith missed a step. How had Gregorius gotten to Tyre and back so quickly? He must have obtained the warrant, or he wouldn't be here.

She would have to go right by Gregorius to get out the front door. Would he recognize her? She couldn't take that chance. She shielded herself behind some of the guests and headed for the servants' waiting area.

Gregorius must have gone to the bishop's residence and learned that the bishop was here. He would give the bishop the warrant. He would see the earl of Trent and show the warrant to him, as well. Ailith pictured Gregorius sneering at Bonjute. With any luck, Bonjute would break a pitcher over his head.

Behind Ailith, a breathless voice said, "Alan."

Odelina.

Ailith acted like she hadn't heard. She entered the servants' crowded waiting area, passing men and women laden with ale and fruit, pressing against the wall and scratching the varnished wood of her lute.

Approaching the servants' entrance to the house, Ailith found her way blocked by Hugoline's steward. She tried to push by him. "I'm leaving," she said.

Grinning, the dough-faced steward stepped in front of her, blocking her way again. "Not till the banquet's over, pretty boy. Can't have you leaving before that—they might need you again." He laughed, because they both knew that wouldn't happen. "Carry on," he said, mocking her earlier dismissal of him.

Ailith couldn't wait until the banquet was over. Gregorius was still at the hall's main entrance, arguing with the guards, who were preventing him from entering. He showed them a sheet of parchment—probably the warrant. They didn't care. To them he was just another cleric looking for a free meal. He would get through eventually, though. And sooner, rather than later. Would any of the guests connect the mustachioed, goateed Alan of the Dale with Ailith?

"Alan."

Ailith turned and Odelina was beside her. Ailith stared at her face. The bruises were worse than they had seemed from a distance; they had been covered by cosmetics. Ailith winced. She remembered to sound gruff, like a man. "What happened? Did your husband do this?"

"Yes," Odelina said. "Josserand made me . . . perform with another woman, while he . . .while he pleasured himself. It was disgusting. I didn't want to do it, but he hit me until I did. I can't take any more, Alan. He's getting worse." Her eyes were wet. "He has three prostitutes waiting tonight when we get home, and if I don't perform with them, he said he'll . . . Please, you must help me. I'm at my wit's end."

She was appealing to Ailith as though to a man, to a lover. "There's nothing I can do," Ailith said. "I'm in trouble of my own just now and I have to get away from here. Here, take my dagger. Don't let him hit you again." As Odelina's husband, Josserand had the legal right to hit her as often and as hard as he wished. Maybe the dagger would make him back off, or at least think twice before he acted.

Odelina took the dagger and looked over her shoulder. "Oh, God, here he comes. If he sees me with you . . ."

She slipped the dagger up her wide sleeve, turned and vanished into the crowd. "Pray for me!" she called back.

The ancient Josserand was heading toward Ailith, a thunderous look in his eyes. He probably suspected that the troubadour Alan and Odelina were having an affair and intended to take his revenge. Two rough-looking men who must be his bodyguards were behind him.

Ailith hurried through the waiting area. Josserand would probably think she was going for one of the exits to the house, and he and his men would block them. She needed a place to hide, and she needed it fast.

There was a small door to Ailith's left. She opened it, half expecting a closet but instead revealing a narrow stairwell. She closed the door and took the stairs, going down, feeling her way in the dark. She would hide down here and leave the house later. Gregorius would be gone by then, so would Josserand. It would be quiet. She hoped Odelina would be all right, but was afraid she wouldn't be. She felt sorry for Odelina, but there was nothing she could do for her. Her plight was no different from that of countless other women.

She went down several levels, until the stairs ended. She found herself in a small room with a single candle burning. As her eyes accustomed themselves to the gloom, she made out a cross on the wall. She was in a chapel of some sort. The chapel was old, with faded mosaic tiles on the walls portraying Christ raising Lazarus from the dead. The house must have been built centuries before.

She removed the lute from her back and leaned against the rough stone wall. If Josserand and his men found the stairwell and came down here, they could murder her with impunity, but that was a risk she had to take. She would wait here until the noise from upstairs abated and told her the banquet was over, then she would try to sneak away. But where would she—?

She heard a sniffle.

She stiffened.

Someone else was in the room.

It was a man, a huge one, only one man built like that. He was on his knees in the shadows at the back of the chapel, opposite the cross.

Ailith scrambled away from the wall. "I'm sorry to disturb you, sire. I'll leave."

"No, wait," said the man from the shadows. "Stay. You're the singer, aren't you?"

"Yes, sire. I'm called Alan of the Dale."

"I want to apologize to you for my behavior earlier, for walking out on you. I've been under a lot of strain lately. The truth is, I greatly enjoyed your singing. And your songs."

King Richard rose and emerged from the shadows into the weak candlelight. He must have used a different entrance to get into the chapel; Ailith saw a door in the back of the room. He wiped a cheek with the back of his hand. "I couldn't remain in that hall a moment longer. I felt like the walls were closing in on me. I felt like the world was closing in on me. I was only there because Bishop Jean insisted that I listen to you sing. Why people think I would be in the mood for celebrating is beyond me."

Ailith didn't know what to say, so she remained silent.

Richard went on. "Jean raved about what a fine singer you were, and he was right. One of the best I've heard in some time."

"Why—why, thank you, sire. That's most flattering."

"Lady Hugoline says you're English."

"I am, sire. From Trentshire."

Richard shook his head. "Is there anyone here who *isn't* from Trentshire?"

Ailith frowned. "Sire?"

"I'm sorry, you wouldn't understand. Those songs—you write them yourself?"

"Most of them." She used the same joke she had used with the bishop of Acre. "Some I steal from others."

Richard didn't respond. He didn't seem in the mood for humor.

"Are you sure you don't want me to leave?" Ailith said.

"No, no. I thought I wanted to be alone with God, but as it turns out, I'm glad of some human company."

Here in the depths of the house, Richard's voice was flat, lifeless. His eyes seemed hollow. Ailith took another chance, remembering to keep her voice low and to talk slowly, like a man. "Are you sick, sire? Do you wish me to fetch a physician?"

Richard laughed, a laugh devoid of humor. "Sick? Yes, I'm sick. Sick of many things. Including myself."

Ailith didn't understand. "Sire?"

"Look at me, Alan. What do you see?"

"I—I see a king. A warrior. A hero."

"No. You see a failure."

Ailith started to protest, but Richard cut her off. "That is how history will remember me, should it remember me at all. The crusade is over, and I must return home in disgrace. And the thought of that is too much to contemplate. That's why I left the banquet and came here, to be by myself and seek guidance from the Lord."

"Guidance for what?"

He didn't answer.

"What happened with the crusade wasn't your fault," Ailith said.

"Of course it was. I was in charge, I bear the blame. You've heard the songs Burgundy's men sing around town, calling me a coward?"

She had; everyone had. "You're no coward, sire."

"But I am. When the time came to march on Jerusalem, to do what we came here to do, I lacked the courage to do it. Twice." He paused. "I was afraid to try because I was afraid to fail. So I failed because I didn't try."

Ailith was uneasy. This was far too—what? Intimate. Personal. She wanted to leave, but didn't know how. Anyway, she couldn't leave. Gregorius would have delivered the warrant by now, and they would be searching the city for her. Fortunately, only Bonjute and Hugoline knew that Alan of the Dale was in reality Ailith, and they were unlikely to give up her secret. This house might be the safest place for her—for the moment, at least. "I don't understand, sire. Why are you telling me this?"

Richard cocked his head. "I'm not sure, really. I suppose it helps to tell someone. I've kept so much bottled up inside me for so long. It's good to get it out."

"But why me?"

"Why not you? It's not like I have anyone else. No one I can trust. Isn't that sad? Amongst all this vast assemblage, there is no one I can really talk to."

"What about your confessor?" Ailith said.

"You think he'd keep a secret?"

"Your wife, then?"

Richard shook his head. "I never talk to my wife."

"Your friends?"

Richard gave no answer.

"But you don't know me. Why do you think I'll keep your secret? I might be the most untrustworthy of all."

Richard eyed her shrewdly. "I don't think so. You're a kindred spirit, Alan—at least I believe you to be. It's a stroke of luck meeting you here, actually. I had planned to send for you tomorrow."

"Sire?"

"To apologize for earlier and to show the world that I meant you no disrespect. Tell me, what would you say to a position at my court?"

Ailith's eyes widened. "Sire?" She knew she sounded stupid to keep saying that, but she couldn't think of anything else. "What—what kind of position?"

"Minstrel, *trouvere*, troubadour . . . companion. Whatever you choose to call yourself."

"Sire, I—"

He flashed his boyish smile. "You can't refuse me, you know. You're English, and I'm your king. I can command you."

Ailith said nothing.

"Well?" Richard pressed.

"I—I don't know. This is such . . . such a—"

He put a hand on hers. "It would mean a lot to me. A bit of brightness before I—after all that's happened."

Before Ailith could reply, a light appeared at the chapel door.

A man with a lantern.

Ailith was so startled, she almost jumped. Was it one of Gregorius's men, looking for her? Maybe even Gregorius himself? Or Josserand?

Then she recognized the newcomer. It was Humphrey of Toron, first husband to Queen Isabelle, now the kingdom of Jerusalem's chief negotiator. He looked around uncertainly.

In an instant, Richard transformed himself. He seemed to grow in size as he sprang forward, arms wide, voice booming. "Humphrey, my boy! Good to see you! You're looking well. How is that wily fox Saladin? Has he given up and surrendered? Converted to Christianity?"

Humphrey was flustered. He looked at Ailith—or Alan—and back to Richard. "Neither of those, sire, I regret to say. Forgive me, I didn't know you were here. I just returned from Jerusalem, and I thought I'd make my evening devotions while I waited for the banquet to end and I could report to the council. There's an unholy row up there just now. Some monk. I don't know what it's about, and I didn't want to get involved."

"Think nothing of it, my boy. Come, let's have a drink and you can tell me what those pesky heathens have to say."

Richard steered Humphrey from the chapel. As they left, Richard turned back to Ailith, his tone regal once more. "Attend me on the morrow, at the Templars' House." It was a command, not a suggestion.

"Yes, sire," Ailith said, removing her cap and bowing deeply.

"Do not fail to present yourself."

"I won't."

"Good," Richard said. "By the way, your sheath is empty. What happened to your dagger?"

Involuntarily, Ailith dropped a hand to the sheath. "I'm—I'm not sure. I had it in the hall. One of the servants must have stolen it from me in the crowd."

Richard smiled. "You must learn to be more careful." Then he was gone, leaving Ailith alone in the chapel.

A position at court?

What had she gotten herself into?

They'd quickly learn she was a woman, and then what?

"Attend me on the morrow . . ."

If she wasn't there, Richard would send men to find her. And Hugoline knew where she lived.

That was if Gregorius didn't find her first.

She had to get out of the city, and she had to do it now.

But how? There would be no ships sailing for Jaffa at night, maybe none tomorrow morning. There was no other choice—she'd have to get a horse and chance the overland route.

First, she had to get out of Hugoline's house, and that was going to be difficult enough. She retrieved her lute and exited the chapel, keeping to the shadows.

Chapter 33

ℑN JAFFA, IT seemed that the war was over. Only a few units of the once-vast Christian army remained, most of them camped outside the city. City and port life had returned to something resembling normal conditions. Trade had even resumed with the Muslim interior. The markets bustled. The harbor was crowded with fishing boats and coastal traders, with galleys and plump cogs from over the sea, come to collect silks and spices.

Roger was returning from the beach. He, along with Tatwine, Pentecost, Ralph the Red, and a number of the other Death's Heads had gone down as a group, as they did most days. Their shirts and hair were wet as they walked.

Roger ignored the badinage and horseplay around him. He was daydreaming about Ailith, about living with her in a great castle far out in the desert. It sounded like a fantasy from those *romans* that rich women listened to, but it would soon come to pass.

His reveries were interrupted by the sight of two men standing before his tent.

"Fauston!" He rushed forward and took his old friend by the shoulders. "How are you?"

Fauston grinned. "I'm not hanged yet, if that's what you mean." He indicated his companion. "You remember Francisco?"

"Of course." Roger pumped the young *morisco*'s hand. "How are you, Franco?"

Francisco smiled, revealing large white teeth. "I am well, Captain."

"None of that 'Captain' nonsense around here. I'm just Roger. How's the knee?"

"I still limp, alas."

"Fauston tells me you're quite the artist. Why did you never show your skills when you were with the Death's Heads?"

"There was little need for art when I was with the Death's Heads," Francisco pointed out.

Roger wrinkled his brow. "Well, you've got me there."

Tatwine came up. "Hallo, Brocky," he said to Fauston. "Good to have you back."

"Why does he call you 'Brocky'?" Pentecost asked Fauston.

"Long story," Fauston said.

Tatwine didn't take the hint and answered. "Short for Brock the Badger. That's what they call him at home."

Fauston tried to keep Tatwine silent, but Slowfoot broke in. "Famous outlaw, he was. Now look at him, all dressed up and respectable, like."

"An outlaw?" Pentecost said.

"Most famous outlaw in England," Ralph the Red bragged. "Lived in the forest, he did, with his gang of cutthroats."

Pentecost, who was a native of Outremer, could not quite get his head around the concept of living in a forest, but he shook Fauston's hand.

"Brocky fought with us at Acre," Fauston explained. "And Franco, here, he was with us at Arsuf. That's where he got his knee busted."

"What brings you to Jaffa?" Roger asked Fauston.

Fauston grew serious. "Your old friend Gregorius."

If Fauston expected Roger to be surprised, he was disappointed. Roger's brow darkened. "I was afraid of that. His protégé, Auberie—you remember him, the one I stabbed—was in Jaffa recently. Turns out he didn't die, after all."

Fauston nodded. "Yes, Gregorius told us."

"He came here to see his father, the count of Vouzin. I expect he's back in Acre with him now."

Fauston went on. "Gregorius has been sent by the Pope to purge the Holy Land of false relics. He was about to arrest us, when the earl's wife, Bonjute, sent him packing. Made him go to Tyre and get a warrant from the archbishop. We took advantage of his absence and hopped it down here."

Fauston paused, then added, "Gregorius saw Ailith."

"Damn," Roger swore.

"He still intends to burn her for being a witch."

"Why doesn't that surprise me? Where is she now? Why didn't she come with you?"

"She'll be here in a few days. She stayed behind to sing for King Richard."

"She did what!" Roger said.

"She's a troubadour now, didn't you know? Writes her own songs and everything."

Roger scrunched up his eyes. "What are you talking about?"

"It's true," Fauston said. "She's cut her hair and pretends to be a man—calls herself Alan of the Dale. Entertains at banquets. She's become the most popular singer in Acre. Bishop Jean contracted her to sing for King Richard before he leaves for England, and she wanted to stay behind and do it."

"What in the seventeen names of God have you all been up to since I left?" Roger said. "It sounds like you've gone mad. Ailith a troubadour?"

Fauston grinned. "It's a new world, Roger. Anyway, we reckon to lay low here till the storm blows over. Like as not, Gregorius will leave when the army goes home."

"I wouldn't count on that," Roger said grimly. "Gregorius isn't the type to give up, especially when there's people to be tortured or burnt."

A young herald approached the gathering. "Pardon me," he asked the men, "where can I find the captain of the Death's Heads?"

"That's me," Roger told him.

"The governor's compliments, my lord, and would you please attend upon him at your earliest convenience?"

"What's this about?" Roger said. He hadn't seen William of Mello since that first interview.

The herald shook his head. "No idea, my lord."

"Very well. I'll go with you now." He turned to Tatwine. "Make our guests comfortable. I'll be back as soon as I can."

Chapter 34

ROGER ENTERED THE hall of the governor's palace. Standing in the center of the marbled floor was dark-jowled William of Mello, surrounded by the usual coterie of hangers on—clerics, merchants, petitioners for one thing or another. There was no sign of the woman in the diaphanous gown, and Roger quickly saw the reason why, probably the same reason that William wore such an irritated look on his face.

Gregorius stood next to William, tall and dark and oleaginous, hands stuffed in his large sleeves, brown cowl partly hiding his face even in this hot weather.

The sight of Gregorius brought memories flooding back, none of them good.

"Here's Huntley at last," William said, relief obvious in his voice. Gregorius was not a man people enjoyed spending time with.

Gregorius looked Roger up and down, taking note of his changed state since last they'd met. "I almost didn't recognize you, Roger," he said in his waspish voice. "It's been a long time."

"Not long enough," Roger said.

"You're a knight now, I take it."

Roger ignored the statement. "I thought you were in Tyre."

"Tyre and back, thanks to that whore of Babylon who styles herself the earl of Trent's wife. And when I came back, I found the rats had fled. I assumed they fled to Jaffa, and when I learned you were here, I knew they would come to you. As they obviously have, since no one else could have told you I was in Tyre." He smiled.

William of Mello said, "Your friend Gregorius is some kind of Papal johnny, it seems."

Roger said, "He's not my friend, Lord William, and that doesn't say much for the Pope. You've come up in the world, Gregorius, I'll give you that. Though it would have been better had you stayed under your rock."

"Be careful how you address me," Gregorius said.

"I'll address you any way I choose. Just because you wear a tonsure doesn't make you a man of God."

There was a sharp intake of breath from the others in the hall. Gregorius fumed.

William was plainly in a hurry to get this over with. "Gregorius says you were a monk at that abbey of yours, not a woodcutter as you told the king."

"And if I was?" Roger said.

Roger knew that William looked down on him because he wasn't born a knight. "I'm a bit hazy on my monkery, but isn't it a Mortal Sin or something to break your vows?"

"Not when you've been unjustly accused of a crime."

"Unjustly, eh? Gregorius tells me you ran away after trying to kill one of your fellows."

"Gregorius is lying."

"Let us get to the point," Gregorius interrupted. "I am a representative of His Holiness the Pope. As such, Roger, I demand that you reveal the whereabouts of the maker of false relics. And of the witch whore, Ailith."

Roger bristled at the description of Ailith, but kept control of himself. "I didn't know your writ ran to witchcraft."

"My writ runs to whatever I want it to," Gregorius said. "I am not only to stop the sale of false relics but to stamp out any other forms of heresy I encounter."

Blandly, Roger said, "I assure you, I have no idea where the people you're looking for are to be found."

"We both know that's a lie." Gregorius stepped closer and eyed Roger balefully from under his cowl. "You realize that by aiding these people, you are as guilty as they are, don't you? You flirt with a charge of heresy yourself."

"Heresy?" Roger said. "You'd like that, wouldn't you? Then you could burn me. After the requisite torture, of course. Tell me, how did a worm like you ever get a commission from the Pope?"

"Since you ask, I have a friend in the Vatican Curia. False relics have been flooding the market. My friend knows my reputation and procured me the charge of stamping out the trade."

"Let me guess. These so-called 'false relics' are undercutting the profit from the relics that your friend sells?"

"You just can't help yourself, can you, Roger? Now you slander a member of the Vatican staff. A charge of heresy seems almost too good for you."

Roger gave Gregorius what he hoped was a bored look.

Gregorius drew himself up, formal now. "I will ask you one more time. Where is the relics maker?"

226

"I have no idea," Roger said.

"And the witch whore, Ailith?"

"Ailith isn't a witch. And if you call her a whore again, I'll knock your teeth out."

More gasps from those in the hall.

Roger expected Gregorius to react with anger, but he didn't. Instead he turned to William of Mello, a smile of triumph on his long face, if the set of those lips could actually be termed a smile. "Governor, I demand that you take this man into custody until he reveals the whereabouts of the heretics. I furthermore demand that he be held for trial for his sins, the trial to be held in Ecclesiastical court."

William of Mello might look down on Roger, but he despised officious clerics. "Who are you to make demands of me, sirrah? I've listened to your ranting long enough, and frankly I find it tedious."

Gregorius pulled a rolled parchment from his long sleeve. He untied the red ribbon and showed the parchment to William. "Do you see that signature? Do you see the seal? I represent the Pope, and the Pope is God's representative on earth."

"We've been through that already. So what?"

"So if you defy my request, *sirrah*, I will begin proceedings to have you excommunicated."

William stood straighter. "You wouldn't."

"Would you care to test me?"

Excommunication was the worst thing that could happen to a Christian. It meant you could no longer partake of the sacraments; it meant you were an outcast from the Christian community. It meant that when you died, you couldn't be buried in a churchyard and you went straight to Hell. It meant your lands and wealth were forfeit to the Church. It meant that William's position as governor of the city would be also forfeit, and that any order he issued would lack authority. It also meant he would have no chance of gaining the post on a permanent basis.

Gregorius went on. "Don't think I'm unaware that you live in sin here with a woman who is not your wife. Two of them, in fact. I'm certain the archbishop of Tyre would be interested in learning about that at your hearing."

Mello swallowed. "Yes . . . er . . . well, perhaps it would be for the best to get this straightened out. Serious charges and all." He cleared his throat and turned to his steward. "Florin, take my lord of Huntley into custody until we can have a proper trial and sort all this out."

"An Ecclesiastical trial," Gregorius reminded him with a raised index finger.

Roger smiled. "Ecclesiastical court, where the accused is always guilty."

"Precisely," said Gregorius.

William grit his teeth. "Take him away."

Chapter 35

𝕿HE GATE OF Roger's cell creaked on its rusty hinges.

Roger came awake.

Feet scraped the cell's filthy, rush-strewn floor.

The intruder hesitated, searching for Roger in the darkness.

The intruder spotted Roger then hesitated again, no doubt figuring a plan of attack with Roger propped against the cell's far wall, something he possibly hadn't expected.

The intruder inched forward.

Roger waited until he was close, then swept the man's feet from under him with a leg kick and leaped on him.

They rolled on the stone floor. Roger's eyes were used to the total darkness of the cell, so he had the advantage. He tried to keep the attacker's knife hand away from him, grabbing it with both his own hands, while the intruder punched him in the face with his left fist. Roger twisted the man's wrist back till it was ready to break. The man screamed and dropped the knife. Roger grabbed the man's head and banged it against the stone floor.

The intruder fell back, dazed. After a second, he tried to raise his head, but Roger swung a right hand that caught him alongside the temple, and the man went down. Roger knelt over him and slammed his fist into the man's face again for good measure.

Roger was breathing hard. His face throbbed where the man had pummeled him. Blood trickled down it. He didn't need a light to know who the intruder was.

Auberie.

Roger felt on the floor for the knife, found it, and stuck it in his belt. He knelt over Auberie and slapped his face. "Wake up."

Auberie shook his head, groggy.

"How did you get in here?" Roger demanded.

"Bribed . . . bribed the guard."

"Why? Gregorius intends to burn me, why not let him do it?"

Auberie's voice dripped with hatred. "Because I didn't want anyone else to have the pleasure of killing you, Foundling. I wanted to do it myself. I've wanted to kill you since I first laid eyes on you."

Roger smacked Auberie's ear, eliciting a sharp cry of pain. "You haven't done a very good job of it so far."

Auberie put a protective hand to his ear. "Anyway, you have friends. King Richard or the earl might save you from Gregorius, and I couldn't take that chance."

Roger hauled Auberie to his feet. "Get up."

"What are you doing?" Auberie asked.

"I hope you'll appreciate the irony in this, Auberie, because you're going to help me escape. And if we're successful, I'll let you live."

Auberie's aristocratic sneer was palpable; Roger had seen it most of his life. "And if I don't help you?"

Roger drew the knife from his belt. "If you don't, I know where to stick this knife and make sure that you have a long and painful death. Now, wipe the blood off your face and move."

They left Roger's cell and found themselves in a kind of lobby facing the dungeon gate. All the cells opened onto this lobby, but Roger was the only prisoner right now, which was why his cell had been unlocked. The dungeon lay in the depths of the citadel, far underground. It was damp down here, moldy. Water dripped. There was the clicking of nails on stone as rats scurried in the deeper shadows.

"Call the guard," Roger ordered.

Auberie hesitated.

Roger jammed the knife in his ribs. "Do it. I'm going to die anyway if I stay here, I'll be more than happy to take you with me."

Auberie cried, "Guard!" but his voice broke, so he tried again, louder. "Guard!"

Roger pulled Auberie's hood over his head to cover the cuts and bruises on his face. "What about Ailith? Were you going to kill her too? Did you want the pleasure of doing that yourself?"

Auberie struggled fruitlessly against Roger's grip. "I never wanted to kill her. That was Gregorius's idea. I wanted to get between her legs, but I had no desire to see her torn apart. Gregorius did it to a girl once before, and that was enough for me."

"Don't tell me you've developed a conscience," Roger said.

"I just prefer my women in one piece."

Roger hit him in the head with his forearm. "You're not supposed to prefer women at all. A good little *omnus* like you? Call the guard again."

"Guard!"

At last the guard thumped down the winding stone steps. "You're finished, young sir?"

"I am," Auberie said, speaking from beneath his hood. Roger poked his back with the knife. "I'm taking this prisoner to the cathedral close for further questioning."

"Dunno, sir, I'm not supposed to release prisoners to—"

Roger poked Auberie again.

"That was part of your fee," Auberie told the guard. "I'm working with the inquisitor, Gregorius. He wants to get started on this one right away. He'll explain it to the governor in the morning."

The guard hesitated.

"You can always give my money back," Auberie told him.

The guard didn't like the sound of that. He scratched his jaw. "The cathedral you say? Well, I guess it's all right. Go ahead."

With the knife still at Auberie's side, Roger played prisoner now, shoulders slumped, head low. Auberie pretended to drag him up the stairs. "Come on, you. A red-hot poker up your ass will get you talking."

Roger whimpered.

Auberie hit Roger, getting some of his own back while he still could. "Move, heretic."

They followed the guard up the stairs for several floors. Roger had to get out of Jaffa. He had to find Fauston and Ailith and go to Deraa. They would be safe at Deraa. Henry would hang Gregorius from the walls if he showed up there.

But Ailith wasn't in Jaffa. Where the Devil was she, and why did she have to stay and sing for the king? Roger would have to find Fauston and hide until she turned up.

At last the guard showed them through a door and into the citadel's courtyard. When the guard was gone, Roger shoved Auberie away. "Congratulations, you get to live. Now get out of here."

"I still intend to kill you," Auberie swore.

"Next time you try, I won't be so lenient."

"Next time, I'll—"

"Shh!" Roger motioned him silent.

"Don't you—"

Roger clamped a hand across his mouth. "Quiet!"

He listened.

There it was again. A cry from the camps outside the city. Another. More.

A distant horn sounded an alarm. More horns and trumpets took up the call.

A church bell started ringing. Soon bells were ringing across the city.

A soldier ran through the citadel gate. Roger grabbed his shoulder. "What's going on?"

"Saladin!" cried the soldier. "Saladin is here, with all his army!"

PART IV

BATTLE OF JAFFA.

Chapter 36

ROGER THRUST AUBERIE aside. "Go. Before I change my mind and kill you."

Auberie hurried off. All around, bells were pealing, men were running in confusion.

Thoughts of escape were forgotten. Roger had to get to his men, see them safe behind the city walls.

He made his way out of the citadel and down the winding streets of the town. The streets were crowded with people and animals fleeing in both directions, and in the dark it was slow going, Roger having to shoulder his way through. He came onto level ground, where he battled a flood of panicked men, women, and children headed for the port, hoping to escape the city on the boats docked there. Members of the city garrison rushed up the steps to the walls. There were screams and shouts and the constant clanging of church bells.

He got through the gate and across the bridge, fighting the mob trying to force its way into the city. Finally he was on open ground and headed for the Death's Heads' camp.

He passed the Turcopole company, which was commanded by his friend Espiart. The white-cloaked Turcos were mounted, and Espiart was calmly placing them in a line to cover the retreat.

"Roger—we meet again," Espiart joked as Roger came up.

"Is Saladin really out there?" Roger asked him.

"He is indeed," Espiart said.

"How close?"

"Very. We'll be the last ones into the city. I wouldn't linger out here were I you."

"I'll see you there," Roger said and kept going.

Roger found his men. They were falling back in good order, drawing wagons and carts piled with hastily assembled gear. Short Peter, Oswy, Slowfoot, and the vintenars chided the men to move more quickly. Tatwine and Pentecost led Roger's horses and Tatwine's horse, Lionheart.

Tatwine looked surprised to see Roger. "We heard you got arrested by the Church."

"I un-arrested myself," Roger told him.

"I packed your equipment in one o' them carts," Tatwine said. "Your tent, too." In the distance could now be heard the sound of hooves and marching feet, underlaid by the rumble of heavy wheels.

Roger accompanied his men as they made their way back, giving a hand with the wagons as needed. They were passed by fleeing merchants or soldiers from one or another of the kingdom's units left outside the city. There were families, too, carrying infants and what meager belongings they could, some with carts piled with goods. A mother and two children struggled to push a heavy wagon across the rutted ground.

"Leave that, madame," Roger told the woman, a dark-haired native Christian. "Get to the city before the gate closes."

The harried woman said, "These are all our worldly possessions. We can't abandon them."

Roger said, "But—"

"We'll be fine," the woman assured him.

Roger kept going. He didn't have time to worry about what was going to happen to the woman and her family. And there were plenty more like them out here.

Dawn was breaking as the Death's Heads neared the city's Acre Gate, which was choked with people trying to get inside. "Keep the men in order!" Roger cried to his centenars. "No straggling!"

Behind them, the sound of the Saracen army grew louder. The Death's Heads pushed their way over the bridge and into the open space, or gate yard, opposite, their order broken by their passage through the crowd. Roger was the last man over. "Get your equipment and form up!" he shouted. "Quickly!"

The gate yard was total confusion. Milling soldiers, civilians running around. Animals wandering aimlessly—horses, mules, donkeys, even a camel. Dogs barked. There was no sign of William of Mello. Rob and his archers were there, looking like they had no idea what to do next. Rob saw Roger and came over. "All right if we throw in with your lot?" he asked Roger.

"Of course," Roger said. "Glad to have you."

The Death's Heads fetched their gear from the wagons and formed up—spearmen, axe men, and a few archers. They stood in ranks and donned their jacks and helmets.

"What are we supposed to do now?" Short Peter asked Roger. Oswy and Slowfoot were with him.

"Buggered if I know," Roger said. "We've been given no instructions on where to go. No one expected an attack."

He thought. Seven towers defended the city, all of them the old square kind. There were two gates—one here, on the road to Acre, the other on the road south, to Ascalon. Saladin was approaching from the north. If Roger were the sultan, he'd try the obvious thing first. Attempt to batter down the Acre Gate—the one directly on his line of march—and scale the walls alongside it.

The rumble of the Saracen army filled the air. If no one was going to issue orders, Roger better do it himself. "All right, Shorty," he said. "Place the men along the walls above the gate, axe men at whatever intervals you like. Archers—stay here."

"Right, Roger," Shorty said, and he and the others turned away.

Roger beckoned Rob close. To Rob and Jumping Billy, who led the handful of Death's Head archers, he said, "Billy, join Rob and his men. Defend the tower that guards this gate. Take as many arrows as you can with you. Rob's in charge."

Rob and Jumping Billy nodded. At another time, Billy might have protested being placed under the authority of someone not in their company, but not now. There was no time; and anyway, Rob and his men had become famous because of the caravan raid.

The two groups of archers merged and began drawing arrows from the supply wagons. The rest of Roger's men were armed and going up the wall. Someone had already planted the Death's Head flag on the battlements.

It was full dawn now. Espiart's company of Turcos rode in. A squad of city guards chopped down the bridge behind them, and the gates were barred shut. From outside came the frantic cries of stragglers, but nothing could be done about them.

Roger had finished getting into his armor. His sword was in his hauberk, his axe in his belt. Tatwine was lacing Roger's helmet when William of Mello and his entourage rode up. Mello was armed but looked bleary, as though he'd had a long night.

"Morning, Huntley," he said. "I sent someone to release you from the dungeon. Looks like they found you."

"Actually, I escaped," Roger told him.

"Good lad. Even better. Can't stand those tonsured twats ordering us around." He pointed to the battlements. "Those your men?"

"They are, my lord. I believe Saladin will attack here, at the Acre Gate, so I sent my men to guard the wall above the gate, and I put my archers in the tower. I'll move them if you—"

"No, no, you did well. I'll put your father's men next to yours, and the city guard and local troops can fill in around the rest of the walls. We'll hold the Turcos as a reserve. What a cock-up this is. God knows how we're supposed to defend this place with so few men."

He turned to a frightened looking squire. "Get to the harbor and commandeer the fastest ship you can find. Take a message to King Richard at Acre. Tell him we're under attack by Saladin's entire army. Tell him if he comes quickly, some of us may still be alive."

The squire was visibly relieved to be out of the coming battle. "Yes, my lord." He galloped off with a pair of men-at-arms.

Outside the walls, the Saracen army grew louder still. Henry of Deraa's scarred second-in-command, Guiles, strode up in full mail, acting as though he hadn't a care in the world. "Thought there was a truce," he remarked offhandedly.

"Nothing's been signed, so technically we're still at war," William of Mello told him. "Guess Old Sidesaddle's trying to change the situation on the ground before the peace is final. Greasy bastard, no idea why everybody likes him so much. Your fellows will hold the wall to the right of young Huntley here. He thinks that's where Saladin's main push will come, and I agree."

Guiles nodded to Roger, then turned to his men. "All right, *mes amis*, up we go."

The sun had risen, though it was not yet visible above the city walls. "We're not prepared for an attack," William said, as much to himself as to those around him. "The hoardings are down, there's no catapults on the towers. The ditch is half silted in, and there's no stakes in it." He swore and turned to his own second-in-command, Thibault of Troyes. "Find every arrow in this city and get 'em to the walls. Find water for the men, as well. And food—they haven't eaten breakfast. Round up those odds-and-sods from the kingdom and post them at the Ascalon Gate. Comb the city for volunteers. Give 'em whatever weapons you can scrounge up and put 'em between the city guards and the Ascalon Gate. If they don't volunteer, make 'em go. Be better than nothing."

Thibault chose some assistants and started off. Mello turned to another knight. "Find some cauldrons and hoist them onto the battlements." He pointed above the gate. "Get wood and start boiling water. Get plenty of buckets, too."

The knight wheeled to carry out his order.

"What about the catapults?" said another knight. "Should we get them—?"

"There's no time," William said, "and we don't have the men to work them. Get any men that Thibault doesn't grab—the old and young—women, too. Force 'em to come. Start building a barricade behind the gate here."

The knight left. William dismounted and, with what remained of his staff, mounted the city wall. Roger slung his shield over his shoulder and adjusted his helmet one last time. Tatwine came up and handed him something. It was Helvise's crossbow and a quiver of bolts. "Thought you might want this."

Roger smiled. "Thanks, Tatty. And thanks for saving them from the camp."

Roger took the crossbow and started for the wooden steps to the battlements. Suddenly Gregorius was there, blocking his path, hand raised to Heaven like a Biblical prophet. Auberie was with him. "You are not allowed in this place," Gregorius told Roger. "You are a heretic, and you are forbidden to fight for—"

"I don't have time for you right now," Roger said. "Why aren't you two helping to defend the city?"

"I will defend it with prayer," Gregorius intoned solemnly. "Prayer is what will save us, not force of—"

Roger grabbed Gregorius by the robe, kicked him in the butt and sent him sprawling. "You do that." He turned to Auberie. "What about you? You like to fight so much. Are you going to pray or lend a hand?" He paused. "Or are you going to run?"

Auberie's jaw tightened with rage.

"Make your father proud of you for once," Roger goaded.

"All right," Auberie said. "I'll fight. I'll show you. We'll settle our differences later."

"If there is a 'later'," Roger said. He looked around, saw Tatwine at one of the wagons, stuffing a second quiver with crossbow bolts. "See my squire there. He'll get you fitted out."

Crossbow in hand, Roger mounted the battlements. The sun was well over the plain now, exposing the vast Saracen army, coming relentlessly on. The Death's Heads' chaplain, Ambrose, appeared. He wore a helmet and armored jack, had a round shield slung behind him and an axe stuck in his belt. He moved along the battlements, blessing the men and sprinkling them with holy water.

Roger crossed himself as Ambrose sprinkled the holy water on him. "Good morning, Roger," Ambrose said heartily. "A fine day to smite the heathen."

"I'd be happier if there weren't so many of them to smite," Roger said.

The chaplain laughed and moved on. Behind him two more men appeared on the parapet, one of them limping.

"Been wondering when you'd show up," Roger told Fauston.

Fauston wore a beat-up mailed jack and a rusty helmet. Francisco had a Death's Heads helmet and a cut-down spear.

"Never miss a chance to get myself killed," Fauston grumbled. "Which seems to be pretty much any time I'm around you. Should've left you in Dunham Forest when I had the chance."

"Brocky!" Tatwine exclaimed as he climbed onto the battlement and saw Fauston. "Now I know we're going to have some fun."

Roger clapped Francisco's shoulder. "Glad to have you back, Franco."

The young *morisco* grinned. "Glad to be back. I'll join my old section." He limped down the line to good natured jeers and catcalls from the men leaning against the parapet.

Roger joined William of Mello and Guiles above the gate. Below them, the Saracens were spread out like a malignant cloud. Bright-colored banners flew, trumpets blared, cymbals banged, men sang. Sunlight glittered off helmets and armor and spear points. The Saracen infantry were in front, the horsemen behind in serried ranks; behind them, dust from wagons. The infantry carried scaling ladders. They swarmed through the gardens, through the houses and orchards surrounding the city, killing any stragglers they came across—men, women, children. They did not stop.

"Jesus Christ and the Twelve Apostles," William of Mello swore. "They're not going for a siege. They're going straight into an assault. To your posts!"

Chapter 37

THE SARACEN INFANTRY advanced in orderly ranks, approaching the city ditch, banners flying, drums beating, trumpets sounding.

On the walls, the men waited. William of Mello stood with the Death's Heads directly above the gate, along with his staff. Guiles was down the wall to his right; Roger, to his left, near the tower. The Death's Heads banner flapped defiantly in the breeze.

Roger placed his foot in the crossbow stirrup, hooked the bow string onto his belt and pulled it tight, nocking it behind the trigger. He slung his shield behind his back, took a quarrel from his quiver and placed it in the bow's tiller. Around him men readied themselves. The joking had stopped. Men were taking deep breaths, running hands along the blades of spears or axes. Men crossed themselves. Lips moved in prayer.

Roger felt a tightening in his gut. This day might very well end with him dead. He might never see another sunrise. Might never . . .

He shook the thoughts from his head. No time for that now.

The Saracens were almost at the ditch. Their archers ran ahead to provide a screen. Roger looked at the tower and cried, "Archers! Fire when targets come in range. Take your time. Try to pick off men who look like they're giving orders."

From the tower, Rob waved acknowledgement. Roger made out Tiny John and Jumping Billy among the bowmen gathered there, along with Will, who refused to wear a helmet in lieu of his red hood.

Behind Roger, cauldrons had been hoisted to the walls by civilian volunteers. A relay line of men passed buckets filled with water to the walls and poured the water in the cauldrons. Other men had built fires beneath the cauldrons, some of the fires already billowing smoke in the sea breeze.

Somewhere a bird sang.

The first arrow flew from the tower, and a Saracen officer toppled into the ditch.

Roger aimed his crossbow and fired. The Saracens were massed so tightly along the ditch that he couldn't miss. More arrows flew from the tower. More Saracens fell. The archers shot deliberately; they didn't want to run out of arrows in the first few minutes.

The Saracen infantry started into the ditch. Roger could see why William of Mello had been so angry earlier. The ditch was so silted in that the infantry crossed it with ease, slogging through the dirt and foul-smelling muck that clogged its bottom. There were no pointed stakes to delay their passage, to trap them and make them targets. The ditch, which should have been a main line of defense, presented practically no obstacle at all.

The Saracens dragged scaling ladders with them, two or three men manhandling each ladder across the ditch to the level ground at the foot of the wall, heedless of the arrows directed at them. At the gate, Saracen engineers worked to repair the destroyed bridge. The defenders only had about forty archers in all, so there was only so much damage they could do to the large numbers of the enemy. The Saracen archers set up at the far edge of the ditch and kept up a steady fire at the city walls. One of the Death's Heads near Roger was hit in the jaw by an arrow. He slumped against the parapet, moaning.

Roger waved at the tower. "Rob! Keep your fire on the bridge!"

Rob waved a reply.

Roger aimed his crossbow at the men working on the bridge. He had to lean through an embrasure between the merlons to do it, and this made him a target for the archers below. Arrows whizzed by. One bounced off his conical helmet, dazing him. Recovering, he aimed at the man directing the engineers. He fired. Missed. Swore, ducked behind the merlon, and pulled the crossbow string taut again, trying to remain calm, trying not to rush and make a mess of the job. Knowing that would only make it take longer. He placed a quarrel in the tiller. Aimed. Squeezed the trigger. The iron bolt pierced the back of his target's mail shirt. The man dropped to his knees, then slumped to one side. He lay on his elbow, the arrow in his back, directing the engineers, exhorting them on, until he fell over, lifeless.

The first scaling ladders rasped against the wall. Men leaned over and pushed them away while Saracens at the bottom of the wall and across the ditch shot arrows at them. The first ladders were easy to dislodge, but once men were on them, they got heavy and the job became harder. Saracens scrambled up the ladders, yelling and cheering.

"Give me a hand," Fauston told Tatwine. Together they pushed a ladder away from the wall, its occupants crying out as they fell back into the ditch, Tatwine's cheek grazed by an arrow.

The bridge had been repaired. The engineers drew back, and a battering ram was wheeled across the bridge, its iron head dangling from chains.

"Where is that God damned water?" William of Mello shouted.

But boiling water took time, and they had to wait. Meanwhile fresh buckets of water kept coming up, and these were lined up to be thrown in the cauldrons when the first load was emptied. More wood was stacked nearby to put on the fires. The civilians doing the work— old men and boys—struggled to ignore the battle and confusion around them and to concentrate on the task at hand.

Roger concentrated on firing his crossbow at the battering ram as it made its way to the gate. A gang of men heaved its head back on the chains, then swung it forward into the stout timbers of the gate. The resultant *bang* was loud above the din.

A bearded face appeared in the embrasure next to Roger. The two men stared at each other for a moment, their eyes meeting. Then Roger hit the Saracen between the eyes with the butt of his crossbow. That stunned him, and before the man could recover, Roger dropped the crossbow and grabbed the axe from his belt. He drove the spike at the tip of the axe into the bearded man's forehead. The forehead erupted in blood and shattered bone. The man screamed and fell back. Roger heard himself shouting as he gripped the axe in both hands and swung it at the next man coming up the ladder, driving its blade through the man's helmet and into his skull. The man got hung up in the ladder's rungs and did not fall, blood and brains oozing from his broken helmet, blocking the ladder for those trying to come up. With a great heave, Roger pushed the ladder away from the wall

Roger bent over, catching his breath. He heard the battering ram at the gate.

Nearby, someone was crying, "Oh God, oh God, oh God."

Roger leaned his axe against the wall and looked for his crossbow. Found it. Tightened the bow string. Nocked a quarrel. Fired. His heavy breathing caused the shot to go awry, and he almost cried in frustration.

"Water's ready!" came a cry.

The water in the cauldrons was boiling. Below, the Saracens pounded the battering ram into the gate. The men on the battlements, wearing thick leather gloves, hoisted buckets of the boiling water. It took two men to lift a bucket. William of Mello helped one of the Death's heads—Francisco. The men rested the buckets on the embrasures, heedless of arrows flying around them, then overturned the buckets on the Saracens below. Boiling water scalded skin and seeped through cracks in armor. The men on the ram screamed in agony and fell back, some of them rolling in the ditch to ease the pain. Others took their places, and boiling water was poured on them with the same results. Mello was roaring like a madman.

There was a cauldron near Roger. A scaling ladder hit the wall. Fauston and Tatwine grabbed a bucket and lugged it to the embrasure. They tipped the boiling water onto the men climbing up. The first man's face dissolved as the flesh melted off his skull, and there was an inhuman scream as he fell from the ladder, taking the next man with him. Fauston and Tatwine pushed the ladder away. Other men quickly emptied the cauldron, dumping water on groups of Saracens at the foot of the wall waiting to get on ladders, burning them. As the cauldrons were emptied, fresh water was poured into them, but it would take a while for it to come to a boil.

Roger ran out of quarrels and reached behind him for his second quiver. Below, he glimpsed civilians throwing together a barricade of stone and wood in the gate yard.

The ladders kept coming. A Saracen jumped nimbly onto the walkway. Aimed a sword blow at Roger. Roger dropped the crossbow, somehow managed to turn his body in time to deflect the sword with the shield slung across his back, then turned back, grabbed the Saracen, and heaved him over the parapet. Nearby, Tatwine was rolling around with a Saracen. Fauston jumped on the Saracen's back and with two hands drove a dagger into the man's head. Bern the spearman leaned out to push away a ladder before its occupants could get onto the wall. He kept one hand on the merlon for balance, put the other on the ladder's top rung. A huge Saracen at the head of the ladder grabbed Bern's arm. As the ladder fell back, Bern tried to free himself, but the Saracen kept a grip on him and pulled him through the embrasure, and they fell to the ground below.

Roger retrieved the crossbow. No time to focus on the battering ram now. He pulled the bow string tight and shot a Saracen looming over the embrasure, putting the bolt through the man's open mouth.

"Arrows!" came a cry from the tower. "More arrows!"

The gate shuddered under repeated blows from the battering ram. They could be felt on the walkway.

"Water's ready!"

Men grabbed the heavy buckets, again dumped boiling water on the crew of the battering ram.

More Saracens clambered over the embrasures and onto the walkway. One sacrificed his hands to turn over a cauldron of the boiling water. Even as the man fell screaming in agony with his hands burned away, boiling water surged along the walkway, burning men's feet up to the ankles. Men from both sides howled and hopped in it; the screaming wounded had it wash over them. Ralph the Red grabbed a Saracen and pressed him onto the red-hot cauldron, searing his face with the smell of burning flesh.

More ladders hit the wall. The soles of Roger's shoes had been burned away by the spilled water, and the bottoms of his feet were blistered. He could still move around, though. His mail leggings had protected the tops of his feet. He gripped the axe in both hands, chopping frantically at the men forcing themselves through the embrasures and onto the walkway. He caught one man as he balanced on the embrasure and pushed him off. All around him was yelling, stabbing, choking with bare hands.

The attack receded. The walkway was filled with bodies, with spilled water mixed with blood, with equipment of every kind, with spent arrows. Men threw Saracen dead and wounded over the walls. The base of the wall was largely blocked by bodies and broken ladders. It was hard for Saracens to find an open spot to put their ladders. They had to toss bodies into the ditch to clear space.

"Water!" cried William of Mello.

"It's ready!" came a shout in reply.

Again the battering ram advanced. More ladders were hurled against the wall. More boiling water was poured on the men manning the ram. More Saracens climbed through the embrasures. Everything became a blur of faces and blood and mad screaming.

Then, from behind the ditch, trumpets sounded. The Saracens at the gate drew the battering ram back across the bridge. The Saracen infantry abandoned their scaling ladders and retreated across the ditch, covered by their archers on the far side, then all of them retreated beyond bow shot of the walls.

Soldiers and civilians collapsed against the wall, breathing heavily, chests heaving, eyes wide with terror and battle madness, some babbling, covered with blood and brains and other gore.

Roger's right shoulder ached where someone had hit him with a mace. He wanted to lie down and sleep, but he was a commander and he couldn't afford that luxury. He supported himself on the parapet, its stone the only thing propping him up. His eyes were blurred with blood and gore—his own or someone else's, he didn't know. Something was caught in the bottom of his helmet. He drew it out. It was a clump of blood-clotted hair. He threw it away. His throat was on fire with thirst, it was hard getting his breath, his heart pounded like an armorer's hammer. His mouth was full of blood where at some point he'd bitten through his lip. He didn't feel like he could lift his arms or move his legs.

He heard the rumble of heavy wheels, the creak of wood, the squeal of metal.

He raised his eyes, and his heart sank.

William of Mello, who was still standing, muttered, "Damn."

"What is it?" asked Short Peter, sitting against the parapet.

Roger croaked, "They're bringing up catapults."

Chapter 38

𝕿HE CATAPULTS WERE laboriously wheeled into place, drawn by gangs of bare-chested, chanting men—slaves, probably—with overseers whipping them. There were six catapults in all, four large and two small. Wagonloads of rocks came behind them, pulled by teams of oxen. It would be some time before they were in a position to fire.

Roger set aside his crossbow and looked at the sun; it was midafternoon. He was surprised by how much time had gone by. Below him, the city ditch seemed to be alive, as the mass of wounded men in the ditch

writhed and called out. Tatwine, his cheek leaking blood from the arrow graze, handed Roger a water skin he'd found somewhere.

"Thanks," Roger told him. He took a gulp of the warm water and passed it back. "You all right?"

"Nothin' a gallon of ale and a whore wouldn't cure," Tatwine said. He handed the water to Fauston. "Maybe two gallons of ale."

Roger said, "You all right, Fauston?"

"Haven't had this much fun since the last time I was hanged," Fauston said. He drank some water and started wiping red muck from his face, shaking it from his fingers to the walkway.

Roger had Tatwine unlace his helmet. He took off the helmet and tucked it under his arm till it was needed again.

Urged on by Ambrose the chaplain, tired men roused themselves to treat the wounded. The man who had been hit in the jaw by an arrow lay nearby, still moaning, his shattered jaw bent in a way it was never intended to go, blood and teeth on his beard and the front of his jack.

"Get the wounded to the cathedral," Roger told Ambrose. "We'll use it as an infirmary."

Ambrose's helmet had a large dent in it, the cloth cover torn where the Death's Head emblem had been painted. "What about the dead?" he asked Roger.

Roger knew they should throw the bodies over the wall, but he couldn't bring himself to do that. "Have them carried below. We'll bury them in the cathedral yard later." He raised his voice. "Lively there. We don't have much time."

He approached the civilians, who rested against the wooden balustrade opposite the parapet, wide eyed, bathed in sweat. "Who's in charge here?"

A grey-haired fellow with a gamey eye, who looked like he might once have been a soldier, glanced around, then rose. "Guess I am, Cap'n. Name's Gautier."

"All right, Gautier. Get some water up here. My men are dying of thirst, I'm sure yours are, too. After that, find food. Anything that's edible."

Gautier knuckled his forehead and turned to the other civilians. "You heard him. Stop playin' with yourselves and get on your feet."

Roger moved down the walkway. The last Saracen bodies were being heaved over the parapet, landing with thuds below. Above the gate, the Death's Head flag was still flying, leaning to one side where someone had fallen into it. Roger straightened it, noted that it was more torn than it had been before, and moved on to where William of Mello stood.

There were dark circles under Mello's eyes, but his jaw was resolute. "Still with us, eh?" he said as Roger approached. "Good." He added. "Deraa's man, Guiles, is dead."

Roger looked down the walkway to where a group of his father's men were clustered around a body. "What happened?" he asked William.

"Arrow in the eye. Bastards killed him while he lay wounded."

Roger didn't know what to say. His father, Henry, would be . . . what? Devastated by the news? Maybe not. Death in battle was the accepted fate of all Henry's men. That fate had caught up with Guiles today. It was his time.

William went on. "Deraa's men will throw in with your lot. That all right with you?"

"Yes," Roger said. He changed the subject. "The rest of the city held?"

"It did. The main attack was here. By the grace of God, the heathens lacked ladders to attack all along the wall, or we'd have been lost."

They turned to watch the catapults spreading out before the city walls, axles squealing, slaves still chanting, overseers crying out.

"I'd better see to the rest of my men," Roger said.

William said, "When you're done with that, tell that Turco Esplanade, or whatever his name is, to have his half-breeds help with the barricade. I have a feeling we're going to need it."

Roger moved down the walkway to where the rest of his men were gathered. The centenar Oswy was badly hurt and was being carried off, along with the rest of the wounded and dead. Altogether, the Death's Heads had thirty-six men out of commission. It could have been worse. Roger appointed bushy-bearded Wulfhere, one of the vintenars, as new centenar of spearmen, replacing Oswy. As before, he sent the civilians for water and food.

He came across young Francisco bandaging a cut on his arm. "Still glad you came back?" Roger asked him.

Francisco laughed. He pulled the bandage tight and tied it. "Of course. Don't tell my fiancé I said that, though."

"Fiancé? I didn't know you had proposed."

Francisco winked at him. "I haven't, but I intend to as soon as I get back to Acre. Not going to wait long for the wedding, either."

Nearby, Auberie was propped against the parapet, covered with gore like everyone else. He had exchanged his brown monk's habit for an armored jack and leather leggings. He glared up at Roger balefully.

"He done his bit," Slowfoot told Roger. Slowfoot had apparently been keeping an eye on Auberie.

"Good," Roger said.

Auberie unbuckled his helmet and threw it to the walkway. "I hate this thing. It's uncomfortable." He took off his arming cap and wiped sweat from his hair and tonsure.

"Where's Gregorius?" Roger asked him.

Auberie shrugged. "How would I know?"

Roger kept moving and reached his father's men, some of whom were still gathered around Guiles' body. The men straightened and moved aside as Roger came up. Guiles's head had been split open; men were waiting for the jam on the steps to ease so they could carry him below. Roger looked at Guiles and crossed himself. "He was a good man."

"That he was," said one of Henry's senior knights, a fellow named Nevelon. "He started as a common foot soldier. Did you know that?"

"No, I didn't."

"He and your father were together a long time."

"The Governor wants your men to throw in with mine," Roger told Nevelon.

"Keep it in the family, eh?" Nevelon said. "Fine with us."

"You'll be in charge," Roger said. "How many dead and wounded?"

"Six dead, ten wounded so bad they can't fight."

"We're using the cathedral as an infirmary," Roger told him. "Get your wounded off the wall before the Saracens attack again."

Beyond the wall, the catapults were in place. They were being aimed and locked into position, ammunition carried from the wagons and stacked for use.

Before leaving the wall, Roger sent a runner to the tower. "My compliments to Rob, and ask him to bring his archers to my banner."

"Aye, Roger," the man said and left.

Roger went down the steps from the parapet, flexing his sore shoulder, picturing the purple-black bruise beneath his armor. He passed the men working on the barricade—slapping it together with rocks, trees, furniture, anything they could find.

Espiart and his blue-clad Turcos waited in a side street. They were fresh, untouched by battle. Roger could only imagine how he looked to them.

"The Governor wants you and your men to help with the barricade," Roger said.

Espiart straightened; Turcos were notoriously prickly. "My men are soldiers, not—"

"We're going to need that barricade," Roger told him, "and the people working on it now aren't doing a great job."

There was a pause, then Espiart smiled. "Of course." He turned. "Come, *mes amis*, stack your arms and equipment. Let's show those civilians how to construct a proper barricade."

"Thanks," Roger told him.

As the groaning Turcos divested themselves of their arms, a skinny priest stormed up to Roger. "Are you in charge here?"

Roger looked to the wall, where William of Mello was in talk with his staff. William wouldn't want to be disturbed. "I suppose I—"

"What do you think you're doing, sending wounded men to the cathedral? The church is a house of God, not an abattoir. The blood, the filth—the church is not to be defiled in such a manner. Get those men out of there this minute."

Roger stared at the man in disbelief. "You do realize that 'those men' were hurt while defending this city? Of which your cathedral is a part?"

"That's neither here nor there. Brother Gregorius is leading prayers to drive the pagans off, and the screaming and stench are upsetting—"

Roger dropped his helmet, grabbed the priest by the front of his cassock and lifted him half off his feet. "You and the cathedral chapter will stop praying and tend to those wounded men. You'll do it now, and you'll do a good job of it. And if I hear any reports to the contrary, you and Brother Gregorius are going to see Heaven a lot quicker than you thought you would." He shook the man like one might shake a miscreant puppy. "Do you understand?"

"Yes," choked the priest. "Yes, I understand."

Roger threw the priest down. The man stumbled backward and fell on his rear. Roger started toward him, and he scrambled up and ran away.

Roger was about to go to the cathedral and wring Gregorius's neck when from the wall came a *thump* and a *bang*.

The catapults had started.

Roger picked up his helmet and climbed the steps back to the parapet, where he joined William of Mello, who was standing near the Death's Heads flag. Rob and his archers waited nearby. "Ah, there you are," William said. "They're taking our range. You see the gouge in the ground there, where the first one hit short, then bounced into the wall. Not bad for a first shot. Those fellows may be heathens, but they know what they're doing."

Roger watched as the Saracen crews, stripped to the waist, loaded and winched down the next catapult. Mello was still talking. "I like your banner, by the way. Used to think it was a bit overdone, but it's kind of grown on me."

Before Roger could answer, the catapult fired. Roger and William followed the flight of the stone, a streak against the sky. Roger heard a heavy *whoosh* as it passed overhead and ducked instinctively, though Mello remained upright. "Long," he said.

There was a crash as the rock landed in the gate yard among some men who were building the barricade. It then bounced twice and took out the awninged front of a shop. The men at the barricade—it was impossible to tell their number—had been smeared into a mincemeat of blood and flesh, guts and bone, cloth and leather. The stone's first bounce had taken off another man's leg just below the hip, and he lay screaming, while his comrades attempted to staunch his wound.

"Stop staring at that mess and get that wounded man to the cathedral!" Espiart yelled to the survivors. "The rest of you keep working."

The next stone hit the wall with a loud *bang.* The wall shook and a cloud of dust rose from it. "Ranged us," William said.

"That was quick," said Thibault of Troyes. He, along with William and some other men, peered through the embrasures to judge the damage the rock had caused.

William pulled back. "It doesn't look good for us," he told Roger. "I'll be honest with you, our only chance is that King Richard comes before the city falls." He let out his breath. "I'd hoped to be made permanent governor here. Have a nice, comfortable old age and get away from my damned shrew of a wife. Oh, well."

Another rock hit short of the wall, landed in the ditch, and gouged the side of it. William said, "Looks like they intend to breach the wall between the gate and the tower. Better get your fellows off the battlements there. Have them wait below for when the wall is breached. Safer that way."

The two small catapults started to range on the gate. They were much closer to the city wall than the large ones. Their first rock hit the bridge in front of the gate with a resounding crash, smashing it.

"The gate's what I'm worried about," William said. "Buggers won't need a battering ram if the gate's knocked in. Won't need the bridge, either. They can just walk into the city."

Roger turned to the archers. "Rob."

Rob stepped forward.

"Have your men concentrate their fire on the fellows manning those two small catapults. See if you can't drive 'em back."

"Right," Rob said. He turned and gave orders to his men. They spread out in a line along the parapet and began shooting arrows at the two small catapults. The catapults were just the other side of the ditch, and were well within the archers' range. Saracen artillerists began falling, then more. Soon the catapults' fire died away because there were no longer enough men to work them. Gangs of men were sent forward, overseers lashing their backs, to drag the catapults back.

The archers started shooting at the slaves, but Roger said, "Let them go. We don't have enough men to stop them. We'd be wasting arrows."

The catapults were pulled back to long bowshot. They could hit the gate from that range, barely, but the stones would lose some of their impact because of the longer distance. A small victory.

Through the rest of the long summer evening, the catapults pounded the wall and gate. Soon the city's defenders were covered with a gray dust that mixed with the blood on their clothes and faces, with the blood from their wounds, with their sweat, until they looked like apparitions from the underworld.

Roger and his men from the parapet waited in the side street where the Turcos had been. Gautier and his group of civilians were with them. Behind Roger, most of the men had fallen asleep, passed out from exhaustion. Fauston and Tatwine seemed to be having a contest as to who could snore the loudest.

Roger struggled to keep his eyes open, but it was a losing battle, and just before he gave up, he realized one thing.

The wall would come down on the morrow, and the gate with it.

Chapter 39

As DARKNESS FELL, the fire from the catapults slackened. The Saracens needed to replenish their ammunition, and they didn't want to waste what they had left by firing at unseen targets.

"No torches on the walls or towers," William of Mello ordered. "Don't give the bastards anything to shoot at. Plus, we'll be able to see them better in the event they try a night attack."

There was still a glow over the walls from buildings in the city, but this gradually died out as Mello sent heralds around the city to order anyone who had lit a fire to put it out.

In the end, there were only two sources of light in the city. One came from the barricade, where men worked in shifts by torchlight. The other came from the cathedral, where the wounded men were being treated. The cathedral's infirmarian, Anselm, and a group of lower-ranking clerics tended to the wounded, much to the displeasure of members of the cathedral chapter.

In the cathedral yard, Ambrose, the Death's Heads chaplain, supervised burials, watched by the skinny priest and robed members of the cathedral chapter. The watchers' eyes blazed with hatred. They were infuriated by this use of their yard, but they were scared to try and stop it.

∾

Roger's eyes popped open. It was dark.

Where was he? He had been dreaming that he was at Huntley Abbey, filing into the church for matins.

Then he remembered. He was in the Holy Land, in Jaffa, lying against a stone parapet. His mouth felt clammy, and his neck hurt where his head had fallen to one side while he slept. Tatwine was near him. So was Fauston, along with the other Death's Heads. They had been brought back to the wall before dawn in case the Saracens attempted a surprise attack.

Last night, Roger and Fauston had gone to the cathedral to look for Gregorius. Roger wasn't sure what he would do to Gregorius when he found him, but in the event, Gregorius wasn't there, and Roger and Fauston had ended up helping with the burials. Now, Roger pulled himself to his feet, chilled by the night and the land breeze. This act made his shoulder hurt where he had been hit by the mace, and he bent sideways until the pain was gone. He peered through an embrasure and saw the fires of Saladin's army spread before him. There was noise from the Saracen catapults as crews worked on them and brought up fresh rocks. A faint lightening in the eastern sky signaled that dawn was not far off.

As light spread from behind the hills and over the plain, the bombardment began again. Thump and bang of stone against the city wall, the higher pitched crash of stones hitting the gates. The sound, the rhythm, seemed to take on a life of its own, as if it had always been there and would always remain. The Saracen camp was fully visible now. That cluster of tents in the hills would belong to Saladin. Over one part of the camp waved a green flag. That belonged to Meshtub, who had commanded at Acre. Over the part closest to the Acre Gate flew Qaymaz's blue banner. The Saracen archers along the ditch returned from breakfast and opened fire, aiming at anyone foolish enough to show himself. Some of their arrows went over the wall and landed among the men and women building the barricade, causing casualties.

Sitting against the wall with the other men, Fauston was resigned. He was thinking of Bonjute. Remembering her smile, her laugh, her perfect body. He would have given anything to be with her now, but Fortune's Wheel had spun again, and here he was. At least he was still alive, though he wasn't sure how much longer that would last. He wondered how Francisco was doing. The young *morisco* was on the other side of the parapet, and Fauston had barely spoken with him since the battle began. They should have gone to Tyre, with Gregory. But that would have meant abandoning Roger.

Why did life have to be so difficult?

Civilians mounted the walls with water for the defenders, along with cheese and fresh-baked flatbread. When his men had eaten and drunk, Roger sent the ones on the left side of the wall below again.

With Tatwine's aid, he put on his helmet and made his way down the walkway, where he found William of Mello urinating against the wall. Only William and his staff were standing—William, to show his contempt for the enemy; his staff, because William did it. Most of the men crouched against the stone wall, safe from Saracen arrows.

Rob and his archers sheltered behind the wall's merlons. Rob and Tiny John took turns loosing arrows at the distant catapults. They were the best shots, the ones who could reliably be expected to hit targets at that range. As Roger came up, Rob stepped from behind a merlon, aimed, let fly, and ducked behind the merlon again. Seconds later there was a distant scream.

"Two for me, one for you," Rob told John cheerfully.

"Hmph," John muttered. "Day's still young yet. See who has the brag of it when the sun goes down."

The other archers occasionally popped from behind the merlons and shot at the Saracen bowmen by the ditch, making obscene gestures and jeering at them. The Saracens lacked shields or pavises for protection, so they took casualties with almost every arrow fired by the English. Unfortunately, there were a lot more Saracens than there were English, and casualties were something they could afford.

The bombardment went on through the morning. Roger waited with William of Mello by the Death's Heads' flag, wishing he could take cover. Everyone was coated with grey dust from the stones hitting the walls. The gritty dust was in Roger's mouth, in his nostrils, in his eyes. It was in the water that he drank, the bread that he ate.

A stone slammed into the wall close by, the shock jarring Roger's teeth. William of Mello turned to Roger with bloodshot eyes. "Not long now. Better get more men ready for when the wall's breached."

"Aye, my lord," Roger said.

Roger made his way down the wall. Arrows whizzed by him, but he had to follow William's example and walk upright, holding his shield up, feeling arrows thudding into it.

By the time he reached his men on the right-hand side of the parapet, three arrows were stuck in his shield. He made a show of pulling them out, waving them defiantly at the Saracens, and tossing them over the wall. "Wulfhere, Nevelon," he called.

The two men came forward, bending low. Unlike William of Mello, they didn't feel obligated to make themselves targets for the Saracen archers. "We have to be prepared for the wall to go down on the left," Roger told them. "Send every second man to the gate yard. Shorty's there, he'll tell them what to do. If the wall goes, the men that remain here will probably face another assault with ladders. You'll have to hold, and you can't expect any help."

Nevelon and the bushy-bearded Wulfhere nodded grimly.

The men started counting off, the designated ones heading down to the gate yard. Auberie was among them.

"Put your helmet on," Roger told him.

Auberie gave him a look, but did as he was told.

Roger started back to where William of Mello stood. As he did, a stone from one of the catapults took off part of a merlon and cut William in half. William's upper body disappeared in a pink froth, while his legs and ragged lower torso did a macabre, twitching dance, then fell over, still twitching, blood and other things gouting from it, the men nearby jumping back to avoid being splashed. The rock landed in the courtyard, bounced once and crushed a wagon bringing material for the barricade.

Roger stared at what was left of William. Then he shook his head. There was no time to dwell on it. "Who's in charge now?" he shouted to what remained of William's stunned staff.

"I believe you are," said Thibault of Troyes.

"Me?"

"You're the senior captain."

Roger's gut sank. He was in command of the city? How could that be?

He swore in frustration, but there was nothing for it. He moved forward, motioning William's men to crouch below the parapet, so they wouldn't be targets anymore. One of William's young pages was vomiting uncontrollably.

Roger signaled three heralds, pointing to each of them in turn. "Go around the city walls—to the city guards, the soldiers of the kingdom, and the civilians. Get reports on their situation and bring them back to me."

The heralds started down the steps, glad to get off the wall. To Thibault, Roger said, "Remain here with my flag."

"Very well," Thibault said.

"And for God's sake, keep your head down."

Thibault managed a laugh at that.

Stepping around what remained of William of Mello, Roger went back down the steps to the barricade. The barricade was being constructed in the shape of a "U," ranging from one corner of the gate to the other. The gates themselves shook heavily when hit by rocks. Splinters sprinkled from the dry wood. At the top of the right-hand gate, a hole let in sunlight where the gate had been cracked open.

The Death's Heads were helping the civilians and Turcos with the barricade. Houses were being knocked down; men were taking their rocks and timber and piling them high, reinforcing them with barrels and sacks of grain and anything else that came to hand.

Roger summoned Espiart and Short Peter. He said, "William of Mello is dead. I command the city." He looked at Espiart. "Sorry."

Espiart was senior to Roger, but for some reason unknown to Roger, Turcos were not allowed to command any men but their own.

"I understand," Espiart said.

"If I go down, William's man Thibault will take over."

Espiart nodded, and Short Peter said, "All right."

"How is the barricade coming?" Roger asked Espiart.

"As well as can be expected," the Turco replied. "We lack the resources to build it high, so we're building it in depth. The infidels will have to claw it apart to get to us, and we will kill them as they do. It's close enough to the gate that they can't get a running start, and their horses won't have room to maneuver."

"Good," Roger said. "If we can hold this barricade. We have a chance of holding the city."

Espiart said, "Let us pray it doesn't come to that."

"I'm going back on the wall. If you need me—"

There was a terrific crash and a loud rumbling, followed by a roiling cloud of smoke.

The wall had been breached. It was falling.

Chapter 40

KING RICHARD STOOD on the balcony of his quarters at the Templars House, looking out to sea. A galley was rounding the Tower of Flies into the harbor at almost reckless speed. He wondered what that was about.

He turned away from the balcony, dispirited. "Is everything packed?" he asked Alart.

"It is, sire. It just needs to be loaded onto the ships."

"Good. And Joanna and Berengaria, are they packed, as well?"

"Amazingly enough, they are."

Richard shook his head. "Two women? I'd never have thought it possible. They must have had help."

"Andrew is with them. He's so excited to be going home that he's practically packed their belongings by himself."

Richard nodded, then winced. He had a sore tooth and was afraid he would lose it. How many teeth did that make since he'd been here? God's blood, he hated this land. "So, there's nothing keeping us here?"

Alart stated the obvious. "Well, the peace accord has yet to be signed."

"Hang the peace accord. I'm tired of playing Saladin's games. Henry of Champagne can sign it, assuming it ever comes to pass. Burgundy, too, if he stays here that long. What's the holdup? Still Ascalon?"

Alart spread his arms. "Negotiations have ceased for the time being. Humphrey of Toron hasn't been admitted to Saladin's presence for nearly a week. Saladin is ill."

Richard snorted. "How many are staying behind to visit Jerusalem when this peace is finally signed?"

"About half the nobles, I'd say." Alart hesitated. "Are you sure you don't want to see Jerusalem, Richard? Like as not, you'll never get another chance."

Richard shook his head ruefully. "I'm not worthy, my friend. I have failed Jerusalem, I have failed God and His church. I would be the worst kind of hypocrite if I went to the Holy City."

He let out his breath. In his mind, the Holy Land was already in the past and he was back in Acquitaine. But first there was England to take care of.

He used to think he was born to be a king, but lately he found himself wondering how much easier his life might have been had his older brother, the "perfect knight" Henry, not died and left him heir to the throne. He felt like the weight of the world had been placed upon him. Would the expectations have been lower had he remained a duke? Fame and glory were cruel masters.

"What about that troubadour, Alan of the Dale?" he said. "Any word of him?"

"None so far," Alart said. "My men have searched the city for him, but he's nowhere to be found."

"You went to Lady Hugoline's?"

"It was the first place we checked."

Richard grew testy. "I told him to meet me, but he disobeyed my command."

"You know entertainers, sire. They are notoriously lax in discipline. There's still time for him to appear before we sail."

"Not much, though. What the Devil's the matter with the fellow?" Richard wanted a new voice, a new companion, to make the coming months a little brighter, to mitigate the sting of failure.

Richard changed the subject. "Will your son be coming back with us?"

"No, unfortunately. His Papal commission won't permit it."

"That's too bad."

"Yes. Incidentally, Auberie told me something interesting. You know Roger of Huntley, the Death's Heads fellow?"

"Of course. What's that scamp up to now?"

"Remember how he told us he was a woodcutter at Huntley Abbey? Auberie says that he was actually one of the brothers."

"Was he! Splendid! So he left the order to serve God with his sword."

Alart frowned. "Actually, Auberie says he left because of a—"

Downstairs, there was yelling and confusion.

Richard said, "What the—?"

Footsteps on the stairs. Shouts. The heavy door flew open. A boy burst in and fell to one knee before Richard, bowing his head. "Sire."

A guard followed breathlessly. "Sorry, sire, we couldn't stop him."

Richard waved the guard off. He peered at the boy. "You're one of William's squires, aren't you?"

The boy beamed, pleased to be recognized by the most famous man in Christendom. "Yes, sire." Then he remembered why he was here. "My lord of Mello sends his compliments, sire, and begs you to come to Jaffa with all possible haste. Saladin has attacked the city with his entire army, and it cannot hold out for long. My lord says that if you get there quickly, some of our men may still be alive."

Richard rounded on Alart. "Now we know why Saladin was 'ill.'"

"We do indeed, sire," Alart said.

Richard's chest swelled. His blue eyes blazed. "Get the army together and start them toward Jaffa by land. Burgundy in command. I will go by sea. Prepare every galley you can find. Have my arms and armor brought aboard *Eleanor*. Alert the lords to see who can accompany us." He looked at the squire. "You'll go with me—right, son?"

The squire looked scared, but he said, "Of course, sire."

"Good lad."

Alart said, "When do we leave, sire?"

"The instant my ship is ready for sea."

Chapter 41

⚓HE BILLOWING CLOUD of dust rolled over the men who toiled at the barricade. They bent their heads, choking, coughing, eyes shut so the dust wouldn't get into them.

Roger knew the next few moments were critical. "Get your weapons, men! To the wall—now! Espiart, you're still in reserve."

With difficulty, because he was coughing so much in the thick dust, Roger unslung his shield from behind his back and pulled his axe from his belt. The Death's Heads, along with Gautier and his civilians, ran through the dust toward the wall. It was hard to breathe, almost impossible to see anything.

They heard cheering from the other side of the wall.

"Quickly!" Roger cried. "Before they get in!"

The men stumbled forward. The dust partially cleared, revealing a breach in the wall in the shape of a ragged "v". The base of the "v" was about ten feet high, with a pile of rubble at the wall's foot. The Saracens would come through that opening.

As commander of the city, Roger should be where he could have an overview of the battle, but it was too late for that now. "Hurry!"

Both sides hit the opening at the same time. Men pitched into the fight without attempting to get into any kind of formation—hacking, clubbing, stabbing. The defenders ran up the rubble to the opening. There was less rubble on the other side, so the Saracens were forced to hoist men onto each other's shoulders to get into the breach. This gave the defenders the advantage at first. They chopped down on men appearing at the top of the breach, splitting open helmets, shattering faces. The Death's Heads fought with cut-down spears and axes and swords. Roger saw Fauston with a sword; Francisco had eschewed his spear in favor of a meat cleaver. Everyone was yelling. Arrows from Saracen archers across the ditch were sent high and fell onto the backs of the Christians.

Even though the Saracens had to climb onto the shoulders of their comrades to get to the breach, there were too many of them. Christian defenders went down. Some of the Saracens started getting through, then more, and soon the Death's Heads and Gautier's civilians were being pushed back. Roger edged out of the line and grabbed Tatwine's shoulder. "Get the reserves!"

More Saracens climbed through the breach, sensing victory. Then there was a cheer, and Espiart and his Turcos rushed forward, flashing their curved swords.

❧

Ralph the Red rolled in the rubble with a big Saracen. The Saracen had a dagger and was trying to stab Ralph. Ralph held the man's wrist and pounded him with his free hand, while the Saracen used his free hand to try and poke Ralph's eye out. The Saracen worked his way on top of Ralph. The Saracen shifted the dagger to both hands and tried to drive it down, while Ralph gripped the man's wrists. Other men struggled around them, stepped on them, kicked them out of the way, but Ralph and the Saracen were oblivious, locked in their own little world.

The Saracen pushed the dagger towards Ralph's chest. Ralph braced himself on the hard stones, held the man back, felt his strength fading. Normally he would have had the advantage over this man, but he was not yet fully recovered from the wound he'd taken at Acre.

The Saracen pushed harder, harder; saliva dripped from his drawn, scabby lips. The dagger inched downward. Ralph strained, trying to kick the big man off him.

The dagger's tip reached Ralph's jack, went through the cheap mail sewn onto it. The Saracen's eyes bulged; Ralph smelled his sweat, his rotten breath, the oil he used on his hair.

The dagger went through the thick leather of Ralph's jack, through the shirt beneath. Ralph strained with all his might to hold the man back.

The dagger deflected off the thick scar that ran down Ralph's chest. It pierced the skin beneath, then his heart. Ralph couldn't believe the pain as the grunting Saracen kept pushing, pushing. And then Ralph couldn't feel anything at all. He lay on his back in the dust, eyes sightless, the faded ribbons in his beard turned bright again by his blood.

Gasping for breath, the big Saracen pushed himself to his knees. As he tried to regain his feet, a Turco ran by and lopped off the top of his skull with a sword.

The Turcos contained the Saracens. They pushed in from the sides of the breach, attacking the Saracens' flanks. Blocked in front by the Death's Heads and Gautier's civilians, the Saracens couldn't spread out and make their superiority in numbers effective. They were gradually forced back, amid screaming and blood and stench in the pall of dust that still hung over the breach.

Roger's right shoulder screamed in pain from the bruise he'd taken from the mace, but he continued to wield his axe. He pushed at a Saracen, the two of them shield to shield, grunting with the effort, neither man with room enough to move his sword arm, Roger gradually forcing the Saracen back up the slope of rubble. The Saracen lost his footing and fell, throwing himself forward onto Roger as he did, his weight knocking them both to the ground. Their shields banged together and became entangled. The Saracen had lost his sword; he tried to hammer Roger's face with a broken rock from the wall. Roger averted his head and the rock hit his helmet. The Saracen hit him again. Roger felt the reverberation through the helmet. Roger turned his face, and the Saracen tried to smash the rock into it, grinding it at Roger's cheek and forehead. Roger fumbled in his belt, found his long dagger. He dropped it as the Saracen bashed his helmet again. He retrieved the dagger and plunged it into the Saracen's side.

The Saracen grunted, but recovered and came at Roger with the rock again. Roger dodged another blow and stuck the dagger in the Saracen's lower back.

The Saracen reared, howling with pain. He raised the rock high with both hands. As he brought it down, Roger thrust the dagger under his jaw and up into his head.

The Saracen fell forward, head impaled on the dagger, the rock hitting Roger's ear, the Saracen's hot blood splashing Roger's face and chest. Roger tried to get the man off him, but struggled because their shields were stuck together. Finally he was able to slide from under the man. The Saracen was still alive, barely, but Roger didn't finish him off. Somebody else could do that.

Around Roger was the din of battle, and above that was hoarse cheering. The Saracens were falling back, scrambling through the breach in the wall and fleeing, with some of the Christians right behind them, hacking and stabbing at their enemies' defenseless backs, killing as many as they could.

Others of the Christians were too tired to chase the retreating enemy. They slumped to the ground or lay against the broken rock of the breach, parched with thirst, panting and heaving for breath, resting heads against any support they could find, some of them going to sleep on the spot, covered in layers of blood and dust from two days of fighting.

Fauston found Roger and helped him to his feet. "Are you hurt?"

"No," Roger said. "You?"

"How do I know? There's so much blood on me, I can't tell if any of it's mine."

"Where's Tatwine? Is he all right?"

"Yes, I saw him a moment ago."

Taking stock of the situation, Roger saw there were not as many of his men on the battlements as there had been before. Ladders were propped against the wall, and dead Saracens lay at his men's feet. The Death's Head flag still flew, though.

He found the civilian with the gamey eye, Gautier. Gautier, who wore a helmet and padded gambeson, nursed wounds to his arm and side. "Gautier," Roger said. "I'm glad to see you're alive."

"Glad to see it myself," Gautier said.

"Do me a favor. I know you're tired, but find some civilians who aren't fighting. Women, maybe. Have them bring water to the men. Are you fit enough to do that?"

Gautier seemed to enjoy being a soldier again. "I am, Cap'n."

"Good. Off with you then."

Many of the Christian soldiers had literally collapsed in the breach, resting and watching the Saracens flee. There was a huge crash as a rock hit the wall right near the breach, and several of the men closest to that spot disappeared as if they had never existed.

"Pull back, men!" Roger shouted. He moved up, dragging men away. "They're going to keep pounding this breach and make it bigger."

He was shoving men back toward the relative safety of the gate yard, when there was a strange noise from the gates. In the back of his mind he was aware that rocks had been hitting the gates all along, but this noise was different, lighter, scratchy. There was a funny smell, as well.

Short Peter ran up to him. "Roger—they're shooting fire at the gates."

Chapter 42

𝕿HE BUNDLES OF firewood, thrown by the two small Saracen catapults, bounced off the gates and fell at or near their base, where they burned, licking at the wood. More followed. One of the large catapults was shooting at the gates now, as well, the rocks crashing into the heavy wood and making it shudder. The other three catapults worked at enlarging the breach in the wall.

All Roger wanted to do was lie down and sleep, but he didn't have that luxury. As he mounted the parapet to observe, Saracen infantry began crossing the ditch with faggots of wood and lighting them at the base of the gates. Rob and his archers shot arrows at them, and other men hurled rocks down on them, but some of the Saracens got through and managed to set the faggots on fire before they were killed. Other Saracens used spears to push the fire bundles from the catapults closer to the gates until they, too, were killed.

"I'll send you buckets of water," Roger told the new centenar, Wulfhere. "Pour them on those fires. Drop these Saracen bodies on them, too. Maybe they'll help smother the flames."

The men on the wall had suffered seven dead and ten wounded in the last attack. Among the dead was his father's knight Nevelon, the man Roger had appointed to take Guiles' place. He picked another veteran knight, named Manassier, to replace him.

Back in the courtyard, Roger searched for the gamey-eyed old soldier Gautier. "Get water from the wells," he told Gautier. "Send some of it to Wulfhere on the parapet. Use the rest to douse the gates. Try and saturate the wood so that it won't burn."

Gautier nodded and went off to organize bucket lines. Wood smoke from the gates blended with the dust already in the air, and it seemed as though everyone was coughing.

The surprisingly resourceful Gautier had already organized women to bring drinking water to the men on the wall and at the barricade. He got them to bring food, as well, bread along with whatever meat they could find—mule, camel, even pork for a lucky few.

Work on the barricade proceeded without letup. Roger saw Auberie there, relatively unhurt and doing his bit with what looked like a will—even joking with his neighbors. Perhaps there was hope for him yet. More wounded were carried to the cathedral, more dead taken to the churchyard.

A passing woman offered Roger a meat pasty from a basket. He suddenly realized how hungry he was, and he gobbled down the heavily spiced pasty as he searched the breach for the weapons he had dropped during the fight. Nearby, Short Peter led a party of men who were dumping the Saracen dead and wounded on the breach's far side. "Make 'em climb over their own men next time," Shorty told Roger with a grin. "Serve the fuckers right."

Roger found his long dagger still embedded in the Saracen's jaw. He pulled it out and cleaned it on the dead man's tunic. It took him longer to find his axe, but eventually he did. He fingered the "A" burned into the axe's handle, wondered again what it stood for, then stuck the axe in his belt.

He turned and bumped into a grey creature. The man's once sky-blue robe and white turban were now the color and consistency of thick ash, his face and short beard the same. His eyes poked through the mask like those of an owl, making him resemble a creature from Hell that Roger had seen in an illustrated manuscript in the Huntley library.

"Espiart?" Roger said, unsure.

"The same," Espiart replied with a dusty flourish.

The two men laughed at each other's appearance. "You look a bit less dashing than you used to," Roger said.

"I could say the same about you," Espiart replied.

Espiart was also looking for a lost weapon, his curved sword, which had been knocked out of his hand during the fight. They both ducked involuntarily as a large rock hit the wall near the gates, raising a cloud of dust. "The infidels are far too accurate for my liking," Espiart observed.

"Let's hope the men who built this wall built it well," Roger said.

Another rock came through the breach in the wall. It crashed on the far side of the courtyard, and two women carrying a kettle of stew on a long pole were turned into pulp.

Espiart found his sword and returned to the barricade, while Roger mounted the parapet again. The parapet's walkway was covered with blood congealing in the hot sun, and Roger's feet stuck to it as he moved. Accompanying the reek of the blood was the stench of men who had voided themselves during the fight.

Wulfhere stood near the Death's Head flag. The thickly bearded Wulfhere, who was about the same age as Roger, had apprenticed as a tanner, so the smell probably didn't bother him that much. The cloth cover on his helmet was in tatters. "D'ye think King Richard will get here in time?" he asked Roger.

Roger didn't, but he said, "He'll be here. We just have to hold on."

Rob's archers were doing their best to whittle down the Saracens at the catapults and the men carrying fire to the gates, but every time one of them peeked through an embrasure they were met by a hail of arrows from Saracens across the ditch. Two of them were already out of action from wounds, and Red Will had a broken arm suffered in the last assault.

Rob loosed an arrow at one of the catapults and stepped back. "Can you stop them?" Roger asked him. "Or at least slow them down?"

Rob's handsome face was haggard and blood splattered beneath layers of dust and grime. "With what—less than twenty men?"

That was the answer Roger had expected. "Do the best you can," he said.

"And pray," Rob added.

"Yes—and pray."

Roger descended the steps. "Tatty!"

Tatwine came up.

"I'm going to make an inspection of the city. Come with me. Shorty!"

Short Peter said, "Yes, Roger?"

"If something happens, find me."

"Got it."

Roger didn't like leaving the gates, but he needed to see what was happening in the rest of the city, not just rely on reports from the heralds. He and Tatwine made their way around the embattled city, sometimes using the parapet walkway, sometimes the street that ran along the base of the wall. He visited the civilian volunteers, then the city guards. As the heralds had reported, all was quiet along their sections of the wall.

Lastly, he came to the kingdom's men. Their commander was named Emo. He was one of Balian's knights, a smallish fellow with a greying beard. He appraised Roger and Tatwine. "You two look like you've been through it."

"We have," Roger said.

"Glad it's you in command then, and not me."

Emo and his men were stationed at the Ascalon Gate, the site deemed most vulnerable to attack if the Acre Gate did not fall. Emo led a rag-tag band of knights, men-at-arms, and footmen, along with a handful of Templars and Hospitallers. Some of his men had been waiting to rejoin their units after recovering from sickness or wounds. Others had been discharged from service and were going home. Still others had missed leaving the city with their lords for one reason or other, or their lords were dead, or they were otherwise unattached. Most were veterans, but they had never fought together before.

Roger and Emo stood on the parapet. Below them was a full Saracen division. The Saracen tents seemed to go on forever, and over them flew a red banner. "Al-Adil," Emo said. He added, "I'm from Jaffa originally, you know. Those fellows in the back there are camped on my family's land. Bastards, I should charge 'em rent."

Close to the wall, companies of Saracen footmen had been placed along the ditch, but there was little movement from them. Their chief duty seemed to be seeking shade. A few Saracen archers directed a halfhearted fire at the city walls.

"What do you think?" Emo asked Roger.

Roger rested a hand on an embrasure and studied al-Adil's force, leaning out and looking in both directions, heedless of the occasional arrow that came his way. "I don't like it. Why aren't they attacking?"

"Our spies say they don't have enough ladders to attack all along the walls," Emo said.

"They've had time to make more."

Emo shrugged. "Maybe their job is to keep us from escaping."

"Where would we escape to?" Roger said. "They'd catch us in the open and cut us down. No, they're up to something, but whatever it is, there's damn all we can do about it. Keep your men alert and let me know if anything happens. I'll be at the Acre Gate."

"I will," Emo said. "Good luck. You'll need it, by the looks of you."

"Thanks," Roger said. "Luck to you, as well."

Roger and Tatwine made their way back. Most of Jaffa's adults were on the walls or helping the men at the gates, but not all, and in parts of the city life went on much as before. Shops were open, as were taverns, though many of the shops had little to sell. A few women fetched water or hung out laundry. Children played, dogs barked and chased each other. A fisherman trundled the day's understandably meager catch on his cart, calling for buyers. There was even music playing somewhere.

"Amazing, ain't it?" Tatwine said, looking around.

"It's war, I guess," Roger said.

As they neared the Acre Gate, smoke and dust decreased visibility. The quiet of the streets was replaced by the crash of catapult rocks hitting the wall and the gate, by the yells of men working at the barricade or around the breach, by cries of the injured.

Roger and Tatwine climbed the wall and approached along the parapet, keeping low to avoid arrows coming through the embrasures. Wulfhere was crouched near the Death's Heads flag, which had been further torn by arrows.

"They've brought up more archers," Wulfhere told Roger. "Looks like they're working up for another go."

Rob's men were still shooting at the Saracens, but sporadically, because they were running low on arrows. Roger chanced a look through one of the embrasures. A steady fire burned at the base of the gate, despite all attempts by the Christians to stop it. An arrow whizzed by Roger's face, and he ducked back.

"That fire's going to burn through the gate," Wulfhere said, "unless it's damn wet on our side."

Roger and Tatwine went down to the courtyard. The first person they encountered there was Fauston, hauling two buckets of water to throw on the gate. "Where've you two been?" Fauston asked. "Thought you must've wised up and left the city."

"And leave you, Brocky?" Tatwine said. "What d'ye take us for?"

As he said that, a rock hit the fire-weakened gate, cracking the wood and bending the iron bar that was used to hold the gates closed. Minutes later, another rock hit the gate in almost the same spot. The wood shattered, and suddenly bright light streamed through holes in it. There were cheers from outside, sounds of cymbals and trumpets.

Wearily, Fauston put down the buckets and drew his sword. "Looks like we're about to find out how good that barricade is," he said.

Chapter 43

ᴅESPITE FAUSTON'S PREDICTION, the weakened gate did not fall right away. It was late afternoon as the Saracens crossed the corpse-filled ditch and attacked the gate with axes and crowbars, trying to widen the holes in the wood and bring the smoldering gate down. Fortunately, the bridge had been destroyed by the catapults, so they were unable to use their battering ram. The men on the other side of the gate fought them, thrusting spears through the shattered wood. Atop the wall, Rob's archers shot arrows at the attackers, while other men poured boiling water on them, but the swarms of Saracen archers across the ditch had the embrasures covered and rained arrows through them, and the defenders were soon forced to keep their heads down.

Meanwhile, the other three Saracen catapults pounded away at the breach in the wall, widening it. Roger gathered Short Peter and Espiart. "Shorty, you defend the breach when they attack. Espiart, you're in reserve, as before. When the Saracens come through, Shorty's men will counter them, and you'll attack their flanks—"

"As before," Espiart finished with a smile.

"As before. Hopefully, with the same results."

The rest of the Death's Heads and the civilians continued working on the barricade, arms and armor handy for when the gate inevitably gave way. Roger would have liked to pull more men from the wall to help at the barricade, but they would be needed on the wall to withstand another assault by ladders. He thought about sending for some of Emo's men, or the city guards, but that would leave the wall in those parts of the city almost totally undefended. He brought Rob, Jumping Billy, and what was left of the archers off the wall and stationed them at the barricade. They would do more good there than they would on the wall, where their every appearance was met by a swarm of arrows.

Without waiting for orders, Gautier had organized the civilians for the upcoming defense of the barricade, appointing vintenars and finding his motley group of old men and boys weapons and bits of armor. "I'm glad you're with us, Gautier," Roger told him. "I don't know what we'd do without you."

Gautier wiped sweat from his brow. "Feels good to be doing something useful again, to tell the truth. It's a lot better than twiddling my thumbs in some wine shop, waiting to die of old age."

"You were a soldier once?"

"I was. Had to quit because of the eye. Odd jobs since then. You know how it is with old soldiers."

Satisfied that the gate would hold a while longer, Roger sent Gautier and Slowfoot and with a party of Death's Heads to the harbor, where they drafted sailors from the boats to come fight—fishermen, mostly, and coastal traders. "What about our boats?" a grizzled fishing captain complained. "Who's to protect them from thieves while we're gone?"

"Them boats won't do you no good if the Goat Fuckers get to 'em," Slowfoot told the man.

291

Gautier added, "They'll make you a slave on one of their galleys—that's if you're lucky."

"I don't care," the captain said. "I'm not leaving my boat. It's all I've got in the—"

Gautier grabbed the man by the neck. "You'll fight, or my men will burn these boats, starting with yours."

Reluctantly, the sailors complied and were marched back to the battle area. Half were sent to Short Peter at the breach; the other half stayed with Gautier and Slowfoot at the barricade. There was plenty of Saracen armor and weapons lying about, and the sailors were outfitted primarily from that.

"What d'ye want us to do if the buggers get in?" asked a sailor whose face looked like a manual of things not to do while knife fighting.

Gautier knew these men weren't trained soldiers. "Pretend they're men from Acre, come to poach your catch."

"Aye, Acre," said the man with the scarred face. "We been stuck in with them before. I hate them bastards."

"Killin's too good for 'em," added another energetically.

While Gautier and Slowfoot were at the harbor, Roger and Tatwine went to the cathedral, whose nave was filled with wounded soldiers and civilians. Roger turned men out of their beds and sent them back to the wall or barricade.

The wispy-haired infirmarian Anselm hurried up to Roger as he helped one of the wounded men from his bed. "This man's hurt too badly to fight."

"If he can stand, he can fight," Roger said. "Better to die on your feet than be killed here on your back."

On their way out, Roger and Tatwine passed through the cathedral yard, where bodies and pieces of bodies were stacked. "You can't just leave them here," the skinny priest, who, it turned out, was the bishop's secretary, told Roger. "The smell is already intolerable." Several well-dressed members of the cathedral chapter who were present nodded assent.

"No time to bury them," Roger said.

Roger made to move on, but the bishop's secretary grabbed his arm. "I insist that you remove them."

Roger's eyes lit with anger, but before he could say anything, a serious-faced young priest came up. "That's all right," the young priest told the secretary. "My friends and I will bury them."

The bishop's secretary didn't look happy—he didn't want any more bodies buried in the yard, at all—but there was little he could do about it.

Unable to break through the gate, the Saracens backed off as the sun was setting and let the catapults work again. A hit on the wall just above the gate took out Jumping Billy and two of his archers, who had gone up there on their own to shoot at the Saracens. Another direct hit on the gate brought down more wood, further bending the iron bar.

Darkness fell. Saracen footmen crossed the ditch to set more fires at the gates, while men on the other side thrust spears through holes in the gates, shot arrows, or threw water on the fires. The Saracens had almost unlimited manpower, so they could send fresh men in waves. Roger had to work his men in shifts, letting the others grab what rest they could. Smoke from the fires at the gates filled the courtyard. The Saracens blared trumpets and beat drums all night to keep the tired Christians awake. Their catapults hurled fireballs into the city, starting blazes that had to be extinguished, drawing precious manpower from the walls, making tired men even more weary. Overcome by exhaustion, Roger managed a few moments of sleep in the relative cover of a side street.

At dawn, the Saracens withdrew from the gate and the catapults started again. Within minutes, it seemed to Roger, though it was probably longer, their rocks smashed through what was left of the gate, breaking the iron bar, leaving huge gaps in the wood through which Saracen infantry now poured.

Men who had been at the gate scrambled back behind the barricade. At the same time, the Saracens attacked the breach and the wall. Roger held back a small reserve, including Tatwine, Fauston, and some of the sailors.

Rob's archers took out the first line of Saracens through the gate, including several emirs, and then the enemy was at the barricade. The barricade had been constructed of rocks from the wall, pieces of houses, tables, tree trunks, anything that would provide an obstacle. Blocks had been placed along the back side to provide a step for the defenders, giving them height from which they could strike down at attackers.

The Saracens tore at the barricade, trying to take it apart, while the defenders threw axes and spears at them, and shot them with arrows. They killed and wounded many, but the Saracens kept coming, regardless of losses.

It took a while and they took a lot of casualties, but the Saracens worked through the obstacles, and there was hand to hand fighting all along the barricade. Men hacking, stabbing, chopping, gouging, and choking each other. Thrusting spears through gaps in the barricade. Dragging men across the barricade to be killed by others. The Saracens brought up archers, and Roger saw a Death's Head go down with a shaft in the throat.

Fighting was also heavy at the breach and on the wall, but because of the dust and smoke, it was impossible for Roger to determine with any certainty how either battle was going.

Eventually the greater Saracen numbers and the weariness of the defenders began to tell, and the Saracens punched a hole in the barricade.

"Come on!" Roger yelled to his reserve. He drew his long-bladed dagger, and he, Tatwine, Fauston, and the sailors joined the fight to plug the gap. The chaplain Ambrose was there, as well, as were Gautier and Slowfoot. They threw themselves at the Saracens, trying to form some sort of line. Roger put his shield up, Tatwine on one side, Fauston on the other. Fauston had abandoned his sword in favor of a cut-down spear. They were met by screaming faces. Roger thrust the dagger into one, felt it crunch through bone, withdrew it, head behind his shield. Stabbed around the shield next time, hitting someone in the side. An axe smashed into his shield, splitting it. Roger thrust the shield forward, closing the space between himself and his opponent before the man could strike again. He reached under the shield and stabbed the man in the thigh. The man dropped to one knee, and one of the sailors jumped on him and drove a dagger into his eye.

❧

Further down the barricade, Auberie fought in line with the Death's Heads, using the cut-down spear he'd been given. He was dying of heat with the metal helmet on, and as soon as he got a chance, he unbuckled the helmet and threw it away. That felt better, and he returned to the fight feeling refreshed. But in an environment where razor-sharp blades were flying in all directions, Auberie's head soon picked up nicks and cuts, until he had trouble seeing through the blood in his eyes. As he tried to wipe his eyes, a Saracen rammed a spear through his skull, and he fell.

❧

Roger could only see what was before him. The press of men around him limited his vision. The Saracens weren't advancing beyond the hole they'd made in the barricade, which was good, but that was all he could tell. He had no idea of passing time; he fought to keep himself alive. Pushing, stabbing, trying not to be knocked down or thrown off balance. A Saracen boy crawled through the mass of tangled legs with a dagger, stabbing Christians in the feet. The boy's blade glanced off Roger's mail hose, and Roger kicked him away. The boy moved along and sliced the tendon behind the knife-scarred sailor's right ankle, eliciting a scream from the sailor that was cut short by a Saracen sword. Ambrose dragged the boy out of the scrum by the back of his collar and drove his axe through the boy's head.

Suddenly the pressure in front of Roger lessened. And just as suddenly, it was gone.

The Saracens were running away.

The defenders were too tired, too stupefied, to do anything but stare.

At last Roger spoke through a throat so parched that it hurt to talk. "We did it," he whispered. "The barricade held. We won."

He looked around. The breach in the wall was empty of Saracens, as well. The upper wall was also clear of them, though there weren't many of Roger's men left up there.

Roger slumped and let out his breath. The ground was littered with dead Saracens, especially in front of the barricade, and the bodies had to be disposed of. His own dead and wounded had to be seen to, as well, but the first thing he needed was a long drink of water and some—

There was distant yelling from his right. A lot of it. It might have been going on for some time, Roger didn't know. He saw a fresh plume of dark smoke to go with the fires started by the Saracen catapults last night.

Civilians came running from that direction, women and children mostly. A woman carrying a baby. A trickle at first, then a lot. Followed by soldiers.

Roger grabbed a weaponless footman by the arm. "What's going on?"

"The Ascalon Gate is taken," the panicked footman said. "The Saracens are over the wall."

The man pulled away from Roger and kept running.

The yelling grew in volume, as did the number of people running away. Roger realized there was no hope of saving the city.

"Fall back!" he ordered. "Fall back to the citadel!"

Chapter 44

"𝕳URRY," ROGER CRIED, "before they attack again."

He waved his men off the wall, back from the breach and the barricade. The civilians, men and women, who had been helping, went too. There were still people fleeing the southern part of the city, most of them in panic, though some of the soldiers—especially the few Templars and Hospitallers—seemed under control.

The attack on the Acre Gate had been a diversion. The real attack had been at the Ascalon Gate and the southern walls. Saladin had waited until the Christians were fully committed to this part of the wall, then he had attacked to the south, and the defenders there had been overwhelmed. Still, what other steps could Roger have undertaken? The defense of the city had been hopeless from the start. There had never been enough men to hold it.

Because of the city's layout, if the Saracens made a straight line north from the Ascalon Gate, they could cut off Roger's force before it reached the citadel.

"Hurry!" he cried again, waving a hand.

Tatwine hauled down the Death's Heads' banner from its staff and handed it to Roger, who stuffed it inside his stained surcoat. Fauston joined them. "Go ahead," Roger told them, "get out of here. I have to go last."

"We'll stay with you," Fauston said.

"Aye," said Tatwine.

"You're either stupid or you're crazy, then. But thanks."

The three of them shepherded the retreating men and women to the warren of narrow streets that led to the citadel. They were assisted by Short Peter and Slowfoot, by Gautier and Espiart, each of whom funneled groups up different streets. If everyone had used one street, that street would have become hopelessly clogged. The men were covered with days' worth of grime and dust and blood. They were all hungry and thirsty and tired. The young *morisco* Francisco was one of the last to leave the breach, clutching his bloodied meat cleaver. His Death's Heads helmet was dented, and he shuffled along on his bad knee.

"Come on, Franco," Fauston yelled at him. "Get moving and stop playing for sympathy."

Francisco grinned at Fauston and made an obscene gesture.

At last the areas around the gate and breach were cleared. "One last stop," Roger told his two companions.

They made their way to the cathedral. Inside the nave, the wounded and sick were packed like fish in a boat's hold. Where once the nave had smelled of incense and candle smoke, it now reeked of blood and urine and feces and vomit. Hymns had been replaced by moans and screams, by cries of pain and whimpers of men for their mothers. Priests and other clerics worked quietly, tending the wounded as best they could under the infirmarian Anselm's direction.

"What a surprise," Fauston said, looking around. "The bishop and his pals are nowhere in sight."

"Probably halfway to Acre by now," Tatwine added. "Cryin' about how rough they got it."

Roger assumed a position before the rood screen. He raised a hand and lifted his voice above the din. "Attention, men! Attention!"

He waited for the noise to subside. "The Saracens have taken the city. I need every man who can walk to get on your feet right now and head for the citadel."

"What about the rest of us?" asked Barnabas the cook, who was wrapped in bandages and lying on a straw pallet. Other men murmured the same question.

Roger looked at them. "I'm sorry," he said.

There was no outcry. These men were soldiers. They knew how the game was played.

"Hurry," Roger told the walking wounded. "The Saracens will be here at any time."

As men struggled to their feet and began to leave the nave, Roger turned to Anselm. "Get your people out of here, too, Father."

"And leave the wounded to the enemy?" Anselm said.

"I'm afraid there's no choice."

The wrinkled, wispy-haired Anselm looked at the other clerics, who seemed to be in agreement with him, and shook his head. "We won't go as long as there are men to be tended."

Roger let out a long breath. Anselm could have gotten out of the city with the higher clergy, but he had stayed. Why? "You know what will happen to you."

"God's will be done," Anselm said quietly.

Roger went to one knee and Anselm blessed him.

Roger rose and took the priest's hand. "God keep you, Father."

"And you, my son," Anselm said.

Fauston and Tatwine likewise received Anselm's blessing, then followed Roger from the cathedral and up the hill for the citadel. Behind them were shouts and cries as Saracens poured through the now undefended Acre Gate and the breach in the wall.

Gregorius joined the panicked crowd pushing its way along the harbor, trying to board a ship, any ship, to escape the Saracens. People were yelling, screaming, holding children and babies in the air to elicit sympathy from the boats' captains. Holding jewelry or sacks of money, those who had no money praying, begging to be taken aboard out of mercy. The mole was piled with litter, adding to the confusion. The wide awnings over the shops and fish mongers' stands had mostly been knocked over, and their swathes of colorful cloth and long, rickety poles hindered passage even more.

Gregorius had been lying low in the church of St. Peter these last days, conducting prayer services. He could have left the city earlier, but he had wanted the church to be empty first. When the city fell and the church emptied out, he had stolen a jeweled crucifix, so he had more than enough wealth to secure a passage. He had also pried all the jewels from an ancient chalice and stowed them in his scrip, giving him something for the future. As he moved through the crowd, he fumed that Roger had been given command of the city. Roger was barely more than a child; they should have known he would never be able to hold it.

From behind Gregorius came distant shouts in what sounded like Turkish. Saracens. He had not expected them to get here so quickly.

He pushed through the increasingly panicked mob, using the end of his staff to jab people out of his way. When a soldier shoved him back, Gregorius used the staff to knock the man off the mole and into the water, and with his helmet and mail shirt, the man sank immediately.

The harbor was in chaos. The fools had known this was coming, yet they seemed unprepared for it, as though they had imagined a miracle would save them. Boats were pulling away, some so crowded that they were in danger of capsizing. Others, probably belonging to men who had been made to serve in the city's defense, had been stolen and left the mole with practically no one aboard. People jumped into the water and swam out to the departing vessels, but were beaten back by sailors with oars. Some were knocked unconscious and sank beneath the water, others tried to swim back to the mole.

Gregorius worried that he had left it too late. All the ships were gone. He should have fled earlier, but he had wanted to get those jewels, and the city had fallen so suddenly.

No—there was one ship left.

It was a stoutly appointed cog. Passengers filed onto its deck via a plank, handing valuables and bags of money to the captain and mate as they got on. Sailors manned the sides with crossbows to discourage a rush from the mob on the mole. The last passengers were selected from the crowd, holding up what they could offer for the passage, and went aboard. Others tried to follow them, unbidden, but they were shot with the crossbows and fell into the water.

Sailors hastily pulled in the ship's boarding plank as Gregorius pushed his way forward. "Stop!" he yelled to the crew. "Wait!" He held up the jeweled crucifix. "Take me!"

The ship's captain, a swarthy Venetian with a drooping mustache, regarded the crucifix and his eyes lit with greed.

Gregorius relaxed. He was going to make it.

The captain gestured to the crewmen, who halted the boarding plank. "Is it real?" the captain asked Gregorius.

"Of course, it's real, you fool," Gregorius said. The two men were close, but the ship was drifting away by inches. "It's worth a fortune."

"Let me see."

The captain gestured impatiently, and Gregorius handed the crucifix across the water. The captain looked at it, then motioned his sailors to continue pulling up the plank. Other sailors began poling the vessel away from the mole.

"Come back!" Gregorius cried. "Come back, damn you!"

The swarthy captain smiled at Gregorius. With the crucifix in hand, he gave Gregorius a little wave goodbye and turned away to oversee the handling of his vessel. Passengers lined the ship's side to watch the fate of the fallen city, the fate they had so narrowly avoided.

Gregorius was going to try and leap onto the boat, but it was already too far from the mole. He'd find another boat, and he'd get to Acre, and he'd see that captain burned as a heretic.

But there were no other ships. He looked around, desperate, and now he saw Saracen troops coming toward him. They were killing everyone they came across, men, women, children—Christian or Muslim, it didn't matter. There were cries and screams, sounds of swords hitting flesh, wails of infants thrown into the harbor. Laughter of the conquerors. Screams of women being raped.

Gregorius turned. Nowhere to run. *Maybe this side street,* he thought. But as he turned into it, his way was blocked by more Saracens, grinning at him with yellowed teeth and yellowed eyes, like wolves.

He backed away, raising his hand in peace. "Leave me alone. I'm not a soldier. I'm a holy man."

But these peasant footmen didn't understand his words. They kept coming, teeth bared.

He took some of the jewels from his scrip. "Here. Take these. Just let me live."

One of the men grabbed the jewels from his hand and spat on them.

"I'm a representative of the Pope," Gregorius pleaded. "He'll pay a goodly ransom for me."

The soldiers grabbed him roughly by the shoulders, beating him about the face, while he lowered his head and tried to avoid their blows.

Laughing, they dragged him to a nearby warehouse. There they found lumber and hastily built a cross.

Gregorius realized what they were going to do. "No!" he cried. "No! No! Please!"

This made the Saracens laugh all the harder. They were still laughing as they nailed him to the cross and raised him screaming on the mole for the departing ships to see.

The citadel lay atop a steep hill, approached by narrow, winding streets. Roger, Fauston, and Tatwine made their way upward. The street was strangely quiet. It lay in late afternoon shadow. They were tired and thirsty, out of breath from climbing the hill in armor after days of fighting. They followed a trail of men, women, and boys who had given up and lay exhausted, unable to go any further. "Get up," Roger told them.

"I can't," complained an old man. "Leave me be."

Roger helped a middle-aged woman to her feet. He had seen her working on the barricade and bringing men food. He draped her arm over his shoulder and kept on. Fauston took a young boy and rode him on his shoulders. Tatwine slung his shield and carried a toddler in his arms. The others they left behind. They had no choice.

Behind them yells and screams and columns of smoke told that the Saracens were pillaging the city. They passed two of the kingdom's foot soldiers passed out drunk in the doorway of a wine shop, but there was nothing they could do for them. Roger went last, with the woman. He stepped around one of the walking wounded from the cathedral, who had collapsed, unable to go further.

Periodically they glimpsed the citadel's tall, rectangular tower, but it never seemed to get any closer. The woman held on to Roger's shoulder tightly. He took most of her weight, and his shoulder and neck hurt.

"Come on," he told her. "Not far now."

If they could reach the citadel, they could hold out until . . .

Until what?

The truth was, King Richard was not coming. They were all going to die here, the only questions were the hour and manner of their deaths.

Shouting ahead. Clash of steel.

They rounded a corner and saw a party of their men fighting a company of Saracens.

They were cut off.

Chapter 45

ROGER SWORE WEARILY.

"What's your name?" he asked the middle-aged woman he was helping.

"Mathilde," she said, breathing hard.

"Mathilde, wait here with these children. If we don't get through, you'll have to save them yourself. Can you do that?"

She swallowed and nodded.

"Good."

Fauston lowered the child from his shoulders. The red-faced toddler was screaming and kicking and beating with her fists as Tatwine handed her to Mathilde, who held her tightly and tried to calm her.

Ahead of them, a mixture of Christians was fighting Saracens in the narrow street.

"Come on," Roger told the others.

The three of them entered the fray, or tried to. The Christians were outnumbered and fighting uphill. It was a vicious little battle, men cramped together, stabbing, gouging, seeking any advantage. Roger had his long dagger out, but he couldn't get to the front of the fight because the street was so packed with men. All he and his friends could do was lean on the backs of the men in front of them, to try and add weight to the line and keep it from being pushed back. "Don't retreat!" he shouted. "If we do, we die."

Brave words, but they didn't help. Slowly the Saracens forced the Christians back, their way impeded by litter in the street and by the dead and wounded from both sides. The exhausted Christians did all they could to hold their ground, but it did no good. Steadily, they were moved down the hill, scrabbling for purchase on the cobblestones.

They were going to lose.

Suddenly, from up the street, came yells in French and the clash of arms. More yells, in Arabic and Turkish this time, yells of fear.

"Our boys are attacking them from their rear!" shouted Francisco, who was at the front of the fight.

"Come on!" Roger cried.

The Christians fought with renewed vigor, driving the enemy before them now. The carnage of the Saracens being attacked from behind in the narrow street, essentially unable to fight back, was frightening. Those Saracens who could, fled down side streets. The others were killed.

The rescue party was led by the gamey-eyed veteran Gautier, along with a hodge-podge of soldiers and civilians.

"Hurry!" Gautier told Roger and his men. He stood amidst the bodies and pointed back down the street. "There's more coming."

Another swarm of Saracens was making its way toward them. Hastily, Roger and his friends gathered Mathilde, the little boy, and the toddler, while Francisco and the rest of the men started for the refuge of the citadel. "You're the last to get away," Gautier told Roger as they made their way up the hill. "The infidels have overrun the city. It's lucky we saw you from the walls."

The exhausted men raced as best they could to the citadel. The Saracens behind them were gaining. The Christians crossed the open space in front of the citadel wall and reached the gate. Roger looked back. Francisco had fallen behind, hobbling on his bad knee. The Saracens were right behind him.

Fauston started back to help, but Roger grabbed his arm. "No."

Fauston said, "But—"

A Saracen threw a knife and hit Francisco in the back. The young Spaniard arched his back and stumbled, and the Saracens fell on him with swords and daggers. One picked up Francisco's meat cleaver and used it on him.

"Inside." Roger pushed Fauston through the gate, which shut in the face of oncoming Saracens. There were tears in Fauston's eyes.

"Close the gate!" Short Peter yelled.

As the gate was barred, civilian women attended to Mathilde and the two children. Slowfoot came up. "We thought you were dead," he told Roger and the others.

"We thought the same thing," Tatwine panted. "Would've been, 'cept for Gautier here."

Pentecost and Yves were there as well. "Glad to see you made it," Roger told them.

"Much good it's like to do us," Yves replied.

"Cheerful sort, ain't he?" Pentecost said. "Think we was all goin' to die, or somethin'."

Roger saw one of the kingdom's soldiers from the Ascalon Gate. "Where's Emo?" he asked.

The man shook his head. "Didn't make it. He stayed at the wall so the rest of us could get away."

The citadel was surrounded by Saracens, but they were content not to launch an all-out attack, probably because of the late hour. The citadel's wall didn't offer much of an obstacle, its only strength lay in its tall tower.

Roger pulled the tattered Death's Head flag from his surcoat and returned it to Tatwine. "You know what to do."

"Aye," Tatwine said and headed for the tower.

Roger appointed a knight named Leuthard to take Emo's place. "You'll command the city guards, as well," he told Leuthard, whose slab-sided face was so deeply tanned he might have been a Saracen himself. Leuthard nodded. These men came and went so quickly. Most were gone before Roger really knew who they were. Already he had a hard time recalling what Emo had looked like.

Roger summoned his commanders—Slowfoot, Short Peter, Leuthard, Gautier, Manassier, and the Turco, Espiart. The few Templars and Hospitallers left from the garrison stayed by themselves in the courtyard.

"What's with them?" Roger asked.

"They're touchy about being commanded by anyone but their own," Leuthard explained.

"Fuck 'em, then," Slowfoot said.

"Agreed," said Espiart. His turban was gone; dust-covered hair hung down his dust-covered face. "Let them do what they choose when the fighting starts. It's not going to make any difference."

"Here's the situation," Roger told the men. "We can't hold this wall, and we're not going to try. When the Saracens attack, we'll slow them up here, kill as many as we can, then retreat to the tower."

"And die there?" Espiart said.

"Yes," Roger admitted. "I'm sorry I can't be more positive, but that's the way it is. Keep your men in good order for as long as you can, and die like Christians."

"Don't get taken prisoner," added Pentecost, who was looking on. "I been one of their prisoners, and death is better."

"He's right," Roger said.

Roger looked at the sky. The sun was well down in the west. Was it only two days ago he had been Gregorius's prisoner here? Or was it three? He couldn't remember. Time had become a blur.

"Roger!" a Death's Head on the wall yelled. "A flag of truce."

Roger snapped out of his reverie. Along with the other men, he mounted the wall. A Saracen rider sat his horse in the open space before the wall, a makeshift white flag on his spear. Behind the rider, Roger had a view of the late afternoon sea, shimmering in the setting sun, with the ships carrying refugees sailing peacefully away. To his right, Qaymaz's blue flag flew from the tower next to the Acre Gate. Dark smoke hung over the city, punctuated by flames; the sounds of pillage continued unabated. Smoke hung in the air, along with the smells of burning wood and burning flesh.

The Saracen horseman shouted in French. "I wish to speak with your commander."

"I command the city," Roger told him.

The Saracen looked behind him to where the city was being sacked, and he smirked. "I rather doubt that, but I will not argue the point with you. The Emir Qaymaz requests an audience. Will you guarantee his safety?"

All eyes were on Roger. "What does he want?" Roger said.

"He will tell you that himself," the rider said arrogantly. "That is why he wishes the audience."

"Very well," Roger said, "we'll hear what he has to say."

The horseman bowed, mockingly it seemed, and rode off. Tatwine joined the group on the wall, tapped Roger's shoulder and pointed. The Death's Heads flag flew from the tower. "Good," Roger said.

A short time later, Qaymaz and another rider appeared at the head of the street facing the gate, followed by the horseman with the white flag. As Qaymaz advanced, the watchers saw that the man accompanying him was a Christian prisoner, his hands tied; Qaymaz was leading the man's horse. The prisoner's clothes were torn, his face had bruises and cuts, and one eye was blackened.

A chill prickled the back of Roger's neck. He stared at the prisoner more closely, and his hands gripped the wall's stone coping. The prisoner wasn't a man, it was . . .

It was Ailith.

Roger's stomach turned.

How . . .?

Ailith held her head defiantly. Her good eye met his.

Qaymaz reined in beneath the wall. He acted jolly. "Death's Head! It is good to see you again, old friend."

"I wish I could say the same," Roger told him. "And I'm not your friend."

Next to Roger, the archer Rob whispered, "Want me to kill him? We can bring the lady inside the gate before they react."

Roger was tempted, but couldn't do it. "No, I gave my word. I'll honor the flag of truce. It's more than that bastard ever did." Besides, Ailith would be killed when the Saracens overran the citadel. She stood a better chance of survival this way.

Qaymaz looked along the wall. He was handsome, with his trim beard and white smile. He nodded toward Pentecost and Yves. "I see two more of my former guests with you. I look forward to renewing our acquaintance. Your other friends that we captured, they did not end up so well. I think they wish they had not escaped."

Roger cut him off. "What do you want, Qaymaz?"

Qaymaz indicated Ailith. "You remember this lady, I believe. She tried to reach Jaffa by riding overland." He shook his head and tisked exaggeratedly. "Not a good idea. My fellows mistook her for a man and treated her with some discourtesy before the truth was revealed, and for that I must apologize."

Roger gripped the wall harder. He spoke through clenched teeth. "I assume you want me to trade my life for hers?"

"No!" Ailith shouted.

Qaymaz laughed. "Not at all, not at all." He turned to Ailith "So gallant, our Death's Head, is he not?"

To Roger, Qaymaz said, "Nothing like that, my friend. I would never trade the lady Ailith. She is going to share my bed tonight and every night thereafter for as long as I live. She will bear me many children. The boys will become great warriors and slaughter feringhees. The girls will be married to emirs. But tomorrow she is going to watch me kill you. It will be a slow process, I promise, as slow as I can make it. And the lady Ailith will enjoy every minute of it. Won't you, my dear?"

Ailith was trembling. Roger tried to sound tougher than he felt. "You talk too much."

"Do I? We shall see tomorrow. And don't expect the sultan to save you this time. I'm so glad we had this little chat, Death's Head. As you feringhees say, *à bientôt.*"

He waved, then turned and led Ailith away. She looked back over her shoulder at Roger, and she was crying.

Chapter 46

𝕴T WAS NIGHT. Roger stood on the citadel's walkway. He should get some sleep, but that would be a waste of his last hours on earth, and he wanted to make the most of them.

In the distance were the twinkling lights of Saladin's camp, looking for all the world like an army of fireflies. Fires still burned in the city itself, but they had abated, which meant that Saladin had gotten control of his people. Traditionally, when a city was taken, the victorious general gave his army freedom to sack it, to do whatever they pleased to the city and its inhabitants. In Christian countries, three days was the usual amount of time allotted for this. Roger wasn't sure about Muslim custom, but Saladin seemed to have reined in his men fairly quickly. Out to sea, a few lights burned in the distance, but to whose craft they belonged, Roger could not say.

Closer was the sound of wheels and creaking axles. The Saracens were positioning a battering ram near the citadel gate. Catapults wouldn't fit in the narrow streets, but Roger saw the Saracens' four big catapults being aligned along the city ditch by torchlight. From that point, they could hit the citadel.

"He intends to make quick work of us," said the veteran Manassier, who stood guard nearby.

"No point in drawing it out," Roger replied.

Roger had removed his hauberk and gambeson. He didn't think the Saracens would try a night attack. Why risk the confusion, when they could take the citadel easily by daylight.

The cool breeze was refreshing on Roger's filthy, sweaty body. His hair felt like it had some kind of crust on it from being under the arming cap and helmet for so long. He tried to run his fingers through it, but it was too tangled. He splashed water on his face from a nearby bucket, to get off some of the caked blood and dust, but he wasn't very successful. He normally wouldn't use precious well water for something like this because that water might have to last through a long siege. But in this case, they wouldn't need the water past tomorrow, so it was all right.

Above him, on the tower, the ragged Death's Head flag snapped in the breeze. Tatwine had set lanterns beneath it, so that it could be seen by Roger's men—and also by the enemy. That was the spot where Roger had picked to die, by the flag. He wouldn't let himself be taken prisoner. He wouldn't let Ailith see him tortured; he would deny Qaymaz that pleasure.

He thought about Ailith, about what she was doing now. It had been a shock to see her like that, bruised and battered, dressed like a man with her hair cut short. He almost envied his fate over hers. She would never escape the Saracens again, Qaymaz would see to that.

And it was Roger's fault.

If not for him, Ailith never would have been here. She would have been raped by Auberie, true, but with luck that would have been the end of it. She would never have been accused of witchcraft, never have been forced to flee her manor all those— how long had they been here, anyway? Was it only a year and a half? It seemed longer.

What would his own life be like if he hadn't taken that fork in the woods? If he'd turned away when he heard trouble instead of going toward it? He'd probably be in his cell at Huntley right now, dreaming of foolish adventures, or at nocturns, praying. His life wouldn't have changed a lot.

Did he regret what he'd done? For Ailith and for those he had gotten killed, yes. For himself, no. He had lived a lifetime out here, seen and done things that most people only dreamed about. Even more, he had met his father, and he had learned who his mother was.

He turned the niello-inlaid ring on his finger. Tomorrow some Saracen would have the ring. He wondered how his father, Henry, would react to the news of his death. It would break his heart, probably. Roger smiled. Henry came across as tough and mean, but he had a sentimental streak as wide as the Jordan River.

Footsteps nearby. It was Mathilde, the woman he'd saved in the street. "Brought you some food, my lord."

A folded cloth held cheese and day-old bread, along with cold bacon—a last snub at the Saracens. "Thank you, Mathilde, and don't call me 'my lord.' I'm Roger."

"Very well . . . Roger."

Mathilde must have been quite good-looking when she was younger. She was still attractive, though her curves had hardened and her hair was streaked with grey. "Thank you for what you did for me," she said. "I—I owe you my life. Or an extra day of it, anyway."

He smiled at her joke. "How are the two children?"

"They're fine. Young like that, maybe the Turks will spare them. Raise them as slaves, or such. Maybe they'll even be ransomed back someday."

There was a better possibility that the Saracens would kill the children outright, but neither Roger nor Mathilde wanted to consider that. "What about your own family?" Roger asked her. "Where are they?"

"Gone, far's I know. My husband's a cordwainer, he was defending the wall. The children are grown and married. Lost touch with them when the fighting started and I began helping on the barricade. Haven't seen them here, so I expect the worst."

"I'm sorry."

She looked up at him, and there were tears in her eyes. "I'll not let them take me tomorrow. I'll not be raped to death or made a slave. When the time comes, I'll kill myself."

Roger didn't say anything. Killing oneself was a sin, but in this case it was the right thing to do. God would understand.

She wiped her eye. "Now I better go look after those children. I may not see you again, Roger, so . . . good luck."

"Thank you, Mathilde." Roger took her shoulders and kissed her cool, damp forehead. "Good luck to you, as well. Perhaps I'll see you in Heaven tomorrow evening."

"It's like to be a bit crowded up there," she cracked.

"I'll keep an eye out for you, anyway."

She left. Roger ate quickly and made a circuit of the wall. Cauldrons of water simmered over fires in preparation for the morrow. Few of the men slept. They were quiet, reflective, talking and laughing in low tones. Reminiscing. Some sat by themselves, staring into the past.

He climbed the steps to the tower. A fire had been built on the tower's fighting platform. Men sat around it, Tatwine and Fauston and some of the old hands. Rob and Tiny John were there, Pentecost and Yves. Wulfhere and Leuthard. In the darkness, the flickering fire illuminated the men's faces from the bottom.

Someone played a mournful tune on a tin whistle.

To Roger's utter lack of surprise, the men by the fire were passing a jug of arrack. "Don't reckon drinking makes much difference this time," Tatwine said as Roger sat beside him.

"Don't reckon it does," Roger agreed. "Ready for the morrow?"

"Got no regrets," Tatwine said. "I should've been dead in that first attack on Acre. Would've been, hadn't been for you. All the rest has been a blessing. Fun, good food and drink, beautiful women."

"You been fightin' the same war we have?" Slowfoot asked him. "Cause I don't remember none of them things."

Tatwine passed the jug to Roger, who took a sip and marveled. "After all this time, you finally found some decent liquor?"

"Better late than never," Tatwine said.

Roger passed the jug to Fauston on his right. Amidst laughter and crude remarks, Tatwine and the others began arguing about whether Wulfhere's voluminous beard contained more bugs or food, and whether there would be so many bugs if there wasn't so much food.

Roger ignored the conversation. He remembered all the men who weren't there. Young Cole, the gongfermer's son, Egbert—poor Egbert, Grandad, Blackie, Hake, Father Mayne, Bald Matthew the cook, James of Claire, Deaf Martin, and William—William, who'd promised to bring his sister a Saracen princess from the Holy Land. Their faces were blurred; he couldn't see them clearly anymore.

And Helvise. Helvise, whom he'd loved.

He'd be with them soon.

The jug came round again. He drank and handed it to Fauston. "Sorry I put you through this," he said to his friend.

Fauston shrugged. "If I'd stayed at home, I'd probably be hanged by now, or dead from cold and wet. Never figured I'd live to an old age." He sighed. "Plus, I got to meet . . ."

"Your woman?" Roger said.

Fauston nodded. "Never knew what love was before her. Not even with Mary."

"Who is she? You can tell me now, it doesn't matter."

Fauston hesitated. "It's Bonjute, the earl of Trent's wife."

Roger's eyes widened. "You're serious?"

Fauston nodded again.

"But . . . how did you . . .?"

"She came into my shop one day. I saved her from a mob, and things went from there."

"But Bonjute is a . . ."

Fauston shook his head. "She's nothing like people think she is. She's warm and loving, sensitive. The other bit is an act she puts on for the world."

"She does a damn good job of it," Roger said.

Fauston smiled. "She does at that."

Roger stared at Fauston. "You really love her, don't you?"

321

"I really do. I want to spend the rest of my life with her, but I guess that's not going to happen. I'd give anything to see her one more time before . . . you know."

They both sat silent. The haunting, mournful tune kept playing on the tin whistle. It sounded familiar somehow, and suddenly Roger knew where he'd heard it before.

It was "Girls of Falaise." Played slowly, like a dirge. Its deep, melancholy air was completely at odds with its usual jaunty lilt. Roger liked it better this way.

Roger realized he had forgotten something.

He rose. "Find Gautier. Bring him here. Quickly."

There was a wait, then Gautier appeared at the head of the stairs leading to the tower. Roger motioned the men around him to rise.

"Kneel," he told Gautier.

Gautier frowned as though he hadn't understood. "What?"

"Kneel!" Roger ordered.

With some trepidation, Gautier got to his knees, obviously wondering what he'd done to incur Roger's wrath.

Roger advanced and slapped Gautier hard across the cheek. "Accept this blow and no others."

Gautier shook his head unsteadily, blinking.

"Rise, Gautier. You are a knight."

Roger handed Gautier to his feet as the men around them laughed and cheered. "Really?" Gautier said.

"Really." Roger smiled broadly. In theory, any knight could make a knight, and Roger was determined to make use of his prerogatives. "No one deserves it more than you."

"Why . . . why, thank you, Roger. This means a lot." He couldn't help but grin. "Me, a knight. Me, who was never more than a vintenar."

"Sorry I've no lands to give you," Roger said.

"That's all right." Gautier jerked a thumb toward the Saracen camp. "Wouldn't keep 'em long, anyway."

As the men crowded round Gautier, congratulating him, a horn sounded the call for Mass. Ambrose said Mass for the citadel's garrison and the civilians in the courtyard. All heard and received Communion, save for the guards on the tower and the wall. When Ambrose was finished, he visited the wall and tower, blessing the guards and giving them Communion, as well.

After Mass, Roger and the other men put on their armor. As Roger's helmet was laced on, the first light of dawn showed in the east. The rumbling wheels of the battering ram could be heard, along with the tramping of feet.

"Not wasting any time, is he?" Fauston asked Roger.

"Didn't expect him to," Roger replied.

They made their way to the wall.

Chapter 47

𝕿HE CIVILIANS AND children had already been sent to the storerooms and dungeon on the tower's bottom floors. Roger held a quick meeting with his commanders in the courtyard, or bailey. "The signal to abandon the wall will be three trumpet blasts," he told them. "Slowfoot, how many axe men do you have left?"

"Eight that can fight," Slowfoot replied.

"Hold the tower doors. Don't let anybody bar them before we're all in."

Slowfoot jogged to the tower entrance; the rest of the men took their places on the wall. Roger's position was above the gate, along with Tatwine, Fauston, and a frightened young trumpeter. "Don't get yourself killed," Roger told the boy, "because I can't play that trumpet."

The scared boy laughed in spite of himself.

From outside the wall, came the long wail of an oriental horn, followed by the rhythmic pounding of kettle drums.

With a cheer, columns of Saracens emerged from the streets. They attacked along the entire wall, with ladders. The battering ram was hauled up to the gate. Roger saw Qaymaz in the midst of the attackers, riding his black horse, urging his men on. Beside Roger, Rob snapped a bow shot at Qaymaz, but Qaymaz wheeled his horse at the last second to give a command and the arrow sailed harmlessly behind him. Rob swore. Roger wished he had Helvise's crossbow, but it was long gone. Alarmed, one of Qaymaz's aides told him that he had just been missed by an arrow, and Qaymaz trotted out of range.

The first ladders to reach the wall were pushed away, the men at the bottom of the wall scalded like bugs with boiling water or pelted with rocks by the defenders. Rob's archers plied their bows, and at this distance almost every arrow hit a target. The battering ram crashed into the gate, making it shudder, before its crew was taken out by boiling water.

The second wave of ladders hit the wall. Some were pushed away, but men made it to the top of others. They were struck down with axes and swords and spiked clubs. A fresh crew manned the battering ram, and the gate cracked from their exertions before they, too, went down.

The third wave of ladders struck. There were too many ladders and not enough defenders, and before long the first Saracens were over the parapet and onto the wall's walkway.

Trying to sound calm, Roger turned to the young trumpeter. "Sound the call."

Following Roger's example and trying to be calm, the trumpeter raised his horn and blew three long notes.

"Withdraw!" Roger cried. The order was echoed all along the wall. "Withdraw!"

The men disengaged and hurried down the steps to the bailey. The wounded had to be left behind. There was a running fight across the bailey to where Slowfoot and his men held the door. A crash signaled that the gate had given way, and Saracens poured through the opening, cheering.

A Saracen rushed up to Roger. Roger bashed the man with his shield, staggering him, then thrust his long dagger under the man's breastbone. The citadel door was up a flight of stone steps, then a right turn into a small outbuilding. Once in the outbuilding, a sharp left turn led to the door that entered the tower itself. Roger stood at the foot of the steps waving his men up them and through the first door. "Hurry! Hurry!"

As Yves neared the steps he was hit in the ear by an arrow. He dropped to the ground, screaming. Pentecost stopped, lifted him to his feet, and half-carried him up the steps.

Roger looked back. The ten or so Templars in Leuthard's command hadn't left the wall. They fought together there until they were all dead, leaving a pile of Saracen bodies around them.

The Hospitallers followed the Templar example, forming a circle in the bailey and taking on the Saracens there. While they did, the last men time raced up the steps and into the tower. Roger was the final one in. "All right," he told the man at the door, who dropped the metal bar. They turned left and entered the second door. Roger left Slowfoot and his axe men to defend the door and he climbed the winding stairs to the tower roof, squeezing past the soldiers manning the stairs.

Below, the Hospitallers were all dead, their black-robed bodies lying in an almost perfect circle, surrounded by the bodies of their enemies. Saracens looted and cut up the Christian corpses, while Rob, Tiny John, and the rest of the archers shot arrows at them.

Other Saracens started for the first door and began chopping at it with axes. The Saracen catapults opened fire from across the city ditch. The very first rock scored a direct hit on the tower's fighting platform, crushing five men, fracturing the platform's floor, and knocking down the pole that held the Death's Head flag. Another Saracen rock hit the tower's side, dislodging stones. A fireball landed on the tower's platform, setting it ablaze. The Saracens in the bailey began shouting and cheering at the flag's disappearance, thinking that the garrison had surrendered.

Roger struggled to his feet through the smoke and dust and confusion. Blood ran across the platform. Men rushed to put out the fire. The tower shuddered from another hit from the catapults. "Help me," Roger told Tatwine.

They untied the flag from its fallen staff and hung it from the side of the tower. The men on the tower cheered now. "We ain't finished yet," Fauston shouted.

But they would be soon. There was a crash below as the Saracens hacked through the first door and started on the next.

"Here, what's that?" cried the archer Red Will. His broken left arm was in a sling, and with his right he pointed out to sea, where a fleet of galleys approached. One of the galleys was painted red, and three gold lions were sewn onto its red sail.

Chapter 48

THE GALLEYS RACED toward the embattled city. They were spread in a fan-like formation, each one making the best speed it could, oars rising and falling, bow waves churning, King Richard's red ship, *Eleanor*, in the lead. There were thirty-four of them, or had been yesterday. Two had disappeared or fallen behind during the night.

Richard stood on *Eleanor*'s forecastle, wearing his red surcoat and new silk slippers, a gift from his wife. His hair was tousled from sleeping in the lee of the ship's bulwark and crusted with sea spray. Beside him were Alart of Vouzin and Andrew of Chauvigny, along with the earl of Leicester and one-eyed Henry of Deraa. Richard's liege men Ralph of Mauleon, Robert of Saci, and about forty other knights were scattered through the fleet, along with a force of Pisan naval infantry and Genoese crossbowmen, about two thousand men in all. *Cats and dogs living together,* Richard smiled as he thought of the Pisans and Genoese, who were traditional enemies. It was all the force he had been able to scrape together at such short notice. The crossbowmen had actually been boarding transports for home when they were diverted for Jaffa. Henry of Champagne was supposed to be following with reinforcements, but Richard had no idea when he would get here.

Northbound vessels had told Richard's fleet that the city had fallen. At first, Richard refused to believe it, but now . . .

The ships slowed. Ahead of them, smoke hung over the city, making it hard to see what was going on. To their left was a large camp—Saladin's it must be, judging by the cut of the tents. Saracen soldiers dotted the shore, watching the ships. There was no sign of the city's garrison or, indeed, of any Christians.

Richard's heart sank.

The wind shifted, lifting the smoke and revealing a large blue flag flying from the largest of the city's towers.

"Qaymaz," swore Henry of Deraa.

Alart said, "We are too late, sire. The garrison is dead or led away."

"We'd best turn back," said Andrew. "We've not enough men to recapture the city, and 'twould be folly to attempt a landing."

Andrew was right. Saladin had outwitted Richard again. He'd outwitted him at every turn, since the day he had arrived in the Holy Land. This was just another humiliation to take home with him.

Richard turned. "Captain, prepare to go about."

Suddenly Henry of Deraa grabbed Richard's sleeve. "Look there, sire. The citadel tower. What is that hanging there?"

Richard squinted. Even with his repeated illnesses, he had the best eyes in the army.

"A flag?" Alart suggested.

"By God, it is a flag," Richard said. "Why, I'd know that banner anywhere." He thumped Henry's chest with the back of his hand. "It belongs to your son's Death's Heads."

Gravedigger Leicester pounded the forecastle rail. "The city hasn't fallen, after all. There are still men holding out."

Richard didn't have to think what to do next. He turned again and shouted to the rear of the ship. "Captain! Battle speed! All the way to shore."

The Cypriot captain scratched his jaw doubtfully. "That's a long pull at battle speed, sire. The men—"

"I don't care, do it. Signal the rest of the ships to do the same."

Across the fleet of galleys, drums beat. Spray flew over the bows as the ships picked up speed. Men hurriedly began arming themselves. Richard only had time to don his gambeson and hauberk. There would be no leggings or mail coif, or even shoes; he would go to battle wearing his new slippers. He placed a flat-cap helmet over a cotton coif.

On the shore, surprised Saracens scrambled to meet them. Footmen hurried to the beach. A few horsemen rode into the water, loosing arrows at the oncoming ships.

The drums beat more loudly. Closer to the shore they came.

"Ship oars!" the captain cried.

The half-dead sailors drew their heavy oars inboard. *Eleanor* drifted to shore, propelled by its momentum and the waves. Richard and his men gathered in the waist, bracing themselves for the shock when the vessel ran aground.

The ship struck the shore with a jarring thud. Men staggered. Gear fell from the rigging.

"Now!" Richard cried.

Grabbing his axe, he vaulted the ship's side, landing waist deep in the warm water. He waded toward the shore, Henry of Deraa, Alart, and the other men following him amidst a hail of arrows.

Chapter 49

SHIELD RAISED TO deflect the arrows, Richard headed for the beach. He stumbled as an incoming wave caught his legs, and he stumbled again as the wave pulled back, but he regained his balance quickly. Henry of Deraa and Leicester were right behind him, followed by Alart, Andrew, and the Pisan footmen from his ship. Behind him was a crunch as another ship grounded on the shore and men jumped from it.

The Saracens might have mounted a successful counterattack had they acted quickly, but their units were too jumbled up, and they were too stunned by this attack from seemingly out of nowhere to organize themselves. Plus, many were exhausted from their sack of the city.

Richard reached the beach and plowed into the Saracens waiting there, flailing left and right with his Danish axe, Deraa and Leicester to either side of him. The Saracens fell back, terrified of these bearded apparitions. Saracen horsemen approached, but crossbowmen from the next ship picked them off.

More ships landed, more men waded into the fight. The Saracen footmen resisted briefly, then fled. Horsemen charged the Christians, loosing arrows, but were driven off by the Genoese crossbowmen with heavy losses.

Richard and his men advanced up the beach, while more men poured from the incoming ships. William of Mello's young squire,

Ançon, the one who had brought news of the attack to Acre, tripped and fell on his face in the surf. He was unable to get back up because of the heavy armor he had borrowed, and, unseen in the confusion, he drowned in five feet of water.

Richard waved Ralph of Mauleon over. "Build a barricade—there, at the head of the beach."

Covered by the crossbowmen, the Pisan naval infantry threw together a barricade made from pieces of abandoned boats, wagons, barrels, driftwood—anything they found along the littered shore. The crossbowmen picked off any Saracen who came within range of this barricade, and pretty soon none dared try. Chests of spare crossbow bolts were being carried ashore from the ships' holds.

When the barricade was in serviceable condition, Richard said to Ralph, "You're in command here. Keep working on the barricade. If we're forced to fall back, this is where we'll make a stand. In the meantime have your archers keep up a fire on those fellows."

Ralph was clearly disappointed at being left behind, but he nodded. "Yes, sire."

Richard left Ralph with the crossbowmen and about a third of the Pisan spearmen. He quickly organized the rest and led them along the pebbly beach to the port. They moved along the mole, which was strewn with mangled, rotting bodies, killing any Saracens they encountered. There was a dead monk nailed to a cross, and they cut him down. Richard didn't recognize the man who had interrupted Lady Hugoline's banquet, searching for a witch.

They found an open postern gate in the city wall and entered. Like the mole, the city streets were littered with bodies—men, women, children, pigs, dogs. The gutters were clogged with congealing blood. In the heat, the smell after four days of battle was overwhelming. The streets were also filled with unsuspecting Saracens, and Richard and his men fell upon them with fervor. Those who weren't killed fled in panic, jamming the narrow pathways and opening themselves to even more slaughter from the pursuing Christians.

❧

The fight for the citadel tower had reached the lower part of the stairs, and Roger's men were being driven slowly upwards. The tower's fighting platform was a shambles, knocked to pieces by rocks from the catapults, repeatedly set ablaze and put out, dead and wounded piled against the battlements, blood and discarded equipment everywhere.

Roger and what was left of his men watched Richard's landing and the fight on the beach. Because of all the buildings and the steep hill, they couldn't see what was happening in the lower town, but they noted large numbers of Saracens fleeing the city.

Roger's blood was up. "Our turn now, lads."

The newly knighted Gautier said, "I know a postern gate that will take us to the courtyard."

"Let's go, then."

Roger led his men past the weary line of defenders on the stairs. They charged down the stairs, pushing the Saracens back, leaving the stairs littered with bodies and slippery with blood, and more than one man fell on the wet stone. They pushed on to the lower floors, from whence they heard screams and cries. The Saracens had gotten down there and were killing the women and children. Roger's men fell on the Saracens from behind, and no quarter was given.

When the Saracens on the lower floors were all dead, Roger and his men continued on to the dungeon. Gautier showed them a passage from there, and Roger realized it was the same passage he'd taken when he'd escaped from the dungeon what seemed like ages ago.

They followed the passage, went up several flights of steps, and reached the door that opened onto the courtyard. Before them, a mob of Saracens pressed round the tower entrance, where fighting still raged. Other Saracens milled behind the first group in the courtyard, waiting for their chance. These men must not know about King Richard's landing. If any of them wondered why their catapults had suddenly stopped shooting, it wasn't apparent.

Roger turned, breathing hard. Fauston was behind him, along with Tatwine, Gautier, Pentecost, and the others—all of them wild eyed.

"Ready?" Roger said. "Let's go."

They charged into the courtyard, attacking the Saracens from behind. Killing them with swords and axes, with daggers and sharpened shovels and cut-down spears. Roger's hauberk was so rusty and clogged with dried blood and gore that he could barely work his arms till fresh blood lubricated the mail.

The frantic Saracens tried to turn around, but it was difficult because they were so packed together, and the vengeful Christians slaughtered them. Roger's men were all jumbled together—Death's Heads, Turcos, civilians, city guards, soldiers of the kingdom. There was no order, just a desire to avenge their dead.

Then Short Peter led a party through the citadel door and attacked the Saracens who had finally gotten themselves turned to face Roger's men. Those Saracens who were not killed fled as best they could, many of them throwing down shields and weapons and helmets so they could run faster. The Christians chased them, cutting them down without mercy. They pursued them through the citadel gate and into the streets. Roger led a party down the Street of St. James until the Saracens he was chasing ran into Christian soldiers advancing from the other direction. The Saracens wailed in despair, seeking side streets, trying to hide in looted shops and houses, from whence the Christians dragged them out to be killed.

Leading the oncoming Christians was a huge, blood-spattered figure in a red surcoat with three lions embroidered on it. Behind him was a rangy knight with one eye.

"Sire," Roger said.

He started to drop to one knee, but Richard caught his arm and lifted him up. "Huntley, it's good to see you. Was it you who hung that flag from the wall?"

"It was, sire."

"Good work. If it hadn't been for that, we would have turned back for Acre." Richard looked around. "Where is William of Mello?"

"Dead, sire," Roger said.

Richard bit his lip, and Roger went on. "I'm the senior captain left, so I'm in command of the city."

"Are you now? You seem to have made a good job of it." Then Richard grinned. "Well, don't just stand there, boy, say hello to your father."

Henry held Roger at arm's length, his good eye filled with joy and pride, and maybe a tear. "I thought you were dead."

"We came close," Roger told him.

Henry noted the grim look on Roger's face. "What's wrong?"

Roger drew Henry away from the others. "It's Ailith," Roger said. "Qaymaz has her. He brought her to the wall before the attack to show me."

"Christ on the cross," Henry swore. "How did he—?

"She was trying to come here overland, and he caught her."

"Overland? That's madness. Was she by herself?"

Roger spread his hands. "As far as I know. She was dressed as a man. I didn't recognize her at first."

"She must have been in one Devil of a hurry to leave Acre if she came overland."

Roger said nothing.

"Maybe we can ransom her," Henry said. "I've got—"

"Qaymaz as much as told me that's not possible. He intends to make her queen of his *harim*. I think the bastard actually loves her, if he's capable of an emotion like love." He paused. "Barring a miracle, I fear she's lost to me forever."

Henry put a hand on Roger's shoulder. "Don't give up, son. Saladin will die soon, and there's going to be a fight for his throne. There must be a lot of people on the other side who want Qaymaz dead. If anything happens to him, maybe we can ransom Ailth back from his son."

Roger wasn't cheered. "His son is as liable to kill her as to ransom her—you know how things go out here. Or to take her for his own."

Then Henry had an idea. "You've been to the Blue Fort. Could you find it again?"

"I think so. Why?"

"Perhaps we could mount a raid—"

Behind them, King Richard cleared his throat. "I hate to interrupt this reunion, but I need a horse."

Roger looked over his shoulder. "Tatwine."

"I heard," Tatwine said. He turned and jogged off.

Richard's burly companion Robert of Saci came up the street, carrying a folded blue bundle that he handed to Richard. "Qaymaz's flag. I cut it down from the tower."

Richard looked at the flag and laughed. "I'll give it to Qaymaz when next I see him. I can't wait to see the expression on his face." Richard looked around and picked out one of the youngsters who had been fighting with Roger. He beckoned. "Boy."

The blood-covered boy came forward, wide eyed and maybe a bit afraid. "Sire?"

"Run down to my ship." Richard pointed to the beach. "It's the big red one. Have my steward give you one of my banners. Bring it back, and my lord of Saci here will hang it from the tower."

"Yes, sire," the boy said.

Richard patted the boy's shoulder. "There's a good lad."

The boy turned and ran off.

Before long, Tatwine and Slowfoot returned with Roger's two horses and a nag they had found somewhere. The king mounted Roger's bay with the black mane, Leicester took the chestnut, and Alart took the nag. "Come," Richard said, "We've tarried long enough. Leave us go amongst the enemy. Huntley, you'll join us?"

Roger was so tired he could hardly stand, but he said, "It will be my pleasure, sire."

Riding his new mount, Richard led the way down the street to the city wall. Horns blew and the men assembled, and, to a great cheer, Richard's banner was hung from the tower by the Acre Gate. On the other side of the ditch, the Saracens gathered, still disorganized, men searching for their units, with Qaymaz and the other emirs riding around and trying to get them back into something resembling an army. The catapults had begun firing at the city again. One rock hit the citadel tower, knocking off a corner.

"Where's that boy?" Richard cried.

The boy who had gone for Richard's banner presented himself, and Richard said, "My compliments to the lord of Mauleon. Have his crossbowmen form behind us. Have him leave his spearmen at the barricade should we be forced to retreat."

The boy took off again.

A rock from a catapult landed in a street just behind a party of Richard's men. "Too close for comfort," Richard said. "All right," he cried. "Cross the ditch and form a line. Lively, now."

The men surged through the destroyed city gate and the breach in the wall, crossing the ditch and lining up on the other side, chasing away the Saracens manning the catapults. The crossbowmen joined from the barricade and fell in behind.

Richard rode in front of the Christian line, axe in his belt, sword raised. "Advance!"

The line moved toward the Saracen army. Richard's force was outnumbered, but the Saracens didn't attack. They were either too disorganized or too scared. Roger and his men were at the far right of the line, where they would have to deal with any flanking attack. Roger's men were all in from days of fighting, but they kept up the pace, not wanting to lag behind in the face of the famous English king.

The line drew closer to the enemy.

"Halt!" Richard cried. "Crossbows! Shoot!"

The five hundred or so crossbowmen fired a volley into the massed Saracens, dropping men all over.

"Advance!"

Spears lowered, the Christian line advanced. The Saracens edged backwards.

"Halt! Crossbows! Shoot!"

Another volley of crossbow bolts.

"Advance!"

Onward the line went. Roger watched Richard. Richard was in his element. He was having fun. This was what he was born for—not negotiation, not statesmanship. War. War, plain and simple.

"Halt! Crossbows—shoot!"

Another volley. More Saracens went down.

"Advance!"

The lines were close. With a cry, Richard spurred his horse at the Saracens, joined by Leicester and Alart. The other knights raced forward on foot, yelling, Roger with them, while the footmen followed, keeping formation. The knights hit the Saracens, weapons flashing, and at that point, the Saracens ran. In the distance, Saladin's camp was being struck, the tents taken down, camels and beasts of burden streaming north.

Richard and his men pursued the Saracens as far as Saladin's old camp, killing any who were not quick enough to get away. Richard halted his men there. He was shown the spot where Saladin's tent had stood that morning. "Then this is where I shall camp tonight," he announced gleefully, like he was playing a joke on the sultan.

Alart of Vouzin said, "Sire, is that wise? We are in the open here, and Saladin has a formidable force."

"Nonsense. Old Sidesaddle won't attack us. Like as not, he'll go haring back to Jerusalem at dawn, before we can finish him off. Besides, where else would we camp? We can't quarter in the city—it's destroyed. And there's water here."

"I suppose you're right, sire."

"Of course I am." Richard peered about. "Where is that squire of Huntley's?"

Tatwine stepped forward. "Here, sire."

"See if you can find us some food," Richard told him.

"Yes, sire," Tatwine said.

As Tatwine started off, Richard shouted after him. "Find me some proper shoes, too. These damned slippers are killing my feet."

Chapter 50

NEITHER ARMY MOVED on the following morning. Richard had expected the Saracens to retreat, but they stayed in place, their camp about five miles distant from his own.

Richard, Alart, and the earl of Leicester studied the Saracen camp from horseback. They armed themselves and approached as near as they dared without provoking the mounted Saracen patrols. They didn't need to do this, but Richard always enjoyed an act of bravado. Then they returned to camp, where they took council with the army's other leaders. Roger was present, as commander of the city. The little group occupied the rise where Saladin had camped the night before and stared over the plain toward the Saracen lines.

"We should build a ditch to protect our camp," Ralph of Mauleon cautioned Richard. Ralph shaved his head to hide the fact that he was going bald.

"No," Richard said. "Saladin won't attack, he's beaten. I'd finish him off, but I can't do that with fifty knights and only three horses." He spoke without rancor. Here was a chance to turn failure into triumph, to right all the reversals of the last year. He could win the war—right here, right now—but fate was denying him the opportunity. That was the story of his crusade, though, and he had resigned himself to it.

"He doesn't look like he's running away," Ralph said.

"He will," Richard said confidently. "This is just for show. He's pretending he hasn't been beaten as badly as he has been."

"So what are we to do?" asked Leicester.

Richard shrugged. "There's nothing we *can* do. We'll have to let them get away."

Leicester still hoped for a fight. "Burgundy's bringing the main army by land, isn't he?"

"Saladin will retreat before they get close," Richard told him. "He's not foolish enough to risk battle with our main force."

Richard turned to other matters. "We'll clean up the city and repair the fortifications, in case Saladin comes back after we leave. That's all we can do."

Roger spoke up. "There's no mortar or lime for the wall, sire. Any repairs will have to be temporary."

"They need only last until the peace is signed," Alart of Vouzin assured him.

The council broke up, and remainder of the day was given to burnishing arms and armor, then cleaning up the city and repairing its fortifications. Henry of Champagne arrived with two ships, bring an extra five knights and a hundred men.

As commander of the city, Roger was in charge of the cleanup, while his father volunteered to oversee the fortifications. Roger put Ailith from his mind as best he could. There was much to be done. He left Tatwine to clean his armor, which was going to be a lengthy job. Tatwine examined Roger's blood-, gore-, and dirt-stiffened hauberk. Roger assumed that Tatwine would wash the hauberk in the ocean, then soak it in oil and polish it. It's what Roger would have done. "Before we leave the Holy Land, I'm knighting you," he told Tatwine.

Tatwine lowered the hauberk. "Oh, come on, Roger, I don't want to be a knight. I didn't even want to be a squire."

"You've been a squire long enough. It's time for you to move up. Besides, being a knight will help with that tavern of yours. You'll be able to attract the quality trade, instead of thieves and murderers."

Tatwine scratched his cheek. "Quality trade? That means quality whores, right?"

"It does, indeed."

A broad smile crept over Tatwine's elfin face.

"Of course you'll need a title," Roger went on. "'Tatwine of—' where's your home, anyway?"

"Shitte Lane."

"That may not work. 'Tatwine of Badford'—that will have to do. No—'Tatwine of Jaffa.' Now that sounds impressive. Mysterious. Should help with those quality whores."

Tatwine thought of something. "What about fighting? Don't knights have to . . .?"

"Lots of knights don't fight. You pay somebody to take your place. Happens all the time. You could even send some whores in your place. Any army would welcome that."

Leaving Tatwine with the armor, Roger gathered his men. Short Peter couldn't be found, nor could Leuthard, and that had Roger worried. The men were still caked in blood and grime. They could bathe in the ocean later, but that would have to wait. Right now, they had to return to the city.

Acrid smoke lingered in low-lying places throughout the city. Buildings had been destroyed—doors and awnings ripped down, roofs charred, broken furniture in the streets. Bodies lay everywhere—Saracens, Christians, civilians—some of the bodies charred, as well. The buzzing of flies was an angry drone. The city smelled of shit and rotting flesh and burning. It was useless to try to avoid walking through all the congealed blood, so Roger gave up. His feet squelched at each step, leaving sticky tracks in the few spots that weren't covered with blood.

The newer men were appalled by what they saw, and a young Turco got sick. "How could anyone do this?" he asked as he straightened and wiped vomit from his sparsely bearded chin.

"It's no different than we'd do if we took one of their cities," the Turco commander Espiart told the boy grimly. "Now pull yourself together."

"Start with the streets," Roger ordered his centenars. "Bury the Christian dead in the churchyards. Throw the Saracen bodies and the dead animals in the city ditch and burn them."

"Aye," snarled the bushy bearded centenar Wulfhere, "mix the Goat Fuckers in with the dead pigs and dogs."

"Some o' them pigs ain't been dead that long," Slowfoot pointed out. "Maybe we could cut 'em up and cook 'em. Ain't all that much food about, and I'm sick of camel."

Wulfhere made a face. "I ain't sure I'd do—"

"It'll be all right," Fauston told Wulfhere. "I ate worse when I lived in the forest, believe me, and all of us had worse during the siege." To Slowfoot, he said, "Just be careful which pigs you choose."

While the men began cleaning the streets, Roger and Fauston made their way to the citadel. Like the rest of the city, the citadel's walls and bailey were littered with bodies. City guards carried more bodies from inside and lay them in rows, separating the Christians from the Saracens.

As Roger had feared, his father's man Leuthard was among the dead. So was Short Peter, his helmet and skull caved in. Roger stared at Peter's body. It seemed like he'd known Shorty all his life. "Poor bastard made it almost to the end," Fauston said, echoing Roger's thoughts. "Then . . ." His voice tailed off.

Yves was in the tower's first-floor hall, with the wounded. Pentecost was with him. The arrow had been pulled from Yves' ear, but he was feverish and pale. "He'll be with his wife and kids by tonight," Pentecost murmured to Roger.

Roger went outside. Voice cracking, he called, "Gautier!"

The gamey-eyed old soldier came up, and Roger regained control of himself. "You're in charge of the citadel."

"Very well," Gautier said.

"Get it cleaned up and ready to withstand another attack, should there be one."

Gautier beckoned with his fingers. The apple-cheeked boy who had brought Richard's banner from the beach came up. "I'd like to make Milo here my squire. With your permission."

"You don't need my permission," Roger said. "You're a knight, you can pick any squire you choose."

And just like that, the street urchin Milo found himself on the path to possible knighthood.

The surviving civilians from the lower floors of the citadel were camped in the wrecked hall of the governor's palace, many with vacant, shocked looks on their faces. Mathilde was trying to get them organized. Roger hugged her. "Mathilde, I'm glad you're alive."

"I'm lucky," Mathilde said. "Beggars didn't have time to get to me before you attacked 'em." Despite all she'd been through, she managed to look fresh, her hair neatly pulled back.

Roger indicated the rest of civilians. "How are they doing?"

"They'll come round. I'll get the ones in the best shape to help with the cleanup and bring food and water to the men. The others can watch the children."

Roger said, "About the children. The ones we brought here with you . . .?"

Mathilde nodded her chin at Fauston. "The wee one he carried is fine."

Roger said, "And the little girl that rode on my squire's shoulders?"

Mathilde met his eyes and said nothing.

Roger hung his head.

Pentecost appeared. To Roger he said, "If it's all right with you, Roger, I'll lend the lady here a hand with the civilians. Then maybe we can both help with the wounded."

Mathilde frowned at Pentecost. "You a doctor?"

"No, but I was a slave to the Goat—to our gallant enemies, and when you're a slave, you learn a lot about doctorin'. Out of necessity."

"I'll vouch for his abilities," Roger said. "Go ahead, then. Stay here with Mathilde."

Leaving the rest of the men behind to clean up, Roger and Fauston went to the cathedral. Roger dreaded what he would find there, but reality turned out to be far worse than anything his imagination had conjured. The stench gave it away before they got there. Roger drew the keffiyeh over the lower part of his face; Fauston buried his mouth and nose in his forearm.

The cathedral nave was a charnel house. Bodies, pieces of bodies, half-dried blood, hordes of plump, green-and-black flies buzzing. The statues in the church had been broken apart, everything behind the rood wrecked. After much searching, Roger found the body of the infirmarian, Anselm. He could only identify him by his wispy grey hair. Anselm's eyes had been gouged out. Some of his fingers had been chopped off to get at his rings. He'd been gutted and his chest cavity crawled with maggots.

Roger crossed himself, bowed his head, and said a prayer. Fauston walked away, unable to look.

The Death's Heads' chaplain, Ambrose, was in the church yard, supervising burial of the bodies. Ambrose wore a filthy linen shirt; he hadn't had time to look for his vestments. The Saracens had disinterred some of the previously buried bodies and chopped them up. Ambrose helped re-bury these men, while volunteers dug mass graves for the new bodies. Civilians were being buried here, as well. Because of the bodies' condition, it was difficult to differentiate between the Christian and Muslim civilians, so they were all buried together, and Ambrose prayed over them. "I'll find a Muslim holy man later and get him to pray over the grave as well," Ambrose told Roger.

"Now I've got to go to the next church and do the same thing. Every church yard in the city will be full by nightfall."

Roger and Fauston left the cathedral. They gazed a while over the city, and beyond that, the clean, sparkling sea. "What a business," Fauston said at last. "Hard to believe either of our gods condones what we're doing here."

After a moment, Roger said, "Everyone says the war is over. Maybe you'll get to see Bonjute again after all."

Fauston nodded.

Roger went on. It felt strange to speak of the earl's wife by her first name. He had always thought of her as "countess" or "her ladyship." "Will Bonjute be returning to England, or will she . . .?"

"I tried to get her to run away and stay here with me, but she refuses," Fauston said. "She won't go back on her marriage vow."

"What if, God forbid, the earl dies?"

"That would change everything, but there's not much chance of that happening."

"At least you'll see her before she leaves," Roger said. "I'll never see Ailith again."

Chapter 51

THE ATMOSPHERE IN the sultan's tent was tense—and nervous. Commanders had been executed for the kind of disaster that had befallen the army yesterday. The sultan paced back and forth, head down, hands clasped behind his back. He wore a tunic of dark crimson silk—so dark it was almost black—with no embroidery. His white turban lacked jewels or adornment of any kind. There was no refreshment for his guests, which boded ill. No fruit, no sherbet, no sugared almonds. There was no incense. No slaves with fans. The sides of the tent were rolled up, which meant that the guards and servants outside could hear what the sultan was saying, as Qaymaz assumed they were meant to. They would report Saladin's rage, and any penalties he might impose, to the rest of the army.

The sultan suddenly halted and wheeled to face his commanders, hand on the hilt of his sword. "We lost Jaffa to a handful of men and three horses. Three!"

He paused to let that sink in. "You ran from them. Ran like rabbits. You have humiliated yourselves, you have humiliated me. Most of all, you have humiliated your faith. Do you for one instant imagine that Allah looks favorably upon any of us today? Do you?"

No one spoke. Most stood with their heads lowered, staring at the carpeted tent floor and hoping the sultan would let them live.

Only Qaymaz, Saladin's brother, al-Adil, and al-Afdal, the Bull, had the courage to meet the sultan's gaze.

Saladin went on. "My lord Qaymaz, I expected better of your men. I expected better of you. Your men bore the brunt of the infidel attack, and they barely put up a fight."

Qaymaz said nothing. There was nothing he could say; it was true. Saladin went on. "Lord Meshtub. Your division took no part in the battle. You could have attacked the feringhees in the flank. You could have attacked them from behind. You could have done *something*. Why did you choose not to?"

Meshtub, former commander of the Acre garrison, bowed humbly. "Your pardon, lord, but my men were in no condition to fight. They had been plundering the city and were mixed in with men from the other divisions. I tried to get them organized, but—"

"So you freely admit you let your men become disorganized in the face of the enemy? How could y—"

Al-Adil interrupted. "In all fairness, brother, Rik surprised us. We never expected him to appear—"

"Do not speak to me of Rik. Rik is one man. One. Can one man so terrify an entire army? And do not interrupt me again, *brother*."

Saladin went on, berating the other generals, pointing out what they could or should have done.

Qaymaz was in more trouble with the sultan than he'd ever been, but he had difficulty paying attention. His mind kept drifting away, to the feringhee woman. She consumed him. He wanted to be with her—he wanted to be *in* her—every moment of every day. It was driving him insane. He had never felt this way about a woman. He would do anything for her. He hated this weakness in himself, and yet he was fascinated by it because he had never experienced anything like it before. It revealed a part of him that he had never known existed. The fact that she hated him made it even better somehow. He would break her, like one breaks a wild horse, and eventually he would ride—

"Lord Qaymaz, am I boring you?" Saladin asked.

"What? No. No, lord. I was thinking."

He was thinking about Ailith, about her pale body beneath his.

"I trust you were thinking about a way to redeem yesterday's failure, since your men were chiefly to blame for the debacle."

Saladin had never spoken to him this harshly before. Qaymaz struggled to compose himself, because he did have a plan. "I was, lord, and I apologize for my men's performance. The blame rests entirely upon me, however, not on them."

That willingness to accept blame seemed to mollify Saladin a bit. Some of the edge went out of his voice. "You were distracted, perhaps?"

He knows. "I was, lord."

"That woman?"

There was a stir in the tent. The others turned and looked at Qaymaz. He held his head higher, refusing to show shame, not because he was too proud, but because he was not ashamed of Ailith or the way he felt about her.

"Yes, lord, and for that I am sorry. I let my emotions interfere with the performance of my duties."

There was a low gasp from the crowd. Men of Qaymaz's position were not expected to be so forthright about such things. Qaymaz went

351

on. "I have an idea, lord. One that, if it works, will more than make up for yesterday's embarrassment."

Saladin gestured for him to continue.

"My spies report that the feringhee camp is lightly guarded. I do not know why; the fools must not fear us. The feringhees have only one tent. Rik sleeps in it, along with his chief emirs."

Saladin leaned forward, eyes gleaming. "Chief emirs? Is the lord of Deraa with them?"

"He is, lord." Qaymaz paused and continued. "A surprise attack could take that tent, lord. We could kill Deraa and capture Rik and his other emirs. Then we could destroy their army and retake the city. Undo all that has been done."

Saladin's son al-Afdal looked scornfully at Qaymaz. He knew about the infidel woman, and he did not approve. "We should kill Rik and the infidel chiefs, not capture them."

Saladin raised a finger. "No. They will be more useful to us alive. I like this plan, Lord Qaymaz. When would you propose to carry it out?"

"Tonight," Qaymaz said.

Chapter 52

𝔉AUSTON HAD TO shit. Again.

The first thing an army did when it made camp was dig latrines. But the camp latrines were full, both with men and with their leavings. Perhaps because of his days of living in the forest, Fauston liked to be by himself at these times. He liked a bit of privacy. Even more, he liked a bit of fresh—and, to be honest, less noisome—air to breathe.

He shrugged off the jack beneath which he had been sleeping, rose from the ground and scurried beyond the camp lines. "Eat the pork," he had told them. "It will be all right," he had told them. What the hell had he been thinking? Bloody Tatwine had found some arrack that tasted like it had been fermented in the guts of a dead camel, and the pig that Slowfoot had cooked had definitely been tainted. And, like a fool, Fauston drank the arrack and ate the pig anyway.

"I had worse in the woods," he had bragged. "I had worse during the siege." He forgot that he had spent half the siege in the jakes, squirting his guts out.

Now here he was, his insides rumbling like a hangman's cart on cobblestones, for the third time since dinner. He picked his way in the dark, stumbling over brush, his joints stiff from sleeping rough. That's the way the army had camped, sleeping on the ground in their battle formation, arms to hand. King Richard and his men had been in too much of a hurry to load any baggage or supplies when they sailed from Acre, and the soldiers' tent city outside Jaffa had been destroyed by the Saracens. The only tent in Jaffa belonged to Roger, the one that had been saved by Tatwine. The king was using that, sleeping in a tent with a red Death's Head painted on it. It was said he quite fancied it.

Fauston found a dip in the earth. He undid his braies and squatted. Just in time.

He was sighing with relief when he heard voices nearby.

Two men arguing in low tones. They had different accents. Probably a Pisan and a Genoese fighting over a spot where they could relieve themselves—or over anything, really. The Pisans and Genoese loved to fight each other, God only knew why.

The two idiots were even further out from the camp than Fauston was. He strained his ears, trying to make out what they were saying. Then he realized they weren't speaking Italian. What, then? Not French. Hungarian, maybe? No. Welsh? Greek? No.

They were speaking Arabic.

Now he heard other noises. Clink of metal. Scrape of feet.

A lot of feet.

Christ.

He finished what he was doing and pulled up his braies, letting his hose hang round his ankles. He scrambled out of the dip and ran back to the camp, yelling as loud as he could.

"To arms! To arms! The Saracens are attacking!"

Chapter 53

ALARMS SOUNDED. HORNS blew.

King Richard awakened instantly. He grabbed his sword and ran out of the tent, clad only in his shirt.

"Arm yourselves!" he cried.

Deraa, Leicester, and the other nobles tumbled out of the tent behind him, carrying whatever weapons came to hand.

"To arms!" came the voice from the darkness again. "The Saracens are here!"

The footmen jostled into line, which was easy for them because they'd been sleeping in the same formation they had held at the end of yesterday's battle.

A figure bolted out of the dark, into the line of footmen. Men reached for him, ready to cut him down.

"Stop, I'm English!" the figure cried. He turned and pointed. "The Saracens are right behind me!"

"Let him go!" Richard shouted.

The figure headed for the Death's Head tent. Behind him some two hundred footmen appeared out of the darkness, chasing the fugitive. They stopped when they saw the waiting Christian line bristling with spears and other weapons. They hesitated, then drifted away, hurling curses at the Christians. Behind them could be heard the rumble of approaching horses.

"What's happening?" Alart of Vouzin asked as he came up. Alart had been sleeping naked and hadn't anything on.

Henry of Deraa, like Richard wearing only a shirt, lowered his sword. "Looks like a surprise attack to kill or capture the king. Looks like the rest of Saladin's army is coming behind them to kill the rest of us and take the city back."

"Cheeky buggers," said Andrew of Chauvigny.

Richard assessed the situation. "My guess is, they planned to attack this tent right at dawn, with the main force following behind. They counted on catching us leaderless and unprepared. Well, we've got a bit to go before dawn yet." He clapped Fauston's shoulder. "This fellow has bought us some time, and likely saved the army."

"It was luck, sire," said Fauston breathlessly.

"How many more are coming?" Richard asked Fauston. "Could you tell?"

Fauston straightened. "Their whole army, I think, sire. That's what it sounded like."

Squires appeared, shaking sleep from their eyes, hurriedly fetching arms and armor. A squire offered Richard a padded leather gambeson, but he pushed it away. "No time for that now," he said.

To Fauston, Richard said, "Good work, son. If we live through this, I'll see you're well rewarded. Now rejoin your unit."

Fauston started off, and Richard strode down the line of men. "Squires—saddle the horses!" In scouring the city, the army had now acquired ten horses. A couple of them were broken down, but they would have to do. "Robert!"

Robert of Saci came running up. "Sire?"

Saci had his gambeson on, but it wasn't laced. The Saracen horses grew closer.

"Find some obstacles to trip up their horses," Richard told Saci.

"What kind of—?"

"I don't care. Find something. Ralph!"

Ralph of Mauleon appeared.

"Have the spearmen plant their spears in the ground at an angle."

"Yes, sire. Double line or single?"

"Single. We need to stretch our line as far as we can. Two crossbowmen between each four spearmen. Count off by twos—shoot odd and even. That way, we won't be caught with men reloading. Quickly now."

"Yes, sire." Mauleon moved off.

By the sheerest of good fortune, Saci discovered some bundles of tent pegs, left by the Saracens when they had camped here. While the other footmen were planting their spears in the ground, the crossbowmen hurriedly knocked tent pegs into the earth in front of the lines. The eastern sky lightened, revealing the Saracen cavalry, banners flying, bearing down on the Christian line at a canter.

Squires tried to get their knights armed. Most of the knights ended up wearing only hauberk and helm. None had time to put on mail leggings, and a number were bare legged, lacking hose.

Alart came up. He'd somehow gotten his hauberk on, and he was holding his new kettle helmet, the kind that covered your entire head, with slits for the eyes and for breathing.

The Saracens were very close.

"Archers back!" Richard cried.

The crossbowmen ran back from putting in the tent pegs and placed quarrels in their previously winched bows. The laggards or men who had gone too far out front were speared or cut down with swords by the oncoming Saracens.

"Brace those spears, men! Get ready!"

Roger and his men were still at the end of the line, on the right flank. Roger had thrown on a jack; there was no time for his hauberk. There were no tent pegs for this stretch of the line, so his archers and the Turcos threw large rocks willy-nilly along the ground to break up the Saracen attack. As they worked, men looked anxiously over their shoulders at the oncoming Saracens. "Nobody told you to watch them heathens," Wulfhere cried. "Get back to work."

Fauston came up, slightly out of breath, hair damp with sweat. "Was it you that gave the alarm?" Roger asked.

"It was."

"Good work."

"Don't thank me, thank Slowfoot and his bloody pig. Weren't for them, I'd never have been out there shitting my guts out."

Roger grinned. "Drink some water and arm yourself. Tell Tatty to hurry up with my axe and sword."

"Archers back!" King Richard cried from down the line, and Wulfhere repeated the call. "Archers back!"

Rob and his men raced back and slid into their places in the gaps between the spearmen. Rob's surviving ten men had been augmented by archers from the city guards and the kingdom's men, but Roger had no idea about their quality. The Turcos took position on the flank. Two Turcos weren't fast enough and screamed as they were ridden down.

"There's not many of us," Rob shouted to his archers. "Make every arrow count."

Tatwine brought Roger's weapons, his shield, and a footman's helmet. The Saracens were on them. The sound of their horses drowned out everything.

Richard had gotten his gambeson on, and he paced back and forth like a great cat on the hunt, watching the oncoming Saracens as though he was about to lunge at them, much to the frustration of the squire who followed him, trying to get the king to put on his hauberk. Henry of Tyois rode behind Richard, carrying Richard's banner, which he had fetched from the ship.

The Saracens increased their pace to a gallop. The noise was like a thunder clap that never ended. Richard saw the lead riders' faces in the dawn's grey light. There were about a thousand in the first line. They had counted on surprise to destroy the camp and rout the Christian army, but now they had a battle on their hands.

"Ready!"

The Saracens reached the tent pegs. Some of their horses tripped on the pegs, snapping legs and throwing riders, making other horses shy away, disrupting the charge and causing confusion.

"Number ones—shoot!" Richard cried.

The crossbowmen fired. Men toppled from saddles; horses reared in pain and fell.

"Ones, reload! Twos—shoot!"

More Saracens fell. The remaining Saracens spurred their horses up to the line of spears, but, despite their riders' urgings, the horses were reluctant to challenge the line of sharp metal points. Points that gashed the horses' bellies, gutting them, points that scored chests and forelegs.

"Twos, reload! Ones—shoot!"

More men and horses fell. The rest hurled their spears or loosed arrows and wheeled away.

"Ones, reload! Twos—shoot!"

A last volley of quarrels plunged into the retreating horsemen, bringing down men and animals. Spearmen ran out to kill the wounded and plunder the dead. But already the next line was coming on, lance points glinting in the rising sun.

The squire was still following Richard with the hauberk, turning and twisting to keep up with his master. He held the hauberk up, pleading, but Richard ignored him. "Bend down, damn it!" the frustrated squire muttered. It was meant to be said to himself, but Richard heard it.

Richard whirled and stared at the boy in surprise. The squire's eyes bulged in terror.

Then Richard burst out laughing. He bent and the squire pulled the hauberk over his head. The next line of Saracens was close.

Alart had the kettle helm on; his squire laced it to his hauberk. "Looks to be a long day, sire," Alart observed.

"Ready!" Richard cried.

Chapter 54

𝕿HE SARACENS LAUNCHED seven attacks at Richard's small force. Saracen arrows and spears brought down a number of Richard's men, but the Saracens failed to break through the line of spear points and the rain of crossbow bolts that faced them.

On each approach, the Saracens were forced to walk their horses through the maze of tent pegs and rocks so that the animals wouldn't break their legs, and because of that, they lacked momentum when they reached the Christian spear line. And as the bodies of horses and men began to pile up, their progress became even slower. If any did make it through the line of spearmen, they were dispatched by Richard's knights, who roamed behind the line, looking for prey.

Richard clapped Robert of Saci's broad shoulder. "Robert, old friend, those tent pegs of yours are making our infidel guests feel most unwelcome."

"The credit goes to whoever left the pegs in camp, sire," Saci replied modestly. "I wonder if he's aware of how he's helped us?"

"Mayhap we'll be able to tell him one day. Hope it's Qaymaz. That would be fun, eh?"

Richard's ten horses were kept well back from the fighting; Richard couldn't afford to get any of them hurt. He would need them for a counterattack. Ralph of Mauleon, who was in charge of the footmen, came up. "We're running low on crossbow bolts, sire. We can bring a few more from the ships, but that will be the end of it."

Next to Richard, the count of Champagne, Henry of Deraa, and the other knights studied the enemy's overwhelming numerical strength. "We'll be in serious trouble without those arrows, sire" Champagne said. "Should we withdraw?"

"I don't retreat," Richard said casually.

At that moment, horns sounded. Drums pounded a steady rhythm. The Saracen infantry started forward, feet tramping the ground. Egyptians and Syrians, it looked like, advancing in good order. The catapults at the city ditch had been turned around by the Pisans, and now they fired at these men. Stones fell among the Saracens, crushing them, bouncing and crushing more, but the Saracens closed ranks and kept coming. They passed through the tent pegs and attacked the line of spearmen, which was considerably diminished. The fighting was fierce. The Saracens pushed the Christian line back, slowly, by weight of numbers. Some of the Christian leaders looked anxiously to Richard, but he appeared unconcerned. He watched with almost preternatural calmness, as if he knew exactly how the battle would play out and what his role in it would be.

Henry of Tyois pointed with Richard's banner. "Sire," he said excitedly, "they're attacking the right flank."

Richard looked in that direction, still seemingly unconcerned. "Wondered when they'd get around to that," he said.

∿

On the right, Roger was worried. His flank was in the air. It was covered by rough ground, but Roger didn't think that would be enough protection. Roger's line ended on a small escarpment. There was a break, or draw, then the escarpment started up again. Espiart and his Turcos were posted in the draw to keep the Saracens from turning the flank. It wouldn't stop a determined attack, but it was the best Roger could do.

Saladin's infantry pushed forward, trying to break through the spear line. It would have been easier to defend if they'd had a double line, but that was life. There weren't enough axe men to cover the gaps when a man went down or a Saracen pushed through, so Roger, Fauston, and Tatwine formed a sort of reserve and went to where the action was hottest to lend a hand. Pentecost had been with them, but Manassier went down, and Roger had Pentecost take his place.

Roger lost track of time; the choking dust hid the passage of the sun. He was thirsty, hungry, tired. His hand hurt from gripping his axe. He was covered with more dust, more blood and brains, more God knew what else. He wished he'd taken the time to put on his hauberk instead of the mailed jack. The jack was so full of arrows that he had to stop and snap them off, so they wouldn't impede his movements.

At that moment, Rob came up. "We're out of arrows."

Roger threw broken arrows from his jack onto the ground. "Maybe the infidels will lend you some. They've got enough of 'em."

Rob grinned. "I'll put my men in the gaps between the spearmen,"

"All right. No—wait. Have them reinforce Espiart in the draw. I'm worried about the flank."

Rob moved off. In truth, Roger was worried about his entire section of the battle line. The Death's Heads were well disciplined and used to fighting together, but the other units had been cobbled together at the last moment, and they were starting to fall apart, men fighting alongside men they didn't know, men they didn't trust. One or two were already sneaking away, running for the ships on the beach. It wouldn't take much more for the whole line to break.

The Saracens began working horsemen around Roger's right flank. Espiart and Rob held them in the draw, but how long would that last? In the distance, Roger saw Meshtub's division bypass the battle entirely and head for the city.

"Buggers are going to take the city back," Fauston said.

Tatwine swore.

"No use worrying about it," Roger said. "We can't stop them."

In the draw, Saracen horsemen rained arrows on the defenders. Some went down, others raised shields above their heads for protection. When they did that, dismounted Saracens attacked their vulnerable torsos. The Turcos and Rob's men pushed the Saracens back, and when they did, the archers shot at them again. Other Saracen archers climbed the escarpment on the draw's other side and poured arrows down on the defenders. Casualties mounted, and the force in the draw was gradually driven back. The Saracens would be able to get behind Roger's men soon.

"We have to turn the rightmost company and face them east, toward the draw," Roger told Gautier. The righthand company was made up of kingdom soldiers, and Gautier was in charge of them. This was going to be difficult. They would have to wait for a break in the attack, then have the line of men swing inwards, as though they were on a hinge, this for men who had never drilled together.

The Saracen attack ebbed. "Now!" Roger told Gautier.

Gautier and his vintenars began giving orders, shoving men into the positions they wanted them in, almost physically pushing the line around, crying to the men to go faster, the men scared because they were defenseless while making their turn.

"Hurry!" Roger shouted. "Hurry!"

The men got into position not a moment too soon. In the draw, Espiart was down. Rob and Tiny John helped him back up the escarpment. The Turcos and archers were retreating. Dismounted Saracens climbed the side of the escarpment right behind them only to face the new line. But more Saracens were coming through the draw and heading further south to tun and attack the Christian rear.

The position was lost.

Chapter 55

ℛOGER'S NEW LINE was on the verge of being outflanked. After that happened, his original line would be attacked from the rear. It was over, but he couldn't give up.

This was going to be even trickier than the last maneuver, especially with untrained men. They'd all die if it went wrong, but they were all going to die anyway. He rehearsed his orders, then, trying to sound calm, as if this were a drill, as if hordes of Saracens weren't all around them, he called, "Gautier's company—remain in place. The rest of you, count off by twos. Number twos—weapons up! Four paces back! Number ones—close ranks!"

It was hard for the men to disengage and carry out these orders while fighting, but by God's grace the Saracen attack on his front had died down for the moment, and, amazingly, most of the men got the movements right. Closing ranks shortened the line, leaving an opening between Roger's men and the next division, but what difference did it make now.

"Number twos—about turn! Close ranks! Weapons down!"

Again, most of the men did it, more or less in unison, and even as they did, the Saracens were on them. Roger joined the new line, Fauston and Tatwine on either side of him, locking shields.

With Espiart down, Rob took charge of the Turcos and the other men who had been stationed in the draw. Tiny John was beside him, with a spiked club he'd found somewhere. He stepped forward, swinging the club with his great strength, literally mowing down men in front of him, holding back the Saracens almost single handedly.

Arrows rained on the Christians from front and rear and from the Saracens on the escarpment across the draw. Men fell. There was screaming everywhere.

"Close ranks!"

The line shortened more. Roger covered himself with his shield and swung his axe at whatever came before him, cleaving heads and shoulders and shields. Next to him, Fauston chopped off a Saracen's sword arm as the man brought it down to strike. The arm went spinning away, and the man stared at the stump, stupefied, until someone rammed a spear into his gut.

Despite Tiny John's heroics, the archers and the lightly armed Turcos were falling back. The Turcos were not meant for this kind of work. Sensing victory, the Saracens pressed them harder. Rob and his archers and the disciplined Turcos kept fighting, but some of the civilians in the line began to run.

"Close ranks!"

Roger and his men were forced to retreat until they stood back to back with the front line. There was nowhere else to go. All they could do now was sell their lives dearly.

Our Father, Who art in Heaven . . .

Shouts. Horns. More shouts, this time from behind the Saracens, and suddenly the Saracens had broken, and they were running, and there was King Richard with a relief force attacking them from the back and side.

❧

Richard, along with Henry of Tyois and Robert of Saci, had gone to the beached galleys and rousted every spare man off them—crew members and those who had previously run away from the fighting.

Richard had taken these men and attacked the Saracens who were overrunning his right flank, striking them from behind and routing them. Indeed, many of the Saracens fled just at the sight of the red banner with its three lions.

With the Saracens in retreat, Richard turned to Robert of Saci. "Robert, take these fellows to the city. Kill any of the enemy you find within its walls."

"But Meshtub has an entire division there," Saci pointed out.

"Trust me, they'll flee. They won't be expecting you. When you have finished, rejoin us here."

"Aye, my lord," Saci said, and he started off with the men from the ships.

Richard rode over to Roger, looking down at him. "Still alive—eh, Huntley?"

"Still alive, sire."

"You appear to have a gift for that. Leave a good man in charge here and come with me."

Roger wanted to ask why, but couldn't. One didn't question the orders of a king. "Yes, sire."

Richard rode off, and Roger turned. "Tatty, with me." He called to the front rank. "Gautier!"

The gamey-eyed old soldier came over. Roger said, "You're in charge here. You know what to do."

"Aye," Gautier said.

Gautier turned and started bawling orders. Before he left, Roger visited Espiart, who lay with the wounded. The Turco captain had several arrow wounds and a sword cut across his chest. Blood welled through his sliced mail shirt. Roger gave him water from his own water skin. "You're out of it now, you'll be all right. The surgeons will fix you good as new."

Espiart swallowed some water. He reached up, touched Roger's shoulder. "Thank you, *mon vieux*."

"We have to leave," Roger told him. "I'll see you when we get back."

There were tears in Espiart's eyes. "Take care of yourself."

Roger and Tatwine joined the army's fifty or so knights, who were assembled around Henry of Tyois and Richard's banner. Robert of Saci had taken one of the army's ten horses to the city; the other nine were ridden by Richard and his highest ranking knights—Henry of Deraa, the count of Champagne, Alart with his new kettle helm, young Andrew of Chauvigny, the earl of Leicester, and Tyois among them. Roger's father touched his helmet to Roger in greeting, and Roger replied in kind.

The count of Champagne said, "Sire, we've lost a lot of men and we're out of arrows. Let us withdraw into the city and await the arrival of our main army by land."

"I told you, I don't retreat," Richard said.

"What are we going to do then?" Champagne asked.

"What we came here to do," Richard said. "Attack."

Chapter 56

ℜICHARD RODE IN front of his little army and waved his arm. "Now, men! While we've got 'em on the run!"

The men cheered. Richard and his eight horsemen started toward the Saracens, followed by the dismounted knights in a loose line, then the spearmen and crossbowmen, who maintained their formation and moved more slowly. The men on foot had to keep formation because they lost their effectiveness in a melee.

Richard and his horsemen crashed into the enemy ranks, followed by the dismounted knights, swords and axes flailing. Whether by design or from fear, the far more numerous Saracens fell back before this force. The Christians waded into the press, pushing deeper until they were surrounded on three sides.

The Saracens tried to kill the Christians' horses, to pull the knights off them. Leicester's horse was wounded by spears and arrows and swords, and when at last it dropped to its knees, a gang of Saracens leaped at the earl and made him prisoner. They were dragging him off when King Richard appeared, swinging his Danish axe. He killed two of the Saracens and the rest fled. Leicester took a sword and shield from a dead Saracen and returned to the fight.

The count of Champagne had not had time to put on his reinforced hose. As a result, his bare legs were worn to shreds by his saddle and his thighs were bleeding. He tried to fight off the mob of

Saracens who surrounded him, but they hacked at him and his horse until the horse went down, trapping the count's right leg beneath it. He was about to be killed when Henry of Deraa and Andrew of Chauvigny came to his rescue.

Alart of Vouzin had a hard time breathing with his big kettle helmet, and the heat made it worse. The helmet's eye slits didn't offer much of a view. A blow from a Saracen mace broke the helm's lacing on one side and knocked the helmet askew. Alart could see nothing but a shaft of light coming from his right. He flailed blindly with his sword. Blows rained on his helm from mace and axe and sword, one after another, denting it, cracking it, smashing it, until he slumped in his saddle. Swords slashed his legs. A group of knights on foot saved him, driving the Saracens off and helping Alart to the ground.

Roger battled alongside the other dismounted knights. Tatwine was to his right; he didn't know the man to his left. The knights pushed forward, deeper into the mass of Saracens, and Roger hoped the spearmen came before they were surrounded. From the corner of his eye, he saw his father break from the group of mounted knights and ride toward Qaymaz's blue banner. Roger tried to go after him, Tatwine following, but their way was blocked by Saracen spearmen. Arrows bounced off Roger's shield and helmet, they stuck in his mailed jack. His eyes were blurred from splashed blood but he dared not let down his guard to wipe them clean. He swore in frustration as his father got farther away.

❧

Henry bulled his way toward Qaymaz's flag, slashing at men trying to stop him. Henry was wounded in several places, including a deep cut to his right side. A war hammer blow to his knee didn't penetrate his mail, but it hurt like the flames of Hell, and he was afraid it had broken his kneecap.

His horse bled from a dozen wounds. The animal slowed. Hands grabbed Henry and pulled him off. Trying to ignore the pain in his knee, he fought off his attackers, sustaining a wound to his right arm in the process.

Qaymaz saw Henry and pounded toward him on his black horse, blue sash trailing from his helmet. Qaymaz aimed a sword blow at Henry. Henry blocked it with his battered shield. As Qaymaz rode past, Henry backhanded his own sword, hamstringing the black horse.

The horse pulled up and Henry hobbled toward it. Qaymaz leaped from the saddle and ran at Henry. Henry had been trying to get to Qaymaz before he dismounted, but because of his injured knee he couldn't get there in time. The two men slammed into each other with no room to swing their swords. Their shields banged together. They struggled, then Henry's knee gave out and they both went down, Qaymaz on top. Qaymaz battered his round shield into Henry's face. Henry had dropped his sword in the fall, and he hit Qaymaz in the face with his mailed fist, opening a deep gash over Qaymaz's eye. Stunned, Qaymaz shook his head. Henry pushed him off, found his sword and stood shakily. Qaymaz scrambled to his feet as well, wiping blood from his eye with his forearm and smearing it all over his face.

Henry was weakening from his wounds. He swung at Qaymaz, but Qaymaz skipped nimbly out of the way, his face running with blood. Qaymaz returned the blow, which Henry blocked with his shield. Henry went low and tried to slice through Qaymaz's ankle, but he was too weak and the move was slow. Qaymaz jumped out of the way and struck Henry across the top of the right shoulder. Henry almost dropped his sword from the pain but regained control. Qaymaz stepped further to the right, slashing behind Henry's shoulder this time, hitting his back, breaking the mail, cutting through the gambeson. Henry felt blood on his back.

Henry turned, sword arm down, weak from loss of blood, unable to put weight on his broken knee.

Qaymaz darted in, swinging for Henry's head. Henry blocked the blow with his shield but it was still powerful enough to drive him to his bad knee, and the pain from the knee seared through him like he had been hit by a lightning bolt. He heaved for breath, unable to rise.

Qaymaz paused for a second to savor his triumph, and that was his mistake. As he did, Henry summoned all his strength, leaped to his feet and brought his sword down on Qaymaz's head, slicing through Qaymaz's blue-sashed helmet, through his skull, all the way to his teeth. Brains and blood fell out. Qaymaz's legs did a spastic dance, then he fell onto what used to be his face.

Henry stood over his enemy, then collapsed in the dust.

Roger and Tatwine ran up. Roger knelt and took Henry's hand while Tatwine shielded them from the battle raging around them. Roger said, "Father . . ."

Henry smiled up at him, his voice wet with blood. "Finally . . . got . . . the bastard."

Roger's eyes filled with tears. "Father, you'll be all right. I'll get you to—"

Henry shook his head. Blood spilled from a corner of his mouth. He took Roger's hand, patted it. "I'll tell Aethelflaed that you . . ."

He choked up a gout of blood and went still.

Roger hung his head.

The noise of battle brought Roger back to his senses. The Saracens were falling back—running, many of them. The Christian spearmen and crossbowmen had arrived. A flight of crossbow bolts hastened the Saracen retreat. The Pisan naval infantry and Roger's footmen took care of any who stayed behind.

Maddened by battle lust, King Richard rode after the Saracens, getting out in front of his men, who were regrouping. Richard's bay horse had been wounded in a number of places; his armor and shield were stuck full of arrows. As he raced toward the Saracens, the horse suddenly gave out. Richard jumped from the saddle as the animal fell.

Richard rolled in the dirt, stood up, and looked around. He was far in front of the army. The Saracens were closer to him than his own men were. A regiment of Saracen cavalry passed through their fleeing footmen and began forming a battle line.

Richard would never be able to reach the Christian line before the Saracens were on him, and he refused to be taken from behind, to be taken while running away. So he faced the Saracens and awaited his fate.

Behind him he heard yells as the Christian knights tried to regroup and support him, but they would never reach him in time.

Richard braced himself, Danish axe ready.

Then, from the Saracen side, a horn blew.

The Saracen cavalry reined in. Behind Richard, the Christians stopped what they were doing, as well. It was as if both sides wanted to see what would happen next.

The Saracen ranks parted, and a figure rode through. It was al-Adil, Saladin's brother, leading two saddled horses.

The battlefield went silent. The two horses were magnificently caparisoned in the Saracen style. The sun glinted off al-Adil's polished mail.

Al-Adil led the horses to Richard and pulled up. He bowed his head and placed his free hand over his heart. "The sultan says it is not proper that one of your courage and skill should meet his end on foot. He begs that you choose one of these mounts for yourself."

Richard stared, his eyes white orbs in a face covered with blood and dust. "What does the sultan ask in return?"

"He asks nothing, it is a gift."

Richard examined the horses. One was creamy white, the other black. The white was bred for strength, the black for speed.

"I'll take the white one," Richard said.

Al-Adil bowed again and handed Richard the reins. "A good choice, my brother." He smiled. "Farewell, and Allah keep you."

"Farewell, and thank you," Richard said. "You've been a good friend."

Richard mounted the white horse, easing into the unfamiliar Saracen saddle. He looked to a distant rise, where a lone figure watched.

Richard raised his hand to the figure in salute, then clenched the hand into a fist.

On the rise, Saladin raised a hand, as well.

Chapter 57

WITH A CRY, Richard launched himself at the Saracen army.

The Saracens didn't expect that. Neither did the Christians. Both were caught totally unprepared. On the Christian side, the few knights who still had horses remounted and followed Richard, but Richard had a head start, and their exhausted mounts could not match the white horse's speed. The Christian spearmen had been hastily pounding the butts of their weapons into the ground in anticipation of a Saracen attack, now they just as hastily pried them out again. The crossbowmen, running out of bolts, had been gathering ones that had been shot previously, and now they ran back to their companies, formed up, and prepared to move forward. The dismounted knights, tired after fighting on foot all day in armor, caught their breath and followed the king.

"Get me a horse," Roger told Tatwine.

"What?" Tatwine said. "How?"

Roger thought of his father, of Ailith. Both of them gone, and nothing left for him but tears. "I don't care. Just get me a horse."

Richard piled into the Saracens, hewing left and right with his axe. This was the way for it to end, in glory, instead of in the ignominy that awaited him at home.

The stunned Saracens didn't know what to do. They tried to get out of Richard's way. *Why would the sultan have given Rik a horse if he intended for us to kill him?* This wasn't what Richard wanted, however. He wanted them to fight. They fell back before him as he pressed deeper into their midst, killing and wounding men and horses, striking at anything he could reach, getting angrier and angrier because the Saracens weren't reacting the way he wanted them to.

He heard himself crying with rage and frustration. An arrow brushed his flat-capped helmet on the left side. Another stuck in the upper shoulder of his hauberk. At least somebody on the other side still had their wits about them. He was deep into the Saracen formation now, with a strength in his right arm that he'd never felt before. His body sang with blood lust and joy and freedom, and the end of it all, and for a moment he felt like Roland, like Charlemagne, like Alexander the Great. He felt like the man he was supposed to be. His horse's white mane and hair were splotched with blood. Richard barreled the horse into another Saracen mount, beating at the rider till he'd broken through the man's shield and hacked off part of his arm.

He became aware of someone fighting alongside him. It was Andrew of Chauvigny. On Richard's other side was Leicester, on a Saracen mount. And Henry of Tyois, banner gone, sword in hand. They had caught up with him, damn them, but someone was missing.

Here came a mounted footman to join them, wearing one of those Death's Heads helmets, and another glance revealed that it wasn't a footman, but young Huntley, wielding an axe and yelling like a madman.

Richard swore. He came here to get himself killed, not somebody else. He wasn't going to have Andrew or Huntley slaughtered to salve his pride.

A failure, even at this.

He hauled on his horse's reins, forcing the others to do the same. "We need to go back," he yelled to them.

Huntley was wild eyed and crying, and Richard realized that the boy didn't want to go back. He was filled with the same rage and despair that consumed Richard, but Richard's rage ebbed as his plan fell apart.

Richard heard horns. The dismounted knights on foot were in action; the spearmen and crossbows wouldn't be far behind.

"With me!" Richard cried.

They cut their way back to the Christian line, Richard in the lead, Roger covering the rear, and the Saracens seemed only too happy to let them go. They wanted no parts of Richard. The feringhee king was invincible and perhaps a madman, as well.

Roger was still crying. Tatwine had brought him his own horse, Lionheart; Roger had no idea where he'd been hiding the animal. Roger didn't know why he had joined the king's attack. He had acted without thinking, acted from emotion, acted out of . . . what? Looking over his shoulder, he regained his concentration. A group of Saracen horsemen were edging closer, hoping to pick off the last man in Richard's party, who was Roger. Gravedigger Leicester dropped back and joined Roger. There was a sharp exchange of blows, and the Saracens lost heart and fell behind. A few shot arrows. Another threw a spear that just missed Roger's head.

Richard's party emerged from the Saracen lines and passed through the dismounted knights and the rest of the advancing Christian army. As they did, a flight of crossbow bolts went over their heads and into the pursuing Saracen ranks. There were cries, and the Saracens turned away to regroup.

Richard wheeled his horse and went back to his knights. They surrounded him, congratulating him, praising him for what they thought had been an act of bravado. The footmen cheered him.

He ignored them and rode over to Andrew. "Where is Alart?"

Chapter 58

ALART WAS BEHIND the Christian line with the wounded. The Death's Heads chaplain, Ambrose, had taken charge of the casualties. He'd removed his armor and cleaned his face and hands as best he could, but his blood-splattered legs gave evidence of how involved he'd been in the day's fighting. He had fashioned a series of awnings out of captured Saracen spears and cloaks, to give the wounded shade. Richard and Andrew dismounted, and Ambrose led them to where Alart lay.

Alart's hauberk had been removed. He was propped against a Saracen saddle, bleeding profusely from the nose and ears. There was blood in his eyes, as well. His usually immaculate hair was mussed and sticky. The sword wounds on his legs were bandaged but not yet sewn.

Richard dropped to one knee beside him and took his hand. "Alart? Alart?"

Alart's head moved slightly, but his eyes were unfocused.

"Alart, it's me. Richard."

Alart's head turned further. He looked at Richard without seeing him. He mumbled, "Blue . . . blue . . ."

"Alart!"

"Blue . . ."

"What is he talking about?" Andrew of Chauvigny asked.

"I have no idea," Richard said.

"Blue . . ." Alart's voice was weak. It didn't sound like Alart; it sounded like someone else, like an old man.

"He just keeps repeating that over and over," Ambrose told the king.

Richard looked up at Ambrose. "Will he . . . will he be all right?"

Ambrose stared at Richard a long moment, then dropped his eyes.

Richard felt his own eyes moisten. He gripped Alart's hand more tightly.

"Blue . . ."

Alart, his mentor . . . Alart, his friend . . . Alart, his . . .

Richard's tears were replaced by rage, towering rage. His thick chest rose and fell, his nostrils flared.

He rose and pushed his way from the shade. "Find me a lance," he told a squire.

"A lance, sire?"

"Yes, damn your eyes. You know what a lance is, don't you?"

"Y—"

"Then find me one!"

The boy shot off. Richard waited, his brow a thundercloud. No one dared approach him. Alart might have, but Alart was dying.

The squire returned with the lance.

Richard took it and glared at the men around him. "This time, none of you follow me."

He didn't wait for a reply. He turned and started back to his white horse. He tossed the lance to the squire who held the horse's reins. He mounted and took the lance back. He wheeled the blood-splattered horse and trotted through the Christian line.

The Saracens had regrouped. They were preparing yet another attack. This time they would use their entire army—Meshtub's and al-Adil's divisions, as well as Qaymaz's. Flags waved; horns and drums sounded. Their horsemen had formed in three battles, with the infantry behind.

The horns and drums and shouted orders suddenly died away.

Because the red king approached.

When Richard got within fifty yards of the Saracens, he turned his horse left and walked it along the Saracen line, facing the enemy and holding his lance aloft, challenging any of them to combat, challenging all of them.

There were murmurs among the Saracens. A few in the front ranks edged their horses back. There were cries from emirs and officers. Richard couldn't understand the words but he knew from the tone that they were pleading for someone, anyone, to accept the challenge, to kill Rik or take him prisoner.

But none dared try.

Richard rode slowly, rage exploding inside him. When he reached the end of the Saracen line, he turned, rode back to the center, and stopped. He faced the Saracens and waited. Telling the Saracens that they would have to go through him if they wanted to attack the Christian army.

Come on, damn you! Do it! What's the matter with you? Here I am. Kill me. Do it!

The sun beat down.

Richard waited.

Nothing happened.

No arrows, no thrown spears.

Richard waited, and hot tears rolled down his cheeks.

He wondered if the man on the rise was watching, knew he was, and wondered if he was upset by his men's reluctance to fight.

Or was this Saladin's final trick? Was he once again denying Richard what he wanted?

Or had Saladin backed down? Had he refused to accept Richard's challenge?

Muffled orders circulated among the Saracens. The rear ranks of infantry faced about and marched away, followed by the middle ranks, then by the front ranks of horsemen. The Saracen army departed in a roiling cloud of dust that billowed and rolled over Richard, obscuring his vision.

And out of the dust, almost sensed rather than seen at first, emerged a figure on horseback.

Chapter 59

ℜOGER RECOGNIZED THE figure right away. She wore an Arab robe and she had been cleaned up, but otherwise she was the same as he'd seen her two days earlier. He threw down his helmet and shield and ran toward her, ignoring the king's previous order for everyone to remain in place, ignoring the shouts of Leicester and others.

"Ailith!"

❧

Richard clenched his jaw. There would be no glory, no redemption through death. Only disgrace. The figure on the rise had vanished, and Richard knew he would never see him again.

"Ailith!" someone was crying behind him. "Ailith!"

Richard wiped his wet cheeks and studied the rider coming out of the dust. The fellow's face was bruised and puffy, as though he'd been beaten, but he looked familiar. His mustache and goatee were gone, and, for some reason, the Saracens had put a woman's robe on him and stuffed it—quite realistically—to make it appear as though he had a bosom.

"Alan?" Richard said. Louder, he said, "Alan of the Dale? Is that you?"

He spurred his tired horse closer to the fellow and took hold of his horse's bridle. "What happened to your face? Why are you dressed like a woman, and . . .?" He motioned awkwardly at Alan's chest.

Roger of Huntley ran up to them, helmetless. "Ailith."

Richard turned. "What do you mean, 'Ailith'? This is Alan, a member of my court. My troubadour."

The rider smiled and spoke in a voice Richard had never heard him use. "Actually, my name *is* Ailith."

Richard stared.

Ailith continued. "I'm a—"

"A woman," Richard said, the truth dawning on him.

"Yes, sire."

"But . . . why did you pretend to be a . . .?

"Some Churchmen want me burned as a witch. I was forced to adopt a false identity and go into hiding."

"A witch?" said Richard. "Why, that's absurd. Though I admit you bewitched me into thinking you were a man. But now that I know the truth . . ." His voice tailed off.

Roger cut in. "Gregorius is dead, Ailith. So is Auberie. You no longer have anything to fear."

Richard turned again. "Do you *never* stop popping up. Huntley? What is your part in all this?"

"We're—Ailith and I—we're to be married, sire."

"Married! This grows stranger yet. When?"

Roger looked at Ailith and they both grinned. "As soon as possible. Today, maybe. Or tomorrow. As soon as Father Ambrose has time."

For a moment Richard let the disaster that was his life fall from his shoulders. For a moment he was happy to assume another role and play the avuncular king. "Well, I'm . . ." He cleared his throat ostentatiously. "If you two are to be married, you deserve a present. I have a number of English estates in my gift. I'll give you one as a wedding boon—a rich one."

"Why . . . thank you, sire," Roger said. "I never . . . I mean . . ."

Richard held up a hand. "Nonsense. A knight must have property. Besides, you've earned it." He cleared his throat again. "Even if you were disobeying my orders most of the time. I assume you prefer to live in Trentshire?"

Roger looked at Ailith again. "Well . . . yes, sire."

"As long as it's not Lower Wynchecombe," Ailith added.

Richard and Roger both stared at her. It was the height of impudence to make such demands of a king.

Ailith explained. "Lower Wynchecombe is my home, sire. I never want to see that place again."

Richard seemed to find enjoyment in her boldness. He leaned his head back and roared with laughter. "I'm not familiar with Trentshire, but I'll make sure your estates are nowhere near this Lower Whatever-it-is. My clerk is on the ship. He's part English; he'll about know that sort of thing. He'll have the charters drawn up before I leave the Holy Land—which, please God, will be soon." He inclined his head gallantly toward Ailith. "Any other stipulations, my lady?"

Roger broke in before Ailith could think of something. "No, sire. You've been most generous. Thank you again."

Richard waved him off. "See that you govern your lands wisely."

"I will, sire."

"Now, if you two supplicants to the Court of Love will excuse me, I have other matters at hand." Richard bowed to Ailith and rode back to his small army.

Roger helped Ailith from her horse and kissed her. He embraced her—gingerly, because of her bruises—the scent from her freshly washed short hair filling his nostrils, the warmth of her body melding with his. Tears ran down his cheeks and dropped onto her neck. "I thought you were lost to me," he murmured.

"Saladin freed me after Qaymaz was killed," Ailith told him. "Somehow he knew I was your . . . your lady. He likes you, you know."

Roger stepped back and took her shoulders. "My father is dead."

"I know. I heard the Saracens talking about it—I understand enough of their tongue to get the gist of what they were saying."

"He was the one who killed Qaymaz. They died together."

"From what you've told me, I suppose that's fitting somehow." Then she realized something. "This means you're lord of Deraa, Roger. You're a powerful baron. You sit on the king of Jerusalem's council."

Roger shook his head. "No. We'll go home, back to England. I committed no murder. You're not wanted for being a witch. And we'll have land to support us."

"What about Deraa? You can't just leave it. Who will be the lord?"

"I have someone in mind." He pulled her to him, staring deep into her eyes. "But that's for later."

They kissed again, a long, slow kiss. They did not hear the cheers and raucous calls from the soldiers behind them who were watching.

Chapter 60

ROGER AND AILITH were married two days later.

Roger bathed in the governor's palace. The palace had been largely wrecked by Saracen catapults, but the marble bathing tub was intact. For the wedding, Roger wore a new, knee-length shirt of white silk, with red hose and an embroidered blue tunic, all procured for him by Mathilde. Ailith, who had been bathed and perfumed the day before by the Saracens, was still bruised, one eye swollen half shut. Her dress was made of red silk, trimmed in gold to match her hair. Each wore a chaplet of flowers in their hair. King Richard's clerk had worked the night away, and before the ceremony, the king presented Roger with a charter for the fief of Ashleigh, in Trentshire. Ashleigh's former lord had died on the crusade without heirs.

The wedding took place on the open plain not far from the Ascalon Gate. The area around the Acre Gate was still littered with bodies of men and animals. The stench of burning flesh from the city ditch hung in the air, but everyone was happy. It was the first positive thing that had happened to most of the guests and onlookers in a good while. Many still bore traces of dried blood and dust, some still had it caked in their hair.

Father Ambrose presided over the ceremony. King Richard gave the bride away. Afterwards, Roger and Ailith danced to music from an impromptu band made up of soldiers from different units. It was a frenetic peasant dance, not a courtly one, and all the more fun because of it.

Richard danced with the bride after Roger. The king was no slouch at peasant dancing, nor was Ailith, and the onlookers cheered them and clapped their hands in time to the music. The count of Champagne danced with Ailith next, then Andrew of Chauvigny—the two nobles much more stiff and awkward than Richard had been. Fauston and Tatwine came next, then just about every member of the Death's Heads and some of Richard's knights, until Roger despaired of seeing his bride again and repaired to the wine tent. Mathilde and other women of the city were at the wedding, as well. Mathilde danced with Pentecost, and the other women did not lack for partners. It became more than a wedding, it became a celebration of Jaffa's salvation from the Saracens. Courtesy of King Richard, there was more than enough drink and food to go round.

Richard, Henry of Champagne, and the earl of Leicester drew off to one side and looked on. The sight of so many people enjoying themselves made Richard happy, a feeling all too rare for him these days. Yet, even now, the real world intruded on Richard's thoughts. He had to decide what to do about the Count Josserand of Bellaire, who had been found stabbed to death at his house in Acre. The count was one of Richard's vassals, and an important one, at that. Richard knew the family would blame the count's young wife, Odelina, and demand her execution. He also knew that the count beat Odelina, as he had beaten his first two wives, possibly killing one of them. Richard despised men like that, and he decided to incur the family's wrath and accept Odelina's story that the death had occurred at the hands of an intruder, probably looking for money.

Next to Richard, Leicester, who would never dance with anyone below him in rank—and with few of equal rank—watched the wedding celebration. "I was against you making that fellow a knight, sire. Don't hold with raising men from the ranks. But now I think you made a good choice."

"How could he not?" said the count of Champagne. "The boy has his father's blood." Champagne was twenty-six, but the crusade had aged him. There were strands of grey in his hair and beard. "Henry of Deraa might have been insolent and loathe to obey orders, but he was a good baron, a good knight, and a better friend."

"Young Huntley takes after him," Richard said, "save for the insolence."

"Give him time," Champagne joked.

⚬

Richard fell ill again two days later. He put his seal to peace terms which included tearing down the fortifications at Ascalon. He no longer cared. He just wanted to leave.

Many of the Christian nobles and common soldiers made a pilgrimage to Jerusalem, as they were allowed to do under the new treaty. Richard did not.

⚬

Roger and Ailith didn't go to Jerusalem either. They didn't have time. Roger was still commander, or governor, of Jaffa, and he had to oversee rebuilding of the city. Ailith joined Mathilde in tending the wounded and homeless, of whom there were many. True to his word, King Richard rewarded Fauston for saving the army, giving him the princely sum of five hundred silver bezants. Fauston left the money with Mathilde to use for raising the little boy he had carried to the citadel on the day the city fell.

Roger dug his father's grave with his own hands, refusing assistance. With his own hands, he lowered the body into the grave. Ambrose prayed over it. Roger was tempted to leave his ring with the body, but realized his father would not want that.

Before Henry of Champagne returned to Acre, Roger pledged fealty to him and to Queen Isabelle for Deraa. He also made a request of Count Henry. Roger then called the remainder of his father's men together. It was the surviving knights' first chance to pledge fealty to Roger as lord of Deraa, and all did. Afterwards Roger told them, "I am returning to England. The count of Champagne has agreed to a new lord for Deraa."

There was murmuring at that. Roger beckoned, and Gautier stepped forward. "Lord Gautier has already pledged fealty to the count and to Queen Isabelle." The men of Deraa had worked with Gautier during the siege, and they respected him. They gave him their allegiance. Gautier thanked them and got right to business. "We need to recruit men to replace those who have been lost. A lot of them." He searched the onlookers and pointed. "Pentecost, how about you? I'll make you my captain of foot."

Pentecost shuffled his feet. "That's good of you, Gautier, but I kind of thought I'd stay here in the city."

"You?" Roger said. He shared a surprised look with Gautier. "Why? You've been a soldier your whole life."

"I know," Pentecost said, "but, you see, well, me and Mathilde, we been working together and, well, I'm kind of hoping that when her mourning period is over, she'll . . . well, you know."

"She couldn't find a better man," Roger assured him.

Berengaria and Queen Joanna departed Acre on September 29. King Richard left on the Ninth of October. He was ill, low in spirit, and glad to see the last of the Holy Land. He wished he had never come here, though he was not looking forward to what awaited him at home. He was taking the white horse Saladin had given him. That was something.

Huge crowds gathered to see Richard off, cheering and singing and throwing flowers. Because of Richard's feats at Jaffa, the same people who had recently excoriated him were now hailing him as one of the great heroes of history. They claimed he had ridden into legend at Jaffa; they didn't know he had tried to get himself killed. They were so enamored of his deeds as a warrior, they had forgotten why he had come here. They had forgotten about Jerusalem.

Fools.

Failure seemed to have been turned into success, but that was an illusion. Richard knew the truth, even if no one else did, and that truth would haunt him the rest of his days.

The earl of Trent's illness had worsened. He was bedridden with fever again, delirious at times, so the burden of packing and arranging transportation for his household fell largely on his steward Pero and on Bonjute. Bonjute hadn't had much time for Fauston, and the night before they sailed, she cancelled all her commitments and came to his rooms.

They spent an evening of frenzied passion. It was as though they tried to fuse their bodies, by some strange alchemy to literally try and make them one. At one point they stopped to catch their breath, covered in sweat, hair matted.

They drank white wine to refresh themselves, and Bonjute ran her finger in whorls across Fauston's wet chest, her eyes half closed, voice dreamy. "Who will you take to the eremite's hut when I am gone?" she murmured.

"No one," Fauston swore.

She teased him again. "Hugoline would go with you, I think."

He smoothed her damp hair. "There will never be anyone for me but you, you know that. I'll always love you."

"I'll always love you as well," she told him, looking up, serious now. "I almost . . . I almost wish Geoffrey would die. I know that's horrible to say, and I don't really mean it, but I want to stay here with you so much. I can't stand losing you. It's tearing me apart to think that I'll never see you again. You've changed my life."

She pressed herself to him, head against his chest.

"You've changed me, as well," Fauston said.

"Will you keep selling relics?"

"For now. But they're going to be real ones. Everything will be authenticated."

"And after that?"

"We'll see," he said. "But it will be something honest."

She smiled. "I'm glad."

"So am I." He gently placed her on her back and rolled his tongue around the outside of her left nipple. "When do you have to be back at the palace?"

"Dawn."

"Dawn?" Fauston's eyebrows shot up. "Everyone will know what you've been doing."

"Since when have I cared what people think?" She pulled him down and kissed him.

❧

The next day, Bonjute stood by the boarding plank as Geoffrey was carried onto the ship that was to return them to England.

Geoffrey was barely conscious. He wanted this dreadful experience to be over. He was going home ill and impoverished—not only impoverished, but deeply in debt. He had won no glory, no honors, but neither had anyone else. Few who had come to this place were leaving with anything positive. But at least they were leaving. Most who had come here were staying. And here they would remain, forever young . . .

From the crowd, Fauston watched Bonjute board. When Geoffrey's litter had been placed in his compartment beneath the stern castle, Bonjute came back to the rail, attended by her maid, Jehan. Bonjute sent Jehan away, which was fine with Jehan, who was more interested in flirting with the sailors. Bonjute stood by the rail, searching for Fauston in the crowd.

Fauston pushed his way through the throng till he was at the front. He met Bonjute's eyes. There was no waving of hands, no shedding of tears, they just gazed at each other, emotion writ large on their faces.

They stayed that way, unmoving, staring into each other's eyes, as the ship was poled from the quay. When the vessel turned and pointed her bow toward the sea, Bonjute moved to the aft rail. She stood there, gazing at Fauston, their eyes still interlocked. Fauston kept watching long after he could no longer see her eyes, long after he could no longer make out her figure at the rail, long after the crowd had gone and the ship had disappeared from view over the horizon.

≈

The Death's Heads began boarding. They were sailing on two ships, and the vagaries of sea travel meant that Roger would never see many of these men again. He and Ailith bade farewell to each of them in turn. Tatwine held the battered Death's Head flag, and many of the men kissed it, some with tears in their eyes.

Rob and Tiny and Red Will, his arm still in a sling, embarked with the Death's Heads. The other men they had come to the Holy Land with were all dead. Tiny still had the loot that he was supposed to buy all of Yorkshire with, assuming he didn't drink it away first. Rob didn't know what he would do when he got home. "Go back to what I've always done, I suppose. Poaching."

"Me, too," said Slowfoot despondently. He still had the problem with is eyes, blinking rapidly in the glare of the sun off the water. "Runnin' from the forest wardens ain't fun, but it beats bein' here."

"You could join up with our bunch," Rob told him. "We can always use a fast runner."

"Even if he's blind?" Slowfoot said.

"I'm sure your eyes will get better when you get away from this Eastern sun." Rob put an arm around Slowfoot's shoulder. "I can't promise you a better life than the one you had before, but the ale in

Yorkshire is a hell of a lot better than that swill they make down in Trentshire."

The four men walked up the ship's plank, bantering about the ale in their respective shires. Wulfhere followed, his bushy beard cut so short as to make him nearly unrecognizable. Then the others, the few that were left. Roger shook each man's hand and Ailith embraced them.

When the men had boarded, Tatwine, duly knighted—and still hungover from the celebration—folded the Death's Head flag reverently and handed it to Roger. "I'd best board," he said. "I need to make sure Lionheart's comfortable."

As Fauston went up the plank to see to his horse, Roger stuffed the flag in the front of his shirt. He would hang it in his hall, so that he would never forget what he had been through out here.

"You'll need a new device as lord of Ashleigh," Ailith told him. "Something better than that skull."

"I know," Roger said. He thought. "Maybe I'll use the emblem on my ring."

"That would be fitting. Assuming you can ever make out what the emblem is."

Roger and Ailith were the last to board. Roger handed Ailith onto the plank, and they walked up to the deck. They stepped onto the deck and took positions at the rail. The captain shouted orders, and the boat was poled from the quay.

Arm in arm, Roger and Ailith watched the city slowly fall away. Behind them, life in Acre went on as normal. Crowds flocked to the Golden Keys, customers came to Fauston's shop, people thronged the streets, vendors hawked wares. Maybe Hugoline was giving a banquet. Roger and Ailith would never see any of it again. It would exist for them only in memories.

They rounded the Tower of Flies, and Roger saw the spot where he had disembarked from the *Quail* what seemed like several lifetimes before. He had arrived penniless, a runaway monk, and he was going home a knight with land and a beautiful wife. He had killed men and seen men killed, and his hands sometimes shook because of the things he'd seen and done.

Roger thought of all those who weren't going home. Had it been worth it? Had anything been accomplished by the expenditure of untold wealth and countless lives?

It all gone wrong from the start, at Acre, and one mistake had followed another. But still they could have been successful. They *shoul* have been successful. That was the maddening part. Roger loved King Richard; he owed Richard much. Yet he was also forced to admit that the crusade's failure had been a failure of leadership, both on the part of King Richard and, before him, Guy of Lusignan. Conrad of Montferrat would have taken Jerusalem if he'd been given the chance. For that matter, Roger's father, Henry, would have taken it had he commanded the army. But it was not to be, and Roger was leaving the Holy Land if not content, at least resigned to the way things had worked out.

It had been God's plan.

Ailith leaned over and whispered something in Roger's ear. He stared at her, wide eyed, then embraced her with joy.

EPILOGUE

Acre

October 1193

𝕿HE BELL OVER the door rang, announcing a customer.

Fauston made his way from the rear of the shop, where he'd been cleaning up.

A hooded figure stood there, her back to him.

"Good day, madame," Fauston said. "How may I . . .?"

The woman turned and pushed back her hood.

Fauston stopped.

It was Bonjute.

Author's Note

This is a work of fiction, and facts have sometimes been changed to fit the story, but in the main the events of the Third Crusade are as I have described them. As in the previous volumes of this series, the cast of characters has been whittled down to avoid confusion, as has the scope of the negotiations between King Richard and Saladin, which went on practically non-stop, and to little effect.

It is perhaps the crusade's supreme irony that Saladin never beat Richard in the field, yet Richard lost the war. Saladin was on the verge of abandoning Jerusalem both times that Richard decided not to pursue a siege, and once he had even given the order to do so. There was a caravan of supplies and reinforcements for the garrison at Jerusalem, and its capture prompted Saladin's short-lived order to abandon the city. Richard arrived at Jaffa just as the citadel was about to fall, and his personal bravery and dash against far superior numbers turned the tide of battle and saved the city. During the battle, Richard was unhorsed, and Saladin sent him a replacement mount. Richard's challenge to the Saracen army is related by Beha-ad-Din and Ibn-al-Athir.

Richard was in a hurry to get back to England, but a swift return was denied him, as he was shipwrecked on the Adriatic coast. In disguise, he attempted to make his way overland, but he was recognized and taken prisoner by, of all people, Duke Leopold of Austria, whose flag Richard had hurled into the ditch at Acre. This seems to be the very definition of *schadenfreude*. Leopold sold his prisoner to the Holy Roman Emperor, who held Richard for a ransom equivalent to two to three times the entire yearly revenues of England. The ransom was eventually paid, and Richard was set free in 1194.

Richard was never the same man after the crusade. He forgave Prince John, as he always seemed to, and even named him his heir. He bedeviled King Philip of France, winning military engagements against him and regaining lost territory, but his name never had the luster it had once possessed. He no longer had that transcendent promise of greatness and accomplished little of lasting significance. He died in 1199, shot by a crossbow while besieging one of his own vassals over an unpaid debt.

Saladin died in March of 1193, six months after Richard departed the Holy Land. As the sultan had predicted, his empire descended into civil war, with his brother, al-Adil, eventually controlling the largest part of it.

Henry of Champagne and Isabelle of Jerusalem were married within days of Conrad of Montferrat's murder. The union was by all accounts a love match, and it lasted until 1197, when Henry fell—or was pushed—from a window of his house in Acre.

Richard's nemesis, King Philip of France, went on to become Philip Augustus, father of the modern French state.

The kingdom of Jerusalem limped along for another hundred years. Jerusalem was actually returned Christian control from 1229 until 1244, and prospects for the kingdom appeared bright. That was not to be, however. The usual bickering and feuding set in amongst the Christian leaders, amidst which Outremer was overrun by the

Mamluks. The last stronghold, Acre, fell in 1291, for all intents and purposes ending the Christian presence in the Holy Land.

The so-called "numbered crusades," of which there were eight, continued until 1291. Most of these were disasters or parodies of what they were supposed to be, such as the Fourth Crusade, which was diverted from the Holy Land to sack the Christian city of Constantinople for the benefit of the doge of Venice. Other, unnumbered, crusades took place, as well, such as those of the Teutonic Knights in northern Europe, the Albigensian Crusade in southern France, the Children's Crusade, and the *Reconquista* in Spain. In one form or another, crusading ventures lasted until the 15th century. This was followed by a period of Muslim expansion into eastern Europe and the Mediterranean, and subsequent efforts to drive them out, so it is possible to say that the crusades, and the events that led up to them, have never really left us. Of all the crusades, however, none possessed the scope, or had what we would today call the "star power" of the Third, which is perhaps why it has lasted the longest in the popular imagination.

Astute readers will recognize Ailith's signature song as coming from the *Lais* of Marie of France, the first great female poet of the Middle Ages. I could have tried composing my own lyrics, but I could never have come up with anything as beautiful as those.

About the Author

Robert Broomall is the author of a number of published novels. Besides writing, his chief interests are travel and history, especially military history, the Old West, and the Middle Ages. He also likes to cook, much to the dismay of those who have to eat what he prepares.

Amazon author page: https://www.amazon.com/author/robertbroomall

Facebook: https://www.facebook.com/RobertBroomall.author

Connect with Bob: robertbroomall@gmail.com

Printed in Great Britain
by Amazon

57211139R00241